J

Chase watched as the mayor brought forward the pretty blond woman.

He stared dumbly down at her upturned face.

"Go on, Linese, give your husband a proper reception," the mayor urged.

"Welcome home—Chase." She rose on tiptoe and touched her soft lips to the side of his face in a self-conscious greeting.

His heart slammed against his rib cage. *Linese*. This was Linese. This was his *wife*.

God, she was beautiful, and younger than his own twenty-one years, if he had his guess. She was the very image of what every soldier wished he had waiting for him at home.

Chase swallowed hard and beseeched God to let him remember her, but nothing happened. He remembered nothing about her.

He was doomed to play out this charade in a life he could not recollect. And this poor woman, who had done nothing to deserve this kind of punishment, was condemned to play it out with him.

Dear Reader,

The Return of Chase Cordell is a poignant new Western from Linda Castle, an author who is fast becoming one of our most popular writers. It's a love story about a war hero with amnesia who is struggling to put his life back together, and rediscovering a forgotten passion for his young bride. Don't miss this wonderful story.

Ana Seymour's sequel to *Gabriel's Lady, Lucky Bride*, is the delightful story of a ranch hand who joins forces with his beautiful boss to save her land from a dangerous con man. Elizabeth Mayne, a March Madness/Romance Writers of America RITA Award nominee author, is also out this month. Her book, *Lord of the Isle*, is a classic Elizabethan tale featuring an Irish nobleman who unwittingly falls in love with a rebel from an outlawed family.

And another RITA Award nominee, Gayle Wilson, is back with *Raven's Vow*, a haunting Regency novel about a marriage of convenience between an American investor and an English heiress.

Whatever your taste in reading, we hope you'll enjoy all four of these terrific stories. Please keep an eye out for them wherever Harlequin Historicals are sold.

Sincerely,

Tracy Farrell
Senior Editor

Please address questions and book requests to:
Harlequin Reader Service
U.S.: 3010 Walden Ave., P.O. Box 1325, Buffalo, NY 14269
Canadian: P.O. Box 609, Fort Erie, Ont. L2A 5X3

LINDA CASTLE

The Return of CHASE CORDELL

Harlequin Books

TORONTO • NEW YORK • LONDON
AMSTERDAM • PARIS • SYDNEY • HAMBURG
STOCKHOLM • ATHENS • TOKYO • MILAN
MADRID • WARSAW • BUDAPEST • AUCKLAND

ISBN 0-373-28948-0

THE RETURN OF CHASE CORDELL

Books by Linda Castle

Harlequin Historicals

Fearless Hearts #261
Abbie's Child #321
The Return of Chase Cordell #348

LINDA CASTLE

is the pseudonym of Linda L. Crockett, a third-generation native New Mexican. Linda started writing in March of 1992, and *The Return of Chase Cordell* is her third book from Harlequin Historicals.

When not penning novels, Linda divides her time between being a wife, mother and grandmother. She loves speaking, and teaching what she has learned to aspiring writers. Her best advice—write from the heart.

Linda believes one of the greatest benefits she has received from writing historical novels is the mail from the readers. She encourages and welcomes comments to be sent to: Linda Castle, #18, Road 5795, Farmington, NM 87401. Please include a SASE for a reply/bookmark.

As always, I thank God for my life and the people that love me; Bill, Billy, Liann, Brandon and Logan. They continue to show patience and understanding when none is earned or deserved. Hugs and kisses to Matt and Will, my grandsons.

There are many unsung heroes who cross my path each day—it is impossible to name all my friends, who read snippets of dialogue and listen to me whine, but please know I do appreciate you all.

Thanks to two extraordinary women I am proud to count as friends, and without whom this book would probably not exist—Margaret Marbury, my editor, and Pattie Steele-Perkins, my agent.

And last, a special note of gratitude to the people who really make this possible: the readers. Thanks to every person who has taken the time to read my books and write to tell me how my words made them feel—this one is for you!

Chapter One

Mainfield, Texas
April, 1864

Linese dipped the quill pen into the ink and tried to put her thoughts on paper before the rush of inspiration left her. Her lace cuff slipped down toward her wrist, and she impatiently took the time to secure it with the stained black garter around her arm. She dared not show up at the train with ink on the sleeves of her frock.

"What time is it, Hezikiah?" She glanced up at the small man swathing ink on the big flat-head printer.

"About ten minutes later than the last time you asked me." He swiped his hand across his face and turned his snowy beard a grizzled gray with a fresh smear of newspaper ink.

"I'm sorry. I hoped to get this editorial finished before the train pulls in." Linese bit her lip and tried to concentrate on the paper in front of her. Chase's homecoming kept intruding on her, leaching off her ability to make coherent thoughts. The war was over for Chase, even though the fighting continued over the question of secession. Linese wanted this editorial, more than any other before it, to be a testimonial to the courage and honor of both sides in the bitter conflict dividing the Union, particularly since she knew it would be the last she would ever write.

"I suppose, with Mr. Chase returning, this will be the last time we'll work together, won't it?" Hezikiah's voice halted the scratch of the nib in mid-sentence when he gave her very thought life.

She looked up at the old gentleman, who, more than anyone in Mainfield, had helped her survive the long separation from her husband.

"Yes, I expect it will." She set the quill aside. "Hezikiah, in case I never get another opportunity, I want to thank you. This paper wouldn't have endured if not for you."

"Nonsense. This paper weathered because you had the grit and determination to make it survive. I've worked with a lot of men, Mrs. Cordell, and there isn't one of them I'd trade for you. You've become a right-hand journalist." Hezikiah blushed bright red before he turned away and busied himself once again with the press.

"I wish more men in Mainfield thought that way," Linese muttered. Her words trailed off. She willed her hand to stop shaking while she added the last sentence to her epitaph as a newspaper editor.

The time Chase had been gone had required her to become a different kind of woman. She feared Chase would be less than pleased to have an independent thinker for his wife. She well remembered the one day he'd brought her to the *Gazette.* His words had echoed in her mind a thousand times over the past two years.

"Women who insist on intruding into a man's domain become shrews and widows. Nothing is so unattractive, to me, as a woman with ideas in her head or ink stains upon her hands."

She glanced at her own stained fingers and grimaced. Linese had managed to acquire both offensive traits while Chase was away. The woman she was now was a far cry from the girl he had married.

Being raised by a pair of aging maiden aunts had com-
elled Linese to be subservient and pliant. In fact, if she had
een any other kind of woman, she never would have mar-
ed Chase after knowing him fourteen short days. But the
ar had changed her and the world around her. Unfortu-
ately, the letters Chase had written home had not reflected
similar change in him. Linese sighed and laid the quill
side just as the train whistle blew.

"They're crossing the bridge at the gap outside of town."
[ezikiah pulled his watch from his vest and looked at it.
Right on time, too."

"Oh, Lord, I'm going to be late." Linese jumped up and
ore off the black garters while she located her gloves. She
early ripped out the seams in her haste to pull them over
er discolored fingers. When she put the bonnet on her head
nd shoved the hat pin through, she immediately felt the
oring heat trapped between the large brim and her neck.

She wished Chase's return could have taken place on a
ay when it wasn't so oppressively hot. This particular April
emed to be more humid and stormy than usual, or maybe
was just her fears about her husband's return as a war
ero that made her feel like a frog on a hot rock.

The bright sunshine outside the newspaper office mo-
entarily blinded Linese when she stepped outside. She
opped open her parasol and hurried toward the train sta-
on. Each step made her boned corset feel all the tighter in
e muggy heat.

Mainfield's proximity to Louisiana had made it strategi-
ally important to the troops on both sides of the present
ostilities. Linese only wished that the citizens of the town
ould enjoy some of the benefits of the community's loca-
on. More and more of late, she had watched people
inching in their belts another notch due to the scarcity of
upplies around town. Only a select few of the local busi-
essmen seemed to be prospering during this hard time. The
ayor and several other prominent merchants grew fat

while all around her she looked into faces grown gaunt from
lack.

Linese turned the corner by the merchants bank and
stopped with a gasp of surprise. Not only had a sizable
crowd gathered at the train station, but cloth banners pro
claiming Chase Cordell a hero were stretched across the
front of the buildings along the tracks.

She had been nervous enough about the homecoming
when she thought it would be a private reunion; now pure
terror snaked around her heart when she looked at the peo
ple who would be observing her every word and deed.

What would she say to Chase? How should she behave?
They had shared a whirlwind courtship of two weeks and
one awkward honeymoon night, before Chase rode off to
war vowing he'd be back in a month. He had never even told
her that he loved her before he left her standing beside his
grandfather on the steps of Cordellane.

Chase Cordell left a shy bride who had dewy-eyed expec
tations of marriage. In order for her to survive, she had
learned to adapt—to grow up. She hoped she would be as
adaptable now and that she would survive the next few mo
ments. Linese bit her bottom lip and summoned up her
courage.

She approached the crowd and several heads turned in her
direction, destroying the flimsy hope that she might blend
in among the mob. One man strutted forward from the
throng, sunlight winking off the stickpin on his barrel chest.

"Mrs. Cordell, come up here. I was wondering what was
keeping you—not trouble with the old Captain?" Mayor
Kerney's florid jowls curled into a false smile.

Linese frowned and fixed a blank stare on her face to hide
her annoyance. She strongly resented the mayor's assump
tion that Chase's sweet old grandfather was in any way a
bother or a hindrance because of his mental condition.

"Not at all. I was . . . detained."

"Oh yes, of course. Well, ma'am, you step up here in ront. We want Major Cordell to see his pretty bride right ff. Yes, we do."

Linese was shoved and jostled to the very edge of the train latform. She tried to retreat backward into the crowd, but le crush of bodies formed an impenetrable wall behind her.

There was no escape. Her first meeting with Chase would e as public as it could get in Mainfield, Texas. Knowing ley would be on display made her all the more uncomfortble.

She told herself not to fret too much for Chase's sake. He as, after all, Major Chase Cordell. He had always been a lan who kept his inner feelings to himself and showed the orld, including her, only his bravado. Now he was the arling of Texas and the Northern army, coming home vicorious from his last battle. He would be as happy as a hitewashed pig, and she would simply have to endure.

Linese glanced around at the faces in the crowd. She saw outhern and Northern sympathizers standing side by side n the platform, waiting for her husband's return. The pinion about which side would ultimately prevail, like the ntire issue of the war, was split firmly down the middle in lainfield. The town leaders had never shown any lasting llegiance to either North or South. Linese thought it was robably because of Mainfield's unique location. A Texas own, yet so very near the Louisiana border. Western ideals lad never really meshed with Southern traditions. In addiion, Mainfield had the odd distinction of being located on major route. Supplies, troops and even fleeing slaves came emarkably close to the town.

In one respect the residents of Mainfield had been lucky. 'ood and goods continued to trickle into Mainfield, when ther towns had nearly perished during the conflict. Still the nonths she had worked at the *Gazette* made her wonder low the town could remain so neutral, and how long that rivilege would last.

Chase had kept Linese updated by letter on each battle—and uncompromising victory—which had ultimately in sured his status as a local champion. Many of those letter had been used to document the news of the war in the *Ga zette*.

It had been Chase's dream to ride off to battle and retur with medals of honor, to the praise of an adoring commu nity after the Union had won the war and settled the ques tion of secession. At least in one respect, he had gotten hi wish. Though the question of secession was unclear, he wa definitely returning home a hero.

Linese sighed and mentally scolded herself for her self ishness. A dutiful wife should rejoice in her husband's re turn, be happy for his achievements.

She fell in love with Chase because he was dashing and bold and knew exactly what he wanted. Now was no time t begin questioning those sentiments, although in her heart o hearts she admitted it would be easier if she didn't feel as i she were greeting a living legend.

A tiny thread of sweat snaked down the nape of her neck Linese tried to ignore the rising temperature and the throng of people elbowing her relentlessly forward, to the very edge of the platform, while she stared down the track toward the dark puff of smoke wending its way through the treetops Each mile it drew closer, the knot in her stomach grew larger.

Chase shifted his position on the hard train seat and peered out the window. The throbbing in his hip had be come a steady pain. He squinted his eyes and searched far out until the features of the land blurred into a shapeless nothingness that matched the formless void in his head. He prayed he would recognize something—anything—abou the landscape outside the train-car window.

A pretty river meandered down the rocky slope and cut a slash through tangled vines and dense forest. It was com pletely unknown to him. He might as well have been a

housand miles from the place his aide identified as his
ome, for all the familiarity it summoned in his brain. He
ubbed the heels of his hand against his eyes. His head hurt,
is leg hurt, and still he had no memory.

Sporadic recollections of certain events in his childhood
attled around in his head, like a few stones in an empty
oucket, but he could not grasp one shred of fact about his
adult life.

He didn't know who he was now or what kind of man he
had been before. Chase Cordell had had no recollection of
anything tangible since the Confederate shell fragment had
orn through his hip, knocked him senseless and taken him
out of the war forever.

He glanced over at the young man in uniform who had
accompanied him from the field hospital. Jeffrey's com-
panionable chatter had filled the hours on the train and
supplied some commonly known anecdotes about Chase's
military life, but Chase had no memory of his own with
which he could confirm or deny anything the young soldier
said.

Jeffrey must have felt Chase's eyes on him, because he
ooked over and smiled uncertainly. "I bet you are anxious
about getting home, aren't you, sir?"

The lad's question sent an uneasy shiver through Chase.
Several times on the journey he had caught the young soldier looking at him with an expression that was close to awe,
out he didn't know why the boy stared, and that clawed at
his insides.

Chase nodded stiffly in answer to Jeffrey's comment.
Anxious was too mild a word for the way he felt. There was
a knot in the pit of his stomach the size of a cannonball and
twice as heavy.

Chase had spent the better part of last night rereading the
stack of dog-eared letters that bore his name on the enve-
lopes. The letters were all signed by Linese—his *wife*—a
woman whose face he could not remember.

He was returning to a town he couldn't remember, to a wife he didn't know, from a bloody war he wanted only to forget.

The irony of it all was not lost to him. Chase leaned his head back against the seat and closed his eyes. He tilted his hat down over his face in order to spare himself further conversation with the eager young soldier.

Images of waking in the infirmary swept over him. At first he had been so heavily dosed with morphine and laudanum that everything had had a fuzzy, uncertain quality about it while he floated between life and death. Days later, when the surgeon told him he would live, Chase realized there was a giant chasm where his identity should have been. While his head cleared, volunteers were busy reading Linese's latest letters to him. Each letter they read brought more dread to Chase.

As the drugs wore off and Chase saw that his wound was mostly concentrated around his hip and not his skull, he tried to reason out what had happened to him.

There had been only a small lump on his head from hitting it on the ground. None of it made sense to him, so he remained silent about his condition, while he listened to the letters from home.

The woman who was evidently his lawful wife carefully outlined every detail of life in Mainfield, Texas, particularly the events concerning his grandfather, Captain Aloyisius Cordell.

It didn't take long for Chase to understand that his grandfather was mad, had been mad for years. In fact, that one memory returned crystalline clear within the first week of his confinement. Since then Chase had slowly regained sundry odd recollections of growing up under the strain of being the only grandchild of "mad Captain Cordell."

He couldn't remember actual events or specific places, but he recalled disembodied voices saying that phrase, "mad Captain Cordell," like some manner of identification that was incomplete if uttered any other way. While bits and pieces of torn memory swirled through his head, he had learned one important thing about himself. He was ashamed of his grandfather, humiliated by his mental affliction and the way the old man had been treated.

Chase swallowed hard and tried to control the anxiety rising inside him. He didn't quite know why, but some deep instinct had compelled him to keep his missing memory secret from everybody, including the doctors who had patched him up and cared for his damaged body. And he had kept his secret.

Through the weeks in the hospital and all through the long train ride home, he remained silent about his amnesia.

He sighed and lifted his hat brim. He prayed that when he opened his eyes, it would all be there—his past, his memory, himself.

But it was not.

Weeks of agonizing and analyzing kept bringing him back to one inescapable thought. The injury sustained in battle did not appear to be the reason for his missing memory. His thoughts kept returning to a question he did not want to ask, but knew he would have to face.

Was the Cordell bloodline responsible?

Had the affliction that manifested itself in his grandfather now touched Major Chase Cordell in the form of his missing memory?

The shrill train whistle jarred Chase from his tortured thoughts. He sat bolt upright in the seat and stared out the window. Green fields and wildflowers dotted the landscape. Mountain laurels shaded lush meadows with their gnarled branches. It was beautiful, this town that had no connection to him, this place that was nothing more than another stop on a long, lonely journey into his unknown past.

The passenger car lurched to a grinding halt while the metal brake screeched against the tracks. A cloud of steam rose up to obscure Chase's view of the station and the town.

He tried to massage some of the stiffness from his leg so he could rise from the hard seat.

Jeffrey appeared in the aisle and smiled. ''Here, Major Cordell, let me take your valise to the platform.''

Chase accepted the young man's offer to help. He adjusted the wide-brimmed Union officer's hat and waited until several other passengers had cleared the aisle before he attempted to reach the door. He was slow and his limp was worse today—the result of the cramped seat, the only partially healed wound, and his long legs being pinched into confinement, he guessed. He rubbed his gloved palm across his thigh and concentrated on getting the blood back into his foot while he limped toward the exit. He did not look up until he reached the outer door of the car.

The metallic rhythm of a brass band starting up froze him in place. A large, cheering crowd of strangers was standing outside the train car waving hats and hankies. They were calling a name—his name.

He felt all the color drain from his face and his knees went liquid. A rotund man with a tall black hat pushed his way forward. Sunlight winked off a huge red stone set in a gold stickpin while he vigorously pumped Chase's gloved hand.

Chase didn't have the slightest idea who the man was. He willed himself to smile and tried to ease the nervous tension he felt bracketing his mouth. The heat intensified beneath his heavy dark blue uniform and moisture beaded his forehead under the sweatband of his hat.

What were all these people doing here? a voice inside his head screamed.

''Major Cordell, it is an honor to receive you home, sir. The whole town has turned out and it is my very great pleasure, as mayor, to be the first one to welcome you back to Mainfield.''

Mayor. The moon-faced man was mayor of Mainfield. Chase tried to conjure up a bit of recollection to go along with that information, but none would be dredged up from the pit of darkness in his head.

Chase stared glumly out across the sea of faces. It was going to be harder than he dreamed, to pretend he was whole and that nothing was wrong with him.

For a moment he regretted not telling the army surgeons the truth—that he had no recollection of his life, or of the many small incidents they spoke of. Perhaps they could have done something, had some remedy, some treatment. At least he would have been spared this farce; he could have remained in the hospital, instead of trying to return to a place where he was a virtual stranger inside his own skin.

"Well, Major, it's been a pleasure traveling with you, sir." Jeffrey's voice wrenched Chase from his misery. Chase turned back to see Jeffrey standing stiff and straight.

"Have a good journey." Chase managed to give the young soldier a smart salute that denied the watery feel of his own legs. A loud cheer rose up from the crowd when Jeffrey returned the gesture.

A bright flash of painful recollection ripped through Chase's thoughts at the sound of the mob. In his mind's eye he saw a group of small boys taunting an old man with silver hair and a long, flowing mustache. The children were chanting a litany.

"Crazy Captain Cordell."

Chase gulped down his emotion and felt the cold, steely resolve sweep over him. No matter what it took, no matter how he might flounder in this strange and unknown place, Chase was not going to let anyone find out the truth about him. He no longer wished he had told the surgeons, he no longer pined for the safety of a hospital bed. Chase would sooner be struck dead than be an object of ridicule like his grandfather.

There was no indecision in him now. His course of action was clear and straight. He would bluff and wheedle and lie to keep his secret. He would inch his way through this nightmare until—by the grace of God—he might regain a tiny scrap of memory, but until that time he would keep his silence.

Chase looked down and saw the mayor's pudgy hands holding a bright scrap of ribbon. The politician babbled without end while he pinned it to the blue uniform. He marveled that the mayor could find an empty spot on his chest among the decorations the Northern army had already bestowed upon him. The small strips of ribbon felt heavy as stone on his Union coat because he didn't remember what they represented.

Suddenly it all became a blur. The crowd, the banners, all whirled in front of Chase without substance. He felt detached, alone, apart from everyone standing in the sweltering April heat.

He stared over the short mayor's shoulder and searched every face in the crowd, hoping against bitter hope that perhaps there would be one face amidst the throng that would spark some remembrance.

A heavy, cold weight grew in Chase's belly when no one was even vaguely familiar.

Except for one.

His tormented gaze kept returning to a tiny blond woman, nearly hidden beneath a straw bonnet and lace-covered parasol. She was biting her bottom lip. As unhappy as Chase was to be a war hero with no past and little hope for the future, she appeared to be even more miserable.

She met his eyes and a tiny quiver of her chin sent his belly plunging to the vicinity of his boot tops. He looked away, but something about the woman reached out to him.

He felt an odd affinity for her. She seemed to be a kindred spirit adrift in a sea of strangers. While all those around him smiled brightly and wished him well, her face held a measure of sadness. He would like to have spoken to the woman, to give her reassurance, but for the life of him he didn't know why he should feel that way.

"Now, Major, I'm sure you are glad to be home."

"Yes—yes, Mayor—I am." Chase found it difficult to pull his gaze away from the clear blue of the woman's compelling eyes. There seemed to be a silent question deep inside them.

For a moment Chase thought he knew what the question was, but it may have been fancy, because it had simply flitted away like a butterfly over a field of sweet, ripe clover like the rest of his past. Every feeling, every thought was no more substantial than a wisp of smoke he could not grasp.

"Come, Major Cordell, don't be shy. It's been a long time. There's not a man jack among us who would blame you for giving your little wife a kiss right here, in public."

Chase watched while the mayor took hold of the pretty blond woman's gloved hand and drew her forward. She stiffened beneath the politician's hold and Chase saw the color in her cheeks intensify when his body and hers abruptly made contact from breastbone to waist. The end of his sword scabbard swung around and hit him in the shin with a plink of sound. Several of Chase's medals poked him through the fabric of his uniform while the mayor shoved the woman with the intense blue eyes tighter against his chest.

Chase stared dumbly down at her upturned face. Heat arced between their bodies while they stood frozen on the platform. All the curious people who were strangers to Chase seemed to be waiting for him to do something, say something, to the woman.

"Go on, Linese, give your husband a proper reception," The mayor urged.

"Welcome home, Chase." She raised on tiptoe and touched her soft lips to the side of his face in a self-conscious greeting.

His heart slammed against his rib cage. *Linese*. This was Linese. This was his *wife*.

God, she was beautiful, and younger than his own twenty-one years, if he had his guess. She was the very image of what every soldier wished he had waiting for him at home. So why did Chase feel the cold wave of melancholy engulf him?

Chase swallowed hard and beseeched God to let him remember her, but nothing happened. He remembered nothing about her, felt nothing for her, except perhaps pity.

He was doomed to play out this charade in a life he could not recollect. And this poor woman, who had done nothing to deserve this kind of punishment, was condemned to play it out with him.

Chapter Two

The disparity in their height made it easy for Linese to look up at Chase and study his face beneath the wide, flop-brimmed hat.

He was older. His jaw was leaner, perhaps sterner than he remembered. There was a determined strength to his chin that had not been there before. Two years had brought him from brash youth to somber maturity. His boyish handsomeness had hardened into the rugged face of a man.

The familiar strand of raven hair was the same, though. It was peeking out from the band of his hat, near his abundant dark brows. There was an unfamiliar look in his gray eyes that made Linese shiver unconsciously while they slid over her face like inquisitive fingers. She could almost feel his probing scrutiny.

She drew back from his broad chest and twisted her hands together until the seams inside the gloves cut into her fingers and made her aware of what she was doing. The crowd around them seemed to be holding its breath, expecting him to say something.

"Linese," Chase acknowledged stiffly.

All of Mainfield seemed to release a collective sigh, as if some action of import had just taken place.

Chase didn't know what else to say to the woman. Any man, particularly one who had spent the past few weeks staring at survivors of war, would consider her a belle. He knew he was lucky to have a woman like this, knew he should feel pride to be her husband, but he did not. He searched his blighted soul and tried to find some memory of her.

There was none.

He found nothing but the same odd, haunted feeling of kinship with her, here among all the strangers who talked too loud and smiled too much. In the end, all Chase could do was stand woodenly on the platform, feeling like a green recruit, while he nervously flexed his fingers inside his soft leather gloves. He sensed Linese was no happier than he was, but she managed to give him a trembling smile before her dark brown lashes fluttered down to conceal her eyes from him.

A tendril of dread entwined itself around Chase's mind. Could she already see the difference in his actions? Had he made a blunder that she would reveal to the crowd of on-lookers? Was there some special word of greeting between them that he had failed to provide? A thousand fears rose up inside him.

He had been a fool to think he could deceive her. A woman would know any subtle change in the man with which she had shared bed and hearth. Chase silently cursed himself as more than a fool to have thought he could pull off his subterfuge. His pitiful deception had not lasted one hour since his return.

He maintained his rigid stance, ignoring the pain in his hip, for what seemed an eternity. Chase knew he was found out, while he waited for her to utter the words that would ring his death knell in front of the assembly. He mechanically worked the muscle in his jaw while the seconds ticked silently by, and yet she said nothing. Finally he could stand the suspense no more. Chase forced himself to speak to her, wishing to put an end to his misery.

"Let's go home, Linese." His voice was hard and flinty.

She looked up and blinked at him in obvious surprise. At the same moment, the mayor stepped in front of Chase as if to prevent him from leaving.

"We planned a little celebration for you, Chase. You can't leave so soon." The mayor's voice held a measure of irritation and authority.

Chase looked down at the man and felt the heat intensify beneath the sweatband of his hat. The last thing he felt like doing was struggling through some celebration where people would be telling him stories about things he didn't remember, and he didn't much care for the mayor's tone. If Linese was on the verge of exposing him, the fewer people around the better he would like it. If by some miracle she had not seen the lie in his eyes, then the sooner he could find a room and shut himself into it, the happier he would be, the easier it would be. Either way, he wanted out of Mainfield as soon as possible.

"I'm going home," he said flatly. Chase saw the mayor raise a brow in surprise, but the crowd obligingly parted in response to his request. He felt a hand on his arm and looked down at Linese, who stood at his side. Her small cloth-encased fingers gently plucked at the blue uniform, until he obliged her by lifting his arm away from his body enough for her to slip her fingers inside the crook of his elbow.

He tried not to limp too much when he fell into step beside her. It was an odd sensation, to be walking beside a woman whom he didn't know, but who knew him, or at least the man he had been two years ago. He allowed her to lead the way and attuned himself to her. Chase saw her staring straight ahead at a small surrey parked beside the train depot, which he suddenly realized was her destination.

Pure panic engulfed him in a cold wave. He would, of course, be expected to handle the horse, as would any self-respecting man. Fool that he was, he had not thought about that inevitability when he rudely refused the mayor's offer of a celebration. Chase didn't have any idea in which direction he should point the beast. He had no knowledge of where he lived, whether it be a house on the next street or a dwelling many miles away. Fear crept upon him like an assassin.

The petite woman, his wife, lurched to a stop beside him when his boots suddenly became anchored to the street. She looked up at him quizzically from under her wide parasol, but he was incapable of willing himself to move.

"Chase? Is something wrong?" she asked.

He looked down and forced himself to meet her eyes. A pang of guilt surged through him. This gentlewoman, *Linese,* did not deserve to be treated like a stranger.

"No—no. I, uh, it's just that I..." he stammered and shot a look back over his shoulder toward the main section of town. Maybe it was not too late to accept the mayor's offer. Maybe he could postpone the disaster awaiting him at the innocent-looking surrey.

His last chance was lost. The crowd had begun to disperse, few people remained. He was going to have to flounder through his confusion and pray he would survive this test. He shut his eyes for one moment and silently beseeched God for a memory, but no one answered his silent entreaty.

He opened his eyes and found her looking up at him. While she patiently watched him, he was struck again by her delicate features. She reminded him of a fragile bit of fine china. Her skin was the color of cream. She was too exquisite for a tall, rangy man like himself.

More questions swirled through his throbbing head. Had he been the kind of man who could sweet-talk a lady like Linese? Were they acquainted since childhood? Did some old friend introduce them? How had he won her affections? How well did she know him? A million unanswered thoughts popped into his mind while they stood staring at each other in the heat.

"Did you wish to go to the office?" Her brows rose into arches over cornflower blue eyes. "Hezikiah will be gone already, if you had hoped to see him, but if you would prefer to go to the office first, we could—"

"Yes, I would like to visit the office." He cut her off abruptly, thanking God for whatever it was she was talking about.

"All right. Shall we walk?"

"Yes." Chase dared not allow himself to be forced into the surrey—not yet. His hip was a steady, agonizing throb, but he summoned his strength and prepared to walk.

Linese paused beside him, and he realized she was waiting for his arm again. It was an odd thing, this possessive feeling inside him that answered her actions. When she looped her gloved hand through his elbow he felt the nearly unbearable heat between their bodies increase, but it was not an altogether unpleasant sensation. Chase tried to ignore her nearness while his mind raced ahead, trying to make sense of the disjointed riddle of his life, and the strange, haunted connection he felt for Linese.

"I think you'll find the office is little changed," she said softly.

What office could she be referring to? Linese had made reference to a newspaper in her letters. Was that what she meant? He plucked up his courage and steeled himself to meet the second challenge of his return.

Linese kept her eyes straight ahead, but her thoughts were only on Chase. The hours she had spent weaving fantasies about his homecoming swam in her memory. She had hoped he would sweep her into his arms and murmur words of affection. How foolish she had been to expect such a display from Chase Cordell. He had not seen fit to put his feelings into words before he left, had not done it by letter, and he seemed to have little inclination to do so now.

Linese frowned at her silly thoughts and lifted her parasol higher. Chase leaned almost imperceptibly into the welcome circle of shade, but she saw he kept his body just short of actually touching her. Her hand rested within his arm, but other than that small point, Chase held himself stiff to avoid touching her.

She tried to remember every letter she had sent him. Had she made some horrible blunder? Did she let something slip about her activities at the *Gazette*, something that caused him to treat her with such cold reserve? Should she ask?

No. There was nothing to worry about, she told herself. Just be patient. She swallowed her fears and forced herself to put one foot in front of the other. A deep intake of breath brought the familiar scent of him to her nostrils, and she experienced a thousand forgotten sensations. She was filled with joy and apprehension at his return.

There was something odd about him though. He seemed different in a way that was hard to explain. Her eyes told her that Chase Cordell had indeed returned, but her instincts told her something was missing. Something had changed drastically in the two years he had been gone, and it wasn't only a maturing of his face and body. There was a reservation between them that signified more than just the time he had been away. He was different.

Chase should have been in his element with the whole town cheering his return. He had always adored admiration and praise, but he seemed anxious to leave the idolization of Mainfield's populace. Even now, while he smiled and nodded to the people they passed on the way to the *Gazette*, Linese sensed a strain in him. His behavior was most puzzling, not at all like the brash young man who had swept into the Ferrin County social and demanded her heart.

He hesitated slightly and appeared to be waiting for her to lead the way to the office, but Linese dismissed that notion as folly. She walked beside him and tried to match her step with the cadence of his limp, without making it obvious she was doing so. His injury was probably the reason for his halting progress. She well remembered his pride. Chase would have walked through fire rather than admit he was in

liscomfort. Yes, that was surely the reason he kept her fingers tightly within the crook of his arm and glanced at her
from time to time.

After she settled into Cordellane, she had realized that
Chase had felt compelled to be a better man than most men,
to make up for the mental frailty of his sweet grandfather.
In the time he had been away, she had come to understand
his need to prove his physical prowess. He had been trying
to prove, to himself and everyone else, that he was not af-
flicted with weakness, not the way Captain Cordell was.

She understood why Chase felt the way he did. Captain
Cordell was ignored and kept out of the mainstream of life
in Mainfield, particularly during this conflict about slavery
and secession. He was patronized and overlooked, treated
like a harmless nuisance by most. Yes, Linese understood
what drove Chase Cordell.

Chase gritted his teeth together and tried to block out the
maelstrom inside his mind. The combination of heat, the
strain of racking his brain for memory, and trying not to
limp beside Linese, made him tired beyond belief. He longed
to sit down, to be alone, to find some peace.

Linese sighed and he knew he should speak to her. He
knew he should be making small talk, to find some way of
reassuring her obvious fears, but he had little confidence
that he could do so without exposing himself as a fraud, so
he remained silent. By the time he and Linese had walked
the three short blocks to a newspaper office with Gazette
painted on the window in bold black letters, he was limping
stiffly.

A wave of embarrassment swept over him when he was
forced to place his butter-colored glove against the building
for support. Linese pretended not to notice, but Chase knew
she did. It sent a bitter feeling through his soul, one he did
not understand but found impossible to ignore.

She unlocked the door with a key she pulled from inside
the small cloth reticule dangling from her wrist. When the
door opened, the pungent odor of ink and paper perme-

ated the still summer air. Chase filled his lungs with the odor and felt his senses sharpen, but still no memory came from the black abyss of his mind.

Linese turned to him as soon as they were inside the musty, warm office. Fire sparked inside blue eyes that had appeared as calm as pools only a short while ago. Chase was puzzled and fascinated by the transformation in her.

"Chase Cordell, I know it goes against your grain to admit any kind of physical weakness, particularly in front of anyone, but it is obvious to me that you are not fully recovered from your injury. Why didn't you say so? If you have no objection, I'm going to send for Toby Sillers to take us home—immediately."

Part of him knew instinctively, without actually remembering, that what she said was true. The man he had been did not easily admit to weakness. But the man he was now, the broken shell of himself, was sensible enough to know he was not fully healed. He also realized with a jolt that his wound could save him further humiliation for a short while.

A wave of relief surged over Chase, followed by mortification. He realized he did not like to feel vulnerable in front of this woman. His cheeks and neck flushed. He didn't want to appear weak in her presence, but he would have to swallow his pride and accept her offer—or risk exposing himself. The choice was not a comfortable one for him to make.

"I am a bit unsteady on my feet these days. I think that would be a good idea—Linese." Her name sounded odd coming from his lips. He said it silently in his head a few times to accustom himself to it.

She nodded curtly and walked out the door. He slumped into a chair beside a table rigged with a large roller and dragged off his wide-brimmed hat in frustration.

How could he hope to keep up this pretense when he could not even remember his wife? How in God's name was he going to accomplish this deception when he didn't even know the way home, or what that home looked like?

Chase didn't know when Linese returned, but he looked up to find her studying him from the open doorway. She stared into his eyes and he felt his soul laid bare. It was a sensation like nothing he had ever experienced, not even in the horror of war.

He stared at the face of the woman he had married, had known intimately but could not remember, and died a little inside.

His gaze sent a frisson of confusion threading through her heart. Here he was, willing to accept help, admitting to his obvious injury, something she would never have thought possible. A wave of compassion flowed over Linese at the new depth she saw in her husband.

"I'm sorry, Chase. I never meant to imply that you were not *able* to drive us home. I—I only meant that it would give me pleasure to do a little something for you—if you would allow it."

Chase experienced a strange contest of emotions. He'd had the same sensation when, two days after he was wounded, soldiers came to his bedside to visit. Major Cordell's quick temper and iron-fisted control of the men beneath him was a constant topic of the lopsided conversation. He had found it disconcerting, but it was nothing compared to what the expression in Linese's blue eyes was doing to him.

Each time she fastened that open, trusting look on him, he felt trapped in a skin too tight, too confining. He was consigned to a life of uncertainty, having to live up to expectations created by himself in a past he no longer knew.

Chase Cordell was in a living hell.

Toby kept the horses at a good pace all the way out of Mainfield. Linese was grateful for the breeze wending its way through the hickory trees and for the shady spots dappling the lane. Soon she was considerably cooler than she had been in Mainfield, but no less troubled.

She found herself sneaking glances at Chase whenever he wasn't looking her way, which seemed to be most of the time. She watched him, puzzled by the enthusiasm he displayed over the most ordinary and mundane things along the old road. He leaned out of the carriage and virtually drank in his surroundings. The gristmill, the same mill he had ridden past a hundred times before, captured his interest.

For a full ten minutes he asked Linese strange, halting questions, then he lapsed into stony silence and fidgeted with his gloves beside her.

Linese accepted the fact he was just plain uncomfortable being with her. By the time they pulled up in the graveled lane leading to Cordellane, she was nearly ill with anxiety, sure that she had done something to betray her secret to him.

Toby halted the horse and she turned to look at Chase, who seemed frozen in his seat. He was staring up at the stately old house with an expression of confounded awe in his smoky gray eyes. It pierced her heart to see such a poignant look on his bleak face. It occurred to her that a man's home would take on great significance in the face of war and possible death. He must have often thought fondly of his home while he was away.

"Big, isn't it?" he said in husky whisper. He continued to flex his fingers inside the thick gloves.

Chase wondered how a man could completely forget his home. The two-story rambling structure was nothing more than board and stone and mystery to him.

He knew with a bitter certainty that he should be seeing an artist's colorful palette of recollection inside his head, but all he found was a dark gray void of emptiness and desolate feelings of loss.

"I told you Cordellane was too big and empty the first time you brought me here. Remember?" Linese gently reminded him.

She saw a muscle in his rock-hard jaw flinch and she cringed inwardly at his reaction to her words. It was as if an invisible wall lay between them in the surrey.

"No. I don't remember that." His words were short, his tone harsh.

Linese tried to ignore the sting of his abrupt reply. Mentally she vowed to do more to make him feel at home and less like a stranger.

Chase jumped down to the dusty driveway and she saw him wince in pain. He reached up his mustard-colored glove and she froze in place, unable to move while she savored the sight of him. She realized, with some awe, that until this moment his return had not fully registered in her heart. She had known he was home, had prepared for it, longed for it, but up until now she had not believed it.

Now, while she stared at him in front of Cordellane, she allowed herself to embrace the happy truth.

Chase was home—he had returned to her.

The dark blue uniform hugged his lean, muscular body. The wide-brimmed hat sent complimentary shadows over his craggy jaw and full, determined lips. New lines were deeply carved around his eyes to add character and depth to his countenance.

He grasped her hand tightly in his own, and her heart fluttered in the same old way it used to. Chase Cordell was still the handsomest man in Tyron County.

She'd loved him from the first moment he'd spoken to her. She loved him now. Linese wanted to make him a good wife and fill up the old house with a passel of laughing children—children that would make him proud and drive the silence from Cordellane's big, empty rooms. Her pulse quickened a little at the thought.

Two years had been taken from them. The sooner she and Chase could begin a family, the better she would like it. No matter how many changes she had to make, no matter how many adjustments, it would be worth it to have Chase home again.

Her young husband's eager lovemaking on their wed
ding night had been almost frightening to her; now sh
longed to know his touch, to return his passion, to bear hi
children.

"Marjorie? Marjorie, is that you?" Captain Cordell'
voice rang out. He appeared at the corner of the stables an
interrupted Linese's thoughts. Chase deposited her on th
ground and she followed his line of vision to the old man.

He was dressed in a dark green coat and high-toppe
boots. Sunlight glimmered along his silver hair and lon
mustache. He was a fine figure of a man, for his advance
years. His body was still straight and tall, and only th
slightly blank look in his eyes would give anyone a clue tha
he was not like any other landowner and ex-Texas Ranger.

"No, Captain, it's me." Linese gestured at him and urge
him forward to join them.

Chase watched the old man. Suddenly he felt the sensa
tion of his scalp shrinking around his skull while a hot tin
gle crept up his spine.

Two things crystallized into painful clarity in one painfu
heartbeat. His aunt Marjorie had died from consumptiv
fever, and his grandfather had been crazy since the day sh
had been laid to rest in the family plot behind Cordellane.

Pity, responsibility and embarrassed shame all welled u
inside Chase. He fought to understand the source of th
emotions.

He heard a sound and glanced at Toby Sillers. The bo
ducked his head and sniggered before he turned away. H
had been laughing at Chase's grandfather.

Realization dawned on Chase in a rush. He did not trul
know the man who stood before him, but he shared his hu
miliation at their mutual flaw. Something else imprinted it
self upon the empty slate of Chase's mind.

Nothing had changed while he had been away. The Cor
dell madness was apparently still the object of ridicule i
Mainfield.

Chase felt resolution harden in his chest like a great chunk of ice. He would never let anyone know of his defect. He would not allow another person to suffer under the weight of a curse that they had no part in creating.

He had no way of knowing with any certainty why he had lost his memory, but the thought that it might be, the hint that it could possibly be inherited loomed thick and dark before him.

Chase swallowed hard.

Would he continue to lose more and more of himself, until at last he was like the man who stood before him? Was he doomed to go slowly mad until he had no reason left at all? He gulped down the horror that washed over him and made a silent promise to himself.

Unless, or until he could be sure this affliction was not the result of Cordell blood, he was determined to do whatever was necessary to make sure he did not sire children—no matter how great the sacrifice, or temptation, might be.

At supper the tension increased. Captain Cordell asked no less than six times who Chase was. Linese had always marveled that his mind seemed to weaken even more when people other than Cordells were at Cordellane. The oldest Jones girl, Effie, had stayed around to help Linese lay out a big dinner to celebrate Chase's return home and her very presence sent the poor Captain into mumbling fits, followed by prolonged periods of vacant-eyed silence.

Linese watched Chase grow more sullen with each word his grandfather uttered. She finally gave up trying to make the old gentleman understand who Chase was, and simply allowed the heavy strain to fall like a dark curtain between them all.

Consequently, the celebration meal was a total failure. She sighed and thought about the days she had spent procuring fresh milk. It had taken all her cunning, but she had even managed to get hold of a smoked ham for the occasion. More food than she or the Captain normally saw in a month sat in front of Chase, yet he picked at his food with little interest. The fact he did not even appear to be aware of her efforts to lay a nice table just for him bruised her deeply. His indifference to her hard work stung almost as much as his peculiar moodiness.

She choked back frustrated tears, refusing to let Effie see her cry, when he abruptly stood up from the table and stalked from the room without a word to either her, or Captain Cordell.

Linese knew Chase Cordell had been known as a bold man around Mainfield, one with a short temper and quick fists, but he had never been regarded as a rude one, and she was not going to give the local gossips any cause to begin saying so now. So she bit her tongue and smiled while she chewed and swallowed, never tasting a thing she put in her mouth.

Two hours later, the lamp illuminated Linese's path up the stairs. Her temples throbbed and every muscle in her body cried out for rest. The chirping of crickets down in the hollow seemed deafening in comparison to the silence that hung in the walls of Cordellane. She put her foot on the stairs and wondered again what had gone wrong with Chase's homecoming.

"Linese?" His deep voice drifted down to her from the darkened landing above and startled her from her musings.

"Yes?" She halted and peered up at him, half-concealed in the quivering shadows cast by her lantern. She had not realized he was standing above her, watching her approach. Her pulse quickened a bit at the notion that Chase had been upstairs waiting for her to come to bed. She caught herself smiling in the dim lighting.

"Linese, I have decided . . . I'm going out for some air. I didn't want you to feel you had to, that is, you shouldn't wait up for me. I will be late." His voice was hollow with meaning.

The impact of Chase's blunt words settled on Linese like a blanket of ice. He did not *wish* for her to wait up. In fact, in his own Texas gentleman's way, he was telling her *not* to wait up. She had walked on eggshells around him all afternoon, wondering what was the matter.

Now she knew. It was not some slip in her letters that revealed her surreptitious work at the *Gazette* that had him frowning at her in annoyance. It was not his grandfather's ramblings, or the food she cooked.

No. His dark and depressed mood had nothing to do with any of those things. Chase did not wish to share her bed, but did not know how to tell her. The dawning realization sent cold gooseflesh climbing along her arms.

Linese fought to control the trembling of her hand lest she drop the lamp and let Chase know how much his rebuff wounded her. Bruised pride and feminine ego forced her to reply as if nothing were wrong.

"Now that the subject has come up, Chase, if you would not be too inconvenienced, I would prefer to move my things into the adjoining room. You've been gone a long time. We both have a considerable *adjustment* to make." She lied to cover her own hurt and humiliation at his rejection.

The last thing she wanted was to force herself on him if he did not want to be with her. Better to cry alone in her own bed than feel unwanted in his, she told herself sternly.

A wall of conflict rose up inside Chase while he listened to Linese's steady voice. He watched her face in the glow of lamplight, searching for he knew not what.

He should be relieved at her willingness to comply with his wishes, but his male pride was offended. No, not offended—hurt?

Could he really be sorry?

Sadness twined its way around his chest and threatened to squeeze the breath from his lungs. For some reason that defied logic, Chase wished things could be different be-

tween him and Linese. He longed to salvage a single mem
ory of the love they must have shared, but found only th
formless void of deprivation in his mind.

"Is that arrangement acceptable to you, Chase?"

Her voice jolted him back to the present. He had secretl
hoped for a chance to get to know her, to find the answer t
his own private hell within her arms.

"What? Oh, yes. That would be perfectly acceptable.
don't wish to impose myself upon you."

He said it but knew it was a lie. He wanted very much t
touch another human being, to feel at home and at peace
but knew he never could as long as his past was a myster
and any mistake could reveal the truth to Linese.

Chase slowly descended each step until he stood on th
same tread with her. She forced herself to look up and mee
his eyes, even though her heart was breaking with the ef
fort. But, instead of the haughty, cold stare she expected t
follow such stern words, his gray eyes were clouded wit
pain and a poignant expression of yearning.

Confusion swirled in her mind and heart. How could h
speak to her so and have such sorrow in his eyes? Linese in
stinctively reached out and laid her hand on his bare fore
arm to offer some comfort. Chase flinched beneath her ligh
touch.

He did not pull away, but he stared at her hand for a lon
moment as if it were the first time he had ever seen it. Sh
wondered if the fading ink stains were noticeable in th
muted, wavering light. To prevent him from seeing them
she lifted the lantern up, away from her hand, but it onl
made his face look more bleak and lonely. He reached ou
one slim finger and slowly traced along the smooth gol
band he had put on her fourth finger himself. His eyes wer
so sad and empty, she felt a painful tightening of her ches
while she watched him.

"Sleep well, Linese." There was longing in the flat tone of his voice. He leaned down and deposited one chaste kiss on her forehead, then he turned and limped down the stairs.

She stood frozen on the spot and watched her husband disappear out the front door and into the humid Texas night.

Chapter Three

Linese sipped the hot chicory and watched Chase over the rim of her cup. She had listened to his uneven pacing long into the night, beyond the door that separated their rooms, after he returned from his walk. Whatever had denied him sleep still lingered this morning, if his creased brow and ravaged expression were any indication. Linese looked away from his stern face and tried to calm her tumultuous emotions.

She wanted to ask him what was wrong, to offer some kind of solace to her husband. But she doubted he would welcome her comfort, since he had seen fit to exile her from his bed. She glanced back at Chase and found him looking at her with a questioning expression in his eyes.

She wondered if he felt the same uncomfortable unfamiliarity she experienced each time she stole a glance at him. Linese's stomach lurched when she finally admitted to herself that two weeks was time enough to fall hopelessly in love, but not time enough to learn about the man who was her husband. In a strange and undefinable way, he had kept her at arm's length during their frenzied courtship, almost as if he were shielding himself from her, or perhaps her from him. Now she wondered if maybe he had been hiding this dark, brooding side of his nature from her. She shook her head to banish the foolish notion, only to have it replaced by a new fear that popped into her head.

Perhaps he was regretting his impulsiveness. Perhaps he now regretted proposing to a virtual stranger. Maybe the two years he had been at war had made him wonder if his choice for his wife had been unwise. That could account for his decision to sleep apart.

The words that sent her into the adjoining bedroom continued to batter her pride, just as they had kept her from rest while she listened to his uneven journey across the wood floor all night long. Linese placed the cup of chicory into the saucer and acknowledged the painful truth. She was married to Chase, but the man sitting at the opposite end of the long polished table was no more than a stranger.

A stern forbidding stranger, a voice inside her head reminded her.

She had never been a quitter. And she would not give up on her marriage. Now was about as good a time as any to begin learning about the man she married.

Did he prefer silence in the morning? Was he the kind of man who wished to start the day with activity, or did he ease into it slowly? He had ridden off the day after he brought her from her home, a county away, to Cordellane, and she had no idea about his likes or dislikes. If she took each day as it came, and learned his moods, she was confident they could begin to rebuild a life together.

"What do you wish to do today, Chase?" She watched his reactions carefully.

Chase looked up at her and grimaced. The gesture was an aspect of pure irony—or dread. Uncertainty shone in his gunmetal gray eyes for the first time in Linese's recollection.

"What have you been doing to fill your days while I've been gone?" He answered her question with one of his own.

She frowned. He focused on her face intently. He seemed to be perched on the edge of his chair, waiting for her answer with as much anticipation as she had been awaiting his reply only a heartbeat before. Much to Linese's chagrin she had somehow traded places, and now Chase was the inquisitor. Panic welled up inside her chest.

Chase's dour warning about women who nudged their way into a man's world rang inside her head. If he learned she had spent nearly every day at the *Gazette* working, would he banish her from his bed forever? Would there be any hope of recapturing the passion they had once shared? Or would it, as she suspected, drive a bigger wedge between them and crush their fragile relationship before it had a chance to live again?

She knew she would tell him the truth about the *Gazette*, but not now.

Her head swam. It was no secret to people in town that she went to the office each day. Chase would probably hear that information from any number of men in Mainfield who would see fit to let him know what had happened in his absence.

The only real secret she kept from him was what she did once she arrived at the *Gazette*—a secret only she and Hezikiah shared. The good people, most particularly the businessmen of Mainfield, would be shocked to learn the words they read calling for loyalty and commitment were her own thoughts and not those of Hezikiah Hershner.

Chase cleared his throat and she knew the silence between them had gone on too long. He was still staring at her with his brows drawing more firmly together.

"I, uh, I spent some time with Hezikiah," Linese stammered.

Chase gnawed the inside of his jaw and forced his mind to link the threads of information together. Linese had mentioned Hezikiah's name yesterday, at the newspaper office. Her letters had spoken of him in passing. Chase searched his mind for some hard fact of memory. Nothing tangible floated to the top of the murk inside his head. He did not know who Hezikiah Hershner was, or why his wife would spend time with him. He took a desperate risk and plunged forward like a blind man on the edge of a cliff.

"Then let me escort you to Mainfield to see him today."
Chase forced a stiff smile to his lips, and even while he was
doing so, a tiny part of his mind mulled over the idea that
his wife had been spending time with another man.

He found himself scowling at the notion while he chided
himself for having such preposterous feelings about a
woman he only remembered meeting yesterday. It was ab-
surd, yet the feeling of annoyance lingered despite his efforts to wipe it from his mind.

Linese watched Chase's face in confusion. He seemed to
want her company. That fact both elated and perplexed her.
If he wanted to be with her, then why did he stay away from
their bed? She felt as if she were trying to balance on the
sharp edge of a sword, one misstep either way would end
their fragile marriage.

"All right. I'm sure Hezikiah will be pleased to see you,
and of course you will probably want to talk to him about
the operation of the paper, now that you've returned."

"Perhaps," he said noncommittally. Each time he opened
his mouth he had the sensation of facing enemy cannon fire.
And mention of this man had brought an unexplainable
edginess to him. He had not expected one thing to lead to
the other.

He had no memory of the paper or what was involved in
the running of it. By going back to Mainfield today he was
setting himself up for possible disaster. Yet, he was going to
have to find out what he had done before the war—and he
had a burning desire to quench his curiosity about Hershner. The question was, could he delve into his past and discover the man he was without revealing to Linese that he
was going mad?

Chase shifted uncomfortably in the narrow buggy seat.
He was acutely aware of Linese sitting next to him. He tried
to keep his mind on the horse, but it was difficult to ignore
his lovely wife. He wrapped his fingers tighter around the
reins and told himself not to steal sidelong glances at Lin-

ese every few minutes like a gourd-green youth, but it did no good. His eyes strayed toward her against his will.

She was wearing gloves again. It was a puzzling habit. Chase wondered how she could keep from withering in the damnable heat, much less wear gloves. He noticed that the oppressive humidity cast a healthy glow across her cheeks and made her lips dewy. Her figure was good and she had a quality of tranquility that drew him like a bee to a flower.

She was pretty, and he was only human. Knowing he had held her in the past, at least on the occasion of their wedding night, only made his dilemma worse. It was like trying to remember the words to a familiar tune only to have your mind go blank and leave you humming off-key in frustration.

He squirmed again and tried to focus on something other than her, but it was useless. All night he had paced the floor and racked his brain, trying to remember her. He forced himself to think of the smooth gold band on her finger, to try and remember placing it there, but he could not. When the pinking dawn found him, he was exhausted and more disheartened than when he'd stepped off the train. There was not one single recollection about the woman who was his wife, or his life in this place he had once called home.

Chase pulled the reins taut and the buggy slowed to a stop in front of the *Gazette*. The heat shimmered up from the hard-packed street in waves. Luckily, he had managed to remember the route young Toby had used to take them home yesterday. Each store and landmark he saw, each face and name, he committed to memory in the hopes he could continue his charade for one more hour, one more day.

"It's too hot for you to walk," he stated. "I'll let you out here and take the buggy back to the livery."

He climbed down from the buggy and allowed himself to look up at Linese. She turned to him and her cool-water blue eyes sliced a path from his head to his belly. He wasn't going to keep his secret very long if he kept falling into the depths of those eyes each time he looked at her.

"That's very kind of you, Chase." She picked up her full skirt and scooted close to the edge of the seat so he could help her to the ground. Linese's voice resonated with obvious surprise at his suggestion.

He was taken aback by her response. Was his kindness something she didn't expect? Another suspicious doubt about the kind of man he had been in the past snaked its way into his consciousness. What kind of treatment had he given his young wife before he left her? Was he exposing himself by extending the most common courtesy?

Chase grasped her gloved hand and prepared to help her from the buggy. He found himself wondering again why she wore the gloves when it was so hot. He wanted to ask her, then choked back the words. What if he was already supposed to know? There were a million questions he had about this woman and what they had shared, and no way to find any answers without subjecting himself to ridicule, or worse yet—her pity.

"Chase? Is something wrong?" Her voice snapped him out of his trance.

He discovered that he was holding her, suspended halfway between the buggy and the ground. Her shoes hovered several inches above the earth. For a tiny fraction of time his brain registered how pleasant it was to have her so near. A hot flush of embarrassment flooded his cheeks.

"No, nothing is wrong. Nothing at all." His voice was gruff with the lie.

She flinched at his tone and he saw her blink rapidly for a minute. Was she holding back tears? Dear God, if she cried he would be undone. The temptation to hold her for another minute or two tugged at him, but he let her down to the ground and tore his eyes away from her face. He climbed stiffly back into the seat without meeting her gaze again.

Chase gathered the reins and drove the buggy down the street, but when he reached the corner, he could stand it no more. He gave in to his impulse and glanced back.

Linese was watching him. For an instant their gazes met and he felt something flit through his mind, but before he could analyze whether it was a memory, it winnowed away. Chase swallowed his disappointment and urged the horse on to Goten's Livery.

The man Linese had pointed out as being Ira Goten was raking manure at the side of the stable when Chase stopped the buggy. A slick sorrel with wild white-ringed eyes poked his head out of a stall at the back of the stable and nickered at the new arrival.

"'Morning, Major." Ira leaned on his rake handle and watched Chase lead the horse and buggy toward the back of the barn.

"'Morning, Mr. Goten. I'd like to keep the horse here while my wife and I are at the *Gazette*—if that's all right," Chase explained.

Ira smiled and gave a little snort. "Mr. Goten? No need to be so formal with me, Chase. I've been wondering when you'd stop by. Come inside. I have something of yours I've been meaning to return to you."

"Something of mine?" Chase swallowed hard. He narrowed his eyes and stared at the man who evidently knew him, and once again found his own memory blank.

"Tie your horse up here, I'll see to him in a bit." Ira placed the rake against the fence and led the way inside the stable.

The mustiness of grain, straw and horse sweat filled the air. Chase paused a minute to allow his eyes to adjust to the dim light. There was a harness spread out on the floor and assorted tools were scattered around in the dirt and grain chaff. Chase watched Ira stride to a corner and move a wooden box out of the way. Then he squeezed his lean body into a dark cranny where he lifted the lid off a staved barrel.

The aroma of cracked corn filled the air while Ira dug through the grain with his bare hands. His arm disappeared nearly to the shoulder before he smiled and started to pull it out.

"There, I've finally got it."

Ira shook the bits of corn off his arm while he extracted it from the barrel. When his hand reappeared, he was clutching an oilskin-wrapped bundle.

"I kept it real nice for you." Ira Goten thrust the bundle toward Chase. "I see your hand hardly scarred at all."

Chase followed the man's gaze to the narrow white scar on the back of his right hand. He didn't know how he got it, but it was plain Ira Goten knew. Some deep instinct inside Chase told him not to touch the bundle the man held out to him, but he ignored the silent warning within his head. Whatever was concealed inside the oilskin, it was a link to his past, a bit of the puzzle he longed to piece together. He reached out and took the object from Ira's hands.

The bundle was hard and moderately heavy in his grasp. He allowed his fingers to wrap around it while curiosity burned inside him. No recall came attached to the object. He wanted to pull back the covering and see what he held, but Ira Goten was watching him, so he forced himself to wait.

"I never did get a chance to talk to you again before you left. We were damned lucky that night in Ferrin County, weren't we?" Ira smiled but it was a cheerless expression. "We did what we had to for the cause, didn't we, Chase? And now you've come home a major with all kinds of decorations." Ira shook his head from side to side as if amazed by the outcome of Chase's time in the war.

Finally, Chase could wait no longer. He turned the oilskin over and untied it. Slowly, to hide his eagerness, he pulled back the covering until the barrel of a Colt appeared.

"Yep, it's just like you left it." Ira reached into one oversize pocket of his overalls and pulled out a small leather bag. Ira dropped the bag into Chase's empty hand with a metallic plop that was surely money. "I intended to give you this, as well."

"What—?" Chase asked under his breath.

"Take it. God knows you earned it. I kept it for you all the while you were gone."

He knew what he would see before he ever pulled the cords at the top to look inside the bag. The sound had been clear and unmistakable. Just as he'd expected, a stack of gold coins was nestled in the bottom of the leather pouch.

Chase yanked the top closed. He couldn't look at the money. Holding the gun in his hand, hearing what Goten said, he was afraid to think of what he had done to get the coins.

He looked up at Ira Goten's lean, weathered face and found himself wondering what kind of man he had been before he rode off to war. What was he involved in that would compel this man to keep a gun hidden for two years? And how much blood stained the small bag of gold coins in his hand?

Chase dumped the gold coins deep into his trouser pocket. He tossed the small leather bag in a heap of manure outside Ira's barn, then he slid the Colt beneath the buggy seat. His head ached from trying to remember what they signified. Now he found himself dreading the moment when he might actually remember his past. Only hours ago it had been the most important task in his life, now he was apprehensive that he might find himself face-to-face with a past he could take no pride in, a past that might shame him more than his grandfather's feeble mind.

While Chase walked to the *Gazette,* he was occupied with nothing but questions about his past life. Each time he searched his mind for answers, all he found were more murky questions. And when he looked at his grandfather, he felt a mingling of fear and an overwhelming responsibility to protect and shield the old man from ridicule.

Chase sighed and ran his hand through his hair while he strode unevenly down the alleyway. He had confronted nothing but mystery since he stepped off the train. First, his wife seemed surprised when he showed her the most basic kindness, which made him question their former relationship, now he'd been given a hidden weapon and Chase knew there was a damned good chance he had used it to obtain the gold Ira handed him.

He was beginning to think returning to Mainfield had been a mistake. Everything and everyone he met made him want to turn around and ride out, to lose himself in obscurity, to forget about finding his lost self. Everyone except for Linese.

Linese made him want to stay. Her shy smile and delicate features lured him toward the unknown. The thought that he could reclaim a past they had shared made him want to challenge his fears, to probe his past. She was an anchor in a sea of doubt and despair. He realized that even though he had no real feeling for her that he could recall, no actual memory of having fallen in love with her, he was glad she was his wife. He was glad she was the woman who had waited two years for his return.

The sudden realization brought a cold fist of sadness to Chase. If not for the fear of his infirmity being discovered, he would gladly seek comfort in Linese's arms. It was a bittersweet truth to face. He would happily allow himself to be a real husband to her, if not for the possibility of her comparing him now to the man he had been.

Chase feared she would find the present persona of himself sadly lacking. She had known him in a way no other person could have known him. Any slip of the tongue, any mistake in action would bring the truth crashing around him like grapeshot. That one fact forced him to keep a rock-solid wall between himself and Linese.

Chase was still lost in his own private hell when he stepped through the door of the newspaper office and found himself toe-to-toe with Mayor Kerney. The shorter man looked up at him. Chase glanced around and found a small group of well-dressed, prosperous-looking men inside the *Ga-*

zette. One man was verbally haranguing a whipcord-thin fellow covered from chin to toe in black ink. Linese was standing in the corner of the room watching the whole scene in tight-lipped but silent disapproval. She still had her gloves on and held her bonnet stiffly in one hand.

The besmudged man turned away from his inquisitor and looked at Chase. His black eyes glittered with intelligent irritation. Chase surmised he was staring at Hezikiah Hershner and he felt a measure of relief.

He knew it was foolish that, under the circumstances, he would have begrudged Linese the company of a young, handsome man in his absence, but he admitted to himself he was glad Hezikiah was twice his age and plain as pudding.

"I'm glad you've arrived, Major. These gentlemen want to talk to the newspaper editor about certain plans they have," Hezikiah told Chase curtly.

Chase saw the printer's gaze slide over to Linese. She lowered her eyes and flushed a pretty rose under the man's pointed attention. Hershner stared at her as if he expected her to say something more, but she remained silent under Chase's gaze. He had the feeling there was much more going on beneath the cool exterior of Linese's proper manners and demure silence. He tried to quell the sharp, yearning desire he had to explore her depths. With little enthusiasm, Chase forced himself to look back at Mayor Kerney and away from the beautiful mystery he was married to.

The mayor stepped forward. Chase remembered the long-winded speech he had suffered through at the train station and cringed inwardly. It was too damned hot, and his head hurt from trying to remember Ira Goten and his mysterious gifts, to be subjected to another political sermon.

"I told you, Hershner. Major Cordell will be pleased to see us and just as pleased to hear what we have to say." The mayor winked at Chase as if they shared a confidence. Doubt about his past came seeping back into his limbs like cold water into a sponge.

Hezikiah turned back toward the press. He mumbled something under his breath that Chase couldn't quite make out.

"Why don't you step into my husband's office, Mayor Kerney," Linese gestured to a door that cut a wall in two equal sections. "I'm sure you will want to speak privately."

Chase didn't have the slightest idea what the men wanted to speak to him about, and he didn't want to speak with them privately or any other way. He grasped Linese's gloved hand in his own and looked down at her. When he stared into her eyes he felt an internal tug. For one moment he thought he might remember her, but he was wrong, and the strange notion evaporated from his mind. Disappointment left him feeling empty and more alone.

He knew it was foolish to want her with him, but he did. When she stood beside him, he felt less like a trapped animal.

"Linese." He lowered his voice so only she could hear. "I'd like you to be with me in case I have any questions about—about the *Gazette*—about what's been going on while I was away." He marveled at how easily the lie slipped from his tongue. Had he been a liar in the past or was this aspect of his murky personality something new?

"You want me to be there while you talk business?" she murmured softly.

"Yes." Chase watched Linese scan his face with innocent blue eyes that turned him inside out. She had the ability to make him feel stripped bare to the bone, make him feel more of a man and less of a man than he was now. His belly twisted painfully while he wondered if he had been a better man in past. Surely he must have been to have won such a prize as her.

Linese studied Chase's face and tried to understand the man who had returned to her. Chase had met with the mayor and the members of the local business association on at least two occasions after he brought her to Mainfield. He had made it plain at both meetings that he did not want her

around, just as he'd made it clear that women should hav
no opinion about business. Her head swam while she trie
to reason out the change two years of war had wrought. Fi
nally she simply allowed herself to answer, even though sh
had no idea how or why his attitudes were so different tha
they used to be. "All right, Chase, if that is what you want."

"It is what I want, Linese." He impulsively gave her han
a little squeeze as a sort of silent thank-you.

Her cheeks flushed prettily when he stared at her a mo
ment longer than propriety dictated he should gaze at hi
wife in front of the mayor and his associates. He heard on
of them clear his throat in annoyance or possibly discom
fort while time seemed to hang suspended. A strange sen
sation began to creep over Chase. It was like witnessing th
first dawn. The feeling flooding through him was lik
watching sunrise turn pitch to a paler shade of gray. Eacl
time he looked at Linese he felt a small part of the bleal
places in his mind recede.

He felt something for her then, something more tha
simple indebtedness, and not only the strong physical at
traction he could not deny. His heart was buffeted by a
emotion infinitely more complicated and undefinable
Whatever the unique awareness was, it was just as poten
and threatening to him as his fear of being exposed. Linese
had a power over him, a power that fascinated and dis
turbed him. He craved her company at the same moment h
feared her nearness. It was a puzzle Chase didn't under
stand, but he would have to think about it later since th
businessmen were waiting to speak with him. Chase tore hi
gaze from Linese and managed a smile.

"Gentlemen," he said, and gestured to the doorway.

All the men who had been in the outer office managed t
squeeze into the cramped confines of the smaller one. Chas
felt his body shoved against Linese while he made room fo
the pudgy mayor.

Finally the door slammed shut and the mayor took a dee
breath that threatened to empty the room of oxygen

Chase, the Businessman's Association met this morning at
my office."

Chase glanced down at the top of Linese's head and noticed the soft, silky texture of her pale hair. The scent of
honeysuckle blossoms and starched cotton wafted up from
her body, while the temperature in the small office rose in
accordance with the hot air the mayor was expelling. He
struggled to listen to what the man was saying, but his mind
was more occupied with the way Linese's body fit next to his
own.

There was a curiosity within him. A need to know her, not
just to remember her, but to know the mystery that made her
so special. He forced himself to focus on the mayor's words.

"...we want you to write a series of articles about the way
the prominent citizens of Mainfield have handled this conflict. We have managed to come out of this with a little
profit, there is no reason why other people in this community can't do the same thing." The mayor looked at Chase
with an excited expectancy shining in his face. "It could
mean real power to Mainfield—and you—if you get my
meaning."

Chase's belly flip-flopped. He didn't understand the
mayor's meaning. "I'm not sure I do."

Kerney looked at him with narrowed eyes. "As long as we
remain neutral and don't get involved with abolitionists or
secessionists, as long as we remember that prosperity can
come out of war, we can turn this to our advantage. It's up
to you, Chase. The people of Mainfield will listen to the
Gazette. You could make a real difference to them. If you
speak out and tell them to refuse to go with either side, they
can all *profit* from this. Besides, do we care who wins? The
real issue is how much *profit* we can make during the conflict."

Chase felt his gut plummet to the bottom of his boots.
What he had seen reflected in the eyes of the men in the infirmary while he was healing were memories he would carry
forever. Those men, both Unionist and Rebel, had given all

they had for their ideals. Now Mayor Kerney was telling him
that as long as men could forget having ideals, and think
only about profit, they could benefit from the war. His mind
rebelled against the notion.

Chase didn't remember the kind of man he was before he
rode away two years ago. But the person he was now didn't
care about becoming powerful, or rich. He could not lie and
say a man's convictions didn't matter—because in the end
they were about the only things that did matter.

Silence stretched on while the men looked at Chase. There
was something in their faces, something dark and familiar
and almost expectant. The chaos in Chase's soul was
matched by the windstorm in his mind. He glanced at Lin
ese and saw nothing but innocence and trust shining in her
eyes. He didn't know what his association had been with
these men in the past, but he knew where his responsibility
lay today.

It was with Linese. She was saddled with a husband who
could not remember her. She had lost so much in the war,
perhaps even more than he had himself.

He wanted to see her smile. He wanted to do something
that would take away the sting of guilt he felt each time he
thought of her waiting for a man who had not returned to
her.

"That is a mighty great responsibility, Mayor." Chase
slipped his arm around Linese and drew her close to him,
partly for effect, partly because he wanted to feel her
warmth against him. Even through the heavy-boned corset
he felt her start at the unexpected contact of his hip against
her. "All I want to do right now is get reacquainted with my
wife."

Linese's head snapped up to stare gape-mouthed at
Chase. The men in the room murmured with surprise. She
fought to control her reaction. She had been raised to be a
lady, and a lady never betrayed her feelings in public, but
Chase had shocked her down to her high-buttoned shoes.

Last night he had sent her from their bedroom. Now he looked at her as if there were no place he'd rather be than beside her. The arm wrapped around her waist felt possessive.

"I know you gentlemen will understand. I just want to live quietly and put the war behind me. I can't take the responsibility of trying to sway other men's opinions." Sincerity rang in Chase's voice. He realized those were the first truthful words he had uttered since waking in the field hospital.

Linese watched the mayor's flabby jowls quiver. Anger flashed in his small round eyes. "You can't do this, Chase. We've been counting on you. We've had certain expectations. We had an agreement...."

Something in the man's tone sent a warning through Chase's mind. A flash of memory hit him like a cold rush of water.

He remembered the mayor's smiling face reflected in the glow of torchlight. It was a time long ago, perhaps two years ago.

"Don't you worry, Chase, we'll keep your secret."

The memory flashed brilliant like a strike of lightning, then it was gone. The fading image and the sound of the man's voice remained lodged in Chase's mind. He tried to remember more, but it was useless. Only that one small fragment had crystallized.

Now when he looked into the angry face of the mayor, he wondered what secret they had shared before he left Mainfield. He felt as if a noose were tightening around his neck. Each day brought only more questions and suspicions about who he was. He found himself pulling Linese closer to his body. He wanted her near him so he could protect her. But from whom? *Himself?*

Chapter Four

Chase limped off the porch and into the hot dusky eve‐
ning. The mayor's words rattled around inside his head like
a stone in an empty bucket. His temples throbbed and his
stomach twisted from trying to bring forth hard facts, when
nothing but smoke and doubt filled his mind.

The Texas thicket was alive with night sounds. Chase
found his eyes traveling toward an overgrown path that dis‐
appeared into the tangled overgrown foliage. Something
about the almost invisible path beckoned to him. He walked
to it and stared while a strange feeling of déjà vu sluiced over
him. Without knowing quite why, he pushed his way
through the plants and went onward, stopping occasionally
to let his instinct take him on a journey his mind had for‐
gotten but his gut still knew. He had to move branches out
of his way, yet some forgotten part of his brain knew that a
path did indeed lie beneath the thick growth, whether he
could see it or not.

The verdant foliage trapped the heat beneath a canopy of
leaves. Chase unbuttoned his shirt and pulled the long tail
from his trousers in the hope it would be cooler. The far‐
ther he went into the unknown thicket, the darker the night
became, but still some feral intuition showed him the way.
He neither stumbled nor faltered while he pushed on.

He stopped and looked back. The glow from Cordelne's lamps was far behind him now. He was alone, with gue sensations of having traveled the path before.

The pain radiating from his hip forced him to halt somene later. Flying insects fed on every exposed inch of his in, but it was too sticky to consider rebuttoning the shirt at hung open and loose. He slapped a mosquito on his ck and saw a flicker of light through hanging vines clingg to the willow and hickory.

"Will-o'-the-wisp," he muttered, but he found himself atching the uneven trail of illumination dancing through e trees with keen interest. Some buried part of him knew ose flickering lights were his destination and not some ystical trick of swamp gas or flitting winged critter.

Chase walked, slower and more deliberately now, toward e source of the flame. When he was no more than a stone's ss away, he saw a group of men in ribald discussion. They rned and recognition flooded him, along with a large easure of dread.

"It's about time, Chase, we were beginning to think you ren't going to show up," The mayor's voice boomed out. But I was pretty sure you would after our talk today."

Chase stepped into the circle of orange torchlight and und himself in the company of the same men who had me to see him at the *Gazette*. He now realized what the an's exaggerated wink signified. The splintered recollecn he had at the *Gazette*, of the mayor's face in the same tie glow of light, came back to haunt Chase.

He had met with them here—before he went to war.

The certainty of that past deed sent chills trailing down aase's spine. He knew if he did not tread carefully these en would learn his secret.

"I wasn't sure I remembered how to get here." Chase told em a sliver of truth and watched their reactions.

"Sure, Chase, whatever you say." The mayor chuckled at aat he thought was a joke. "Now tell us what you're up
"

Chase focused on the faces of the men. A dim memor[y]
appeared in his mind. For a brief flash, he saw them as h[e]
had seen the mayor in his forgotten past. And as he remem[-]
bered them, a feeling of shame wended through him. Th[e]
men were dark spectres of past sins. A sick feeling of guil[t]
or something much like it, twined its way through his bell[y.]

At first there was Ira Goten's mysterious pistol and th[e]
gold that Chase was sure was stained with blood. Now ther[e]
were meetings in the woods with men whose politics h[e]
could not stomach.

What kind of man was I? Chase's voice screamed insid[e]
his head. What horrible things did I do?

"Listen, Chase, Hershner has had too much leeway sinc[e]
you've been gone. The *Gazette* has been printing things w[e]
don't like. When do you intend to take over and get it bac[k]
on track?" The man who had been introduced today as M[r.]
Wallace, from the local merchants bank, stepped forward[.]

"What exactly is it you want me to do?" Chase felt h[is]
anger rising each minute he spent in the men's presence. H[e]
didn't like the way they acted or how they looked. Chas[e]
didn't know if it was a memory or a premonition, but h[e]
knew these men were capable of his ruin.

"We want you to start printing the kind of informatio[n]
we want the people of Mainfield to have," Wallace said.

There was a hint in those words that Chase could not i[g-]
nore.

"You mean the kind of information you wanted printe[d]
before I left?" Chase bluffed again and prayed he had n[ot]
said too much.

"Exactly. We've kept our word about your little secr[et]
and we wouldn't want to think that you've changed you[r]
mind about our arrangement. There are dirty secrets, thin[gs]
that have happened you wouldn't want people to know, e[s-]
pecially that sweet little bride you brought home and su[r-]
prised everybody with." Wallace grinned.

Chase's instinct for survival made him hold his fists at h[is]
side. He wanted to pummel them until all the murky susp[icion]

cions they raised about his missing past were gone. But he could not. Whatever he had done in the past, it was his responsibility, his burden. He drew in a resolute breath and forced himself to stay calm. Chase acknowledged that he was faced with this situation because he had no idea what they held over him. He needed to pry information from them, he needed time to dig into his past.

"Mayor, I've just returned from war. Give me a little time to recover from my wounds before I undertake these heavy responsibilities." Chase tried to relax, but it was a hollow attempt. He prayed the anger he felt was not mirrored in his face. The men looked at one another as if weighing Chase's argument.

Finally Mr. Wallace turned toward Kerney. "I told you it would be fine. Chase Cordell is a man who stands by his word. He's a man who's true to his politics and his friends. We can count on him."

Chase swallowed the bitter taste in his mouth. If these men counted him as a friend, then he certainly hoped he didn't run into any of his enemies.

Linese was sitting in the window seat of her new bedroom, staring at the silver-ringed moon overhead, when Chase suddenly appeared like a shadowy phantom at the edge of the thicket. She watched while he slid one of his hands through his thick hair. He only did that when he was stiff with anger, it was one of the little things she had learned about him before he left. She wondered where he had been, how he could have materialized at the edge of the woods, and why he seemed to be bristling with suppressed fury.

Chase leaned one palm against a gnarled mountain laurel and tipped his head up toward the night sky. His shirt was open and the long loose tail fluttered in an unseen breeze. Spring moonlight and the soft glow from the windows of Cordellane turned his hard, muscular chest into a work of art.

One strand of his tousled hair was touched by the breeze and he turned his head slightly. She saw the glint of violence in his eyes. He was dangerous, wild, and a bit improper. Memory flooded through her.

"Just like the night I met him," Linese muttered.

Chase Cordell had come uninvited like so many other young men to the Ferrin County Presbyterian church. He had smelled of brandy and gunpowder, with a fresh wound on one hand. He had been a handsome, mysterious stranger that made the women, both married and unattached, whisper behind their fans while their pulses quickened at the very sight of him.

Linese had been one of those women. She had stood frozen to the floor as he came into the church. She had watched, mesmerized by his hard gray eyes, while he searched the room, as if he had been looking for someone. As if he had been looking for her.

When he pinned her with eyes as hard as rain-slicked granite, she had nearly swooned on the spot. He had continued to shock her by defying propriety and the codes they lived by. He had walked straight up to her and spoken boldly, without a proper introduction, without a care for the consequences. Linese's heart had nearly hammered its way through her chest.

She had felt every eye in the room fasten on the tall man who none dared to question or oppose. He had been Lucifer fallen to earth, a beautiful archangel whose ember-hot attention had been focused on her alone.

It was the most stimulating experience Linese ever had, and it had not stopped there.

She unconsciously rubbed her ink-stained fingers against her throat and remembered the way his voice had rippled over her like a lover's intimate caress. In those first shattering moments she had fallen completely under his spell.

But then what woman wouldn't have? Any man with the confidence to stride across a crowded room and tell a perfect stranger she was going to be his wife was a man that few women could resist.

"Lord knows I couldn't," Linese whispered to herself.

She sighed and thought about it while she watched him below. Chase had simply told her that *he* had chosen her. He had never asked her what she wanted, he had simply told her how it would be, and she hadn't been able to resist his will.

In the feverish two weeks that followed that meeting, as when they stood in front of the same Presbyterian minister, Linese had given her heart to him without asking for anything in return. Then, in a blur of activity, he had packed her up and moved her from Ferrin County. He had swept into her life like a blue norther.

She had waited, expecting him to tell her he felt the same way before he rode off to war. But he did not. Then she waited at her new home, Cordellane, for letters he would write home, expecting some declaration of affection, but it never came. Now as she stared down at the man who had given her his name, she began to wonder. Did Chase Cordell care for her at all? Had he ever, or had he simply chosen her for his wife for other reasons entirely?

She wrapped her arms around her ankles and rested her chin in the space between her knees. The fact that she was sitting in a bedroom all alone instead of sharing one with Chase, while she watched him through a cold pane of glass, was a hard truth to ignore.

While she swallowed the burning lump that constricted her throat, Chase leaned away from the tree and strode toward Cordellane. Linese listened for each of his uneven footfalls while he limped stiffly across the veranda and through the house. She heard him begin to climb the stairs, heard him pause on the landing.

Her heart quickened with hope. Maybe, just maybe, he was going to fling open the door to her room.

Maybe Chase would open the door and stride in with the same bold confidence he had displayed that night in Ferrin County. Maybe he would envelop her in his strong arms, hold her close to that glistening expanse of chest and make sweet love to her. How she yearned to have him pour his heart out, to tell her how much he had missed her while he was gone, to reveal his inner feelings to her.

But he didn't.

She heard his steps carry him one door farther down the hall, and into the room that had been hers for the past two years. A few moments after the bedroom door shut with a heavy thud, the uneven tempo of his footsteps began again. Her aching heart matched its lonely beat to the uneven stride of his limp.

Major Chase Cordell sounded like a caged animal and Linese wondered if she had become his reluctant jailer.

Chase watched Hezikiah Hershner from under his lashes. It was damnably hard trying to observe and learn, all the while acting as though he knew everything there was to know about the complicated process of setting print and running the big awkward press.

Frustration rolled over him. Chase had only managed to remain idle today by using his recent wound as an excuse. Hershner was eager for Chase to resume his duty of getting the weekly newspaper out, almost as eager as the mayor and his cronies, but he suspected for entirely different reasons.

After the meeting in the woods, after nearly wearing the polish off the hardwood floors in his bedroom, Chase had reached a decision. He had to find out what those men were threatening him with. Bile rose in his mouth each time he thought about the secret they held over him, and the gun and gold.

Were they somehow connected? Or was he such a rogue that he'd left many terrible deeds behind when he went to war?

Chase sighed and wondered which secret would undo him first: his lost memory or the grim and unrecollected act the mayor was holding over his head. He had to find a way of learning about the *Gazette* and his past, and he needed to do t before the mayor and his friends grew impatient and forced him into a corner.

He got up and stretched. His hip ached from sitting, but he had hoped that just being in the newspaper office would ar some part of his mind. He had prayed that he might blink and find the last hellish weeks were no more than a nightmare.

While he massaged his leg, he moved near untidy stacks of papers in the corner. He scanned them quickly and saw random dates scattered among the unordered piles.

"These are back issues of the *Gazette, yes?*" he asked Hezikiah.

The older man looked up and frowned. "Oh, yes. I've been meaning to put them in some kind of order, but I never have the time."

Chase picked up the top paper and read the headlines. It contained news of the skirmish that had ultimately led to his wounded hip and return home. Could reading the old papers shed some light on his own personal history? Hope sprang up inside his chest at the thought.

"I'll take them home." Chase heard his own voice. "I'll bring them back when I have them in order."

Hezikiah's head snapped up. "Well, not that I'm turning down the offer to clean up the office, but I thought you might be anxious to start. The *Gazette* was your pride and joy before you left...."

"Two years have changed me. I need a little time to get to know myself again." Chase felt the irony and poignant truth of his own words slice through him.

Hezikiah nodded. "I understand, Major. Must be difficult coming back when the conflict is still unsettled. You were so determined when you left...." Hezikiah's words trailed off.

Chase looked at Hezikiah and blinked. If only he could understand what kind of person he had been, what drove him and why he had left Linese to go fight. It might help him uncover the truth.

* * *

Linese stood on the steps of Cordellane and watched Chase unload string-tied bundles of newspapers from the buggy. She wanted to ask what he was doing, but his dark brows were furrowed into the distinctive slash above his eyes. If he was even aware of her there, he hid it well. Each trip he made from the buggy to the library was done in total silence. He walked past her like a man in a dream. Finally, when the last haphazard stack was removed, he walked into the library and closed the door behind him. The cold sting of once again being shut out of his life bit deeply into the raw wound of her pride. Linese sighed and stared at the library door. She had to find some way of finding her husband beneath the cold exterior of the man who had returned.

But how?

Chase stared up at the portrait on the library wall and felt a hard knot form in his belly. Vague, disjointed images floated through his mind. His pulse quickened its tempo at the notion that he might remember *something*.

The face he stared at in the painting was his father's, yet it was a face so like the unfamiliar one he found staring back each morning when he shaved, it sent a shiver through him. The same dark hair and serious gray eyes stared down dispassionately from the old canvas.

Chase turned around and looked at the other paintings lining the walls between the shelves of books. A pale woman with soft brown eyes smiled at him.

It was his mother. He knew it, even though he couldn't dredge up a single recollection of her. He also knew, from some deep spring of hidden information, that she had died in childbirth when he was very small.

The irony of feeling some happiness, or relief, at such a melancholy memory did not escape Chase. He sighed and concentrated on each portrait.

Above the fireplace was the likeness of a young girl with raven locks and porcelain skin. Her eyes were similar to hose of his father, with a youthful promise of great beauty n the childish face. Her name suddenly popped into Chase's nead as if conjured up by a magician in a snake-oil act.

Marjorie, his aunt, the apple of his grandfather's eye. Chase had an obscure remembrance of her funeral and the nadness that took his grandfather's mind away following he somber occasion.

"Am I the next Cordell to lose his mind?" he muttered vhile he stared at the young girl's gray eyes. A conflict of emotion ripped through him and a strange high-pitched inging filled his ears. Was his grandfather's affliction omehow responsible, or was it something else that took his nemory?

He tore his gaze from the painting and slouched into a all-backed chair in front of the cold fireplace. The sound n his ears had taken on a lower tone, but it was still evident. With a slight unsteadiness of his hand, he poured nimself a large brandy from the glass decanter on the side able. The liquor blazed a hot trail down his throat toward is empty belly.

Maybe the alcohol would silence the buzz in his ears or numb the ache in his hip. He prayed it would at least dull the aw need he perceived each time he thought about Linese and how much she had lost during the past two years.

Chase returned the glass to the table and picked up the irst issue of the *Gazette* from the mound at his feet. With a little luck, perhaps he could find a part of his missing self n the words. If nothing else, maybe he would stumble upon ome clue that would unearth the mystery of what he had lone before he went to war. Then, even if he was doomed o follow in his grandfather's footsteps, he would have some iny bit of himself, a shadow of the man he used to be. Maybe it would be enough.

Linese sat in the rocker beside Captain Cordell and vatched the moon rise above the treetops just as she had lone for the past two years. Funny, Chase's return had made little difference in the day-to-day existence at Cordel lane. Her reality was nothing like the dreams she had spur in Chase's absence. She was still sleeping alone, still sittin with Captain Cordell in the evenings, watching the moor and the stars, while she longed for the company of her hus band.

"I'll be taking some food over to Doralee's sportin house," Captain Cordell said suddenly. He never looked a Linese. He just continued to stare up at the twinkling arra of stars overhead.

She turned to him in amazement. It had never occurre to her that the Captain went to the local bordello. She kne that almost every other able-bodied man left in Mainfiel did, but she had never even thought of the Captain that way In truth she had never given much thought to the fact he wa still a healthy man who probably had physical desires. Sh caught herself blushing with the thought.

When she first arrived at Cordellane, in the first lonel weeks, she had wondered if he was as out of touch as peo ple believed. Slowly she had come to realize his conditio was changeable. His mind seemed to ebb and flow like th tides. There were times, like now, when he blurted out th most outlandish statements, for instance, about going t Doralee's house of ill repute.

"Now why would you do a thing like that, Captain?" I it had been anyone else but the dotty old Captain she wa speaking to, she couldn't have continued this conversation The very notion was so improper her cheeks burned wit embarrassment. But he was not right in the head and had n way of knowing it, poor dear, so she smiled pleasantly an waited for his answer as if they were talking about the crop or the weather.

"Melissa, one of the girls, is going to have a baby in a fe weeks." The old man squirmed a bit but he continue speaking without hesitation. "She can't work. I never coul abide seeing someone go hungry if I could prevent it."

Linese blinked back her amazement. Only someone like Captain Cordell, who was so far removed from the restraints of proper behavior, could get away with such an opinion. For a moment she almost envied him the freedom his mental infirmity allowed him. He could say things, do things other people would never be allowed to do.

"You're a kind and generous man, Captain. We have a bit to spare. Is there anything else she might need?" Linese knew there were many worse off than she and the old Captain—and Chase, she reminded herself.

Captain Cordell's face pinched into a series of wrinkles. It seemed he was putting a considerable effort into his answer. "There is some old furniture stored in the attic. I might take some of it over."

Linese's breath froze in her chest. She stared out into the dappled shadows of the thicket and tried to blink back the hot sting behind her eyes. Chase's cradle and his old baby clothes were in that attic. She had hoped her own children would use the treasured Cordell heirlooms.

She sat in stunned silence and argued with herself. It was selfish to deny anyone the use of anything when so many had so little. It was small and petty of her to repudiate any kindness the Captain wanted to give the unfortunate woman.

Linese swallowed hard. It hurt, but she made herself face the real reason for her distress. Linese finally formed the idea that had been taking shape in her mind for days. It was likely she was in a loveless marriage, one that would never provide her with the children she wanted so much. She feared she would never have need of the baby furniture.

She told herself it was as much her fault as it was Chase's. She should find a way to bridge the rift between them, but when she thought about it, she felt ill-equipped to win her husband's affection. She had been a green girl when he had married her, and even though she had grown and matured in every other aspect, when it came to matters of the heart she was still hopelessly out of her depth.

The Captain cleared his throat beside her and Linese wa
wrenched from her thoughts. Part of her rankled at the self
pity she was wallowing in. She leaned over and planted a kis
on the side of the Captain's face. His long silver mustache
his only vanity, tickled her chin.

"My mama once told me a pretty girl could get anythin₁
she wanted from a man with a kiss or two." He winked an
patted Linese's hand.

For a sobering moment Linese wondered if he were a
addled as everyone believed. Then she wiped the notio
from her mind. Why on earth would any man *want* peopl
to think he was crazy. Still, his easily offered words made he
think. Perhaps there was a way to win her husband back
Perhaps Providence had dropped the solution into her la₁
like a fat, ripe plum.

"If you need any help gathering up the food and such
just let me know." She rose from the rocker and entered th
house. A glimmer of hope sparked inside her chest while sh
walked across the entryway.

A shaft of light shone from under the library door an
drew her like a moth to a candle. Linese itched to know wha
Chase was doing in the room all alone. She stepped up to th
door and listened.

It was quiet as a tomb on the other side. She nearl
knocked on the closed door, but a flare of stubborn prid
prevented her from doing so. Cordellane had been her hom
for two years. She resented suddenly being made to feel a
if certain rooms were no longer open to her. First her bed
room and now the library had been shuttered and locked i
her face. She felt a small spark of emotion—not anger, bu
perhaps resolve. Linese opened the door and walked i
without warning.

Chase was sprawled in a chair with the litter of *Gazett*
pages scattered all around him. His long legs and booted fee
were stretched out in front of him on the old hooked woo
rug. He was rubbing his temples with his fingers. A half-ful

glass of amber liquid sat on the table beside him and the brandy decanter was three-quarters empty.

"Chase?" Linese wondered if he was too drunk to move from the chair. Could it be he had returned to her so shattered by war that he was trying to drown his memories in drink?

"Mmm." He never looked up. He just continued to rub his fingertips against his temples in small circles.

"You've been in here for hours. Are you hungry?" Linese approached his chair warily, half-expecting a sharp rebuff for invading his territory.

He looked up and fastened a remarkably sober gaze on her. A single dark strand of hair rested across his thick eyebrows. His eyes were hooded and languorous, but the rough-etched contours of his face were still distant and hard.

He reminded her of a wolf—ravenous and feral. The narrowed gaze he fastened on her was a mixture of suspicion and distrust. It pulled at her heart.

"No. I am not hungry." His speech was softly slurred from the brandy.

"Is there anything you require?"

"No." He sighed heavily and looked away. "There is nothing that I *require*." His sardonic reply held a measure of poignancy.

It intrigued her, drove her onward. She took a halting step toward him. "Chase? What is it? What is wrong?" she whispered.

"My head hurts from reading so much." His deep, throaty explanation stopped her only inches from his leg.

She looked down at him again. Suddenly the hard lines of his face didn't seem so harsh. In her eyes, as she wanted so desperately to believe it, he wore only the lines of strain and fatigue. He had seemed so aloof and independent before. He now displayed a vulnerability she had never seen.

A wave of compassion and love swept over Linese. She bent down and grasped his boot top at the ankle. She lifted his leg with both hands.

His head came up with a start. "What are you doing?" His eyes narrowed down to gray slits. The sole source of Linese's courage to persist in the face of his scowling expression was her deep love for Chase.

"I'm taking off your boots." She grabbed her skirt with one hand and shoved it out of the way, while she knelt in front of Chase to take hold of his heel and pull off the tight-fitting boot.

Chase started to protest, then Linese bent toward him in front of him. Her position allowed him a completely unobstructed view of her breasts. One golden curl hung down beside her swanlike neck. Chase tried to look away but the sight was hypnotic.

He stared at the creamy swell of her flesh and imagined what it would be like to touch her. Heat danced up his legs toward his belly while he observed her. He could almost feel her flesh in his palms, could imagine what it would be like to bury his face in her pale hair. He could practically smell the combination of soap, honeysuckle and his own passion.

His boot came off.

His foot hit the floor with a thud. Pain radiated up his leg to his damaged hip. He drew a hiss of breath between his clenched teeth and tried to master the ache in his leg—and his heart.

"Did I hurt you?" she asked.

The concern in her voice shamed him. He wanted her to believe he was impervious to pain and hurt. He wanted her to admire him. God forgive him, he wanted her.

"Of course not," he growled. His mouth was sour with the taste of the lie. Another in a series of lies he kept telling her. It struck Chase that his life had become one long, bitter untruth.

He disgusted himself. And the more he wanted Linese, the more disgusted with himself he became, because she embodied truth and goodness and a past he yearned to remember.

Linese paused to look at him. Chase devoured her body with his eyes. Then she smiled and picked up the other boot and slid it off. When she was finished, she sat down on the floor beside his outstretched leg.

A tingling sensation began to burn his thigh where it was touching Linese's back. The spiraling heat traveled up the length of his body and into every muscle and sinew. The feeling gathered and pooled in the pit of his stomach only to send fingers of desire swirling back out to his limbs, his hands, his fingers.

The top of her golden head was so close, if he flexed his fingers, he could touch her. He cursed himself for wanting her, but it did no good. He wanted her anyway.

"I'll read to you for a while. Maybe the pain in your head will go away."

"I don't need to be read to." He could not trust himself to sit here while she was so close, so appealing. She had no notion of how perilous it was to remain with him. She could not know—he did not know himself—how deep his affliction ran.

"I want to read to you, Chase." Her soft words contained steel. She glanced up at him and he saw something new in her cool-water blue eyes. He saw determination harden within their depths. To protest further would put him at risk of exposure. He was, after all, married to her.

Married to her.

"Fine." Chase sighed in disgruntled capitulation. He reached for the glass, tipped it up and drained it. If he got drunk enough, maybe he could ignore the way her skin looked or the softness of her lips. He would simply close his eyes and let the brandy numb his brain and his need.

Linese felt a tiny shiver of satisfaction at Chase's grudging response. She wondered if this was how a general felt when he gained the hill or took the river. She bent her head and tried to hide her smile of pleasure. She was Chase's wife, she should sit and read to him of the events in Mainfield. She should pull off his boots and linger with him over a glass of spirits, and then maybe they would be able to find what had been lost in the two years he was gone. Linese picked up the first paper and read the date aloud.

"'June 22, 1861. The citizens of Cooke County have formed a home defense and are calling themselves the Cooke County Home Guard Cavalry.'" She glanced up at Chase. He had leaned his head back against the chair and his eyes were closed. She started to read again.

Chase listened while Linese read about Texas and the campaign to secede. Reports of the weather and the escalating war took most of the space, with an occasional tidbit about a birth or death. Her voice was pleasant and somewhat soothing to him. He found himself actually enjoying the sound of it.

After a few minutes he heard the paper crinkle and realized she had stopped reading. The room seemed empty and cold without the sound of her voice. He raised his head and looked at her.

She was neatly folding the paper away. "Do you wish for me to continue?" She tipped her head toward him and raised her eyebrows in question. The lamplight glinted off the clear azure color of her eyes.

His heart thudded painfully inside his chest cavity. It took some effort to keep from reaching out to touch the silken strands of her pale hair.

"Yes, please do." Instead of closing his eyes this time, he watched Linese with intensified interest. He was powerless to do anything but watch her, and want her, and die a little because he could not touch her.

She picked up another paper from the disorganized pile and opened it. Light glimmered on her hair when she bent her head toward the page. Chase knew he was courting his own disaster, but no matter how he argued with himself, he could not force himself up from the chair, or his eyes away from the vision of his wife.

"'June 1, 1862. The provost marshal is looking for the person responsible for the murder of Alfred Homstock, a new resident to Ferrin County.'"

Her face became animated and her brow crinkled slightly while she read the old news item. Soft lips curved, bent around the sound of the words, in a manner Chase found exotic and sensual.

"'...unsubstantiated rumors abound that Homstock's death was in retaliation for Unionists being lynched by suspected secessionists recently in Cooke County. Unverified reports indicate he may have been part of the Underground Railroad and could have been the victim of the runaway slaves he was trying to help, but so far there have been only rumors. The sheriff in Tyron County will be handling the investigation.'"

She stopped reading and laid the paper down in her lap. A soft flush filled her cheeks, she swallowed hard and blinked. Her pink-tipped tongue darted out to moisten her lips. Chase could see she was embarrassed about something. He was struck by a sudden feeling of satisfaction to know that about her, but he realized it was obvious, and was not a memory returning to him.

"What is it?" he asked.

"Hezikiah decided it would be proper to formally announce our wedding since we were not married here in Mainfield." She squirmed a bit.

"So?"

"Since we married without anyone in Mainfield being present, he wanted to announce it." She blushed deeper.

Chase felt the unmistakable bite of sorrow and raw grief pour over him. He grieved for the loss of something precious that he must have treasured, and he grieved for himself because he could not remember the special moment of marrying Linese. Suddenly the need to remember the Colt and gold and what had gone on with the mayor paled beside his anguish at not remembering his wedding day.

"Read me what he wrote." His voice sounded hard and flinty to his own ears. Chase nearly choked on the bitter fact that the only way he would learn about their wedding was through a pitiful two-year-old account written by an aging bachelor who was not even present.

Linese cleared her throat and began to read. "'Chase Cordell, grandson of Texas Ranger Captain Cordell, surprised the citizens of Mainfield by bringing home a bride. The former Miss Linese Beaufort, of Ferrin County, will be residing at the family home, Cordellane. Mr. Cordell, a Unionist, has joined the Northern army....'" Her voice trailed off and she looked up at him with a beseeching look on her face.

"Is that all?" Hearing the dispassionate article filled with nothing more than hard, cold facts left a hollow ache inside Chase. He longed to know everything that involved Linese.

She sighed and avoided his searching gaze. "Only some silly reference about you missing from Mainfield two weeks prior to our wedding, and how people were speculating about what—or who—had kept you away from Mainfield."

Chase's brows shot up when he grasped the implication. "Is it the general opinion of Mainfield that you bewitched me and held me prisoner?" He sloshed another portion of brandy into the glass and cursed his missing memory.

"As I recall, it was the other way around." She said with a tremulous smile. "You most certainly took me captive, as you well know. There are still ladies in Tyron County who are disappointed that their most eligible bachelor up and married a girl from another county." She blushed bright red at the confession.

She dipped her head and avoided his gaze. This brave, delicate creature, who had the misfortune of being joined to him by marriage, gave him a moment of unexpected happiness. He found himself smiling while he succumbed to the urge to run his fingers down the side of her face.

She trembled visibly beneath his feather-light touch. It buffeted him, the way she closed her eyes like a house cat and leaned into his tentative caress. A hard, hot vortex of desire swirled inside his gut and threatened to uncoil like a roused water moccasin.

"Tell me what you recall, Linese." His request was a throaty growl. "How do you remember our meeting?"

Her eyes widened and she smiled up at him. It was a timid expression, one of love and memory, one he could only share through her recollections, since the damnable loss of his memory had robbed him of the past.

Her smile became wistful and full of feeling. "You swept through the door of the Presbyterian church like a blue norther. The women whispered about who you were and where you had come from. I remember thinking you were probably a riverboat pirate on the run from the law." She laughed softly under her breath, but Chase wondered if she was closer to the truth than either of them knew.

Had he been running from the law? Is that what had driven him to join the army? Had he chosen a slightly honorable way to retreat from the consequences of some terrible act? Is that what compelled him to leave this precious female to care for his feeble grandfather and fend for herself in a harsh climate of hostility? He clenched his jaw against the thought and realized if that were the case, then he hated the man he had been.

"You near shocked the Presbyterian minister to death when you—when you said what you did...." She was still speaking softly, lost in her world of memory and emotion.

"And what shocking thing was that?" he asked while he allowed his eyes to skim over her face.

"You said I was the one. You said I was the girl you'd been waiting for and you were going to make me your wife."

He could almost visualize it. It was not a memory, nothing as clear and firm as that, but he could picture the scene in his mind.

She would have been standing by the wall with her eyes shyly diverted, like the lady she was. He probably had mud spattered on his breeches from hard riding, and God knows what other wicked deed. Linese would have blushed slightly, like she was now, when he spoke directly to her. He could understand how he wanted her, but to his great hopelessness he couldn't remember it.

There was a hunger eating at his soul while he watched her. Something was happening to him. He was being consumed by more than just the need to remember his past. Whatever powerful thing wrapped itself around him, it revolved around Linese.

Chase felt deprived, starved. He longed to slake his starvation with the taste of Linese's sweet lips, to sate his appetite with her love.

"Did I shock you, Miss Linese Beaufort?" The name she had revealed to him from the *Gazette* rolled off his tongue like warm honey. He liked the way it sounded. It almost had a flavor, like rich Creole cooking, like Linese herself. She was unique, sweet with a little spice that made a man hungry for more and more.

His hand still rested against the curve of her jaw. She rubbed against his fingers. "No, you didn't shock me. You intrigued me." She looked straight into his eyes. "I loved you from the first moment I saw you."

The heartfelt admission hit Chase like a fist. She had loved him then, probably loved him now, but would she find him so desirable if she knew the secret he kept from her or the dark mystery hidden in his past?

Chapter Five

Emotion ripped at Chase.

He reached for the glass of brandy and finished it off in one gulp. Each time Linese looked at him with that loving, trusting expression clouding her eyes, it shredded his insides. He couldn't stand it anymore.

"It's late, Linese. You should go to bed." The terse sound of his voice fell a little shy of being a command.

She pierced him with a cool gaze. "I think I will sit with you awhile longer. If you don't mind." Her refusal was just short of outright disobedience. He scanned her face and saw defiance and passion written there.

He sighed and slumped back in his chair in sheer defeat. She wasn't going to make it easy on him. This sweet belle had iron beneath her silken exterior.

No submissive shrinking violet sat at his feet, no matter how it might have looked to an outside observer.

If he wanted to be away from her as much as he kept telling himself that he did, all he need do was rise from the chair and leave the room. It was just that easy, and just that complicated.

"Read to me some more then...." he said gruffly. "Since you are going to stay." Perhaps the key to his past was hidden in the old copies of newspaper. At least if he concentrated on the words, maybe he could think about something besides her soft mouth and sensuous eyes.

Linese felt as if she had won a tiny battle of wills in the past few minutes. Chase had not stalked away from her, as she half expected him to, when she did not give in to his demand. It was a small start, but enough to give her encouragement. Her hand was trembling slightly with excitement, and hope, when she picked up the paper and started to read.

Chase listened to the accounts of war and sporadic news about himself that he had apparently provided in letters home, but no memory emerged. He was still lost and confused and becoming more frustrated with each passing minute. Linese paused in her reading and he found himself oddly disappointed.

"Are you finished?" His tone was sharp with the pain of wanting her.

She turned to look at him. Her searching eyes had the same effect on him as being pierced by an enemy bayonet.

"Yes, Chase, I'm finished." Her voice held a faint tone of frustration, or he chose to think it did.

She stood up and shook out her skirt. He caught a whiff of female warmth and the lingering trace of flower blossoms that seemed to surround her.

Perhaps it was the brandy—maybe it was his madness—but he reached out and jerked her onto his lap. She settled onto his thighs with a soft swish of fabric. The weight of her bottom against his legs sent an explosion of desire through him.

"You smell nice," he murmured. He tilted his head back in order to see her face, now only a few inches above his own, and sighed in restless contentment.

"Chase, you've been away so long...." She sighed. "I missed you."

Chase felt his soul being ripped in half. He wanted to try to find the words to explain his erratic behavior, even though he knew he could never explain what he had become, what he could never be again.

"Don't, Linese, don't talk." He knew what he was doing was wrong, but he chose to deny it.

She bit her bottom lip and blinked rapidly.

It was his undoing.

He pulled her face down to him and claimed her lips. They tasted like clear spring water. She was not heady and robust like Creole cooking, not as he thought she would be. She was more pure, like life-giving nectar to a dying man.

Her body was somehow soft and familiar in an odd, dreamlike way. It gave Chase hope that perhaps if he explored her and the life he had led, maybe some tiny piece of his memory would return. At least that is what he told himself as he allowed his mouth to linger on hers while crushing her to him.

She moaned softly.

He realized that he was holding her in a most intimate fashion. One hand was sprawled across her bosom. The warm fullness of her breast excited him and he grew bolder. Chase devoured her lips as hunger and brandy-induced daring spurred him on. He kissed her savagely and allowed his body to respond to her. When he released her mouth, she nuzzled into his neck.

"Chase, let's go to our room."

Her words had the same effect on him as falling into a winter river would have. His ardor chilled in his veins like shards of ice.

He stood up, practically dumping her on the floor in the process. "Go to bed, Linese." His voice was even more harsh than it had been minutes before. "I'm going out for some air. Just—just go to bed."

He turned and stumbled out into the hot Texas night. He felt the burden of his own guilt and the sting of Linese's eyes on his back with every limping step.

Chase watched the big round-faced clock's pendulum tick away the minutes toward noon. A fly persistently kept annoying him. He slapped it absently, wondering for the fifth time in as many minutes when, or if, Hezikiah went home for dinner. Surely the man had to eat—Lord knows it didn't seem as if he ever slept.

He glanced over at the printer in annoyance and saw him making no effort to cease his labors. Chase had been waiting for Hezikiah to leave him alone so he could experiment with the machinery, to see if he could figure it out.

Chase was fairly sure he had the basics, but unless he tried it he would never know.

Frustrated with Hezikiah's lack of interest in the noon hour and leaving the *Gazette,* Chase rose from the desk and stretched out his leg.

His hip wound grew better daily. He was able to move easier, with less stiffness. It pleased him that he was limping less and that he was rapidly regaining his physical strength. He wondered if Linese had noticed, then he chided himself for being so foolish that he wanted her to. He shook his head and the annoying buzz intensified with the movement.

"Going to get some dinner, Major?" Hezikiah's voice boomed over the steady creak and drone of the big newspaper press.

Chase snapped his head around and looked at Hezikiah's ink-stained visage. Evidently the man did work through the entire day and far into the night. He would find no opportunity to be alone today.

"No—no," Chase said in disappointment. "Maybe I'll stroll around Mainfield a bit and reacquaint myself with the town."

"Good idea. There've been a passel of changes since you left. You'll scarce recognize the town."

"I imagine you're right about that," Chase replied under his breath.

Chase squinted against the bright noon sun when he stepped outside the newspaper office. In defense of the unrelenting rays, he pointed his face in the opposite direction and started walking. He had no particular destination in mind, and the annoying ringing in his ears kept him company.

Several store owners spoke to Chase and remarked on the weather and the events of the war while they turned the signs on their front doors over to read Closed. Chase soon found himself nearly alone in the town at midday. It gave him a measure of freedom, walking through Mainfield while everyone was at home eating. He could stop and stare at sights that would normally cause others to look at him curiously. It was a constant worry, that he would make some foolish remark about something that he should have known since he had grown up in Mainfield. He was on guard every minute.

While he walked, he studied each building, tree and house. He sifted through his brain for a memory, but none came. Since his return, he had remembered little besides the mayor's face and his haunting words, but that dim recollection gave him hope that he might find more.

Chase walked to the wide square and sat down on one of the benches under a large spreading oak among a sprinkling of spring's first flowers. It was so hard to believe, sitting in the quiet square, that only weeks ago he had been on a bloody battlefield. He scanned the empty walks and tried to see the town through dispassionate eyes.

It was a pretty place, with well laid out lots and plenty of trees for shade. But it meant nothing to him. No feeling of belonging or roots was in him while he looked at Mainfield.

His eyes came to rest on the *Gazette* office. An invisible clock seemed to be ticking in his head. He was running out of time. The mayor and his friends had made it plain they wanted Hezikiah out as soon as possible. Chase had no idea what hold they had over him, but he had not missed the implied threat in their words. He had to hurry, even if he didn't know what secret they kept. Just knowing they had one was an effective incentive to probe deeper into his faulty brain and try to grab hold of one solid piece of memory.

If he could get Hezikiah out without arousing suspicion and if he could relearn the complicated machinery, and if he could bring himself to start writing editorials that condoned profit at any price . . .

It was a lot of *if*s. Still, what choice did he have? Wallace, Kerney and the rest of those coyotes were biding their time. He had to do what the men asked in order to keep his secret and protect Linese.

For the first time, Chase realized that he did want to protect her, more than he wanted to save himself.

The passion he had felt sweep over him last night left him aching with raw need. She had a way about her, an ability to make him forget his resolve and his caution. Bittersweet mixtures of emotion swirled through his chest while he recalled the moments he had spent with her in the library.

He had forced her from their bed, yet last night he had kissed her and allowed himself to come dangerously close to doing more. Much, much more. If she had not spoken, Chase realized, he might have forgotten himself completely.

She was a fine woman and she deserved better than to have Chase treat her warmly one minute, then coldly the next. She also deserved more than to give herself to a man who had returned as little more than a shadow of the person she had married.

"What kind of man am I?" he asked. Chase was beginning to think the answer to that question was one he wouldn't like.

The strange association with Kerney, the pistol and gold Ira Goten gave him, even the account of how he proposed to Linese, all made him sound like a man who lived fast and loose. The image he was seeing of his past self was not a flattering one.

Chase sighed and lolled his head back on the hard bench. The ringing in his ears seemed to have lessened a bit and he savored the minutes of peace.

A flash in a store window across the street drew his attention. He moved his head a little to one side and watched the sun strike an object and ripple over it like the reflection of a mirror. Curiosity brought him from the bench and across the quiet dusty street. He approached the store window where he had seen the metallic rainbow, and looked inside.

It was a cameo. Rich gold filigree and delicate pearls surrounded the exquisitely carved silhouette. The feminine cream-carved face rested against a soft rose-colored stone background. Fragile features and fine wisps of hair framed the classic profile of the woman captured in stone.

He tilted his head and looked at the jewelry from another angle. "Linese," Chase muttered. Yes, it did remind him of her. It was feminine and refined, beautiful and exquisite. Much like the woman who had the misfortune to be married to him.

Suddenly Chase had the overwhelming urge to give it to her. He shoved his hand inside his pockets and touched the hated gold coins from his past. Some deep, forgotten knowledge told him it was blood money. He could not even bring himself to look closely at the coins. He kept them hidden in the darkness of his trouser pocket, much like the dark secret he kept hidden about himself. If he could get rid of them and do something for Linese in the process, he would consider it a double blessing.

A man of small stature, with thick chin whiskers, paused and glanced curiously at Chase before he stepped around him to unlock the door to the jewelry shop. Chase closed his fist around the coins and entered right behind the little man.

The carpet was threadbare in places, but the color was still vibrant and spoke of a more prosperous time before the war.

"May I help you?" The little man looked up at him and smiled doubtfully.

"Yes, I'd like to buy the cameo in the front window, please."

The man's eyes widened in obvious surprise. He recovered quickly, but Chase could see by his initial unguarde
reaction that business had been slow. The prospect of har
cash made the shop hum with the salesman's anticipation

Chase watched him cross the store and open the bac
glass of the window. The cameo had been there for a whil
and he blew a thin layer of dust from its face when h
thought Chase wasn't watching.

"It's a fine piece. Italian. Hand-wrought gold. I had
brought in before the hostilities broke out," he explaine
proudly.

Chase ran his fingers over the row of tiny pearls at th
medallion's edge. It would look beautiful lying agains
Linese's flawless skin. He glanced at the price tag. He wa
sure the gold coins would cover the cost, and the thought o
being free of them filled him with an inner peace.

"Could you wrap it?"

The little jeweler blinked a couple of times. "Uh, I hop
you won't think me impolite, sir, but since the war, yo
know." The little man turned his hands palm up, as if i
apology for the hard times he had been forced to endure.

Chase shoved his hand into his pocket and brought ou
the gold coins. He dropped them into the little man's out
stretched palm without looking and continued to examin
the cameo, visualizing how it would look on Linese.

The jeweler held one coin to the light and examined i
more closely. Evidently satisfied, his face broke into a smile
"If you will wait, sir, I have a box in the back."

Chase told himself this impulsive act was more to fre
himself of the money, but deep down inside, he knew h
wanted to give Linese a token of his growing feelings. It wa
the least he could do since he and the war had taken her lif
and smashed it to pieces. He would like to have given her
life filled with love and children, but he knew he would hav
to settle for giving her this small bit of gold and stone in
stead.

Chapter Six

Chase looked up at the tall, rambling structure of Cordellane, graying in the shadows of the setting sun. Lamplight
cast pale fingers of muted illumination over a lawn that was
in need of a good clipping. He had seen no other help
around the place, except for the girl who helped Linese with
dinner that first night. He wondered how his grandfather
and Linese had managed alone.

His eye skimmed over the peeling paint on the eaves of the
house. A pang of guilt gripped him. They had been left to
fend for themselves as best they could, while he rode off to
war. Chase made a mental note to go in search of a scythe
tomorrow morning, to begin to put Cordellane to rights.
First, though, he wanted to see Linese.

He climbed the staircase with confidence, but when he
was at her door, he hesitated. Now that he was only a few
feet from her, he regretted his impulsiveness and weakness.
He turned away, ready to leave, to spare himself the embarrassment of showing her what he had done, when a soft
voice coming from behind her closed bedroom door drew
his attention. He realized it was Linese reading aloud.

She had a lovely voice. The soft, gentle sound of the
words flowed over him with the same hypnotic appeal they
had in the library the night before. For a fleeting instant,
everything around him seemed almost familiar. Faint images of her face, smiling and animated, filled his head. He

remembered the way she felt and tasted, even through th
brandy-induced, fogged memory of last night. When th
vision faded away, he was left with a deep void so raw it wa
physically painful.

He knocked on the door.

It opened within seconds, then he found himself bitterl
regretting his decision to see her in the very next instan
because what he saw took the breath from his body.

Linese was wearing a voluminous white night rail. Th
lightweight fabric clung to her petite curves much like
lover's hands, as he wanted his hands to mold to her bod
Chase's muscles grew taut and contracted around his bone
until he was painfully aware of the lovely creature that wa
his wife in name alone.

Chase ordered himself to ignore the newly scrubbed an
fresh-as-morning-dew look of her skin. The aroma of hon
eysuckle blossoms threaded its way around his head and int
his starved soul. He could sooner ignore his own beatin
heart than to deny the attraction he felt for this woman.

"Chase?" Her voice brought his thoughts crashing t
earth quicker than a pigeon with a broken wing.

The painful void inside him cried out for comfort. Ever
part of him wanted to hold her, to recapture what they mus
have shared but what was lost in time to him alone.

"I'll come back tomorrow." He choked on the words. H
turned away and took one halting step. The soft weight o
her fingers on his bare arm, below the rolled-up shirtsleeve
sent a hot frisson of sensation rippling though him.

"Please stay," she invited.

His heart slammed against his ribs like mortar fire. Wh
did she have to be so sweet?

"I didn't mean to intrude." he apologized awkwardl
"You are busy. It can wait...."

"I was only reading." Linese gestured to the lamp on th
small writing table and the slender book lying facedowr
"You are hardly intruding."

"Please, don't let me interrupt." He gulped down the hot lump that grew larger with each glance at her appealing form. "I can see you are preparing for bed."

He felt a hot wash of embarrassment in his cheeks at the mention of her obvious state of undress. She glanced down at her body and back to him as if only now becoming aware of her nightdress.

Linese felt as if a curtain had been drawn back to reveal a bright new canvas beneath it. Each day this man showed her layers of character she had never known existed. The quick courtship and one honeymoon night had not allowed her to explore his personality. For the first time, she realized he was embarrassed to see her standing in her night rail. It occurred to her then that maybe he felt as ill at ease as she did, maybe he was unsure and afraid of failure after so long a separation. Last night had proven to her that Chase had feelings for her, or at least physical needs that involved her. If only she had the feminine skill to bring them together in flesh and spirit. She felt a flood of heat in her own cheeks at the thought.

"I'm sorry I bothered you." He took another faltering step toward the door in an effort to retreat from the tender warrior who stared at him with soft blue eyes.

"Does it pain you much?" Linese wondered if his wounds had anything to do with his reluctance to share her bed. Could it be his male vanity that forced him to deny her companionship?

"What?" Chase frowned and looked at her blankly.

"Your leg. Does it cause you much pain?"

"Not much." Chase self-consciously rubbed his palm over his scarred hip. He felt inept standing there with Linese staring up at him. Her skin was aglow in the uneven lamplight. He thought of how nice it would be to kiss her.

"I hope you know how proud I was when I read the letter from your aide. He told me about the men whose lives you saved before you were wounded. It was a brave thing you did."

Chase swallowed hard. He had heard the account of hi actions in the hospital. At the time he thought it sounde like foolish recklessness, not bravery. But now, when Lin ese said she was proud of him for the same reckless deed, took on a new meaning for him.

"I hope you know... that is, I mean to say, I am happ to be married to such an honorable man."

Chase groaned inwardly. She kept using words like brav ery and honor. If he was so damned honorable then wh didn't he get down on his knees and tell her the horrid truth Why didn't he have the courage to tell her what had hap pened to the man she had married, so she could free hersel from him?

Chase realized at that moment he would do just abou anything to make this woman proud of him again. He hun gered to find a way to make her admire him for the man h was *now* and not the legend he was in his forgotten past, an that hunger was liberally spiced with bitterness.

"Did you wish to speak to me about something, Chase?" Her query brought his thoughts to an abrupt halt.

"Linese, if you are free, would you accompany me t Mainfield tomorrow?" He swallowed hard and hoped sh could not hear the clumsiness in his voice.

Linese averted her eyes and tried to hide the rush o pleasure she got from his invitation. "I would be pleased Chase." This was the first indication Chase had shown tha he wished to spend time in her company.

"Good, good." He turned away, then stopped, frown ing. "What time?"

She smiled at him. It was an indulgent expression tha made his belly clench with satisfaction. He wasn't sure wha he had done to bring the smile to her lips but he wished h could do it again—often.

"Whatever time is good for you. I'll be ready—an Chase?"

"Yes, Linese?"

"Thank you for asking me."

Chase turned away and opened the door. He found himself smiling at Linese's unexpected compliment. For the first time since he had woken up in that hospital, he actually felt a sensation of well-being. He had a renewed sense of hope and it was all because of Linese Cordell, his forgotten wife.

Linese was staring at the ceiling, wide-awake, and soon the sun would be rising. Funny, last night was the first night she had not heard Chase's steady pacing behind the door that separated them. She had lain awake, listening for the jerky sound of his tread, but it hadn't come. He had remained silent on his side of the closed door. It was ironic that she had tossed and turned all night, when he had found peaceful slumber for the first time since his return to Cordellane. She rose from her bed and lit the lamp on the small table. On impulse she threw back the curtains to allow the first faint streaks of mauve and gray to find their way into her room the moment they peeked over the treetops.

She wondered what had changed for Chase. She wondered why he appeared to have found a sense of calm when she was sinking deeper and deeper into a confusing vortex. A tiny voice inside her head whispered that perhaps it was her, that perhaps in some way she was helping Chase work his way through the horror of war.

She wanted to believe it might be true. She longed to believe this invitation was the first step on the long road back to each other. Linese tossed a pile of dresses onto her bed and, for the first time since Chase had come to her room, she felt a true moment of dread instead of giddy anticipation.

The war had been difficult for everyone, including the Cordells. The family had managed to avoid financial ruin— so far. Unfortunately, she had not been able to find an extra dollar to make any new additions to her wardrobe. Each frock was what she had brought with her at the time of her marriage. They were all out-of-date and inappropriate as a day dress for a trip to Mainfield. Her sturdy gray dress was fine for secretly working at the *Gazette,* but for a day with Chase, she wanted to look special. She wanted him to think she was the most fetching woman he had ever seen, whether it was true or not.

Linese held up a burgundy twill and peered skeptically a[t] her reflection in her looking glass. The deep wine color wa[s] flattering against her pale hair, and the scooped neckline wa[s] tempting in the muggy April heat, but Linese finally admit[t]ted to herself that the dress had been designed for a mor[e] festive occasion and was definitely not appropriate for da[y] wear.

She sighed and pulled the material taut against her sli[m] waist for one last look. It did compliment her form, and sh[e] was almost giddy at the prospect of spending the day i[n] Chase's company. On an impulse, she decided to be bol[d] and wear the dress, even though the wagging tongues o[f] Mainfield would probably rip her reputation to shreds fo[r] wearing such a gown before sundown.

"Silly goose," she told her grinning image. "He's you[r] husband, for goodness' sake. You don't have to fret so muc[h] about dressing up for him, or what people might say abou[t] how you look."

But the fact that Chase had asked to spend time with he[r] was no small consideration. It was a new beginning in he[r] eyes, one she was going to treasure. And she hoped the tim[e] they spent together today would lead them into a romanti[c] night, when at last perhaps, Chase would welcome her bac[k] to his bed.

Chase stretched and opened his eyes. The sun was blaz[-] ing through the windowpanes opposite his bed. He real[-] ized, with no small amount of amazement, that he had slep[t] the whole night—slept well, in fact. When he moved his leg[,] he found no stabbing pain in his hip. It seemed like an omer[n] that he could slumber peacefully and wake feeling almos[t] whole again, at least physically whole. He wondered ex[-] actly *why* he felt so good. Then it came to him.

"Linese." He was going to spend the day with Linese. His eyes slid over to the small wrapped package sitting by the lantern on his chest of drawers. He had been tempted to give it to her last night, but for some reason he held back.

The small cameo was a special secret, different from the other things he kept from Linese. It wasn't dark and depressing and he prayed the small gift would make her happy. He savored the unique feeling of doing something nice for her. It assuaged some of his guilt about deceiving her.

There was a light knock on the door. He strode across the room in his stockinged feet and opened the door.

Linese looked up at him and smiled. He was jolted by a ribbon of emotion. It was odd how this woman who was still a stranger could bring out the deepest response in him with no more than a look or a smile.

"Good morning," she said.

"Good morning, Linese." He stood there awkward and electrified while she looked at him. A strange sort of knowledge coursed through him.

He had thought she was pretty at the train that first day. Now he looked at her and knew she was nothing less than magnificent.

Her hair was pulled up and caught in soft, loose curls of gold by a wide black ribbon. Several flaxen tendrils had managed to escape and now they flirtatiously brushed along the sides of her face, as he wished his own fingers could.

The dress she wore was the rich hue of wine, and the effect it had on Chase was nearly as intoxicating. A low neck done with tiny close stitches of dark thread complimented the texture of the flawless skin on her throat and upper chest.

She looked like the image on the cameo. She looked too perfect to be real, and more than he deserved.

"Did I disturb you?" Her eyes traveled from his coat, still tossed on the bed, to the lack of boots on his stockinged feet.

"No, not at all. Come in." He stepped aside and gestured with his hand. He thought she must think him a complete fool, inviting her into her own bedroom, a room she had been forced to leave, because of him.

"I was on my way downstairs. I thought you might like to have a cup of chicory with me before we go to Mainfield."

A flutter of his pulse proved how much the small invitation meant to him.

"Just give me a minute to put on my boots." Chase sat down in the chair and picked up one boot. He saw Linese flick a quick glance around the room. A swelling of anticipation filled his chest when he saw her eyes linger on the small package.

"It's for you. You can open it now, if you like."

Linese's gaze snapped back to his face. "For me?"

Something in the breathy question made Chase think he had not been much accustomed to giving her gifts in the past. Was he a miserly husband, a man who cared more for his purse than the happiness of his wife? He jerked on his other boot and stood up.

In three long strides he was beside her. He picked up the box and placed it in her hands. Her fingers were trembling. It shamed him to know such a small gesture could affect her so profoundly, shamed him to think he had done so little for her in the past. He held her hands around the box and did not let her fingers go.

She looked up at him. "But why?" she asked. "It's not my birthday, or any special day."

For one insane minute, Chase nearly blurted out the sorrow he felt. He nearly apologized for not bringing her more gifts before the war. He wanted to ask pardon for slights he did not remember, and make promises about a future that was uncertain.

But he could not.

"You're my wife. A man should buy presents for his wife." Chase was stunned by the force and conviction of his own words.

For the first time since his return, he actually felt Linese was his wife, and not some beautiful stranger who knew him better than he knew himself.

A burst of pride expanded in his chest. He meant it, a man should give his wife little tokens of—*affection.*

Did he feel affection for her? a little voice in his head asked.

"Oh, Chase, you shouldn't have," she murmured. "It is too dear—how can you afford it?"

"That's not important. I did it and I'll probably do it again. Open it." Chase released her hands, but the warm softness of her touch lingered inside his palms. It was nice, the way it felt to hold her small hands within his own rough fingers.

He wondered what it would feel like to lie beside her, to caress her throat and listen to the steady beating of her heart. The thought brought a wave of heat rising through him.

Linese blinked twice and turned the small box around. She seemed hesitant to open it. He longed to know what kind of relationship they had shared in the short time between meeting and marriage.

But he could not ask.

Chapter Seven

Linese glanced once more at Chase, then she ripped the tissue paper off the box. Hesitance and incredulity shone in her eyes when she lifted the lid and saw what he had given her.

It made Chase squirm inwardly. He tried once more to concentrate on the past, to dredge up some memory of their time together. The strange ringing started in his head once again. He blinked hard and shook his head, but though it became less pronounced, the eerie sound remained with him.

"I—I never expected—never thought," Linese stammered.

"Open it." He couldn't stand to watch her hold the box with such reverence any longer. Every time she blinked her eyes to keep the glistening tears at bay, he cursed himself silently.

Linese gulped and stared at the cameo. The tears made her eyes more blue, more luminous, more wrenching.

Chase struggled to swallow the hot lump in his throat.

He wanted to say something, do something, but for the life of him, he didn't know what to say or do. This should have been a small event in the life of a married couple, but with each passing minute, it took on more significance. Why did she have the power to turn him inside out when he knew so little about her?

"Oh. Oh, my." She bit her bottom lip.

"Is that a good *oh,* or a bad *oh?*" He wanted to tease another grin from her to lighten the moment.

Her lips trembled.

"Linese, I'm sorry. I didn't want to see you cry. I never intended to make you cry...."

He had given her the gift to please her. He never dreamed it would make her unhappy. He closed the distance between them and took hold of her shoulders. She felt small, and appealing to him in a way that challenged explanation, defied logic, sundered his control. He had no idea why touching her should make his blood rush through his ears like a rain-swollen river overflowing its banks, or why the temperature in the room should suddenly have risen ten degrees, but it did.

"I love it. I will treasure it—" she sniffed "—always. I will keep it near me—forever."

Her lips curved into the most poignant expression of happiness Chase could have imagined.

It was his undoing.

In the tiny space of time it took for her to say those words, he had been conquered body and soul.

"Would you pin it on for me?" Her soft request made his knees weak.

Chase gulped down the flood of emotions and rubbed his sweaty palms along the front of his pants. Lord Almighty. Could he stop his insides from trembling long enough to pin the cameo on her dress—on her *low-cut* dress?

"If you'd like," he managed to croak out.

He stepped closer to her and reluctantly took the cameo from her fingers. Suddenly his own hands were clumsy and refused to manage the clasp. He felt his cheeks flame with heat while his wide fingers failed to open the simple mechanism.

"Let me help." She giggled and reached up to assist him. When their fingers met, he felt a sensation of charged air between their hands.

"Maybe I'd better not—I'm too awkward," he stammered. He took a step back, retreating again from his sweet, soft adversary. A voice inside his head told him to turn away, leave her, escape before it was too late. The personal hazard from being too near Linese was greater than any peril he faced at war.

"You have never been awkward, Chase. Pin it on me and I'll wear it today." Linese tipped her head to better expose her bodice, a bodice that was seductive, scented with the indolent odor of flowers, warmed by the ambient heat of Chase's own yearning.

Chase slowly drew in a calming breath. He tried to ignore the feel of her creamy, soft flesh against his skin while he stuck two fingers behind the fabric to shield her, lest he blunder with the sharp pin. The flowery fragrance that he had come to associate with her wafted around his body and made him light-headed.

He stuck the pin through and made the mistake of looking at her face. A temptress stared back at him.

"How does it look?" she asked.

He groaned inwardly when he looked back at the cameo. "It's crooked."

"Well, try again," she suggested.

He stifled the moan that nearly escaped his lips, while he steeled himself to make another agonizing attempt. When he glanced up, he found Linese watching him with a languid expression on her lovely face.

She looked like a cat in cream. Her lips were alluring. Her eyes were sultry and perceptive. The hollow of her throat above his hand pulsated with life.

Instinct and smoldering desire drove him toward her against all reason, against all hope. When their lips met, an icy-hot electricity jumped between their bodies. It was mystifying to Chase. Having no memory of ever having kissed any woman before, the experience was singular. Feelings and passions that were completely new to him, because he had no previous recollections to judge them against, sprang forth fully formed while he drank in the essence of Linese's mouth.

The stupefying sensation traveled down Chase's limbs and pooled around his toes. He was sure the floor was going to open up beneath him.

If this was a sample of what they had shared in the past, if this was how he had held her and kissed her...

Chase jerked his head up as if stung by a yellow jacket.

Fool, he silently cursed himself.

Chase stared at Linese, gauging her reaction, watching for some indication she knew about his madness, his missing memory, *his flaw,* but she seemed lost in her own world. Her fingertip traced an imaginary line around the row of tiny pearls on the outer edge of the cameo.

"Thank you, Chase." Her voice was satiny in his ears.

He gulped down his confusion. A part of him wanted to flee the room and find a place where Linese could not affect him so. Yet all the while he wanted to kiss her again. He wanted to run his hand down her throat and hold his palm over her breast. He wanted to feel her pulse quicken and watch her blush with each bold advance he made. He wanted to explore her personality and learn all the secret things about her.

"Do I look all right?" She brought him out of the clouds with the simple question.

"What?" Chase felt like a man trapped in a dream. This could not be happening, he should not have allowed this to happen. The more he permitted himself to care about her, the more risk he took—and the more at risk he put her, in the bargain.

"How does it look?" She lifted her fingers and met his own, which he had not realized were hovering near the cameo at the juncture of her breasts.

"You look beautiful, Linese." Chase gulped down the lump in his throat. "I can't remember you ever looking any more beautiful than you do right now." The poignancy of his truthful statement sent a lance of pain through his heart.

He didn't remember her at all, before he stepped off that train, but dear God, how he wanted to remember everything about Linese Cordell.

The buggy ride from Cordellane seemed to be going by faster than usual. Linese touched her fingers to the cameo and felt her smile return. She didn't want Chase to think she was being foolish, but his gift meant so much to her. He was finally acting as if he had missed her.

The unexpected token made her feel as if she were being wooed for the first time, since their meeting and marriage had been so quick. She knew that she and Chase had not been unusual in that respect. Many young men had chosen brides and married quickly before they went to war. It was human nature, Linese suspected, to grab happiness desperately with both hands, especially when death lay just over the horizon. Or perhaps each couple prayed for a son to carry on the father's name, in case.

She sighed and thought back to that magical time two years ago. When Linese had met Chase and he had announced she would be his wife, it had been like being swept into a raging river. She had been so mesmerized by his forceful nature and strength of will that she had yielded to his wishes without question. She had never realized how much she had missed. Not until today.

She had missed being wooed. She missed the charm and the courtship every girl dreams of having. Now it appeared that Chase was doing his best to make up for that lacking in their relationship. It gave her just that much more incentive to find a way to span the narrowing gulf between them. Linese felt her thoughts changing, growing bolder each time she found Chase staring at her surreptitiously from under his thick, dark lashes. And she smiled again, knowing that inch by inch she was making the journey to his heart.

Suddenly Chase jerked the reins up sharply on the poor startled horse. Linese blinked and grabbed the edge of the seat to keep from sliding out of it. The horse had nearly run over a group of men gathered in the street. They were huddled over something on the ground. It took her several seconds to realize the form was a man.

He was lying in a bloody heap in the center of a circle of men. Linese wondered what on earth had happened. Then she saw two men deliver bone-breaking kicks to the man's ribs, and the cause of his distress became apparent to her.

Before she even had time to react to the incredible situation, Chase leapt from the buggy, spun one assailant around and hit him straight in the face with his clenched fist. She watched in amazement as a hairline of blood appeared horizontally on the bully's square chin.

Chase's healing hip didn't seem to slow him down in the least while he strode to the other attacker and hauled him up by his shirtfront, until their faces were scant inches apart.

"Damn you, I'll not tolerate any man being kicked when he's down." Chase spat out the words. The tight circle of onlookers opened in the face of his furious wrath and gave Linese clear view of the events.

"You gutless curs," Chase growled.

"He's nothing but a dirty Southern sympathizer," the man with the bloody chin blurted indignantly. "His kind don't deserve your help, Major Cordell."

Only when Linese heard the man address Chase by name did she realize she knew them all. Most of them were neighboring landowners, merchants, people she had come to know while Chase was fighting for the Union. The thought that she had lived among them and yet never knew they were capable of such savagery sent a chill of shame up her spine.

"Whatever his loyalties, the war is not being fought here in the street. Not like this, not with a mob on one single man." Chase let the man's shirt go and he shoved him away in disgust. "Don't you have any honor?"

Linese watched Chase flex his empty hands tightly at his thighs. Silvery flames of fury burned in his eyes. The passionate, reckless part of him she had first seen in the Presbyterian church had burst to life in front of her. Indignant

violence raged within him. The look on his face sent her
heart beating a rapid staccato.

He was quite a man—and he was her man.

The group of men began to filter away and disappear into
the alleys and adjacent streets rather than face Chase's
fierceness. He bent down and helped the beaten man up.
When he was more or less standing, with Chase's assis-
tance, Linese saw it was Ira Goten.

"Thanks, Chase. This is sort of like the first time, ain'
it?" Ira wiped his torn sleeve across the blood dripping from
his mouth. He inhaled slowly and winced from the effort.

"The first time?" Chase had no idea what Ira was talking about, but he glanced over to see Linese sitting in the
buggy, listening intently. Her bottomless blue eyes focused
on him.

He wondered if she was the type of woman who might
swoon in such circumstances while he damned his missing
memory for not knowing something so simple about his
wife.

Ira grimaced again and leaned closer to Chase. He lowered his voice. "I know we made a pact not to speak about
that night, even if our lives depended upon it, but I ain'
forgot, never will. I owe you—we all owe you. God willing
I'll be able to repay that debt someday."

Ira's words were like a knife blade turning in his gut.
Chase's entire life seemed to be made up of secrets. Secret
meetings, secret deeds and the horrible secret that would
forever keep him from Linese.

He had to remember, he needed to remember.

"Are you hurt bad?" Chase grated out the words. He
wanted to steer the conversation in another direction. Everyone he met seemed to know more about his mysterious
past than he did. It angered and frustrated him.

"I'll be sore in the morning, but I'm not hurt." Ira spit
out a mouthful of blood. "Let me take your buggy and
horse. And thanks again, Chase."

"It was nothing. Forget it."

Linese saw a strange expression of sadness wash across Chase's face while he spoke to Ira Goten. A profound feeling of gloom hung in the air around the stable.

She was determined to win him—in spirit and in flesh.

"Linese, I'm sorry you to had to see that kind of hatred." Chase's deep voice rippled over her. When his hand touched hers, as he helped her down from the buggy, she felt his body stiffen with tension.

"I'll be all right. Chase, are you hurt?"

Flecks of blood were on the knuckles of his right hand. Tiny bits of flesh curled up on each one where he had made contact with the abrasive whiskers on his opponent's chin. She reached out to touch his hand, but he jerked away as if he didn't want her kindness.

"It's nothing. These kinds of wounds heal quickly. It's the ones you can't see that remain raw."

Linese puzzled over his meaning while she walked beside him to the *Gazette*. She noticed that his limp was completely gone, and she wondered if it meant that all of Chase's war wounds were healing.

Chapter Eight

They reached the newspaper office a few minutes later, only to find Mayor Kerney pacing up and down the boards outside the door. His flabby jowls were florid with color from his unaccustomed exertion in the heat. His thick neck appeared nearly lacerated by the stiffly starched collar and neck scarf he wore at his throat. The fat red stickpin shone with inner fire almost as vivid as his face.

"Chase, I've heard some disturbing news this morning." The mayor's body practically vibrated with pent-up agitation.

"Really, Mayor, and what would that be?" Chase's expression darkened. His voice had dropped to a deliberately controlled tone that sent shivers of apprehension up Linese's spine.

Chase stepped around the rotund official and opened the door for her. She stepped inside before she paused to look back at Chase and the mayor. Hezikiah glanced up briefly from behind the table holding the proofing press, but never acknowledged their arrival with more than a curt nod in their general direction. The air in the office crackled around her with suppressed anger, and she wondered what in the world was going on.

"There is a rumor going around town that you might have stepped into a situation involving a known secessionist."

One corner of Chase's mouth curled up. His face was still a swarthy portrait of anger. Silver fire leapt within his iron gray eyes.

"What are you talking about, Mayor?" The same deadly calm flavored his voice. It was yet another aspect of his persona that Linese had not seen before.

"This would be better spoken of in private." Mayor Kerney cut his eyes toward Linese.

The threat to Linese was clear to Chase. "All right, step into my office." Chase walked through the door and shut it behind his back. He faced Mayor Kerney and disgust filled his mouth with bitter bile. He didn't like the man, but beyond that he hated whatever the politician held over him, hated him for knowing things about himself that he did not.

"What have you got to say about it, Chase?" the man demanded. "I thought we made it clear—"

"If you're talking about the mob kicking Ira Goten in the street, then yes, I stepped in." Chase cut him off before he was forced to hear any more about secret meetings and pacts. "I would do the same for any man—without regard for his politics."

Mayor Kerney's small eyes narrowed. He pulled out the only chair in the room and sat down. He leaned back. His smile was confident. "I hope I don't need to remind you of the, uh, incident that took place two years back? At the time we all agreed making such matters public could be detrimental to the old Captain's health. Is there any possibility you may have changed your mind? If you have reconsidered our arrangement, then we might have to reassess our previous decision to spare the old ranger the public scandal."

Chase swallowed hard. He had no memory of what Kerney was talking about, but he understood the mayor's meaning, his threat. His grandfather was in jeopardy. Defensive feelings blossomed inside him. Most of the sporadic memories about his grandfather were of his humiliation at having the old gentleman for a relative, but

now in the face of Kerney's threat, he knew he would risk all
to keep the old man from harm.

"I'd do anything necessary to keep my family safe."

"Good. I thought as much. So now what can we do to
heal this breach between us, Chase?" Kerney tented his fingers over his abundant belly.

"What is it you want from me?" Chase felt disgust when
he asked the question. He did not want to bind himself to
Kerney further, but if it meant keeping his grandfather or
Linese safe, he would willingly make a contract with the
devil himself.

"First, get rid of Hezikiah Hershner." The more the
mayor smiled, the more Chase wanted to knock all the shiny
white teeth from his fat mouth. "Second, I expect to see
some editorials in the *Gazette* that voice the right opinion—the opinion of Mainfield's Businessman's Association."

Chase swallowed his pride. "And just what is the opinion of you and the businessmen? That you have no allegiance? That profit is the most important thing?"

Kerney smiled and looked at Chase as one might look at
an errant child. "You need not sound so indignant."

Frustration filled his chest. Chase had to regain more of
his memory. He had to find out what his grandfather had
done. The question was, could he solve the puzzles in time
to save them all from the growing threat?

Linese watched the mayor leave the *Gazette* office with a
rising sense of doom. Something about the smug, self-
satisfied smirk on his face made her heart thud inside her
chest. She looked up and found Chase studying her and
Hezikiah with troubled eyes.

"Chase, is anything the matter?" She took a half step
toward him, until his glowering expression halted her in
midstep.

"Nothing I can't handle." He turned and shut the door
to the office.

Once again she felt the sting of being shut out of his life. Linese felt the first spark of anger. Their special day together had just gone up in a puff of smoke.

Something was going to have to be done, and soon. She had taken about all the rejection she was going to stand. She had waited silently for about as long as she would wait.

Later that day Linese watched Captain Cordell saddle his horse with deft, sure moves. A wave of pity swept over her. The old gentleman could do so many tasks, seemingly without effort, but when it came to his mind, he was like a child.

"Going for a ride, Captain?" She rubbed the velvet muzzle of the tall black mare.

"Yep. I think old Tess could use some exercise. She's been acting like she needs a good gallop."

She smiled. More than likely it was the Captain who missed the feeling of the Texas wind in his hair. He had carved a reputation almost as big as the country itself during the Indian wars. But that was before his mind went, when Chase was just a sprouting youth, from the tales Hezikiah had told her during the past two years.

"Don't wait up for me. Tess and I may be out quite late, we're going for a good long gallop." He swung into the saddle.

His agility made it hard for Linese to believe he was nearing sixty. She watched him disappear into the thicket, taking the same overgrown path Chase had emerged from the other evening. She had not seen the Captain take his horse down that path in many months.

If she had not had business of her own, she would have taken a walk into the woods to investigate why they both would use it when it was little more than a faint trace. Surely there were other paths and game trails that offered less resistance into the thicket. It was a puzzlement, these Cordell men and their strange ways. But she pushed the thought from her mind.

Linese turned away, busy with other plans. She was determined to sunder the wall around Chase, and she was going to begin tonight.

It was plain he found her attractive. In the library his body nearly hummed with sexual hunger. When he gave her the cameo, she saw desire and yearning smoldering in his eyes. The way his hand trembled when he touched her breast left no doubt that he still wanted her. He had never expressed his feelings in words, but he had shown her his ardor on their wedding night.

Whatever obstacle was keeping them apart, it was not a lack of passion. His limp was gone, and he no longer paced his room at night. She simply had to find a way to give him a little nudge in the right direction.

While Linese walked back to the house, she thought about his wound. Chase's aide had described it in some detail in the first letter she received while Chase was in the hospital. His hip must be badly scarred. She worried her bottom lip and wondered. Could such a thing as that be enough to keep him from her bed? Could his strange, changing moods be no more than male pride?

Linese shook her head. No matter. Whatever the cause, she intended to attack it like a general and remove it from their lives—tonight.

Linese placed the last of the dozen candles she had boldly decided to sacrifice into the quadra-plate silver candelabra and placed it on the dining room table. The smells floating from the kitchen made her salivate. She caught herself grinning when she looked into the wavy mirror hanging above the squat oak server.

"Tonight, Major Chase Cordell, you are in for a surprise." She took one last critical look at the table and felt her body tingle with anticipation. The sensation was much like the one she had felt on her wedding night—expectant, eager, yet oddly shy. It was still two hours until Chase would come home, two hours in which she could plan and hope.

She had Toby Sillers bring her home early in a rented buggy after she had finally plucked up her courage and decided on this plan. The tall clock in the corner chimed.

Linese checked the food simmering in the kitchen once more. She had only one more task to complete. A fresh dress was laid out on her bed and a bath was waiting in the hip tub upstairs. Tonight she wanted to look her best. Tonight she wanted Chase to gaze upon her and find her too appealing to resist any longer.

Chase put his horse in the stable and turned toward the house. He had left the *Gazette* early, hoping to find some clue about the incident Mayor Kerney was holding over his head like a sword. For the past two days, he had hammered at his faulty mind to no avail. Then today, when Linese had gone of on some vague errand, he decided to return to Cordellane and use his time alone in the big house to further delve into his missing past.

He stepped inside the empty house and for a moment thought he smelled food. Chase shook his head in annoyance. If the annoying buzz in his ears was not bad enough, now he could no longer trust his senses. Disgust at his imperfect body rushed over him while he strode toward the library. Like the rest of the house, he knew it would be empty, since the Captain had been riding off into the thicket at sunrise and not returning until after dark.

Chase's eyes swept over the stack of *Gazettes* strewn across the old rug. Memories of Linese reading to him came unbidden, threatening to steal his flagging concentration. He fought the temptation and bent over to look closer at the papers. Some nagging voice inside his head told him the answer lay before him. If he could only decipher the puzzle.

He scanned each page, searching for something, anything that might trigger a memory. Whatever his grandfather had done, it had taken place shortly before he left Linese and went to war. Surely any event serious enough to allow Kerney to blackmail Chase would be recorded in the *Gazette*.

While he stared at the row of inked pages, his thoughts turned to the old man who was the father of his sire. The Captain seemed harmless enough, but who could say what form his mental affliction had taken in the past or would take in the future. A feeling of pity mingled with an odd burst of affection. The old ranger might be mad as a hatter, but he was still Chase's blood, and he would fight Kerney and his cronies to keep him safe.

A muffled sound on the stairs made his head come up with a jerk. The humming in his ears was growing worse, but he was sure he had indeed heard something. Without a sound, he slipped from the chair and went to the library doors to investigate. The threat Kerney made about his grandfather and Linese was real and had resurrected all the soldier's instincts he had honed while fighting for his cause.

A shadow fell across the hallway. Chase lunged from the library and felt his fingers dig into familiar flesh. At the same instant, he heard a soft cry of pain that made his gut wrench.

"Chase—" Linese gasped. "You're hurting me."

"Linese?" He stared down at her in shock. Her cheeks were flushed, her eyes were wide with fear and surprise at his rough treatment. "Did I hurt you?" Chase was horrified that he might have injured her.

"Chase, you're home early." Her voice was breathy with disbelief. "I didn't expect you for a couple of hours."

Something about her manner made his belly clench. She was acting almost guilty, an emotion he had become intimately acquainted with lately. A tendril of suspicion wound its way around Chase's heart. Why would she act so disappointed to see him home? Why was *she* home? He was certain she had said something about needing to run an errand in town, that she would not be returning from Mainfield with him. Suddenly he realized that he had seen little of her over the past two days.

Why?

A prickly, uncomfortable feeling, something a whole lot like jealousy, rose inside him. He had been gone a long time. Many women found the separation from their husbands impossible to bear alone. The possibility that Linese might have found, could still find, solace with another man made him crazy, crazier than he already felt without the security of a past life with her.

The thought that another man could have her, might still have her love, clawed at him. His gut twisted painfully. Images of Linese with a faceless but whole man filled his head.

"Is there some reason why I shouldn't have come home early?" He stared down at her lovely, oh so beautiful face and felt his heart rend in two. Those uncanny blue eyes slid over him and left chills in their wake.

She was so desirable. How many men coveted his pretty wife? How many men, who were free of secrets, could give her all that he could not?

"Don't be silly, Chase. Of course not." Even while she denied it, there was a sly tone in her voice. "I just didn't realize you were home." Her smile trembled a little, as if she were the one with all the hidden secrets.

Heightened passion mingled with the aura of suspicion while he stared at her. She intrigued him, this vixen who was his wife. One moment she was meek and blushing, the next her eyes held the promise of some forbidden treasure.

There were so many mysteries to this lovely creature. He wanted to take her in his arms to kiss her, to truly discover all the riddles of his wife. Regret swirled through Chase's soul when he reminded himself that he could never know those secrets, that he could not risk her discovering he was but half a man.

"Where were you going just now?" He forced his hands to his thighs so he would not touch her, though his palms itched to mold themselves to her body. "I thought you were in Mainfield."

"I, uh, decided to come home. I was on my way upstairs to dress for dinner," she stammered.

Her words were like a bucket of water in his face. Suddenly his suspicion evaporated and his wariness about his missing memory rose up. "Dress for dinner? Is it a special occasion?" The unending obstacle of having to feel his way through each unknown day came back to haunt him.

"Perhaps." She stepped away from him and turned to look back at him with a mysterious smile on her face. "It might be a very special day." Then she darted up the stairs.

Linese pulled the yellow gingham over her head and wriggled the full skirt down over her hips. She could thank the war for not increasing the size of her slender form. As it was, the dress was tight as a glove and pushed her bosom up into a deep cleft above the ruffled flounce. She didn't recall its being quite so revealing, but perhaps she had grown a bit fuller in her chest since her marriage. After all she had been barely seventeen when she and Chase stood before the minister. She leaned toward the mirror and pinned the cameo at the juncture of her cleavage.

"I wonder if he will remember this dress?" Linese asked her reflection. It was silly, she supposed. Men were not sentimental in the same way women were, but in her heart of hearts, she hoped he would remember it. She dabbed a bit of scent behind her ears before she summoned her courage and went downstairs.

Chase poured himself a tall brandy. He had read and reread every paper in the stack. Nothing in any of them brought one shred of recollection forward. The slim hope he had pinned on regaining at least a small portion of his memory was fast dwindling and he felt a growing sense of doom.

His own past was nipping at his heels, but the worst part was knowing he was helpless to protect his grandfather and

Linese without the memory of his own deeds. He could face his own destruction, and probably deserved to pay the price for a thousand forgotten black sins. But his grandfather and Linese were different—they were innocent.

He had to protect them. His earlier conversation had intruded on his thoughts the entire time he had been searching the back issues. A part of him knew that he had only given them part of his attention and that his real interest had been at the top of the stairs with Linese.

He sipped the brandy and allowed the sensation of holding her slim shoulders in his hands to wash over him. Touching her had been a bittersweet thing.

When the ringing in his ears grew louder, he took another gulp of the brandy. Then the scent of spring blooms and the sound of crinoline swishing brought him spinning around to see the source of the noise. A bright, painful flash of memory ripped through his head when he caught sight of Linese. . . .

It was her, yet it was not Linese here in this time.

She was younger, more childlike, untouched. Her face held the same sort of promise the first rosebud of spring contains—soft, pristine, achingly beautiful. The memory of fiddle music and loud conversation surrounded her misty image and nearly drowned out the sound of ringing in his ears while he stared at her with his mouth agape. In his mind's eye, he saw a distortion of himself, as if looking through a cracked telescope lens.

His remembered self walked into the crowded room and focused on her. She looked up at him with eyes bluer than a robin's egg.

He knew he had to have her. There was a makeshift bandage on his hand when he reached out and took hold of hers.

The scar Ira spoke of.

The information suddenly popped into his head. Though he had no idea how he had gotten the wound, he now knew it had resulted in the scar. He heard his own voice, echoing up as if from the bottom of a deep dry well.

"Allow me to introduce myself. I am Chase Cordell."

A million missing and unremembered emotions ripped through his head in the space of one thudding heartbeat. He remembered what it felt like to know he had to *have* Linese. He remembered what it felt like to be driven to win Linese. But the thing that tore him apart, the one emotion he wanted to feel, was still missing.

He couldn't remember loving Linese.

He forced himself to face the specter of himself. Had he married her because he had to have her? Had he married her when he did not love her?

The ringing in his ears rose in pitch and intensity. Chase felt his knees go liquid. The brandy glass slipped from his hand. He heard the glass shatter into a million pieces on the stones in front of the fireplace. Then his vision shrank into nothing more than a black tunnel almost as stygian as the pain in his heart.

Chase paced his room and tried to keep his eyes off the connecting door between his room and the room that was now Linese's. It was a futile effort. He could not ignore the door or the pain lingering in his soul. Humiliation and sadness warred with a bittersweet joy inside him.

He had remembered. Not much, just a tiny heartbeat of time, but in that time, a million lost emotions were resurrected.

He remembered what he had felt like the first time he had laid eyes on Linese, but nothing followed or preceded it. The memory was hanging there in his mind, disjointed, unconnected like a spider's web in a dim corner.

He walked to the door and placed his fingertips against the wood, then he leaned his forehead against the solid mass.

He wanted to knock, wanted to open the door, wanted to remove the barrier of wood between them. He sighed and told himself the obstacle between them was not of wood or stone.

If only he could hold her and kiss her.

He could hear her moving about beyond the wide oak door. Each tiny sound brought images of her luminous eyes and moist lips. He squeezed his eyes shut against the pain and passion he felt and slumped into the rocker beside the too-large, too-empty bed.

The pounding in his temples matched the throbbing of his heated blood. His head hurt from thinking about her, and his arms ached to hold her.

A light knock at the door brought Chase back up to his stocking-covered feet. He stood there, rigid, sure he imagined the sound. Then it came again. Hesitant, timid—the knock of someone plucking up her courage.

He crossed the room in three long strides and stood frozen, staring at the door. He had to draw upon his tattered reserve of determination before he could reach for the glass doorknob and turn it. She was there, exactly as he had pictured her.

"Linese." He heard the happiness in his greeting and cringed a little for the weakness she brought out in him.

"I hope I'm not disturbing you." She looked beyond him to the untouched bed. A bright flush of color invaded her cheeks when she faced him. "After what happened, I wanted to see if you were feeling better. Is there anything you need? Should I fetch Doc Lukins?"

He wanted to go to her, to take her in his arms. He wanted to recapture the magic of holding her. But fear kept him rooted to the floor by the doorway.

"No, I'm fine, except for my bruised pride. I had a headache. I lost my balance and fell...." He allowed the lie to trail off. It had been the sight of her in the dress, the recaptured recollection that had put him on his knees before her.

"Oh," she said.

He knew she doubted his flimsy excuse. She swept past him into the room without invitation and he did indeed catch a whiff of flowers and clean cotton emanating from her voluminous gown, just as he imagined. Chase squeezed the knob tighter and tried not to notice the seductive sway of her womanly hips while he drank in the sight of her, there, in his bedroom.

How could he not remember her?

In a moment of pure panic, Chase realized he was falling in love with his wife. He remembered wanting her for his bride in the past, but if he let himself, now, in the present, he could worship her.

It was not just the recollection of their meeting and the thrill of those first heart-pounding minutes when he knew he had to have her, had to possess her. It was so much more.

New feelings of affection were being layered on top of the old ones he barely remembered. Old feelings of wanting to possess her.

She was everything he could desire—beautiful, intelligent, caring. He wanted her. He wanted her in his bed, in his arms and in his heart.

It rocked Chase to acknowledge it, but locked deep inside his soul, waiting to spring free, was a love for Linese so strong, so powerful, it was frightening to him. And to his great sorrow, he was beginning to think he was powerless to prevent it from emerging before the secrets of his past destroyed him.

Chapter Nine

Linese took a sip of hot chicory. She stifled another yawn and fought to clear the cobweb of fatigue and frustration from her mind. Last night, she had lain awake wondering what on earth had happened to Chase. For a fleeting moment she had thought he was ready to allow her back in his life, but if he was willing, he certainly had not been able. She wondered if his blackout was another aspect of his injury, or if it might be something else.

He had made an awkward excuse and taken another walk into the night after she had finally plucked up her courage and entered his bedroom. In fact, he had acted like a man evading a mortal enemy and now this morning, he had left before she even woke.

In a way, she was happy he had left before she had to face him. The dismal failure of her attempted seduction last evening stung her pride. Linese was embarrassed to think of what she had hoped would happen. Her attempts to seduce her husband with a fine dinner, and then lure him to their bed, had ended in failure. But, for one moment, when she found the courage to confront him in his bedroom, he had looked at her with restless eyes full of longing and need. Then he had strode from the room without a word.

He wanted her, he desired her—she was sure of it.

"What am I doing wrong?" she asked herself.

There had to be a way to regain her husband's bed—hi passion and affection. But how? She had been raised by tw maiden aunts who never spoke of the things between me and women. She was ignorant of the little wiles othe women used instinctively. She felt the heat of a blush work ing its way up her neck and cheeks. If only there was some one, another woman she could ask.

Linese sighed and rested her chin in her palm. For the life of her, she didn't know a soul who could help her with thi extremely difficult problem. She had spent most of her time at the *Gazette* with Hezikiah and had made few real friends fewer female friends, since her arrival in Mainfield a Chase's bride. She had no female relations left alive. The bright morning sun illuminated the room and, from Lin ese's point of view, her plan to win Chase looked hopeless.

"Good morning." Captain Cordell's cheerful greetin made her start.

"Good morning." She sounded as glum as she felt. Sh looked at him and saw sunshine shimmering on the spider webs covering his shoulders. His long mustache was gilt wit dust and there were more webs in his white hair.

"Captain? What on earth have you been doing?" Linese frowned. She had never felt his mental condition was to the point that he might hurt himself, but he frequently went of on adventures that would seem odd to other people. The ol gentleman always seemed to be bustling around, busy wit some task or another that neither she nor anybody she knew in Mainfield ever actually witnessed.

"I've been in the attic," he explained cheerfully.

"Why?" She envied him. He never seemed to have a minute's worry or concern. "What are you up to today?"

"I'm heading over to Doralee's." He swiped a long trailing web from his coat sleeve and smiled at Linese. "You look like you could use a change of scenery. How abou coming with me?"

Linese felt her eyes widen in shock. It wouldn't be prope for her to be seen at a house of ill repute. Tongues would vag. Well brought up ladies simply did not consort with women of that ilk. She opened her mouth to speak, then abruptly snapped it shut.

Women of that ilk.

Her own words threaded through her mind while a completely insane idea began to form, one that threatened to make her blush.

"I would like to go with you, Captain. Give me a minute. I have something I want to take, as well."

Linese darted up the stairs and flung open the clothes press in Chase's bedroom. She dug to the bottom of the cedar-lined drawer until her fingers identified the feel of lace. Her fingers closed around the delicate crispness and she pulled out a pale pink silk bed jacket. The delicate embroidery and tatting was more fragile than butterfly wings.

"Forgive me, Aunt Hesta, but giving away this jacket may do more for my marriage than keeping it ever could." She turned and raced back down the stairs.

A part of her was appalled that she could even consider crossing the threshold of the sporting house, while another part of her was tingling with anticipation of what it could mean to her and Chase.

Doralee's infamous house was multistoried and in need of paint, like most of the homes around Mainfield. The weathered eaves had once been a bright green, but peeling strips of faded color that hung sadly were all that was left to testify to that truth. Looking at the building made Linese gloomy. The run-down condition of the bawdy house brought into perspective how the war had tainted everything around them all.

"Whoa." The Captain pulled up on the reins and the old wagon lumbered to a stop. He climbed down and began to untie the ropes holding the cradle, the rocker and small chest in place.

Linese had to look away. Seeing the baby furniture being given to some other woman felt like a prophesy that she and

Chase would never have need of the items. A hot sting o
tears made her bring her chin up a notch to counter th
negative thought.

No. She would not accept defeat so easily. She would no
give in to the dismal thoughts and thereby make her fear
bitter reality. Linese intended to fight for what she wanted
Chase was not the only stubborn, determined Cordell.

If there was a chance she could win her husband, and fil
Cordellane with round-cheeked babies, then by God, sh
was going to take it. No matter how improper it might be
No matter how it mortified her to think about it.

Linese gathered her skirt in her hands and jumped dow
from the wagon. She swallowed her pride and put her foo
on the warped bottom stair. She had decided she would b
carrying Chase Cordell's baby in the spring.

Captain Cordell hefted the cradle up on his shoulders an
carried it into the house. Linese timidly followed him up th
stoop. When he stepped over the threshold, she sucked in
breath for courage and followed him in.

The house looked just like any other house, except fo
several humidors she assumed were full of fat cigars, and
counter well-stocked with whiskey and brandy. Dorale
must have paid a ransom to have such an ample selectior
smuggled in. Other than those small details, the house wa
similar to Cordellane in age and size. Linese allowed he
curious gaze to look into the parlor beyond. She smelle
chicory and women's toilet water.

She realized half a dozen women had stopped in the mid
dle of drinking chicory and were looking at her with th
same surprise she was sure was written on her face. Had the
been occupied with the current gossip and news of the war
like other women in Mainfield, Texas? She watched th
scene with a growing sense of awareness.

"Why, Captain, what have you got there?" A woma
with unusually large brown eyes asked. She held herself erec
while she left the group and came to stand by Captain Cor
dell.

"'Morning, Doralee,'' he said. "I brought some things I thought you could put to use.''

Linese couldn't help but stare. Doralee's reputation had reached all the way to Ferrin County. Long before Linese had ever met Chase she had heard about Doralee's sporting parlor. She felt her cheeks blaze with heat when the woman's eyes slid over her and caught her gawking.

"Who is this?" Doralee's face was unreadable while her eyes coolly assessed Linese from head to toe.

"This is my granddaughter-in-law, Linese,'' Captain Cordell said matter-of-factly while he swept by the two women and up the stairs.

"Welcome, Linese." Doralee held out her hand and Linese accepted it shyly.

Only after the old Captain had left them did Linese realize that he had identified her correctly, for the first time since Chase had brought her to Mainfield. It was a puzzling awareness he seemed to have found.

"I—I brought a present for Melissa. The Captain told me about her condition." Linese felt her cheeks grow warmer than hot muffins. She wanted for all the world to disappear into the floor. What had she been thinking? This plan was ridiculous.

Doralee smiled wistfully while she touched the bed jacket with her fingertips. "She fancied herself in love. I tried to explain how difficult it would be...." The woman's voice drifted off. "Well, no matter now—done is done. Go on up. Captain Cordell knows the way." She gestured toward the winding staircase. Captain Cordell was maneuvering the cradle up the stairs, avoiding the banister where it curved.

Linese wondered how many times he had visited the house. The Cordell men were more of a mystery to her each passing day. She picked up her skirts and followed him, all the while telling herself, if she had a lick of sense, she would go sit in the wagon and spare herself any more humiliation.

At the top of the stairs, Captain Cordell stepped aside and nodded toward an open door. Linese hesitated for a moment, but then he smiled and she finally entered a room flooded with sunlight.

A brown-haired girl, huge with child, was sitting by the window reading a copy of the *Gazette*. She looked up and surprise registered on her young face when the Captain set the cradle in the middle of the floor.

"Look what I found lying around, Melissa," the Captain said with a wink.

"That is the finest-looking cradle I have ever seen. I can never begin to thank you." Her well-modulated voice was spiced with a lilting trace of a Southern accent.

"No need for thanks...got to have a place to put the little rascal when it gets here." The Captain cleared his throat and turned away. He stroked his fingers through his long mustache. "I'm going to go have a drink with Doralee. Linese has a gift for you too, I believe."

"Captain?" Linese was not sure she could finish what she had begun, now that she was here and actually facing the task.

"Stay, get acquainted. I'm in no hurry." The old man turned back to Melissa. "This is Linese." With that short introduction of sorts, he patted Linese on the shoulder and walked out of the room.

Every muscle in her body tensed up. She had no idea what to say, how to begin. The whole idea was madness. She must have lost her mind to even consider such a preposterous notion. Before she lost the last speck of her courage, she thrust the pink silk forward awkwardly.

"This is for you."

Melissa narrowed her green eyes and looked up at Linese. "What is it?"

"It's a bed jacket. My great-aunt Hesta made it. She said a woman should look her best on the occasion of her first child's arrival. I want you to have it."

Melissa took the garment and held it to her cheek. "Soft as down. It's fine, too fine." Her fingers skimmed along the rows of lace and tatting. It was obvious she liked it.

She abruptly handed it back. "I thank you, but I can't accept such a gift. I have no way of repaying such generosity."

This was her chance, this was her opportunity.

Linese gulped down her pride and her fear. She summoned up her courage and forced herself to take a step forward.

"As a matter of fact there is a way you could repay me." The words came out in a self-conscious tumble. "If you—if you would that is."

"What can I do—for you?"

Linese saw a trace of wariness and suspicion in Melissa's eyes. She could not blame her. What Linese was about to do was beyond the boundaries of acceptable behavior. There was no telling what Melissa would think of Linese's request. But Linese had to try to salvage her marriage.

"I want you to tell me how I can seduce a man." Linese's face flamed with fire. Her mouth went dry. She wanted to sink through the floor and disappear, but she held her head up and acted as though she knew what she were saying. She prayed she hadn't gone as mad as the Captain.

"Is that all?" Melissa said evenly. She folded the bed jacket and placed it in what was left of her shrinking lap. "I'm sorry, Linese. I have been a poor hostess. Pull that rocker over here and sit a spell while we get acquainted." Melissa smiled warmly and her face lit up. She was a pretty thing, and younger than Linese.

"Where are you from, Melissa?" Curiosity and relief that Melissa had not laughed at her made Linese grow more bold.

"Georgia. My family was all killed when the fighting broke out." Her eyes took on a faraway look. "I—I was—violated when our plantation was overrun." She shrugged as if it didn't really matter, but her eyes were misty and her voice held the taut control of someone fighting to remain apart from a hellish memory. "It didn't seem to matter much whether I lived or died. Luckily, Miss Doralee found me and brought me here.''

The impact of war's price settled on Linese like a shroud. Fate had forever altered Melissa's life by a chance encounter, a happenstance of destiny. Under different circumstances, Linese might very well be the woman sitting by the window in the house of ill repute, waiting for the birth of her child.

''I don't believe in dwelling in the past. Now let's figure out how I can help you. Who is it you want to seduce, Linese?'' The girl was obviously puzzled by Linese's request, but she kept a straight face and acted as if the question were an everyday occurrence.

''My husband.'' Misery settled in her stomach when she forced herself to voice the humiliating truth.

''Your husband?'' The young woman's eyebrows rose. She looked at Linese with equal portions of pity and disbelief in her face. ''I don't understand. Is your husband an old man?''

Linese sighed heavily. She didn't understand, either, but she was determined that she would. ''No. He's young. He went to war right after we were married.''

''Was he injured? Is that why he's back?''

Linese nodded. ''Yes. His hip—he was in the hospital for some time.'' She looked at the young prostitute hopefully. ''Do you think the problem could be his wound?''

Melissa shrugged. ''Is he—whole?''

''Yes.'' Linese thought about the letter from his aide, describing the wound in detail. She wished her cheeks would stop burning.

Melissa frowned. ''Men are mystifying creatures. Who knows what drives them. If he's well healed, then I doubt it would keep him from, well, keep him from performing naturally. I have, uh, known of men who were ashamed of their bodies. But your husband doesn't have any peculiarities, does he?''

"No. He's a handsome, strong man." Linese thought of her honeymoon, the only time she had seen him partially clothed, and of the injury to his hip. "I haven't seen him unclothed since he returned."

"Maybe his pride is keeping him from letting you see him. Maybe he is shamed by the scar." Melissa rubbed her palm over her belly. "My baby's papa is off fighting. He's as vain as a leghorn rooster. Could be your husband is, too."

Linese smiled. They were not very different, she and this young woman who earned her living by selling her body. If you scratched deep enough, it was plain to see, the love of a man was the most important thing in their lives. If this worked it would be well worth the effort.

"I want you to explain to me how—how I can make him want me."

"Easy as falling off a log. If a woman goes about it the right way, there aren't many men who can stand up against their own weakness. Not for long, anyway."

Chapter Ten

Linese finished her scented bath and stepped from the big brass tub. All the things Melissa had told her swirled through her head. She had had no idea women held such power over men. It was intoxicating to think about it, mystifying, to realize God had given her such ability.

A smile tickled the corners of her mouth while she slipped on the sheer night rail Melissa had sent home with her. When she stepped in front of the mirror to assess herself, she gasped.

Every contour of her body was evident. She could see the dark rings of color around her nipples and the honey-colored triangle of hair between her legs. She had never seen herself like this before. It was a bit shocking. For a moment, her courage nearly failed her, while hot color rose from the low neckline to the roots of her hair, but she steeled herself with all the stern teachings of her aunt.

"Whatever it takes," she told herself. After all, she was Chase's wife. Anything they did together was blessed by the Lord. It wasn't as if she were trying to seduce him outside of marriage. If she had to act a little wanton in order to see their marriage back on solid ground, then so be it. She was more than prepared to play the harlot for her husband. In fact, a part of her was actually looking forward to trying some of the shocking things Melissa had explained to her, just to see if they were true.

* * *

Hours later, Linese heard the front door close with a soft thud of air. Captain Cordell had long since retired. She wondered if Chase had eaten anything before he came home, then she wiped the thought from her mind. The last thing she wanted to do at this moment was cook for him. She wanted him hungry—for her.

She listened to each footfall on the stairs and felt her pulse quicken. There was no limp in his step tonight, and she breathed a sigh of relief. If, as she and Melissa surmised, the wound was the problem, it made her confident to know it was not bothering him tonight.

The louder the steps grew and the closer he came, the more her body burned with desire and anticipation. She gasped when she watched her reflection in the mirror and saw her own nipples rise up against the soft fabric like tight little buds. There was a feeling in her lower belly that was beyond description. She didn't remember ever feeling all the parts of her body in such vivid detail before.

Linese felt predatory.

Chase's door shut with a thunk.

Linese swallowed the lump in her throat and took one last look at her reflection. On impulse she picked up the cameo she had laid on the low chest and pinned it at the neck of her gown.

"For luck," she told herself. Then she turned and stepped toward the connecting door with the sound of her own pulse thrumming in her ears.

Chase had just taken off his coat when he heard the knock at the door. The thought of seeing Linese made his heart pound. Each day the temptation to hold her became more and more unbearable. He had started staying at the *Gazette* until late at night in order to refrain from touching her.

At least one good thing was coming of it: he had managed to figure out part of the printing process. He was almost able to perform the tasks necessary to run the *Gazette*. The knock came again and his mouth went dry.

He knew he should do something to fortify himself against the feelings he had for his wife. He was weakening more each day. He decided not to respond to her knock, hoping she would go back to bed and leave him in his desolate misery.

The knock came again, a third time.

She was not going to give up and leave him in tortured peace. He dropped his coat onto the rocker and walked to the door.

Chase told himself he could withstand it one more time. He lowered his eyes and hoped he could avoid looking into hers, while he opened the door between their rooms. His knuckles were white on the glass knob when he pulled the door open.

All the air compressed from his lungs in a painful whoosh. The light from his lamp, and the one burning beyond in her room, bathed her form in a golden silhouette.

He could see her ankles and calves in clear relief. He was afraid to allow his eyes to wander any further up her body, but travel they did. The smooth contour of her womanly hips sent his heart pounding at double its normal beat. A dusky triangle between her legs made his throat constrict painfully. He gulped down his growing passion and forced himself to look only at her face.

"Did you want to talk to me about something?" Chase suddenly felt a hundred years old while he tried to ignore the beauty of his wife. His eyes drifted from her face again, even while he tried to stop them.

She was wearing the cameo, clipped at the neck of her nightgown. It struck him as an odd thing to do, but it pleased him in some silly private way that made his knees liquid and his heart ache. The cameo rested in the dewy valley between her ample breasts. He ached to hold them, ached to see his children suckle them, cursed himself for the thought.

"I've made a decision. I'm going to move back into our bed, Chase." There was not a trace of indecision in her shocking declaration.

Chase gulped down his surprise and tried to stop the flock of butterflies that had suddenly taken up residence in his middle. Move into this room? Lie beside him in the bed that appeared to shrink to half its former size while he stood there with his heart on his sleeve?

Equal measures of dread, bliss and randy lust marched through his chest. Torment, sharper and more raw than anything in his memory, ripped through his soul.

"What?" He gulped incredulously. She was his wife and it was her right. She deserved better than him. Yes, he agreed bitterly with himself, she deserved more—more than he could ever hope to give her.

"I'm moving back into our bedroom—tonight."

Chase couldn't think of anything else to say. There was nothing to say. She had told him how it would be. She did not ask his permission. He felt as if he had been struck by an iron fist sheathed in a velvet glove.

"You can't, Linese," he declared loudly. He turned away from her beautiful image and the bitter taste of unanswered need filled his mouth.

"Chase, I don't think you heard me." Her voice was calm and unruffled. "I said, it is time. We need to begin to rebuild the bonds between us. I will sleep in here tonight and every night, from now on."

A swish of cloth brought Chase whirling around in time to see her slip between the crisp white sheets. Her nightgown was lying in a heap on the braided rug. The pearl-rimmed cameo winked in the lamplight from the chest beside his bed.

This conversation was over.

Many hours later Chase sat in the rocker and stared at her in complete astonishment. He tried not to notice Linese's soft, even breathing coming from the bed, tried and failed.

He was still numb with shock at her actions. She had fallen asleep within minutes of climbing into his bed. She had simply slipped between the sheets and gone to sleep as if she didn't have a care in the world.

If only God would grant him the solitude of sleep. But he could not sleep, not when the object of his desire was mere feet from him. It was hell, knowing she was naked and willing, and forbidden as the fruit in the garden of Eden.

Chase yawned and raked his fingers through his tousled hair. He was tired, so tired, and the annoying buzz in his ears had returned sometime while he stared in astonishment at Linese.

Around midnight he had finally accepted the fact she wasn't going away, she wasn't some apparition that would disappear if he willed her to. She had said she intended to sleep here every night, and he had no doubt she meant what she said. For better or worse, he was obliged to find a way to deal with this latest complication in his sordid life.

In defeat, he blew out the lamp and crept toward the bed. Linese never stirred while he quietly took off his clothes. When he was standing beside the bed, naked and partially aroused, he realized that he had no nightshirt—apparently had never worn one—since he had found none among his old clothes.

He cursed harshly under his breath.

At this moment he would give just about anything to have a thin layer of cloth between their bodies. But like most things, wishing would not make it so. He grated his teeth, lifted the sheet and slid into bed beside her.

She moved.

The soft firmness of her bare thigh settled against his own. Warm, pliant flesh touched him. A thousand needles of desire and knowledge came alive and coursed throughout his tense body from that single point of contact.

For a fleeting moment, he remembered, or thought he remembered. A cloudy image of holding her beneath him in physical ecstasy filled his mind. Then it flitted away. He had probably imagined it anyway, he told himself sourly. Just because he wanted to know the delight of making love to her, he was probably concocting pictures of it in his twisted, perverse mind. He socked his pillow with his closed fist and cursed aloud again. Then he flopped over.

It was a mistake. The heavier weight of his body on the down mattress brought her petite body rolling closer to his side of the too narrow bed. It sent him into a heart-pounding quandary.

God in heaven. This could not be happening. What horrible cruel deed was he guilty of to be tortured in this way?

All he need do was turn over, lift his leg over her hip, and they would be touching intimately. Images of her silhouetted in the light between their rooms assaulted him again. He now had a tantalizing idea of what her body looked like. He longed to know what it felt like.

His loins burned and his palms itched to know her. He wanted to mold her breasts to fit his grasp. He wanted to taste her mouth and hear her sigh. He wanted to brand her with his desire and make her his wife in more than just name.

Chase's heart cried out to remember claiming Linese's body. He wanted to remember her soft sighs. He wanted to have the memory of filling her to the hilt.

He wanted all there was of Linese.

He tossed back the sheet and stalked from the bed half-mad with lust. Chase looked toward the sanctuary of the adjoining room. Perhaps he should move into the room she had been using.

No.

He could not, would not, hurt her like that again. He was stuck. Stuck with the most beautiful, desirable woman he could imagine, and he couldn't allow himself to touch her.

With a frustrated groan, he flopped into the window seat in the room she had been occupying. He rested his feverish forehead against the cool panes of glass while he stared out into the night in frustration.

The sound of galloping hooves broke the silence around Cordellane. Chase squinted into the night. The image of a lathered black horse emerging from the thicket was the first thing his brain registered. The next was the fact that his grandfather was the man riding the horse.

"What the devil?" Chase looked at the tiny porcelain clock on the mantel. It was well past three in the morning.

"What is that old madman doing out at this time of night?" Chase muttered to himself. An odd feeling of affection, pride and annoyance blended inside his chest.

If the old fellow were sane, Chase would go down and ask him what the hell he was doing, but he was not. He knew he would only answer him in gibberish, and Chase was confused enough tonight, with Linese's soft breathing coming from his room. No, Chase could not ask what the old ranger was up to, but he would have to find out. The mayor and his cronies would like nothing better than to have more leverage over him. He had to remember the night they were threatening him with—and whatever terrible thing his grandfather had done.

He snatched up an old quilt and settled naked into the window seat again. He knew he wasn't going to get a wink of sleep, so he resolved to use the time to sift through the muck in his head and try to find the answer.

All of Mainfield seemed to be in the street when Chase and Linese rounded the corner and stopped in front of Goten's Livery. Mayor Kerney flashed a menacing look at Chase and her heart constricted. She didn't know what business was going on between them, but her instincts told her Chase was not a willing party.

"Have you heard the news?" Kerney asked.

"No, I guess we haven't." Chase turned and helped her down from the buggy. His gaze lingered on the cameo at her bosom. His relentless gray eyes softened for a moment and she remembered the passion she had seen within their depths last night. She hoped Melissa was right about men not being able to stand against their own weakness. Last night had not gone exactly as she had planned, but she was hopeful with a bit more prodding, she would be victorious.

"Some abolitionists managed to sneak some runaway slaves north into Kansas last night," Kerney said sharply. "News like that should be in the *Gazette,* along with an editorial for the citizens to remain neutral—for the sake of the town, don't you think?"

"I suppose that's one point of view," Chase said flatly. He placed his hand in the small of Linese's back and picked a path through the milling crowd. She glanced back once to see Kerney glaring at them.

"Chase, is there some difficulty between you and the mayor?" she asked while they walked to the *Gazette.*

"No, Linese," he lied. He knew she was waiting for some kind of explanation and searched his mind for one that would suffice. "I've had enough of war and politics. All I want is to live quietly. I want some peace." A half-truth was better than no truth at all.

"I want the same thing, Chase. A quiet life with our children and grandchildren growing up around Cordellane."

Her words were a bayonet that went straight through his heart. How could he tell Linese that to remain his wife would mean she would never have children. How could he live without her if she learned the truth and left him?

Hezikiah appeared in front of the *Gazette* and wiped the question from Chase's thoughts. A large bandage was around his right hand and wrist. Chase's mind was forced in a new direction.

"Hezikiah? What happened?" Linese rushed forward to administer comfort.

Hezikiah shook his head. "I was coming out of the storeroom this morning. I guess I tripped over a bundle of paper and must've knocked myself out cold on the press. I have a lump as big as a hen's egg on the back of my head," He looked sheepish, embarrassed about his accident.

"When I woke up, I found the copy press on my hand. It's broke. Doc Lukins says I'll be out of action for at least six weeks." He looked up with his sharp blackbird's eyes. "Sorry, Chase. I guess you'll be doing all there is to do at the *Gazette* for a while."

Had Hezikiah fallen? Or had Kerney and his friends made sure Chase started printing their opinions immediately? He felt his impotent rage flare. He had to remember—must remember.

Chapter Eleven

Chase crumbled up the paper in his fist. He tossed it into the corner, where it landed atop the sizable mound of discarded editorials.

"It's no use," he groaned. He laid the pen aside and closed his eyes. His head was aching again, the ringing in his ears had become nearly constant, and he was frustrated beyond human endurance. He had finally managed the press, the typesetting and the proofing roller, but he could not write an intelligent editorial.

If he had once possessed the skill, it had left him with his memory. Or perhaps it was his desire that had disappeared in the face of the mayor's request. Whatever the reason, he could not find the words to parrot the businessman's opinions of neutrality for profit. Chase looked out at the deserted dark street and sighed.

Mainfield was deep in slumber. He had stayed at the paper for two reasons. He hoped to avoid his beautiful wife, and he was determined to compose an editorial that would keep his secret safe and pacify the mayor and his friends at least for a while, until he could *remember*.

But the more he tried, the more futile it seemed. There was just no way for him to straddle the fence on the slavery issue, the violence surrounding their community, and write something that would keep his grandfather's mysterious secret safe. He didn't remember exactly why he rode off to war, but he knew deep in his gut that slavery and secession went against his grain. He could not lie about that even to save his own skin, it seemed. But time was running out. He could feel it, sense it.

Chase had a sickening suspicion Hezikiah's accident had been engineered. Just how far would the paunchy politician go to see his self-serving ideas printed in the *Gazette* each week? Linese and his grandfather could be in great danger if he didn't find a way to save them.

The hollow sound of running footsteps echoed on the sidewalk. Chase blew out the solitary lamp on the cluttered desk. He flattened his body against the wall beside the window facing the street. He leaned over, far enough to peer out into the night.

A tall shadow fell across the walk, illuminated by the street lamps. Chase held his breath waiting to see who else was up at this late hour. He half expected to see the mayor outside with some of his friends. Perhaps their patience had run out and they had decided to confront Chase, to give him some physical persuasion along with the blackmail.

Much to Chase's surprise, it was Ira Goten who stole across the street. He paused by the telegraph office and shot a nervous look over his shoulder. Chase wondered what the man was hiding from. A moment later, two forms materialized from the shadows. It didn't take Chase long to figure out these were the runaway slaves Kerney had been so upset about. He saw Ira direct them into the darkness at the edge of town.

Chills crept up Chase's spine along with a new question.

If Ira Goten was such a strong Southern sympathizer, what was he doing helping runaway slaves? And did this have anything to do with whatever thing had happened two years ago? Was this somehow connected to the secret that compelled Ira to keep the Colt and a bag of gold for him? Chase turned the questions over in his mind a million times, but no answers, and no more memories came to fill the void.

* * *

Chase was already up and partially dressed before Linese stirred. He had spent the night in the rocking chair again, trying to ignore the soft fullness of her mouth and the heat of his own desire.

She opened her eyes and smiled as soon as she saw him. It had the effect of holding gunpowder too near an open flame. Something hot and profound exploded inside his chest. The terrible heat spread throughout his body and set off a hundred tiny explosions in its wake.

"Good morning." Linese stretched her arms up above her head.

Chase was mesmerized by the creamy swell of her breasts appearing at the top edge of the sheet.

"'Morning." His voice was tight and dry. He felt scorched by the sight of her, dry to the marrow of his bones.

He wanted to devour her.

She smiled again and licked her lips.

He gulped hard. If she knew what that innocent gesture was doing to him, she would not lie there and stare at him like a well-fed house tabby without a care in the world.

"You're up early, Chase. Didn't you sleep well?" Her voice had the intoxicating texture of well-aged whiskey. "I must've fallen asleep before you came home last night."

Hot shivers shot up his back. He caught a glint of playful teasing in her seductive blue eyes. Something about her appeared less innocent in a way that was almost carnal. Could it be that Linese knew what she was doing? Surely she would not taunt him with her body.

Not Linese. She was too pure, too innocent, and yet there was a certain knowledge in her eyes that he didn't recall being there before. It puzzled and intrigued him.

Chase was loath to believe she would use her abundant feminine attributes on him, but now with her blue eyes winking in the morning sun, he began to think perhaps she was toying with him. The thought annoyed him slightly, coming as it was on the heels of his stifled desire and sexual frustration.

A voice in his head told him to get up and leave. But there came another voice behind it, stronger and more forceful. It said to face her down, cure her of the silly notion once and for all and be done with this game before she got hurt by it.

He decided to give her a tiny, completely innocent taste of her own medicine. Then when he had shocked her with his lust, he would be spared at least a small measure of this torment. She might even decide to move back to the sanctuary of the adjoining room.

Chase rose from the chair and started to unbutton the shirt he had just finished buttoning. He stepped closer to the bed and looked at her with a new scrutiny.

"I did have a restless night, but I think I know the cause of my distress." His eyes fastened on her face, and he gauged her reaction, waiting for her confidence to slip.

The smile did slowly disappear from Linese's soft, full mouth. Her eyes followed the slow, deliberate movement of his fingers and he saw her swallow hard.

He cringed inwardly at what he was doing, but it was for her own good. Any minute now she would stop him. Any moment now she would blush bright red, snatch up her gown, and cover herself in ladylike embarrassment.

A part of him prayed she would not.

He slid his hands to his waist and unbuttoned both sides of his breeches. He allowed the front to fall open and he slipped his hand into the sides of the fabric, as if to shove them down.

Chase was certain she would turn away when she realized he intended to bare himself to her full view. Even among married couples, this kind of behavior in broad daylight was shocking to consider. Chase knew Linese was too well brought up to allow such a crude display without objecting loudly.

She didn't turn away. She didn't blush. She threw back the sheet and rose up on her knees, bare, buck naked and nore beautiful in the morning light than his wicked mind had envisioned she ever would be.

It jolted Chase down to the deepest core. He was lost. He was powerless to do anything less than reach out to her and step into her waiting arms.

When he pulled her nude body up against him and felt the warmth of her still drowsy flesh against his form, a deep, biding hunger began to gnaw at his insides. A throaty moan bubbled up from somewhere inside his chest.

He tipped up her chin and covered her lips with his own. She opened for him and the invitation was accepted. There was no part of Chase's primal male instinct that Linese left untouched. Her tongue darted into his mouth and teased him. Hands that were soft and sure touched and caressed him in ways he had never dreamed of.

She was Eve, she was a temptress, she was innocence, and yet she was not. She was *everything*— and more.

He tumbled her onto the bed and lay over her, savoring the way her body melded to his, marveling in the way it felt to be on top of her. He kissed her again and drank in the sweet wine of her lips. She was rejuvenation to his desiccated spirit and he had to have more.

Chase slid his lips down her jawbone and neck. Tiny nibbles brought a shudder through her when he reached her breasts. They were taut and full. He cupped them in his hands and gloried in their beauty.

"Oh, Chase, it has been so long." Linese's voice was husky with passion.

He could not remember lying with any other woman, could not remember this woman, yet some part of him led the way down the dim and forgotten path toward the passion and satisfaction he knew awaited them both at the end.

Chase shoved his breeches down to his ankles and kicked them out of the way while he shifted himself against her. The abrasive hair at the juncture of her thighs rubbing against his flesh nearly drove him wild. She gyrated her body against him with abandon.

The last of his frayed control snapped.

He was going to take her. He was going to drive himse
into her willing body and savor what he knew they bot
wanted. Damn the consequences, he could not go on li
this.

He raised up and looked at her face. Her eyes were close
her lips pink and moist from his kisses. He was going to ta
what she offered and forget all the reasons why he wasn
supposed to touch her.

She opened her eyes and looked at him. Trust, faith an
all the good emotions of her love for him shone within h
eyes. The pure, selfless sentiment condemned him for
bounder—cursed him as an animal who would seek h
pleasure in her flesh when he could give her nothing in r
turn. Chase died a little inside those blue depths.

"Linese," he groaned. "I can't." He rolled off her su
ple body and snatched up his clothes.

He tried to avoid looking at Linese, but he couldn't avo
seeing his own accusing reflection in the mirror before h
walked out of the bedroom with his trousers in his hand.

Linese watched Chase stalk from the room through a ha
of unquenched yearning. One hot tear slid down her chee
For a moment she nearly despaired. Then she swiped at h
damp cheek and brought her chin up a bit higher.

"He wants me, I'm sure he wants me. Why did he stop?
she whispered aloud. "Soon, Chase Cordell. Soon yc
won't be able to resist me."

The trip into Mainfield was made in uncompromising s
lence. Chase gripped the reins with white-knuckled fierc
ness. His lips were a thin taut line and his eyes were hard an
relentless as granite.

Linese studied him from beneath her lowered lashes. SI
honestly couldn't tell if he was angry, or if Melissa was rig
about what a woman could do to a man, and the effect
had upon their moods when they tried to fight their phys
cal needs.

He did look as if he were sitting on a powder keg that might explode any minute. She prayed her plan was working, prayed that Melissa was right.

Chase chewed a hole in the side of his jaw. He felt like a tough, old rooster in the stewing pot. He was tortured over what he wanted to share with Linese, and the lie that kept him from her. This morning he had come dangerously close to making love to her. The thought sent a sobering chill through him.

What could he have been thinking of?

He carried on a silent argument with himself the entire trip into town. When they rounded the corner, Chase was surprised to see Goten's Livery was closed. The door was latched and nobody seemed to be about. The memory of Ira creeping across the street, with the runaway slaves in his wake, made Chase's belly clench. He hoped that the fool had not been caught.

Linese saw Chase's eyebrows slam together in a straight black slash. His eyes were as hard and remote as iron. A terrible feeling of doom swept over Linese. For a moment she saw something like concern wash over Chase's lean features, but it quickly disappeared and he turned to her with a bland expression in place.

"We'll leave the horse. I'll come and check on him later, Ira is bound to be back presently." His words were short and clipped. She was acutely aware that he helped her down without ever looking at her. Could it be she had gone too far? Had her actions disgusted and appalled him?

"Major Cordell?" A male voice called out and wrenched Linese's thoughts away.

She turned around and saw Sheriff Rancy Thompson striding down the sidewalk toward her and Chase.

"Yes?" Chase's voice was taut and flat, almost guarded. He closed his fists stiffly at his sides as if he were bracing himself for bad news. It occurred to her that he knew something, feared something, but she could not imagine what.

"I wanted to warn you and Mrs. Cordell, Major. There
been some trouble last night. Those runaway slaves are st
on the loose. Most of the businessmen in Mainfield a
staying home with their families. I advise you to do t
same, sir. There is no telling whether they might still
about. I suggest you get back to Cordellane and guard yo
property."

"Slaves? Runaways?" A hot, hard lump formed in Li
ese's throat. The war was crashing over them like a gre
destructive wave, sweeping away her fragile security an
hope.

"Yes, ma'am. There's been several men injured over
Denton County."

Chase thought about Ira Goten again. Where was
now? Was he home like most of the townspeople, or was
off doing something else?

"What happened, Sheriff?"

Rancy grimaced. "Someone tried to stop them and got h
head smashed for his trouble. Just to be on the safe side,
suggest you leave the *Gazette* closed for a day or two and g
on home."

Chase sighed in strained relief and the irony of the situ
tion almost made him smile. This sad calamity bought hi
a few more days of peace, a few days before he had to wri
the editorial.

"Whatever you say, Sheriff." He unconsciously placed h
hand in the small of Linese's back to escort her back to t
buggy. He could avoid the *Gazette* for a few days, but ho
was he going to avoid Linese if he was at Cordellane wi
her? Maybe he should leave and go somewhere else.

"Do you think we'll be safe?" Linese's words inte
rupted Chase's worry. Distress was written across her pret
face. How could he even think of leaving her alone if the
was any possibility of danger?

"Linese, one thing I can promise you—I'll do whateve
have to, to keep you and Grandpa safe. Always. You ca
count on that."

Linese was in his arms before he had time to react. He felt her breasts rub against his chest through the layers of their clothing. His aching heart thudded painfully inside his rib cage while he fought a silent battle between desire, passion and his flagging willpower. Without conscious effort his own hands wrapped around her tiny waist, as if they belonged there, as if they had a right to be there.

"Oh, Chase, you are the most wonderful man...."

Chase felt the noose of hypocrisy tighten around his neck. He couldn't let her go on like this. He unlaced her fingers from behind his neck and held her away from him, even though it cost him dearly to do so.

"Linese, let's go home."

Linese looked up at Chase's stern face. The muscle in his lean jaw was working spasmodically. Anxiety crept over her, but she forced herself to nod in agreement. She held her head high while she walked beside him back to the buggy. She couldn't become fainthearted now. She had to believe that Melissa was right, and keep doing what the young woman had told her to do. Their future together depended upon it. They were in front of Goten's Livery when the mayor appeared from a nearby alley.

"Chase, we have to talk—now."

Linese felt tension telegraph its way through Chase's fingers and into her back. "Chase?" She detected something sinister in the mayor's face.

"Get in the buggy, Linese. I'll be right there." Chase turned and followed Mayor Kerney to the side of the stable. The mayor hitched up his leg and leaned against the building. His round face was lost in the shadows cast by the overhanging eaves. She could neither hear him nor see the expression on his face.

"What is it now?" Chase growled. It was almost impossible to be civil to the man who held his past over his head.

"I, that is, *we* have been patient, Chase. We kept the old Captain off the gallows two years ago, and for that, we expect something in return. When you decided to run off and

join the fighting, you must've thought that would be the en
of our bargain. It's not. When do you intend to start prin
ing the editorials we want?''

Chase followed the tangled conversation as well as h
could. New information settled in his brain. So, he ha
made a devil's bargain to keep his grandfather from hang
ing before he left.

But why? His grandfather didn't seem capable of doin
anything that would earn him a hemp necklace. Chas
grappled with his lost memory, praying he could find som
spark of recollection about what his grandfather had done

"Chase? Are you listening? When you provided the alib
for your grandfather, we let it be. The investigation wa
stopped. We never looked any further when you told us yo
were with the old man, whether we believed it or not. If
don't see something in the *Gazette* this week, I'll see to
that the investigation is reopened. I'd hate to think what th
law would say about you lying to protect him.''

Chase swallowed his anger and choked back the urge t
smash his fist into the man's face. "I have to take Lines
home. I won't have her in danger," he said truthfully.

"Fine, Chase, but you remember what I said." Th
mayor leaned away from the stable. "Your grandfather'
alibi is you, and we both know you lied. You couldn't hav
been with him at Cordellane like you said. I'd hate to see a
old ranger brought to such shame.''

Chase watched the pudgy man turn and walk away. H
didn't have any idea what his grandfather had done—but h
was willing to do whatever was necessary to keep him an
Linese safe from Mayor Kerney and the pack of coyotes th
tubby politician called his friends.

Chapter Twelve

Chase slammed the library door shut behind him so hard the portraits on the wall shook. He lit a lamp and slumped into a chair. He couldn't keep this up. He had to remember.

With a sigh of frustration, he began to pick his way back through the old issues of the *Gazette*.

"There has to be something here that I will remember," he whispered under his breath. "There has to be."

He was desperate to find the truth. Even if his past was tainted with sinister deeds, he had to face them. He had to be a man and help his family. He had to keep them safe. It was all that mattered to him now. Damn his pride and his worry over what kind of man he might have been. He was of little consequence, but Linese and his grandfather were.

Chase got on his knees and arranged the old newspapers in order of date, beginning with the issues just before his wedding announcement, in June of 1862. After a few minutes of quick reading, he leaned closer and squinted at the print. He had finally noticed something.

"What the devil?" He changed them around and rearranged to *Gazettes* in three rows.

The first row of editorials, dating from March 1861, had a strong, opinionated style. It was bold and uncompromising, called for the people to make a stand. Chase assumed those were the ones he wrote before he went to war.

The next row, from May through June of 1862, was different. It was short, clipped, factual and concise. The style was another person's voice entirely. There was no emotion in the words, just dry facts without flavor or opinion.

The third row, starting in September of 1862 and ending around the time he returned, was the one that captured his interest. Intrigued, he read the editorials several times.

Each editorial was eloquent, impassioned, almost lyrical in its plea for sanity amidst the conflict of Unionist against secessionist. For every account of butchery and violence in the neighboring counties, the *Gazette* editorial provided balance and reason in a world gone mad with politics and war.

Chase leaned closer and focused on the words. Without a doubt, the editorials were the best he had ever read, and they were most certainly not Hezikiah Hershner's. They couldn't have been his—so just who had written them? He stared at the pages and pondered the question, focusing all his concentration on the new, unfolding mystery.

Linese eased open the library door and peered in. The thin weight of Melissa's nightgown did little to block out the chill that crept over her, when she realized what Chase was doing.

His long legs were stretched out on the old rug in front of the cold fireplace. Three neat rows of the *Gazette* back issues were on the floor in front of him. She could see he had them folded open to the editorial page. Her stomach tightened into a ball. He was so deep in concentration he had no idea she was watching him.

She could not go on this way. She had to tell him the truth and remove at least one barrier from their path. If she couldn't find the courage to tell him the truth, how on earth could she be brave enough to see her reckless plan through to the end? Besides, if she was no longer the same timid girl he married, he deserved to know it. If he could not reconcile her new liberated thoughts and actions, then she should know it now before she ensnared him with the tricks Melissa had taught her.

Linese gulped down her dread and padded forward on bare feet. Chase continued reading, he never heard her, never looked up. Perhaps, she thought, it would be easier to get the words out if he were not looking at her. She took a deep breath and forced herself to find her voice.

"I wrote them, Chase."

His head snapped around. He looked up at her and his eyebrows pinched together while the truth registered on every plane of his austere face. Her nerve nearly faltered then, but she summoned the strength to face his disappointment at the kind of woman she had become.

"Hezikiah needed help, Chase. I could not stand by and watch your family business fail like so many others."

He still had not spoken, so she knelt beside him on the old rug and tried to explain.

"I remember what you said, about women with opinions in their head, but Chase, the war made it so hard to remain that simple, sheltered girl you married." She peered into his gunmetal gray eyes and prayed he would not hate her. "I didn't plan it, Chase, but I'm glad it happened.

Linese sighed and felt a great weight ease from her shoulders. She had admitted the truth. She liked working at the *Gazette* even if it was unladylike and not proper. Now she would have to face Chase's wrath and disillusionment.

"With the war and all, the *Gazette* was nearly going under financially. Hezikiah had not been paid for months. He needed someone to help so he could get circulation up again. We wouldn't have made it at all, but the Businessman's Association suddenly came forward and loaned us some money, until we got on our feet. We managed to show a small profit and got them paid back, right before you came home."

Chase narrowed his eyes at that information. The mayor and his friends had been tightening the grip on Chase's family even in his absence. If he had not returned when he did, or if Hezikiah had failed to repay the loan, what would their next move have been? Fury boiled inside him to know his family had been used—even subtly—while he was not here to shield them from the malignancy of Kerney and his greedy philosophy.

"Chase, say something. Are you disappointed in me?"

Chase stared at her for a few long minutes. Watching Linese's face in the uneven glow of the light had done strange things to his insides. Hearing her parrot the words he had so carelessly flung at her about how a woman should behave and think shamed him. It was more than he could withstand.

He reached out and pulled her closer to him. He turned her away from him, so he didn't have to fight the lure of her eyes. When her back was pressed hard against his chest, he wrapped his arms around her waist and held her there, tight against him. The soft, warm weight of her breasts on his forearms sent a shiver of desire through him. Chase knew what he was doing was madness, but he did it anyway.

"I could never be disappointed in you. Not in anything you do or say."

With a sigh of prickly contentment, he rested his chin on the top of her head and held her. The silky hairs tickled his throat. He needed to hold her. He needed to feel her strength of spirit against his body while he gave her a small portion of the comfort and approval she so richly deserved.

"That was why you wore gloves in this ungodly heat, wasn't it? You were trying to cover the ink stains on your hands." He kissed the top of her head and hated the man who had left her to go to war. "I left you with a great responsibility when I went away."

Chase decided he must have run away, been a coward and gone to war, rather than face the threat Kerney and his allies held over him. How could he have been so stupid? Nothing was worth leaving this remarkable woman.

"Taking care of Grandfather, and the *Gazette*. You did a fine job, Linese. I'm proud of you, and I'm sorry I left you with such a burden. Can you ever forgive me?"

Linese blinked rapidly to thwart the tears, but a hot, hard lump lodged in her throat. She didn't want to cry and was determined not to cry. "Forgive you?" her voice trembled.

He heard the harsh rasp of pent-up feeling in her voice and emotion bubbled through him. "You did what needed doing. If I had been more of a man, stayed here and taken responsibility, then you wouldn't have been faced with the task." Chase's voice was hard with self-recrimination.

Linese pulled out of his arms and swiveled around to look at his face. She saw his eyebrows pinched together, but they no longer seemed to be an expression of disapproval. She saw a crack in his hard shell, and what she saw beneath brought a river of love spilling forth.

"Chase, I understood why you had to go. I've never regretted your decision."

He looked into her clear blue eyes and saw love and forgiveness written there. He didn't deserve this woman, but he was damned glad he had her. Even the tiny bit of her he could allow himself was more than worth the price not having all of her was exacting upon his soul.

"How can you say you understand what I did?" he asked.

"On our wedding day, when you told me that one more man fighting for the Union could turn the tide, I understood. You have always felt strongly about your convictions. It's one of the things I love about you."

She lowered her lashes and her cheeks flushed. The need to taste her lips was so strong he could not ignore it. Chase placed his thumb under her chin and tipped her head up. He leaned forward and brushed his mouth across her lips.

They were soft and warm.

A harsh groan escaped his chest. He knew he was courting disaster, but the lure of her goodness reeled him in like a hapless trout. Chase crushed her to him and heard the soft sigh of satisfaction from her mouth.

When her arms wrapped around his neck and she pressed her breasts against the bare flesh exposed between the unbuttoned section of his shirt, an inferno ignited inside him.

Dear God in heaven. He loved her. It wasn't just the poignant, bittersweet need to remember loving her. It was real and immediate.

It had happened. After all the warnings he had given himself, he had allowed it to happen. He had fallen hopelessly in love with Linese.

Chase felt the power of his devotion roll over him in a huge, all-consuming wave. He could no more disregard the longing he felt for her than he could stop the sun from rising. It was a need, a hunger, that made him tremble inside from the force of it.

"Oh, Chase, I was afraid you would be angry with me."

"I could never be angry with you, sweet."

Chase cupped her slender throat in his palm and looked at her beautiful face. Her lips were red and dewy from his voracious kiss. He smiled at the sheer wonder of holding her.

"Linese, how did I ever win such a prize as you?" he asked softly.

She smiled and touched the side of his face with her fingertips. "By sheer strength of will. How could I do anything but fall in love, when you all but dared me not to?"

Impulsively he kissed her again. His tongue traced the outline of her teeth and, in a weakening moment, Chase allowed his hands to roam freely over her form, cherishing the way her flesh felt beneath the thin layer of cloth. He committed to memory every soft nuance of her body, telling himself he would have this one precious memory to hold.

He rubbed his thumb over the hard peak of one nipple and cupped his hand beneath the weight of her breast. His flattened palm sculpted over the smooth valley of her waist. His fingers sought the warm skin of her inner thigh.

"Oh, Linese," he moaned while his desire unraveled the thread of his reason ever further.

His lips moved over her chin and down her throat. She tasted richer than aged brandy, sweeter than sugarcane. He twined his free hand in her hair and savored the feel of it. It was like holding a skein of the finest silk. She closed her eyes and leaned into him.

She was his wife. He loved her. His body ached to know all of her mystery.

"Chase?"

He heard the longing question in her voice. Every nerve in his body cried out to say yes.

But could he? Could he actually allow himself a small ration of ecstasy in her arms and remain strong enough to prevent doing anything that would show himself for the fraud he was?

He would have to try. He could no longer neglect the famine inside him. If he did not taste some of her goodness, he would surely die. Chase eased her back down to the rough texture of the rug. Her eyes were wide and luminous.

"Linese—"

Fists banging on the door brought Chase to his feet in an heart-pounding leap. Linese made a startled sound of surprise. He looked down her and saw her gown shoved up to her thighs. Her alabaster flesh looked smooth as satin in the lamplight.

Shame at what he was about to do swept over him. He adjusted his clothes and tried to ease the aching in his groin. Chase grabbed the lamp and strode out of the library doors. He reached the big front door of Cordellane just as his grandfather appeared at his side. Light winked off the barrel of a pistol the old ranger had concealed in the folds of his nightshirt.

"Anyone out at this hour of the night is bound to be trouble," Captain Cordell commented dryly.

Chase nodded in agreement at his grandfather's lucid observation and unbolted the door. Sheriff Rancy Thompson was standing outside, blinking against the glare of the lamp Chase held in his face.

"Sheriff?" Chase said. "What brings you to Cordellane in the middle of the night?"

The man shuffled his feet. It was obvious he was not happy to be standing on the veranda of Cordellane, regardless the reason. Chase sensed Linese standing behind him in the shadows by the library door.

"I'm real sorry about this, Major Cordell." Rancy grimaced. He took a deep breath and then his explanation spilled out in a rush. "Dang it, I've come to arrest the Captain."

Chapter Thirteen

"Arrest him? Why?" The hair on the back of Chase's neck prickled.

"I don't take any pleasure in this, Major, but there has been—well, I got some new evidence brought to my attention about an old case." It was plain Mayor Kerney had set the wheels of political machinery turning, just as he had promised he would.

"What kind of evidence?" Chase swallowed the sick feeling. He was walking on quicksand again. He didn't even know what the crime was, and now there was *evidence*. If this new evidence was anything solid, and he could not remember his past and what part he had played in keeping his grandfather safe, then the old man was surely doomed this time.

"Some anonymous statements place your grandfather in the area of a murder, in Ferrin County. The whole thing happened about two years ago. I had almost forgotten all about it. One of the few cases I was never able to solve."

Impotent rage began to simmer inside Chase. If only he could remember something—anything—about that time, but at least now he had a reference point from which to begin, and a crime.

Murder.

"Well, Sheriff, can I put on my britches first?" Captai[n] Cordell's voice made Chase start. When he turned aroun[d] he was shocked to see his grandfather grinning broadly.

The old soul didn't realize his life was in peril. It mad[e] Chase even more furious to know that the mayor and h[is] friends would victimize someone who wasn't mental[ly] competent, in their quest to get their point across.

"Sure, Captain. You go get dressed," Sheriff Thompso[n] allowed patiently.

For the first time Chase saw his grandfather's afflictio[n] as a twisted blessing. At least he was oblivious to the da[n]ger he was in. It was hollow comfort to Chase while [he] watched the old man turn and walk away with the pistol st[ill] secreted in his striped nightshirt.

Chase was waiting outside the jail when dawn brok[e.] Rancy didn't seem to be in the least bit surprised. He s[i]lently unlocked the front door and stepped aside. He m[o]tioned Chase toward a door at the back of the office.

He found his grandfather sitting on a crude iron cot wit[h] his manacled leg attached to a chain and ring in the cent[er] of the rough mortar floor. It sickened him to see the gent[le] soul in such dire circumstances.

"Can I be alone with him?" Chase asked Thompson.

"Sure, I can't see no harm in letting you talk with hi[m] alone for a few minutes. He never said a word all the way last night. Hope he hasn't slipped further—well, y[ou] know—further away." The sheriff cast a sympathetic lo[ok] at Captain Cordell before he turned and walked to the out[er] office and closed the door behind him.

The minute Thompson was gone, the Captain rose fro[m] the cot and stepped as close to the iron bars as his leg cha[in] would allow. He gestured for Chase to come near while [he] leaned far enough to wrap his fingers around the vertic[al] iron bars.

"It's about time you got here, Chase. I was beginning [to] wonder."

Chase was taken aback. In all the time he had been home, his grandfather had never acknowledged his identity by using his given name. He put his face against the bars and listened intently.

"These fools have got some trumped-up charges about that Ferrin County killing a couple of years back. I heard Thompson talking to the mayor and some of those other idiots that call themselves the Businessman's Association, last night after he put me in here."

"What?" Chase was having a hard time absorbing the lucid way in which his grandfather was speaking. The vacant, out-of-focus look in his eyes had evaporated like dew on a hot morning the moment the outer door had slammed shut.

"I had never planned for you to learn the truth this way." The old man grinned sheepishly. He ran his fingers along the silver mustache that hung beside his mouth. "But I guess there never would've been any *good* time to tell you. I ain't quite as touched as everyone thinks. I never wanted to bring you in on this, but it looks like I got no choice."

"You—you're—not mad?"

"Not any crazier than any other fool that settled this country. Hell, we had to be a little insane to come to a place where we had to fight Santa Anna, Comanche, and the weather all at once." The Captain's grin widened.

Chase felt the color drain from his face. He tightened his grip on the bars when his knees went liquid.

"Well, don't look so damned happy about having a sane relative instead of a crazy one, boy."

Chase shook his head and blinked. "Sorry, it's not that. Of course, I'm glad you are sane."

A million thoughts swam through his head at once. He could not manage to grasp one single idea and sort it from all the others in the face of this information.

"You've never been crazy?" he asked in a doubtful whisper. "Not even a little?"

His grandfather sighed and shook his head slowly. '
buried your grandma, your ma, your father, and my swe
Marjorie in the ground behind Cordellane. That is enoug
to make anybody a little crazy. There was a time when gri
made me . . . odd. Gossip and human nature, being what
is, just kept building it up, making it worse, until finally
was known as 'crazy Captain Cordell.' ''

The Captain looked away and continued to speak. ''Pa
ents were never intended to outlive their children, Chase. It
an unnatural thing, something I hope you never have to g
through. No sadder thing on God's earth, than for a pare
to put his child in the ground. For a time I couldn't acce
what happened, especially to Marjorie. Then, as thin
turned out, it became a blessing in disguise. People ignor
me. I was able to come and go, do certain things witho
having to explain.''

''The charges against you are serious. You could hang.

''It's just some nonsense cooked up by Kerney. I could'
cleared it all up in the beginning, but then you blundered
and lied about us being together that night. I had to keep n
mouth shut to keep you safe.'' His grandfather frowned
him a bit suspiciously. ''I don't suppose you'd like to tell n
where *you* were that night.''

Chase gulped. This was his opportunity—he could tell h
grandfather about his missing memory. He considered it f
one heartbeat.

''No,'' Chase grated out. If he had not been with h
grandfather, then he had no notion of where he was—b
the Colt Ira had returned to him made him wonder if he w
a murderer. The unknown kept him silent.

His grandfather's mustache twitched. ''I won't ask agai
You'll tell me if you want to. I don't supposed you'd care
tell me why you told them I was with you?''

''No.'' Chase felt his heart begin to pound and a pain b
hind his eyes made him wince. A new flash of memory fill
his brain.

He remembered his father's funeral and his aunt Marjorie's funeral and how his life changed forever after that.

He could feel his own sorrow and humiliation in the regained memory. He felt the bleak isolation and heart-ripping loneliness that he had known as young man, because from that day on, he heard laughter and jeers behind his back. In defense of the mockery, he had pushed himself to excel at everything, hoping the stigma of his grandfather's madness could not hurt him. But it did. It hurt him in too many ways for a green boy to understand.

Chase felt himself shudder inside while he gripped the cold iron bars. He had lived under a dark cloud of shame that kept him separate from the rest of the world and made him different from other young men. He remembered every painful slur and slight with aching exactness.

A wave of hot anger flowed through him. For the first time since his return he felt hostility toward his grandfather. Now that he remembered the terrible ordeal of his adolescence, his grandfather's confession of sanity took on new significance for him.

He could no longer look at his aging relative with cool detachment and pity. His raw memories made him very much an unwilling participant in whatever his grandfather had tried to protect with the lie of madness, and Chase wanted—burned for—an explanation.

"I want to know why? How could you have let me grow up thinking you were crazy?" Chase heard the pain in his words.

Captain Cordell sighed and moved back toward the huge ring in the center of the floor. He was so still, for a time Chase wondered if his grandfather had heard him. Then he turned to face Chase.

"I've known this day would come. I've thought about it for years, but now that it's here, I don't know how to explain to you what I did or what compelled me to do it."

"Do you know what it's like to grow up under something like that?" Chase's voice was a harsh whisper. There were still huge holes in his collection, but the memory of his grandfather's mental collapse was now crystal clear.

Captain Cordell looked at the floor and ran his fingers over the long, drooping mustache. "I saw the effect it had on you, but you were well on your way to being a man, Chase. I thought—I hoped what I was doing was important enough to justify what you were going through."

"I was still young, little more than a boy. It mattered what people thought. What could possibly have been so important that you would inflict that kind of pain on your own flesh and blood?"

His grandfather looked up. He narrowed his eyes as if trying to picture it in his own mind. "The lives of hundreds, possibly thousands, of people were that important. Keeping them alive tipped the scales, Chase."

"What are you talking about? Just what are you involved in?"

He pierced Chase with intelligent eyes. "I don't want you involved in what I'm doing, for your sake and Linese's."

"I'm a grown man now. I believe I have a right to know."

Captain Cordell moved back toward the bars and lowered his voice. "All right, Chase. I'll tell you what I've been doing. I just hope to God I don't end up regretting it."

He whispered so softly Chase had to hold his breath in order to hear the answer. "I have been helping the abolitionists for years. Long before the hostilities broke out, Cordellane was part of the Underground Railroad."

"Helping get runaway slaves up North?"

"Yep. Mainfield is one of the towns along the way to freedom."

"Why didn't you tell me?" Chase felt the sting of being left out, of being apart.

Captain Cordell shook his head. "Put you in danger? No. I decided it would be better if I was crazy for as long as it was necessary. Nobody was supposed to know this secret. I wouldn't have told you now, except for your recklessness two years ago. You should come clean right now and tell

Thompson where you really were that night. It's going to come out eventually."

For an instant Chase panicked. He had no intentions of letting his grandfather know about his amnesia. Perhaps it was only pride. More likely the reason was the horrible possibility that Chase had not been half the man he wanted to be—not until he remembered. Whatever the reason, he resolved not to tell him.

"I can't tell him."

His grandfather glared at him. "Suit yourself, but it isn't going to be long until somebody starts asking you some hard questions."

Tiny fragments of new memory swirled in his head but nothing was tangible. He could not tell the sheriff what he did not know himself. He was still dancing on a knife edge, bluffing his way through each day. But while those memories floated, just outside of his reach, he had a hope.

"You probably thought I was a fool for lying for you." Chase dragged his fingers through his hair. The ache in his head was growing worse, the ringing in his ears more high-pitched, while the memories floated like leaves in a dust devil.

"I thought you were a brave man doing a selfless thing."

Chase looked up and saw his grandfather swipe at his eyes. The old man sniffed and cleared his throat. "I'm proud of you, boy. Going away to fight has turned you into the man I always hoped you would become. You helped those people just as much as I ever did."

Chase felt a lump in his throat. It was funny, how the old man's approval sent a flood of satisfaction through his body.

He thought about all the secrets he had been confronted with since coming home. This was the first time somebody had said something that made him feel good about the man he used to be.

Chase realized he was happy his grandfather thought well of him. The anger at his grandfather's deception slowly drained away and he was left with a warm affection for the old man.

"I'm proud of you, too, Grandfather." Chase reached his hand through the bars and touched the old man's cheek. "What can I do to get you out of here?"

"I heard Rancy mention a date to Kerney last night. May 30, 1862."

"What difference does the date make?"

"Get a message to Doralee and her girls. After Thompson talks to her, I'll be free as a bird, and just as crazy as I ever was. On your honor, you must swear not to let anyone, including Linese, know any different—not yet."

"I swear, on my honor," Chase said softly. For the first time since his arrival, he felt he might truly have some honor.

Chase turned and reached for the latch on the door. The need to exact some revenge on Kerney was searing his insides. It was all he could think of. He was going to write the editorials the mayor had been wanting. And he couldn't wait to see the reaction of the Businessman's Association when they read them.

Linese stopped her buggy just as Doralee and a half-dozen painted ladies stepped out of a fringe-topped surrey parked in front of the jail. Doralee glanced Linese's way but quickly averted her eyes and acted as if she hadn't seen her. Linese wrapped the reins around the brake and jumped down to the street.

"Miss Doralee, wait." She picked up her skirts and hurried forward, while the May heat shimmered up her legs and made her feel like a wilted flower.

Doralee turned and lifted her parasol as if to protect herself from the sun. She lowered her voice to a whisper. "Mrs. Cordell, you shouldn't ought to speak to me in public." Doralee looked up and down the street, as if she thought the local gossips would already be busy documenting Linese' social blunder. "I wouldn't want you to be shamed 'cause you spoke to me."

Linese's cheeks burned with guilty shame. Up until recently she would have felt the same fear—that speaking to a soiled dove would ruin her reputation. But, lately, she just didn't care about that so much anymore. Perhaps it was her gratitude for Melissa's help, or perhaps she was learning that people were just people, that their circumstance didn't really make them better or worse than anyone else, just different.

"I'm not ashamed to say I know you, Doralee, or any of these women." Linese stared down the row of painted faces behind Doralee. Melissa was not among them, and Linese wondered with a tiny twinge of envy if her baby had come yet. "Are you here to see the Captain?" Linese asked.

"You might say that." Doralee winked in a way that made Linese's pulse quicken. Curiosity made her follow Doralee inside Rancy Thompson's office. He was leaning over his desk, thumbing through a stack of wanted posters. He looked up and a frown creased his face.

"Doralee?" He jumped up from his chair. Astonishment was written across his face while the women squeezed into his office and shut the door. "Mrs. Cordell?" Obviously he was incredulous to see Linese among the prostitutes and did little to hide his surprise. "What is this all about?"

Doralee closed her parasol with a snap and proceeded to take off her black lace gloves. Linese could not help but grin at the way she took command of the situation by the simple task of taking off her gloves and making Rancy wait until she was finished.

"Do you have Captain Cordell locked up in there?" Doralee nodded toward the dim hallway and wrinkled her nose in distaste.

"Yes, I do."

"Then I suggest you get the key and let him out."

Silence fell so heavy in the room Linese swore she could hear her own heart pounding.

"And why would that be, Dora?" Sheriff Thompson eyed the line of women suspiciously.

"I have heard you are accusing him of some silly nonsense that happened on May 30, 1862. Is that right?" Doralee's voice resonated with impatience.

Thompson's initial astonishment was fast turning to irritation. "Yeah, so what?" His words rang with offense.

"Well, then let him out, Sheriff. He can't have possibly have done whatever it is you say he did on May 30."

"And why is that?" Thompson's tone was almost belligerent now.

"Because Captain Cordell was at my establishment that night." Doralee grinned broadly "The whole night, Sheriff, if you get my meaning."

He wiped his hand down his face and turned toward the hallway. Linese hoped she didn't look as shocked as Sheriff Thompson, but she was fairly sure she did.

"Wait a minute, Doralee, how is it you are so sure about that date?" Rancy questioned.

"Because that is my birthday, Sheriff, and that is the night the Captain tossed his hat up on my weather vane. Then he proceeded to climb up to get it—" several girls stifled giggles behind their hands "—in the altogether. It is not an event one sees every day in Mainfield, Texas. We are not likely to forget the sight—or the date—of that occurrence anytime soon."

Thompson's brows shot up and his face turned a bright crimson, but within seconds his skeptical frown returned.

"You expect me to take the word of—of—you and these women?"

Doralee was unaffected by his veiled insult. "No, Sheriff, I don't. All of us are fully prepared to sign statements listing the names of the other Mainfield gentlemen who were there... enjoying the festivities and hospitality of my establishment."

A murmur of agreement spread over the line of women. "I'm sure there are more than one or two wives who would find the list most interesting reading. And I will be sure to tell them that they have you to thank for the privilege." Doralee batted her long eyelashes and smiled pleasantly.

Thompson went pale. Then he cleared his throat and looked at the floor. "No, Miss Doralee, I'm sure that won't be necessary." He turned and grabbed a key from a metal hook, gave the women one more glance, then disappeared down the hallway.

Linese grabbed Doralee and hugged her as hard as she could. "Oh, I could just kiss you."

"Don't you dare!" Doralee said in mock horror. "The Captain has always treated me like a real lady. I remember my friends—my enemies, too." She smiled and touched Linese's cheek affectionately. "What you can do is get over to the *Gazette,* and let that good-looking man of yours know what has happened. I made him a promise it would be all right. He need not fear for the old Captain's safety anymore."

Chapter Fourteen

Chase watched the last paper go through the big flat-head press. Accomplishment swept over him in a rush when he picked it up carefully by the edges so he wouldn't smudge the damp ink.

His editorial contained none of the beauty Linese was able to put on paper, but he had succeeded in saying what he felt. It was stark, visceral, and painted a picture of war that made Chase's belly twist when he read it.

He had poured his heart into the article and the result was the sad truth. After all the parades were over, the brass bands gone, a soldier was left to face enemy fire on the battlefield alone. In the end, a warrior was faced with one task—his own survival.

While he had been writing, faint memories came floating back. The horror of watching young men puke their lives away haunted him. Images, like dim tintype pictures, assaulted him. They had perished by the hundreds from lack of nourishment, lack of sanitation, lack of proper medical care.

Lack.

If he could sum up his slim recollections of two years of war in one word, it would be that word—*lack*.

He stopped reading. There was a bit of moisture at the corner of his eye. He swiped at it with ink-stained fingers and then stared at them in wonder.

Chase was weeping. Not only for the young soldiers who died, but for himself, for the survivors. He had been grieving for the men who came home and tried to pick up the broken threads of their lives. Chase realized that up until this moment, he had been hiding from one more sordid truth about himself. He felt guilty for surviving when so many others did not. But he was glad he had lived. He didn't want to hide anymore.

He couldn't do anything about the past—about the man he had been in the past, about the young men who didn't make it back home. But he could change the kind of man he was now and would be in the future.

He was pretty sure he had been less than he would have wished before he went to war, but he had a chance to atone for that lack in himself now. He intended to change the small corner of the world around him.

This editorial was the beginning. He had found his taste for battle was not wholly gone, it had simply changed forms. He was ready—no, he was anxious—to take on Mayor Kerney and his friends.

Chase sighed and felt a great weight ease from his mind. He knew that in part it was because he had started to heal, to forgive himself for a thousand unremembered faults, but it was deeper than that. His grandfather's shocking admission gave him a glimmer of hope for a future with Linese.

The skeptical part of his brain didn't completely believe it yet, but he was turning over the possibility that there was little substance to his belief that the Cordell blood was somehow responsible for his missing memory. If it was indeed something caused by his injury, then he could heal.

If it was because he could not face some horrible deed he had committed with Ira Goten, then maybe he would not regain his memory.

He asked himself a million questions, tried on hundreds of possibilities to see if they fit, discarded and replaced them in his mind. He was weighing all the options, when suddenly the door flew open. At first he thought a dust devil had forced it, then he saw Linese standing in the doorway.

She was out of breath and her eyes were wide. Her hair had tumbled down around her shoulders and her cheeks were flushed from the heat.

"God in heaven, what's the matter?" He was across the room and beside her in three long steps. "Are you hurt? Is everything all right? Is it grandfather?"

"The Captain is free!" She stood on tiptoe to deliver a series of excited kisses to his jaw. The scent of flowers wafted around them like a clinging vine and drew him ever nearer to her. The feel of her warm form against his chest made his pulse quicken.

Chase felt the smile begin somewhere at the corners of his mouth, but it spread like fingers of flame throughout his body. Affection filled his heart, expanded, swirled, grew.

Her happiness was contagious. He picked Linese up and spun her around like a giddy child. She laughed and clung to him until they were both overheated and out of breath. When he placed her back on solid ground, he paused to gaze into her eyes. The look of happiness in her face blazed a trail straight to his soul.

"Chase, isn't it wonderful? Doralee and the girls were with the Captain that night. He is free."

"Good, good. Now I want you to get him at the jail and go home, Linese. Go straight back home to Cordellane where you'll be safe."

She raised her eyebrows and the brightness in her eyes faded. "Are you working late again?" Disappointment rang in her question.

"No, not tonight. I'll be along soon. I just have to deliver a very special paper first."

The love in her eyes reached out to him. He adored her, and he intended to be the kind of man she deserved. He only had to clear away the last traces of shadow and doubt from their lives and embrace the hope that he would eventually regain the rest of his memory. He was ready to believe it, he needed to believe it, if he was going to reclaim his life and his wife.

When Linese was gone, Chase turned his thoughts to Mayor Kerney. He and his group had been jabbing a hornet's nest since the day Chase stepped off the train. Now they were going to see the results of their actions firsthand.

Chase picked up the fresh issue of the *Gazette* and stepped outside. He locked the door behind him and took off down the walk. By the time he reached Kerney's office, his shirt was stuck to him from the heat and the humidity and the restless anticipation pulsing through his veins.

Chase flung open the door to the mayor's office without bothering to knock. Kerney looked up in astonishment from behind a huge carved desk. The paint on his walls looked fresh and clean, the carpet on his floor bright and new. Everything around him spoke of prosperity and wealth, and it served to make Chase even more angry when he thought of the gaunt faces of men who lived by their convictions. It wasn't fair that a man who had no loyalty should prosper, while better men did not.

"Well, now. Chase Cordell, I've been expecting you. Come in, come in." Kerney leaned back in his chair and laced his hands behind his head. He was the picture of contented victory amid the opulence of his official office.

"I wrote an editorial," Chase said mildly.

The mayor's smile grew wider. "I thought you might. Seeing your grandfather behind bars would be just the impetus you needed to get you going. Some of the other boys didn't think you'd give in so easy. Guess I'm a better judge of character than most, eh, Chase?"

Chase felt as if someone had taken a key and unlocked manacles from his wrists. This moment was going to take away whatever threat the mayor had held over him from the past. His grandfather was free and clear. The Cordells were no longer going to be blackmailed by the Businessman's Association. Chase was going to be able to live his life without fear, just like anyone else in Mainfield, Texas.

"Here's a copy for you, mayor. I wanted to be the one to deliver it, personally, to be sure you got the first look at the *Gazette*'s stand on the issues of the war."

Chase tossed the folded paper across the polished surface of the desk. It slid to the edge, where Kerney's ample belly prevented it from falling to the floor. Kerney picked it up and opened it to read the bold black headline.

The smile began to slip from his flaccid lips. It was soon replaced by a frown, then a bright red flush of pure rage. Kerney's head snapped up. His small eyes narrowed down to slits.

"I guess you've forgotten your grandfather is behind bars. I hold all the cards in this little game, Chase."

"Not anymore. Seems he had been seen by a number of people on that night two years ago. You have no more leverage, Mayor. You can no longer threaten me with my grandfather's safety."

"You made a big mistake, Cordell, a dangerous mistake. There are other possibilities—involving your wife and grandfather. Their continued health and security is in your hands." His voice was a menacing hiss.

"Not hardly." Chase strode forward and placed his palms flat on the desk. He leaned forward and stared into the man's eyes until his nose and Kerney's were mere inches apart.

"If anything—I mean anything—happens to Linese or the Captain, I'll kill you. I don't care if it's an accident, my fault or simply an act of God. If they come to harm, or even come close to harm, I'm coming for you. Then I'm tracking down each and every one of the Businessman's Association. You tell them that, Kerney, tell the association what I said." Chase raised one brow. "So I suppose you could say Linese's and my grandfather's lives, and your own, are in *your* hands, Mayor."

Chase watched the color drain from the mayor's face and experienced a moment of pure, cold satisfaction. But the mayor rallied and dredged up one last particle of bravado.

"Then perhaps it would be safer for all concerned if you should be the one to have a small accident, Major Cordell."

Chase grinned and focused on Kerney's narrow little eyes. Facing his own fears and weaknesses had awakened a part of him that had been in slumber since his return to Mainfield. He felt the warrior inside him spring forth at the threat.

"As you may have noticed, Mayor, I'm a hard man to kill. Several thousand Southern soldiers have already attempted to do that very thing, but if you've got a notion to try, I'll be waiting. You come a-running anytime you're ready."

The mayor sat in stunned silence while Chase leaned away from the desk and stood up straight. He walked to the door, but stopped with his hand on the knob.

"Have a nice evening, Mayor. And I'm sure you will be interested in the editorials I'll be putting in the *Gazette* from now on. I'll see you have one delivered to your door every week—no charge—a gift from the Cordells."

Chase rode home with his thoughts running faster than a swollen river. So many things had changed since Rancy had come to arrest his grandfather. He had finally emerged from a long, dark tunnel and at the end there was Linese, with her love shining like a beacon in the dark.

Images of her face swirled through his mind. Some of his recollections were old memories, disjointed pictures that Chase could not sort into any particular order. Some were new. It gave him a measure of peace to know that he was slowly regaining his memory. It was enough to make him start to believe he could become whole again. For the first

time since he had stepped off that train, he felt confiden
enough to let himself love his wife—completely.

Cordellane was quiet and dark. Chase walked into the li
brary, lit a lamp and sloshed brandy into a glass. The liqui
swirled in a dusky vortex. The crescent moon was jus
peeking through the tall windows at the back of the house

It had taken him longer to get home than he had antici
pated. He glanced toward the darkened staircase and won
dered if Linese was still awake.

There was one more thing he had to do before he could b
completely free of the dark cloud that had followed him fo
too long. He had to tell Linese about his loss of memory
She was the one person in this world who deserved to hea
the entire truth.

Chase didn't feel compelled to let anyone else know, bu
Linese merited his honesty. He wanted her to know exactl
who he was now, and why.

He sighed and slammed back the glass of brandy. H
dreaded telling her. He wanted to avoid it. Revealing hi
horrible weakness to her was going to be the hardest task o
all, because he was afraid of losing her. But he loved her s
much that no matter what happened, he had to be hones
with Linese. It wasn't fair for her to make decisions abou
their future without having all the facts. He regretted no
telling her before. Guilt, fear and slumbering emotions s
powerful they made his knees liquid had prevented him.

He turned the wick down until the flame guttered an
went out, then he turned toward the stairs and took the firs
step toward his future.

The bedroom was dim. The sliver of moonlight comin
through the open window provided enough light for him t
undress, but little else.

Chase nearly gave in to the impulse to wake her, almos
reached out and touched her in his desire to unburden him
self now, tonight. But his concern for her well-being, he

omfort, won out. He could wait until morning, wait until he woke rested and doe eyed from sleep.

The mattress sagged a tiny bit under his weight when he ot quietly into bed. With a flick of his wrist, the sheet set-led back upon his bare legs and hips. Chase was instantly aware of Linese's body heat dancing evenly down his houlders, backside and thighs.

She is not wearing her nightgown.

The information was telegraphed to his brain with utter ertainty. He squeezed the feather pillow in his clenched fists nd fought to control his rising passion. He had waited this ong, he could wait one more night.

Soft fingers suddenly touched the top ridge of his shoul-er and he started at the unexpected contact. Linese trailed hem, teasingly, seductively, down his spine, toward the mall of his waist. There she paused and flattened out her and. Chase's astonished breath stuck in his throat.

She was not asleep. His temperature soared to a feverish tate. Fire ignited beneath the petite expanse of her smooth alm when she started inching forward, molding her hand) fit each inch of his flesh, while she sculpted his body as n artisan might mold clay. She moved relentlessly toward he front side of his ribs, just above his hipbone. Her hands ere roaming over his skin in a way that paralyzed his mind nd his body.

Sweet Lord, give me strength, his mind screamed si-ntly, for Chase seemed to have lost the ability to speak, as ell as the power to move. He was frozen and mute be-eath the electric touch of her hand.

He must have breathed, but he wasn't conscious of it. The nly thing he was aware of was Linese's fingers inching wer, closer, searing a path toward the throbbing heat at the ore of his plight. His body vibrated with yearning and an-cipation.

A scraping sound accompanied her nail's contact with the air on his belly. She twined her fingertips in a curl of hair e encountered below his navel and swirled her seductive,

smooth fingers in the whorl. The muscles in his gut jumpe
involuntarily and he heard his own breath hiss through h
clenched teeth.

Never in his wildest dreams would he have thought Li
ese would touch him so. His heart fluttered with delight, b
he was still too stupefied to move.

Linese's hand shifted again. Lower, slower. Each hear
beat was pleasurable torture while she relentlessly move
toward the hard, pulsing core of his manhood.

Then she reached out and grasped the most rigid part (
him with firm determination. It was an action that shocke
and titillated him to the very marrow of his bones. His hea
lodged in his throat like a stone.

"I am only human, Linese," he growled. "Do you kno
what you are doing to me?" The question ripped from hi
in an anguished rush. Before she could reply, he turned ov
and pinned her beneath his aroused body in one deft mov

"Show me, Chase." Her voice was deep and sensual ar
sent a frisson of chills over his burning flesh. "Show n
what I am doing to you."

Moonlight fell across her face in a silver shaft from ;
open window. The redolent smell of honeysuckle and loan
earth mingled on a warm breeze and heightened his ple
sure in some undefinable primal fashion. She was mo
beautiful than he could have imagined. Her lips were sligh
parted in a sensuous smile.

Chase buried his face in her hair and inhaled the fre
clean smell of her, while he showered kisses over her fo
head, eyes, cheeks and down her throat. It didn't seem I
would ever get enough of Linese. He realized what I
yearned for most in all the world was to love this woma
fully.

She shifted positions and he settled himself between h
thighs. It jolted him to realize how well they fit togethe
how he knew he belonged with her. She gyrated her hi
against him slowly.

He shuddered with pleasure and surprise. ''Lord Almighty, Linese, where did you learn such a thing?''

Linese slid her hand between their bodies and stroked the velvet length of him. She felt powerful, in control. She was still inhibited, but she kept telling herself it was right—they were married, they belonged together.

Butterflies filled her belly each time Chase's body responded exactly as Melissa predicted he would. She moved her hand over his hip and felt the raised network of scars on his skin. For a moment he did stiffen beneath her curious touch, but she rubbed and caressed and his muscles began to relax.

It was quite a revelation to Linese, to find out she had such domination over this man who had always seemed so impervious, so unreachable.

She found his mouth and touched her tongue to his lips. He jerked at first, unaccustomed to her boldness, but soon he opened his lips and speared her with his own. Linese felt the very essence of her being cleaved to Chase.

''I missed you,'' she murmured. ''I missed you so much.''

Chase shivered inwardly. He knew he should say the same thing, but he could not continue the hypocrisy of his silent lie. She nuzzled his throat and moaned softly in contentment.

He could no longer check the molten lust surging through his body, not when Linese and his heart beckoned him to go on. But, if he was going to do this thing—and by all that was holy, he was going to make love to her tonight—then he *had* to be honest with Linese.

''Linese, I must tell you. Something happened while I was gone....''

She opened her eyes. In the muted light from the summer moon, he could see her watching him, searching his face, seeking his soul. It sent an arrow of emotion tearing through his heart.

''Later, Chase, no matter what it is, it can keep.'' She ground her pelvis against him again.

He loved her.

He didn't *remember* loving her—but he *did* love her. Th person he was at this moment in time, the aroused man wh arched his body above hers and held her close in this bed loved her. He adored her with every particle of his blighte soul and he feared losing her.

"Tell me tomorrow," she said with a throaty sigh. "Fc tonight, let's forget about the war. Let's forget about th time we've lost. Tomorrow will be soon enough to face th harsh world again."

Linese reached up and twined her fingers in the hair at h temples. She tugged him toward her. A hot core of nee flowered inside her. She leaned into Chase's wide chest mo with each passionate caress.

This was what she had wanted since Chase stepped off th train. She had waited two years to feel his arms aroun her—two years to know the completeness of giving hersel to her husband without the hurried embarrassment she fe of their first time. Melissa had given her a measure of ur derstanding she had lacked before. Now, because of wha she had learned, she knew she would enjoy Chase in physical way that had been a sweet mystery on their wec ding night.

"Now, Chase. Make love to me now," she pleaded.

Chase tried to make his thoughts coherent. He tried t ignore her request and tell her the truth, but the need to te her right now was weaker than his passion and desire to lov her. He finally gave up the effort to resist her and kissed he with wild abandon. Chase closed his eyes and allowed h hands and his mouth to worship this extraordinary woma without restraint.

Linese felt Chase's fervor intensify. It was like a dai breaking, spilling life-giving liquid over a barren land scape. She felt him change within her arms as a chameleo changes its color. He was no longer holding back. Ther wasn't anything kept in reserve, as she had so often fe when she was with him. For this night, for this magical moment, he was hers completely.

Her husband was an expert lover. He touched her gently in secret hot places. Nerve endings in her body thrummed with feelings she had never known existed. His eager mouth nibbled and suckled her ears, her throat, her nipples.

He was not like this before he went to war. A voice inside her head declared. Not only was she a changed woman, Chase was different in some mystical, profound manner. He was utterly devoted to her pleasure, her gratification. It was as if he were a different man.

The difference went beyond the awkwardness between them on their wedding night, but she could not define it. That night had been more an embarrassing exercise for the newlyweds than an occasion of shared pleasure. This coupling promised to be heaven on earth, the fulfillment of all her dreams and two years' worth of longing.

To her surprise, a soft mewling sound escaped her lips. Without conscious thought, she arched against his chin when he grazed lightly over her belly. It occurred to her that, somewhere along this extraordinary journey, she had surpassed what Melissa had told her and her body had taken over with a secret knowledge of its own.

"Don't stop," she whispered in a breathy voice.

A husky moan of exultation accompanied Chase's exploration of her silken skin. She twined her fingers in his hair and pulled him near again. She wrapped her legs around Chase's waist and encouraged him to mount her.

"Now, Chase, now..." she moaned.

"Linese, I want you so badly it hurts," he whispered at the moment he filled her body.

Her heart soared. She had regained what the war had taken from her—and more. Chase was back where he belonged. Happiness blanketed her heart.

Chase caressed the soft weight of Linese's breasts and he heard her gasp. He fought to master his physical need, intending to hold back until Linese was satisfied. That was what he longed for—to see her shatter in ecstasy beneath him. He shifted positions slightly, willed himself to hold back his own pleasure, and trailed kisses down her chin and breasts while he rocked his pelvis against her. A slick sheen of sweat covered both their bodies and heightened his pleasure. Chase kissed, fondled and basked in the wonder of his newfound intimacy.

It was all a wonderful experience of discovery. Each new touch brought astonishing results. Each new treasure was also a reassuring whisper that told Chase he was finally free of the past.

Chase had never known such bliss existed in this earthly world. It was like finding a part of himself that had been lost, a part of himself he never wanted to relinquish.

Linese dug her fingernails into his shoulders and her body went stiff with her cascading release. For a blink of an eye, he saw them in his memory. He and Linese, locked together awkwardly, in their first attempt at love. He recalled their wedding, or at least a tiny fragment of their wedding night. His mind shouted happily at the recaptured memory while it blended and merged with his present physical rapture. He thrust harder—once, twice, three times and felt her name on his lips like wine.

Linese was lost in her own realm of pleasure, already satisfied once but enjoying the feeling of having Chase hard inside her. She felt all the muscles in his back flex and expand beneath her palms while she held him, an anchor that she clung to while her mind and body floated somewhere above her.

"I love you, Linese," he said with a harsh moan.

She had truly overcome all the obstacles between them. Her husband was in her arms, he voiced his love for her. No specter of doubt could ever come between them again, not now. Not when he had finally said the words that she had longed to hear, not when they had picked up the pieces of their lives. Nothing could take her happiness away now that she finally won his devotion.

Chapter Fifteen

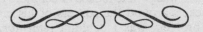

"Oh, my darling Linese." Chase balanced on one forearm while he tenderly stroked the sweat-dampened hair around her face. "You are everything a man could ever wish for." He kissed her deeply. "There is something I wanted to tell you before this happened."

The foreboding in his gray eyes surprised her. How could Chase look so troubled when they had just shared such magic?

"Chase?"

He gently placed his fingertips over her lips. "Shh." He leaned down and kissed her eyes, her nose, her forehead. "Linese, you must listen to me now. It's important."

"All right."

"When I was gone, during the last battle I was in, something terrible happened to me."

She moved aside the dark lock of hair grazing the top of his thick brows. "I know—your aide wrote about your hip. The scar doesn't bother me, Chase. I felt it—"

He shook his head and his habitual frown appeared. "No, I'm not talking about the damage to my hip. Something else, something I never told the surgeons or anyone."

A trail of gooseflesh began to work its way up Linese's arms. Her breath caught in her throat. Fear that Chase had been more severely wounded than she knew wrapped around her heart. Terror that she might yet lose him gripped her.

"What happened to you?"

"When I woke up in the field hospital, at first I was heavily dosed with morphine." He looked deep into her eyes. "When I was able to realize what was going on, volunteers were reading your letters to me."

She smiled, remembering how many hours she spent pouring her love and longing into those letters.

"The problem was—" He looked at her more intently and the deep brackets around the corners of his mouth hardened. "The problem was I couldn't *remember* anything about what you mentioned in your letters."

"I don't understand."

Chase stroked her face. He gently moved a strand of her hair away from her temple and kissed where it had been. Love shone in his eyes, lingered in his touch, yet he was troubled.

"My memory was gone, Linese." His voice was a harsh whisper. "I couldn't remember going off to war or marrying you. I couldn't remember anything—anything at all."

She swallowed hard and blinked. The room had begun to shrink around them. There was no air in her lungs. It was difficult to breathe, difficult to absorb what he was saying.

"When did it return?" she finally asked.

He grimaced as if in physical pain and gave her a sad smile. "It hasn't really. I still have no solid memory about my life before I woke up in that hospital. The day I stepped off the train in Mainfield and Kerney pinned that ribbon on my chest, my life began anew. That day was the first time I ever remembered seeing you."

She felt the warm emotions of victory fade away while cold doubt and fear replaced them. A thousand tiny incidents and moments that had made her wonder about Chase's behavior now fell into place like a child's puzzle. Linese didn't want to believe it, but she knew it was true.

He was different. He was not the man she married. Now she knew why. He was a better man, a more loving man, because he was a different person.

"You didn't remember me?" Her voice was a pained whisper.

"I'm slowly getting better. Small fragments of memory have recently returned." He smiled hopefully. "The memory of the first time I saw you came back to me just the other day. Linese, I have to know." His gaze was riveted on her face. "Does knowing this change the way you feel about me?"

Conflict rose up inside her like sharp shards of broken glass. His tender dove gray eyes rent her heart in two. He was not the man she married, but he was certainly the man she adored. If his memory were to return completely, would he be the same? Or would the recollections of his old self take away the perfect husband God have given her?

"I love you, Chase. Since you have been home, I have fallen more in love with you every day," she whispered truthfully.

"I was afraid knowing would change the way you felt about me." He placed his palms on either side of her face and kissed her. "I was afraid I might lose you. Now there is no cloud, no threat hanging over us. We can rebuild our lives. Each day I remember a little more. I believe it will all come back eventually."

A cold chill made her shiver beneath his loving gaze. She didn't want Chase to remember any more of the past. She didn't want him to remember the man he used to be, because she wanted him to remain the man he was now.

The fact sank into Linese like sharp claws. She tried to tamp down the cruel fear and the smoldering anger that came without warning while Chase lovingly turned her over and spooned their bodies together. He nuzzled her ear and sighed contentedly. She felt a hot lump grow in her throat.

She had finally achieved her goal, had finally regained her husband's bed and heard him declare his love, and she felt as if her world had just collapsed around her feet in a pile of rubble.

* * *

Linese lay awake, curled in Chase's arm, until the rosy glow of May's early dawn crept through the open bedroom window. All night she had hated herself for making comparisons between his past behavior and the man he was now, but she had done it anyway.

Where the old Chase was reckless and daring, his personality was now tempered by patience and warmth.

The old Chase lived by a rigid code of rules that centered around his grandfather's madness, his need to prove himself, and the popular belief that women were only an extension of their husbands. The man who stepped off that train was not afraid to do what was right without regard to how others would react, and he was secure enough to allow her to have independent thoughts.

If he only knew. If only she could tell him that she secretly prayed he would never remember anything more.

He stirred restlessly beside her. He looped his arm around her waist and pulled her closer to the heat of his chest. Warm kisses were trailed down the back of her neck and she felt the subtle change when he moved from sleep to wakefulness.

"'Morning, sunshine," he whispered in her ear.

"'Morning."

"You smell like honey and clover on a summer's day." His breathy compliment sent a frisson of chills down her neck. When he cupped her breast in his big hand, she nearly moaned with pleasure and need. He made her quake inside and brought an abundance of emotion ripping from within her.

"Would you think I was a beast if I wanted to love you again?" his husky voice implored from behind.

"No, Chase. I want you to love me as many times as you get the notion to." She turned over and into his strong arms. Linese slipped her arms around his neck and heard a clock ticking inside her head. She didn't know how long a time she would be allowed to spend with him—the Chase he was now—but she wanted to capture and hold every possible moment she could. Knowing it could all end without warning swept away her anger and any hesitation that might have remained.

And she wanted to have a baby conceived with the tender, gentle man who now held and loved her, even if he ultimately vanished like a puff of smoke and remained only in her memories.

Chapter Sixteen

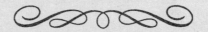

Chase left his horse at Ira's stable and walked toward the newspaper office. The summer sunshine warmed his face and made him squint against the brightness. One strand of his hair fell across his forehead on an errant breeze and he swiped at it halfheartedly.

He caught himself whistling a tune, some forgotten melody that he knew without knowing how he knew it. There was a smile tugging at the corners of his mouth and he knew it was because of his wife.

His wife.

He liked the way it felt to think about her in that fashion. She was more than he dreamed in every way, and she loved him. She loved him in spite of himself.

For a moment, he thought about turning around and going back to Cordellane to spend the day with her. The past couple of months had been like a sweet dream. They had settled into a wonderful domestic routine. Linese showed no interest in coming with him to the *Gazette,* even though he encouraged her to do so. He had tried to get her to write some editorials at home, but she seemed distracted and not really interested.

In a way, it gave him a degree of satisfaction that she didn't feel it necessary to come with him, that she had confidence in him, even though he admitted that some things were still a black void to him. If she missed the work she had done so well in his absence, she denied it each time he tried to get her to write an editorial. She would tell him, with a smile, that his call to duty and honor had jolted most of Mainfield from their lethargic stupor. Linese claimed that Chase had become the catalyst and that the Union would benefit from his convictions. She insisted that he should do what must be done without her there to distract him.

A whiff of wood smoke floated on the breeze of autumn. Alarms went off in Chase's head. It had been quiet these past perfect weeks—too quiet. He had been lulled into unguarded bliss by the harmony he had experienced each night in Linese's arms since their first coupling. Now he felt his belly contract and knew that his world was about to change. Chase quickened his step and turned the corner, knowing somewhere in his gut what he would see before he got there.

Mainfield's bucket brigade was busy tossing water through the shattered door of the *Gazette*. Black smoke rolled out of the smashed front windows. Chase was relieved to note there were no live embers, but the smell of charred wood and seared metal filled the air with choking smoke. He scanned the sooty faces of the men who had tried to save the office. Hezikiah Hershner was among them. He handed his empty bucket to another man and walked toward Chase.

"What happened, Hezikiah?" Chase knew what had taken place, and why, but still he asked.

"I thought I'd come over to see how you've been faring. Doc Lukins says I'm healed." Hezikiah held up his mended arm to show Chase. "I saw smoke coming from the back of the office."

"Is the press ruined?" Chase's mind was flying ahead, already figuring out a way to keep the weekly *Gazette*s coming out without interruption. It was a twisted consolation that his editorials were upsetting the Businessman's Association so much they attempted to silence him by burning him out. The same tactic had been used successfully in Cooke County only the month before. That newspaper had folded and the man who owned it had fled into Kansas with the shirt on his back and little else.

"That hunk of metal is almost indestructible," Hezikiah said. "It'll probably need a good cleaning, but it can withstand a lot more than a small fire. You will be needing a new supply of paper though. Smoke and water damage wiped out everything. Ink's ruined, too, from the heat."

Chase nodded and rubbed his palm down his face. The closest place to find any paper would probably be in Bartlesville. The trip would take at least a day and half. He was reluctant to leave Linese and his grandfather alone for that long, and it was going to be difficult to find the money since the local business community no longer purchased ads in the *Gazette.*

"I could go to Ferrin County for you. See if I can find what you need there, if you could use the help," Hezikiah offered.

A sigh of relief escaped Chase's lips. "I'd appreciate that, Hezikiah, if you feel up to it. I don't want you going if you're not fit."

"The trip will do me good. I've gotten downright lazy since you took over. You've been doing a fine job, Chase, and stirring up some of the local politics in the bargain. I've been keeping up with the news in each *Gazette,* and the reaction of, uh, certain people."

The compliment made Chase smile. "There is still a place for you. Lord knows I could use you, but there is something you should know first." Hezikiah followed him to a more secluded area at the side of the office where the bucket brigade was not throwing water on the smoldering timber. "I have stepped on a few toes with my editorials. It could be dangerous for you to be associated with me."

Hezikiah looked Chase up and down with his glittering blackbird eyes. "So I see." He looked at the charred ruins of the office. "Life has been boring as hell lately. I could use a little excitement."

"I hope you don't get more than you bargained for," Chase said while he watched a puff of smoke head skyward.

Chase slumped into the big chair and poured himself a brandy. He was tired to the bone, but felt alive and full of purpose. The past few days he had been up before the dawn and home long after dark. He had barely seen Linese or his grandfather.

Setting up temporary quarters for the newspaper had been an almost impossible task, but he had done it. Thanks to Ira Goten. Chase grinned and thought of Mayor Kerney and his group. No doubt they were meeting somewhere right now, cursing him to the everlasting fires of hell for thwarting their efforts. He chuckled aloud when he thought about it.

At first, every vacant storeroom and shanty in Mainfield had become suddenly occupied, rented by a nameless, faceless phantom with plenty of money. There had not been a single unused shed that could be had for the purpose of housing a printing press. Chase had come close to moving the press and everything else back to Cordellane, just to be able to see the issues continue, but then Ira Goten offered space in the building next to his stable.

Chase had moved grain, cleaned out wasp nests and stared into the beady eyes of disgruntled field mice for two weeks. Now at last, the *Gazette* was churning out papers again.

A pain behind Chase's eyes made him wince. He had noticed more and more the relentless pain and ringing in his ears that accompanied every small flash of memory that he regained. He picked up the glass and brought it to his forehead. He closed his eyes and held the smooth, cool surface there, hoping to numb some of the pounding. Then he slowly opened his eyes.

Just as he expected, the image of the fireplace swam before him. It shifted, distorted. He was transported to another time long ago.

It was his father's image, dark haired and youthful. Chase knew he had been watching his father in secrecy. His father was wearing black arm bands. The remembered feeling of sorrow and great loss swept over Chase.

He was remembering the day of a burial.

"Whose?" Chase asked himself.

His father was red eyed, grief stricken, shouting at Captain Cordell. Chase heard his father's words echo in his mind.

"It's the damn Cordell curse. I never should've believed we'd be free of it. Now it has taken my wife, my love."

The hair prickled on the back of Chase's neck while the memory slowly began to fade away.

"Now it has taken my wife."

Chase gulped down his sorrow while he allowed himself to remember back to his childhood, back to the day his mother had been put into the ground.

Chase remembered Captain Cordell stepping inside the library. His arms were laden with split logs. He too was younger, his mustache an iron gray instead of snowy white.

He set the logs beside the hearth and laid the first fire of the season on the grate. Chase remembered the way it felt when the blaze ignited and filled the room with heat, yet he shivered now with the old emotions washing over him.

"You look like you've seen a ghost." Captain Cordell's voice jarred Chase back to the present. He looked up to see his grandfather standing beside the hearth, his arms again full of split logs. A feeling of déjà vu sluiced through him.

"What's troubling you, Chase?" Captain Cordell tossed the charred broom straw he had used to start the blaze into the hearth. A golden glow filled the room.

"Grandfather, tell me about the Cordell curse." The haunting memory of his father remained with him. What did it mean? Was there something wrong with this family?

"Where on earth did you hear that?" The old man rubbed his fingers over his mustache and glanced up at his son's portrait as if he too were remembering the day from the past.

"I heard my father, standing right here in front of this fireplace, shouting at you. What exactly is the Cordell curse? Is there such a thing?"

"You were just a little fry when your mama died. I wouldn't have thought you'd remember that terrible night." The old man looked sympathetic. "It was so long ago."

"I've been thinking about the past quite a lot lately." Chase said with a weary sigh. He still stubbornly kept from telling his grandfather the truth about his memory. Linese was the only person he trusted and loved enough to tell.

Captain Cordell walked to the window and stared out at the salmon streak above the treetops. "Your father said all those things out of grief, Chase. You shouldn't be putting any stock in it, not now."

"Tell me about it, please."

A heavy sigh escaped the old man's lips, but he nodded in understanding. He moved to the long sofa and sat down.

"When your mama died, he was brokenhearted. He thought it was some sort of omen. First your grandma from the fever, then your mama and newborn sister—it was a difficult birth. He had the notion, the unshakable belief, the Cordell men were doomed to lose the women they loved. A curse, if you believe in such superstitions. I guess your father grew up hearing about such things on a regular basis, being as close to Louisiana as we are. Those people are steeped in beliefs of that kind. I never could put any stock in it, myself."

Chase shivered inwardly. "You don't believe it?"

The old man squared his shoulders as if preparing himself to take a crushing blow. "I admit when Marjorie died there was a time when I wondered if it might be true. But it's foolishness, Chase. We are no more cursed than any other family. I finally came to terms with that sad fact. I've seen many a family bury too many of their kin in these sixty years, especially since this damnable secessionist trouble began. It's a fact that death is a part of life, but it ain't no curse."

Chase stared into the flames of the fire and prayed his grandfather was right. The best part of himself would never live again if anything happened to Linese. He had done his best to shatter the barriers that kept them apart, and prayed that he would eventually become a whole man again. That was the only reason he had finally allowed himself to love her totally. He wasn't sure he could live with himself if, after all was said and done, there really was a strange hex upon his family. He wasn't sure he could go on if his selfishness put Linese in danger, no matter how farfetched the notion might be.

Linese hung her head over the chamber pot and retched violently. Her churning stomach felt like a roiling river about to overflow its banks. She closed her eyes against the sickening feeling and tried to focus on a happy thought.

She was pregnant.

The happiness of her condition almost made her present dilemma endurable. Almost, but not quite. She had been suffering with the morning sickness several times a day. She could barely hold down weak tea or broth. The thought of solid food sent her into violent episodes of vomiting. It had been a chore keeping her present predicament from Chase, but she didn't want him to know. Not yet.

She had, however, decided to see Doc Lukins. By her counting she was more than three months' gone, and she had never heard other women say they had the kind of sickness that lasted this long into their time. It was a worry to her and she wanted the kindly old physician to reassure her. And, she supposed, she wanted to share the happy news with someone. If it couldn't be Chase, then it would have to be Doc. Linese rubbed a cold cloth over her brow and opened her eyes. The nausea was over for a little while at least.

She stood up and caught her own reflection in the mirror. There was a puffiness to her face that concerned her. She had not put on any weight. Lord knows that would be difficult with the war lingering, making it hard even to get enough to eat each day, yet she had the notion that her face was fuller.

If Chase had noticed any difference in her appearance, he hadn't mentioned it. He treated her as if she were the most beautiful, precious woman in the world. Each night he had brought her to physical ecstasy and held her within the circle of his arms until dawn forced him to go try to find a new location for the *Gazette*.

If only she could feel safe and secure.

Chase hadn't mentioned any more of his returning memories, but there were times when she would catch him unaware. She could almost see him reliving some forgotten moment. Whenever it happened, he became quiet and somber, more like the man he used to be. Each time she looked into his eyes, she felt a little of her heart die with the fear he was changing and leaving behind the man she adored, once again becoming the old Chase.

She turned sideways in front of her mirror and pulled her night rail smooth over her middle. She rubbed her hand over her belly and imagined what it would feel like when she was big with his baby. As it was, she had been forced to unlace her corset a bit to accommodate her filling waist.

"I'll have to tell Chase about the baby soon," she told her reflection. The prospect of telling her husband she was carrying his first child should have brought her deep satisfaction. Instead, it was a bittersweet secret she wanted to keep from him just for a while longer, just until the situation with the *Gazette* was settled and Chase was less distracted.

And she was waiting to see if more of his memory returned. She worried that when Chase regained his past, she would lose him, or at least the best part of him. She just couldn't allow herself to believe the change in him was due to two years of war. It had to be his missing past.

If only she could believe it. But the Chase Cordell wh
had stepped off that train *was* a different man. And he wa
the man she wished to be married to for the rest of her life
In some ways she felt almost unfaithful to her husband, bu
it was a foolish notion. She tried to wipe the negativ
thoughts from her mind while she dressed to go see Doc.

Doc Lukins peered over his wire-rimmed spectacles an
ran his hands over Linese's body beneath the big sheet.

"Mrs. Cordell, are you sure about your dates?"

"Quite sure." Linese vividly remembered the first nigh
Chase had touched her, the night she had finally manage
to batter his resolve with Melissa's tricks.

His face pinched into a deep set of creases. He stood u|
and dipped his hands into the basin of water and then drie
them. "I'm all finished with my examination. You can si
up."

"Is something wrong?" Linese's heart constricted pain
fully when she saw the tense look on his face.

"No, not at all." He smiled reassuringly. "You are mos
definitely pregnant.

Linese wriggled up and adjusted the sheet over the lowe
half of her body. "Is that all?"

"I have a list of instructions I want you to follow. N
lifting, no hanging wash on the line." His smile broadened
"Have you told your husband he's going to be a father?"

"Not yet."

"Well, you best do it today. I'd like to talk to him abou
getting you some help around the house. You've used th
Jones girl before, haven't you?"

Linese nodded and scanned the old physician's face
Worry and fear gripped her with fingers of ice. "Doc, i
there anything you're not telling me?" He seemed reluctan
to meet her gaze straight on.

"No. I just like to pamper new mothers. There will neve
again be a first baby, Linese, no matter how many you have
We want this to be a happy and safe time for you. Go tal|

to Chase now, why don't you, then have him come and see me. Today."

Every nerve in her body was tingling, thrumming while she waited for Chase's reaction to the news. The lingering smell of leather and grain warred with the pungent odor of printer's ink and served to make Linese's stomach churn. She twisted her hands together within the folds of her dress and willed herself to fight off the feeling.

He stood there, staring at her wide-eyed while her heart pounded in her chest. She could not read his thoughts and it was making her almost as sick at the stomach as the smells in the building.

"Say something, Chase," she begged finally.

"A baby? In the spring?" Chase repeated her own words. Linese's heart thudded inside her chest.

"Are you pleased, Chase?"

His mouth snapped shut and he blinked as if waking from a dream. Then he strode across the room and started shoving loose papers from the desk and chair.

"Oh, Lord, honey, sit down." He grabbed Linese's elbow and gently ushered her to the chair and eased her down as if she were fine china that might break any minute.

"Do you need anything? Water? How about milk? Do you want a pickle?" He didn't know why he said that, but some half-forgotten part of his brain said pregnant women had a craving to eat cucumber pickles and saltwater taffy. Could he find any if she wanted them? Maybe the mercantile, or perhaps Hezikiah could go to Bartlesville. His head was spinning, traveling a million miles a second. The need to pamper his wife wiped every other thought from his head.

Linese looked up at her husband's lean face and blinked rapidly to prevent the tears in her eyes from spilling over. She saw love and concern etched into the brackets around his mouth. The need to reassure him filled her heart and wiped away all thoughts of her own discomfort.

"I'm fine. Doc Lukins would like you to come by his of fice, though." Linese tried to banish a niggling worry from her mind. The old country doctor probably had some silly little thing he wanted to tell Chase, about how emotional she was going to become, or some such male nonsense. She told herself not to fret over imagined problems.

"Are you sure? I can see him later. I don't want to leave you alone if you're not sure.

"I'm positive, I'm just fine. Go." She smiled.

"Will you be all right until I get back?" Chase asked.

"Chase, I'm only having a baby. I'm a little tired, but I'm fine. I left the buggy right next door, at Ira's. I'm going to get it and go home."

He shook his head and the heavy strand of dark hair grazed his eyebrows. "No, you are not. You sit right here. I'll go tell Ira to bring it around and pick you up. He can drive you home and then use one of our horses to get back to Mainfield. You are most certainly not going to drive a buggy by yourself, not anymore."

"Chase—" She stifled the grin that wanted to break out.

"I won't hear of it." He walked back to her and went down on one knee in front of the chair. He picked up her left hand as if she were delicate and precious to him. He brought it to his lips.

Linese glanced at her hand and noticed her wedding ring was cutting into her finger. It also occurred to her that her shoes were pinching tight today.

"I intend to take very good care of my child's mama, and I want no arguments from you about it. Understood?" His face was stern, but his voice was gentle with affection.

Linese blinked back more tears of joy. She had noticed of late, the least little thing, good or bad, moved her to the brink of tears. "Understood, Major Cordell," she conceded softly.

Chase smiled at her then he stepped through the door that led to Ira's livery. When he was gone, Linese looked over the stack of papers lying on his makeshift desk. There were several half-finished editorials on top. She picked one up and read part of it.

His strong, blunt style impressed her. The tone was similar to the editorials he had written before he went to war, but there was a sensitivity and a compassion within them that had not been there before. It was yet another layer of the new character he had returned home with.

Linese sighed and laid the paper down. She mentally willed herself to be happy about Chase's trying to regain his memory. No matter what the future held she loved him as he was now more than she had loved him before, even though she could not tell him so.

Guilt flooded over her again. It was almost, in some crazy unexplainable fashion, like having been unfaithful to the man she had wed.

The man who had come home from war was truly a separate man, and the love Linese felt for him made her feelings for the old Chase pale in comparison. How could any wife tell her husband such a thing and hurt him, as it surely would?

She pushed herself up from the chair and felt a twinge in her lower abdomen. Terror snaked through her while she slowly eased herself back down into the hard seat. Linese drew in gulps of air and tried not to grow more anxious with wild imaginings. Soon the pain spread across her back and dissipated slowly into her thighs where it settled with a dull ache.

A million fears about the complications of childbirth flitted through her head, but she forced herself to remain calm. Chase had only gone for Ira, he would be here in a moment, she told herself. Ira was close by, she could call out if she needed to. He was no more than a stone's toss away.

The outer door opened. Linese sighed and looked up gratefully, expecting to see Ira or Chase, but found Rancy Thompson staring at her.

"Ma'am." He took off his hat. "I was hoping to find Major Cordell here. Is he around?"

Linese shook her head. "No, Sheriff, he stepped out of the office for a moment." She shifted on the chair, trying to find a position that would ease the ache in her lower back.

"I see." Thompson's forehead crinkled into a frown. "I was hoping to ask him a few questions." He held the hat between his fingers and was methodically worrying the brim through them. "Perhaps you can help me, Mrs. Cordell."

"I'd be happy to try, Sheriff." She felt the color draining from her face as the pain grew sharper.

"I was wondering if you could tell me when it was, more or less, that you met Major Cordell? It's nothing official, you understand, I just need to clear up some unanswered questions." His frown deepened.

The question seemed odd, but she was preoccupied with trying to master the growing pain, so she did not examine the sheriff's reason for wanting to know such a thing.

"I met Chase Cordell on May 30, 1862."

"Now how is it you can remember that date so precisely Mrs. Cordell?" Something like disbelief flitted through his eyes.

"It was the Presbyterian church's annual social. I always helped with the baking, decorations and such. It's held the same time each year—on May 30."

The sheriff nodded and looked more thoughtful. "That's just over the line into Ferrin County, isn't it, ma'am?

"Yes, it is."

"I see. Well, thank you, Mrs. Cordell, you've been a great help." He turned then turned back. "Are you feeling all right?"

"Yes, Sheriff, I'm fine," she lied.

The door came open and Ira Goten stepped into the new *Gazette* quarters.

"Sheriff?" Ira flicked a quick glance beyond the sheriff and met Linese's eyes. "Mrs. Cordell."

She nodded in response to Ira's crisp greeting.

"Goten. What brings you here?" The sheriff asked.

"I came to take Mrs. Cordell home." Ira stepped past the sheriff. "If you're ready, ma'am. Major Cordell said to get you home right away."

"He's not with you, Mr. Goten?" Linese felt a moment of disappointment. Having Chase nearby made her feel less apprehensive about the baby, and the pain in her legs and back seemed to be worse.

"No." Ira glanced toward the sheriff. "He said he had an appointment to keep. He said you knew about it."

Linese nodded. Chase had gone over to Doc Lukins and he would be back soon, she told herself. "Yes, of course. It slipped my mind."

She pushed herself up from the chair and the strange biting pain shot through her with greater force. To her embarrassment, a whimper of pain escaped her lips. Linese found herself mighty grateful for Ira's strong arm. The sharp cramp came again and her knees almost buckled beneath her.

"Ma'am? Are you feeling all right? You are a bit peaked." Ira peered into her face while he supported more of her weight.

"I am feeling a bit woozy all of a sudden." Ira's face was swimming before her as if she were looking at him through fast-running water. Suddenly the whole room tilted and she fought to catch her breath. "I think perhaps you should send for... my... husband," Linese whispered. Then the room disappeared.

"I'm concerned Linese may have a bad time of it." Doc Lukins took off his spectacles and rubbed his fingers on the bridge of his nose where two small red marks remained. His old face was a network of weather-roughened creases.

"Is Linese in immediate danger?" Chase's heart lodged in his throat when he heard his own voice asking the question he had been trying to avoid.

"Probably not any more than any other women in Mainfield. Just call me an old worrier. She is a tiny woman and you Cordells are big men, combined with the poor diet we've all had due to the war. That in itself is no cause for concern, but I detected some swelling in her face and extremities. I'd just like to take the extra precaution of seeing her take real good care of herself. It's going to be up to you to see she follows my advice."

"I'll do anything to keep Linese safe, Doc."

"That's what I wanted to hear." The old physician slipped the glasses back on his nose and smiled. "I'm sure it will all be fine, Chase. The first thing I want you to do is get somebody in to take care of the household chores. Effie, the oldest Jones girl, is good. I believe she helped Linese out once or twice while you were away. I can send her over, if you like. I'm going out that way later."

Chase nodded numbly. Guilt and worry mingled in his chest. He had been so afraid to touch Linese, perhaps his fears had been founded. While he was wallowing in his misery, the door swung open so hard it hit the wall behind it with a loud thump.

Chase looked up to see Linese laying limp and pale in Ira's arms. Fear such as he had never known galvanized him to action. He bolted from his chair.

"Oh, my God, Linese." Terror constricted his voice.

"Put her in here." Doc Lukins directed Ira through the maze of his small, crowded office and into his own bedroom. Linese's limbs seemed almost liquid when Ira gently laid her down.

"She fainted dead away, Chase." Ira rubbed his palms together nervously while he explained. His eyes were round with alarm and sympathy. He faded back into the other room, leaving Doc and Chase alone with Linese.

"What is it, Doc? Is it the baby?" Chase's knees were weak as water while he stared at Linese's lovely pale face. "Will she be all right?"

"Don't get timid on me now, Chase. Loosen that damned corset more to give her air." The doctor was pressing his fingers to her neck and opening one of her eyelids with his thumb. "She's just passed out. Could be the heat, could be this confounded garment. Now I wish I'd told her to leave it off after the exam," Doc muttered. "Still, she's not even showing."

Chase's fingers moved automatically to loosen the dress and the corset laces beneath while he listened to Doc's muttering. Guilt covered him in a heavy, suffocating blanket. His lust had brought her to this.

"Please, don't let her die, please," he prayed over and over. He was ready to make whatever bargain was necessary to keep her and his child from harm.

Linese was practically lost in the huge bed Chase and his grandfather had carried down and set up in the dining room. Her golden hair fanned out like a halo on the pillow. Doc had given her some herb he said would make her groggy.

Chase kissed her lightly on the forehead and moved to the old rocker. He intended to watch over her and keep her safe, even if he had to do it by strength of will. He shifted positions in the hard chair and pulled the old faded quilt up over his shoulders. Only the flickering flame of a single lamp drove back the darkness of night.

Images, distorted and warped, rattled around inside his head while he kept his vigil. What if his father had been right? What if his love for Linese would be the very thing that took her from him?

Linese stirred and moaned. He was instantly on his feet beside the bed.

"Chase?" Her voice was slurred with sleep and the potion Doc had given her.

"I'm right here." He reached out and took hold of her fingers. Her hand felt so tiny inside his own. She seemed to be little more than a frail child herself, too young and fragile to carry a baby inside her body for nine months.

Guilt and regret flowed over Chase. He loved and wanted their baby more than he had thought possible, but to put

Linese at risk was unthinkable. He loathed himself for not protecting her from himself, from the dangers of life.

"Do you need anything? Are you thirsty?" He stroked the strands of pale hair from her face. Her eyes opened and began to focus in the flickering glow of lamplight.

"What happened?"

"You fainted, honey."

"Is the baby all right?" Alarm telegraphed through her fingers and up his arm when she gripped his hand harder. She tensed and raised a few inches off the mound of pillows as if to get up.

"Yes, the baby is fine. Doc checked you over." Chase gently but firmly held her.

She smiled and sighed in relief. "Did I make a complete fool of myself?" She relaxed back into the mound of pillows and the feather mattress.

"No. I'm just glad Ira was there when it happened." Chase tried to smile to give her reassurance, but it wasn't easy when his heart was lodged in his throat. "Honey, lie back down and rest."

"I'm terribly sleepy." She relaxed a bit more.

"Good. Doc wants you to take it real easy. You go back to sleep. We'll talk in the morning."

She gave him a smile full of trust and love before her eyes fluttered shut. Chase continued to stroke the soft hairs at her temple until she was breathing deeply again.

Chase rose stiffly from the rocker and tried to stretch the stiffness from his neck and back. He yawned and blew out the lamp. The sun was peaking over the eastern horizon. A flickering movement outside the window caught his eye. He rubbed his palms against them and squinted, trying to figure out what it was he saw.

When the cobwebs began to clear from his head, he realized it was his grandfather. The old man was leading his tall black mare out of the thicket toward the barn behind

Cordellane. The first rays of sun cast weak fingers of light on the unlikely pair. The horse's head hung low and her chest and shoulders were flecked with white lather. Captain Cordell seemed to be carrying himself oddly and Chase frowned, trying to force his sleep-deprived brain to know why the old man's movements seemed so awkward.

A cold fist wrapped itself around Chase's heart when it registered. Then he saw the dark stain on his grandfather's shirt. The maroon blotch started at his shoulder and faded downward and toward his ribs. Chase had more than enough memory of war to know it for what it was—blood.

"Oh, Lord, what has happened now?" Chase whispered. He yanked on his boots and crept silently from the room to find out.

"Are you all right?" Chase demanded when he found the old man unsaddling the mare.

"I'll live. At least the slug went through clean." His grandfather's voice was harsh with fatigue.

"What in the hell happened?" Chase didn't know whether he should be furious or relieved. "What were you doing out in the middle of the night?"

"It's best you don't know about what happened tonight."

"Damn it, there have been too many secrets, too many mysteries. Tell me what in God's name you're up to now?"

Captain Cordell grabbed his bottle of whiskey by the slender neck and took a swig. His silver mustache looked droopier than usual. There were dark hollows under his eyes that made Chase all too aware of his age. "There was some trouble at the Jennings' place."

Chase didn't know where the Jennings' place was. His frustration with his missing memory was rapidly reaching the point of combustion. The old man unwrapped an oilskin that contained all the necessary supplies to take care of his wound. Chase impatiently took over the task while he questioned him further.

"What kind of trouble?"

Chase packed soft cotton batting against the bullet hole and pressed until he saw a white line of pain appear around his grandfather's lips. He bound the wound in his grandfather's shoulder with strips of cloth he found in the bundle.

"Some night riders tried to burn them out. Seems they thought the best way to deal with an anti-secessionist was to kill him. Luckily, somebody involved with the railroad heard about the plan. There were women and children in the house, Chase." Captain Cordell shivered. He was a staunch Unionist, but he didn't wage war on innocents, whether they were secessionists or not. It sent a frisson of chills up his back to know there were people who would kill without remorse.

"Who did the attacking?" Images of the Businessman's Association floated in his mind, but they had no allegiance—no loyalties and no convictions. Their one and only motive for anything they did was pure greed, if greed could be said to be pure.

His grandfather shrugged and tipped the bottle to his lips again. When he finished drinking, he wiped the back of his hand across his mouth. "They were wearing something over their heads—looked like flour sacks or some such cowardly nonsense. Too dark to see much anyway." Disgust rang in the old man's voice.

He looked up at Chase and his eyes were hard. "Listen, boy, I don't want you involved. You've stirred up a hornet's nest with those editorials as it is. Calling for each man to take a stand and get this war over with has been more than enough to earn you enemies. Think of Linese. Right now that little lady needs all the peace and care we can give her."

"I'll take care of Linese." Chase bristled at the suggestion that he might not. "Don't you worry about that." Guilt warred with indignation. He still felt he was the reason she was lying in bed, but hearing his grandfather's words made him angry.

"I know you'd do everything possible to keep her safe, but things are getting mighty ugly." Concern glowed in the old man's weathered face. "What if something were to happen to you, Chase?"

Chase remembered Kerney's threats, but they held no more power over him now that his grandfather had been cleared. Still, there was the mysterious gun and gold Ira had kept for him. What if there was something else he didn't know about? He felt the cloud of his unknown past looming over him again.

He could not continue this way. There had to be a way to trigger the return of his memory and stop Kerney once and for all.

"I intend to be around to raise my child. Nothing and nobody is going to take me from Linese."

His grandfather patted his shoulder and winced in pain for his effort. "I know how you feel, but do me a favor. Don't ask me any more questions about what I'm doing. I'm not the only one at risk."

A part of Chase rebelled. He wanted to know what was happening now and what had happened in the past. The unanswered questions nagged at him daily. It kept an invisible wall between him and everyone. He had been foolish to think he could have a whole life without first having all the answers.

"How do you intend to hide that bullet hole?" Chase asked his grandfather.

"I've been feeling a bit peaked lately. I think I'll have to take to my bed with the ague for a few weeks," the old man said with a wink.

Chase grated his teeth together until his jaw pinched in protest. The crazy old fool was going to get himself killed

and there wasn't a damned thing Chase could say or do to
stop him. Not unless he could do something to remove Kerney permanently as a threat.

Chapter Seventeen

Linese adjusted her gown and fluffed her pillow. She had only been confined to her bed for one full day and already she was chafing to be up and busy.

Chase was acting like a fussy old mother hen. She had woken and found herself in the dining room. In the dining room! It was enough to shame a body into never holding their head up again.

The tender care she was receiving from Chase was flattering, but she had things to do. Linese refused to entertain the thought there could be anything wrong with her. It had just been the heat, she told herself, just the heat. She could not allow herself even to think something could happen to her baby.

She could hear the Jones girl humming tunelessly in the kitchen. It sent a ribbon of melancholy through her. Linese wanted to be the one who cooked for Chase. She wanted to serve him chicory in the mornings and listen to his plans for the day.

Gold-and-crimson-colored leaves outside the dining room windows sent a shaft of longing through her. She yearned to walk along the creek with Chase and hear the brittle foliage crunch beneath their feet, to breathe the crisp, pungent odor of fall while their child grew inside her. An invisible clock ticked inside her head. It was ruthlessly marking the minutes she had been given to cherish the man God had changed

Chase into—before he regained his memory and became th man he used to be.

"I'd give anything to know what you are thinking righ now." Chase's deep voice floated over her.

She turned her head and watched him maneuver a hug tray through the dining room door. It was quite a picture t behold. Chase's lean, craggy face was wreathed in a happ grin. He carefully placed the tray holding the teapot an cups on the table near her bed. An old, faded apron ha been secured around his lean middle, but on his large fram it looked comically no larger than a small kerchief.

It made her smile in spite of herself. She averted her eye before he saw how his appearance amused her, fearing sh might wound his masculine pride and embarrass him.

"I was just noticing how the seasons are changing. Sum mer is gone. This is our first fall together." Linese plucke at the embroidery on the edge of the sheet. She had deco rated all their linens in the two years while she spun dream of how their life would be when he returned from the wa This was not how she had envisioned it.

"Where is the old Captain today, Chase?"

"Uh, he is in his room. He's not feeling well." Chas turned away so she could not see his face, could not detec the lie.

"Not well?" Linese tossed back the sheet. "Perhaps ther is something I can do. I'll go see to him,"

Chase shook his head. "No you won't. He said it was touch of the ague. You are not going anywhere." He strod across the room and pulled the sheet back over her an tucked it under her chin. Something about the way h avoided her eyes made her heart contract.

"What is it, Chase?" Alarm snaked up her back. "Ther is something you are not telling me, isn't there? It's som thing bad about the baby."

His dark eyebrows drew together. She could see th brackets at the corners of his mouth deepen into the tellta signs of distress and her heart skipped a beat.

"I don't want you to get upset, Linese."

The minute he said that, she did, of course. "I am not upset," she snapped. "Now tell me."

"Doc wants you to take good care of yourself." Chase's lips flinched. "You are not to be out of bed at all." He paused and sighed.

The impact of his words settled on Linese. "He wants me to stay in bed?" All the worry she had been ignoring came collapsing in on her.

"Yes, and there is more. We can't have relations."

"What?"

"Doc said it could be bad for the baby."

"How long does he think we should remain apart?"

"Until the baby is born."

"Chase, that is five months." Her bottom lip began to quiver.

"Linese, it will be all right. I promise I'll keep you and the baby safe." He managed a smile. "And I can hold you, even if we can't do anything else."

A single tear flowed over her lashes and trickled down her cheek. Seeing his brave wife cry cleaved Chase's heart in two. He wrapped her in his arms and felt his love expand and increase inside his heart. Her petite body was racked with wrenching sobs. It tore him apart to know there was nothing he could do to keep her from hurting like this.

"Oh, Chase, I—I don't want to lose our baby."

"We won't honey, we won't," he promised with complete conviction.

Chase held her until the sobs became ragged sniffles and finally gasping hiccups. She clung to him as a drowning man clings to a branch. In that march of time, while he held her, he knew he had no choice but to defy the Cordell curse, if indeed it did exist, and to defeat it with the strength of their love.

When she was finally quiet, he leaned away and looked into her face.

"I brought you something to eat."

"I don't want it. I'm not hungry."

Chase stroked her forehead and cheeks. "Linese, you have got to eat. You are no bigger than a minute and I won' have you wasting away on me." He took her fingers from the embroidered leaf she had ripped apart. Green thread hung in tatters on the sheeting. "Linese, what can I do to make this better for you? Tell me and I'll do it."

She felt the lump grow in her throat. Just having him ask was enough to make her want to cry. How could she put into words her terror? It was more than just the baby. It was the threat of losing him, the worry that his regained memory would somehow steal her happiness. It was an unreason able fear, but no matter how hard she tried, she could no banish it from her mind.

"I know I'm being silly. I just can't seem to shake off the blues." She could not reveal her fears to him. There was simply no way to tell the man she adored that she was afraid of his becoming himself again. The notion was ridiculous yet it held her in fingers of iron.

He took her chin and tipped it up. She had no choice but to meet his steady, unrelenting gaze.

"I think you are the most beautiful, perfect woman in the world, and I love you with all my heart."

He leaned near and kissed her. It was gentle and protec tive, and filled Linese with a longing that started some where within her soul and spiraled outward until i consumed every particle of her being.

She sighed and leaned into the hard expanse of his chest A sprig of coarse hair tickled her nose. They sat there in si lence, him holding her gently, while she felt loved and cher ished.

A knock at the front door jarred them apart.

Chase's brows furrowed together into a forbidding frown Linese felt the tension in his body before he released her to rise from the edge of her bed.

"Are you expecting anyone?" she said as she watched him jerk off the apron.

"No."

She sensed an urgency in him when he flicked a quick glance out the dining room window. The sound of the Jones girl opening the front door drifted into the dining room along with the unmistakable smell of autumn leaves and chill air.

Chase tilted his head and Linese could see he was listening hard to the murmur of voices.

"I'll see who it is. You rest. I'll be right back, I promise." His voice was light, but she knew he was concerned. He took a single step toward the door but before he could reach it, Rancy Thompson stepped inside the room. The sheriff swept off his hat and blushed pink at the sight of Linese lying in bed in the dining room.

"Ma'am?" His voice was flustered. He turned a darker shade of rose. Linese pulled the covers up under her chin as far as they would go, but she still felt as if she were standing buck naked. Heat flooded her own face. She couldn't remember ever feeling more mortified than she did at this moment.

"Rancy, what brings you here?" Chase asked, but there was little hospitality in his clipped greeting. His jaw and his shoulders were rigid. Something was clearly not right, and it was more than the sheriff seeing Linese in her nightgown in bed.

"I went by the *Gazette,* but you weren't there, and Mrs. Cordell wasn't well. So I came out here to see you." Thompson turned slightly in her direction, but his eyes didn't linger. "Ma'am, I hope you recover soon."

"Thank you, Sheriff."

"It's a long ride for a social call." Chase moved back to the tray and picked up the teapot. "Would you like some tea, Sheriff?"

Rancy blinked and looked self-consciously at Linese again. "No, no. This isn't exactly a social call, Major."

She saw Chase glance at her out of the corner of his eye. She tried her best to look relaxed under his knowing gaze, but it was difficult and she chided herself for not being a better actress. The last thing she wanted to do was have him worry more about her than he already was doing.

"I think it would be better if we talked in the other room, Rancy." Chase set the pot down with a clink. Linese knew he was leaving because of her.

"Chase, please." She wanted him to know how important it was that she not be shut out of his life, but all she could manage were those two pleading words.

He turned and stared at her. The thick black eyebrows furrowed together. She could see him considering the odds, weighing the outcome, wondering if she was too weak. The muscle in his hard, lean jaw jerked. Finally he walked back to the bed and sighed heavily.

"All right." He sat down in the chair and picked up her hand.

It was a small victory that made her heart swell with love. He cared about her feelings in a way the man she married could never have understood.

"Tell me, Rancy. Why are you here?" His voice was soft yet hard as iron.

The sheriff frowned and looked down at his feet. He held his hat in his hand like a shield. "There was some trouble last night."

"Really?"

Chase's voice was unusually mild and uninterested, in contrast to the tension Linese could feel in the fingers he had wrapped around her hand. She had the uneasy notion he was not entirely surprised by Thompson's visit or the news that there had been some kind of disturbance, but that made little sense.

"What kind of trouble?" Chase inquired.

"There was some shooting at the Jennings' place last night." Rancy's eyes narrowed.

"Sounds like something Hezikiah should put in the *Gazette*." Inquisitive eyebrows rose over his gray eyes. Chase was the picture of composure but Linese felt the opposite in his hand.

"That's not why I'm here." Rancy shook his head. "This is not my idea, Major, especially after that nonsense with the old Captain. I have ignored the suggestion that I arrest you. Obviously you lied to protect the Captain—and that I will ignore. But there is a rumor that you were there last night—at the Jennings' place, I mean."

"What?" Linese blurted.

"Honey." Chase's voice was full of concern for her. "I assure you, Rancy, I was not out last night."

The sheriff sighed. "I'm real sorry, Major, witnesses say you took a bullet in the left shoulder during the altercation."

"That's ridiculous. Chase hasn't left me for a moment." Linese could not believe that Sheriff Thompson could consider such a preposterous accusation against her husband.

"I need more than your say-so to satisfy the witness, I'm afraid, ma'am," he apologized, but his meaning was clear.

Linese had never before had her word questioned. It was a new experience, one she found decidedly distasteful, but when she leaned forward, there was Chase's strong hand, guiding her down, compelling her to rest.

"It's all right, honey. This is easy enough to clear up, right now." Chase allowed his eyes to linger on her face for a minute. "I don't want you to be worrying about this or anything else."

Chase stood up. His face was stony while he quickly unbuttoned his shirt and roughly yanked it from his breeches. He tossed it onto the bed and turned one full revolution in front of a red-faced Rancy Thompson, who scanned every inch of Chase's body with his eyes, in spite of his embarrassment.

"As I said, Rancy, I was with Linese all night. So now you can put the rumors to rest and assure the *witnesses* they were obviously mistaken."

* * *

Chase paced in front of the dining room windows like a trapped animal. His grandfather's fears about his safety had been correct. Even though the so-called witnesses had been mistaken about which Cordell had been riding the black mare, and which Cordell had been shot, it was plain there were people who would do anything to stop Chase and his editorials.

Old issues of the *Gazette* made him aware that Rancy Thompson was appointed to his office by the Businessman's Association back in 1862. Chase was damned sure he knew who was pressuring the sheriff to come to Cordellane and see if Chase had a bullet hole in him. He raked his fingers through his hair.

Only his grandfather's canny deceptions kept everyone from looking in the right direction, at the right Cordell. He felt a burst of pride in the old man. He was so good at play acting, he continued to fool everyone and do whatever it was he did, right under their noses.

But how long would it continue?

There was only one way Chase could be absolutely sure he had eliminated the lingering threat of Kerney and his thugs.

He had to remember his past. He had to know what he had done with Ira Goten.

He had to regain his memory.

It tore Linese apart to see the look on Chase's face. He had been staring silently through the dining room window into the darkness for half an hour. She knew instinctively what was wrong even though she did not want to admit it.

Chase was desperate to remember his past. He was trying to put the shattered pieces of his life back together. The dread of what she risked losing clashed with the pain etched in his face. The reality of their shared yet conflicting plight tore a deep cleft in her heart.

Did she love him enough to put his happiness above her needs? Could she risk losing the strong, devoted man he had become?

He turned to her then and she felt a warm swelling inside her. God, how she loved him.

"Linese, I have to ask you something." He strode to her bedside and knelt beside her. "I need your help."

She swallowed hard. "What?"

"I need you to help me fill in the missing parts of my memory." The sorrow in his eyes was unchecked, unveiled.

"I'll help you to regain your memory." The words spilled out. "Whatever you think might help, I'll be there to help you try it." The war raged inside her. She didn't want him to regain his memory completely, but she couldn't stand seeing him struggle in vain. She loved him more than she feared losing him. "I hope you don't expect too much. It might not work...."

He tenderly cupped her face within his big rough hands. Eyes softer than a gray winter cloud roamed over her face.

"With you by my side, I can do anything." He gently laid his wide palm on her stomach. "Thank you for loving me, even though I'm only half the man you married."

He bent his head and nuzzled her throat. Linese blinked back the tears. He believed she loved him *in spite of* his lost past, when in her heart she knew she loved him *because of* it.

He wasn't half the man she married—he was twice the man he was two years ago—but she could not tell him that.

"Were all my letters home to you like this one?" Chase frowned at Linese over the top edge of the dog-eared paper. Her expression sent his pulse thrumming through his veins and made his belly clinch tight.

For the past week Chase had the unshakable feeling there was something hanging right there at the tip of her tongue that Linese wanted to say, or perhaps did *not* want to say.

He wasn't certain he possessed the courage to ask or th
strength to hear the answer.

"Most of your letters were accounts of what had hap
pened during the battles and such."

He heard her words over the ringing in his ears that ha
refused to go away. He willed himself to ignore it while b
focused on her sweet face, even though he knew it heralde
a memory.

"Didn't I ever tell you how much I missed you?" Chas
asked in a husky whisper. A faint voice in Chase's hea
warned him he would not like her answer, but he presse
forward.

A melancholy smile curved Linese's lovely mouth. Sad
ness reached out to him from behind the implacable depth
of her blue eyes. "You were never a man to wear your hear
on your sleeve, Chase. It wouldn't have been like you to sa
such personal things in your letters."

Her diplomatic words brought an unexpected flash o
anger at himself. He frowned and folded the paper away i
irritation. Chase picked up another page and began to rea
it. Linese's words layered more questions on top of the ol
ones.

How could he have left her so soon after their wedding
How could he have not told her how very much he misse
her? How could he have sent exact accounts of each victor
and not declared his undying love on each page?

The more he learned about his past self, the more he re
solved to be a better man. Could it be the man he had been
the man he was trying so desperately to resurrect, had no
loved Linese when he married her? Was there even a ghos
of a chance remembering could erase the feeling he had fo
her now?

No. He refused even to consider the notion. Nothing, no
even death itself, could quell the feeling he had for her.

Linese lay in the bed and longed to penetrate the barri
of Chase's mind. He had been so silent, so pensive, while h
read the old letters. Was he remembering some forgotte

moment right now? Were the words he had written on the battlefield pulling him into the past, away from her while she watched helplessly?

Linese wanted to feel his warmth and strength, but the more she saw his face transform into a dark portrait of concentration, the more she was afraid to reach out to him.

The last dry leaves of autumn swirled past the window on a capricious breeze. The crackling fireplace sent a pleasant glow throughout the dining room, but Linese couldn't shake off the chill of worry. Would spring see her and Chase happy parents, or would she find herself mourning the loss of the person who had returned to her from war?

"Well, Doc, how are we?" Linese watched the old physician's expert hands roam over the growing swell of her belly.

"So far, so good." He pulled the sheet and quilt up to Linese's chin and patted her shoulder as if to reassure her. "Don't look so worried. Every week that passes, that little mite is gaining strength. He certainly is growing at a good clip."

She sighed and felt some of the tension leave her body. Linese took some comfort from Doc's words. Each day she watched her body expand and grow. The baby kicked and she flinched unconsciously, not from pain but from surprise. As if by magic, Chase was beside the bed.

"Do you hurt? Do you need anything?" He touched her face with his palm and she felt love spill over her like a warm waterfall.

"The baby kicked." Linese said softly.

Doc grinned and turned to busy himself with putting his battered black medical bag in order for the long buggy ride back to Mainfield. No matter how many times he saw this scene played out, it still gave him a thrill. He glanced back to see Chase's usually grim face transformed into a bright canvas of wonder. He timidly placed his wide hand on Linese's stomach and waited like the expectant father he was.

Suddenly his eyes widened and his eyebrows shot upward. Doc knew Chase had felt his child kick for the first time.

"She's going to be a scrapper," Linese said with a grin.

"Or he," Chase corrected firmly.

Doc frowned. Chase seemed almost obsessed that the child not be a girl. He had seen fathers who wanted sons badly, but this was something different. He would swear Chase Cordell was afraid. It was as if he feared something terrible would happen if the baby were a girl.

"I'll walk you to the door, Doc." Chase deposited a kiss on Linese's forehead before he stood up and stepped into the hallway.

When they were alone outside the dining room door, Chase paused. "How is she, really, and don't sugarcoat the truth." His voice was a tense whisper.

The old physician dragged his hand over his face and sighed. "I just don't know, Chase. Her ankles and face are swollen more each time I see her. She insists she is not having pain, but I don't believe it. The baby is large for her time. I just don't know." Fatigue and worry showed in every crease and deep line in the physician's face.

"She has to be all right. I can't let anything happen to her or the baby," Chase whispered intensely. "I won't."

Linese watched the first snowflakes swirl by her window. The Jones girl bustled through the house, tending to the chores she longed to be doing. While she lay in bed and watched her body change, the world continued to spin and time marched by the dining room window.

News of the war drifted past her doorway on whispered lips and tiptoeing feet. The sun rose and set and the only time she left her bed was to use the chamber pot and to indulge in the occasional—and too infrequent—sponge bath.

She knew Chase had ordered everyone to wear a smile in her presence and only speak to her of good things. It both gladdened and infuriated her. She felt like a potted plant— too delicate and fragile to live outside in the cold, short days of winter. Linese had been wrapped in a loving cocoon that kept her secure from the outside world. Chase seemed intent on keeping her safe, even if he had to use his body as a physical shield in order to do it.

In February, Linese heard Effie whispering to Doc Lukins about General Robert E. Lee becoming commander of all the Confederate troops. A few short weeks later she heard them talking about the Union forces entering South Carolina, but when she asked about the news, Captain Cordell and Chase pasted unreadable expressions on their faces and ignored her questions. Her frustration grew to the point where she finally stopped asking about anything.

When she asked about the mundane day-to-day news of Mainfield, Chase skillfully changed the subject. She had never received an explanation for Rancy Thompson's mysterious visit, and Chase had abruptly stopped talking to her about his missing memory. She felt as if she were wrapped in cotton and yet there was nothing she could do, nothing she would do, for fear of risking their child.

Instead of the hale and hearty woman she had always been, had strived so hard to be when Chase was away, she was becoming soft and useless. Linese had never been of delicate constitution and her present fragility both frightened and angered her. Tears of anger seemed to be a heartbeat away most of the time. And through it all Chase was loving and kind.

The more she wallowed in her self-pity, the more he patted her rounding tummy and reassured her. It made her fears about losing him increase a thousandfold with each kind word and gentle caress.

She waited, like an eager girl, for Chase to walk through the dining room door each day when he returned from his toil at the *Gazette*. His smile lifted the blanket of concern from her shoulders and for a few hours she was completely happy. It was the pattern of her life through the long weeks and months of the winter of 1864 and the first cold days of 1865.

* * *

Chase slumped into the chair beside the big flat-head press. One good thing had come from Linese's confinement to bed. His grandfather had been forced to stay close to Cordellane and see she was safe, while Chase was in Mainfield at the *Gazette*. At least it had prevented the old fox from getting into more trouble.

His gunshot wound had healed and, so far at least, Rancy had not been pressured into making any more visits or accusations involving the Cordell family.

Chase yawned and thought again of his child. Only another month or so and they would be parents. Linese's body had changed so much Chase was in awe. Her bravery made Chase want to weep with pride. Inside he glowed with happiness while their child grew within her.

It was a portent of hope. One that Chase clung to while the war raged on. Both sides of the conflict had been so sure they would beat the other into submission in only a few months, yet Chase read the date on his latest editorial and sighed wearily.

"February 19, 1865." Who would have thought it would go on for so long? Neither side seemed inclined to give up or give in. Rumor had been circulating in Mainfield, about General Sherman sweeping through South Carolina and sending the Southern troops flowing toward Texas. So far the telegraph office continued to receive reports, but Chase wondered how long that would continue.

Many Unionists were nervous about so many Southern troops in Louisiana and had fled north into Kansas. Local politics were calling for order at any cost, for the profit it would bring to the town. A large segment of Mainfield was still perched firmly atop the fence on the issues of slavery and the only hope Chase had of dislodging them was to continue writing his impassioned editorials calling for victory with honor.

Clusters of people with like opinions clung together for safety. Chase knew he was making enemies on both sides of the slavery issue with his blunt editorials, but he also knew that the war had to end soon. And the Union had to be victorious—there was no other possibility he would consider.

Mayor Kerney and his group had been unusually quiet, on the surface at least. He yawned again. He set the editorial aside. Tomorrow Hezikiah would set the type and by the next day another issue of the *Gazette* would hit the streets of Mainfield. He looked at the round-faced clock and was shocked to see it was nearing midnight.

"Linese will be worried sick." He chided himself for not noticing the time. He snuffed out the lamp just before he heard a dull thud outside the door. Chase opened his desk drawer and brought out the Colt Ira had kept for him. He crept to the door and opened it. Warm air rushed outside and swirled in front of him in the frosty night. His breath came in foggy white puffs.

The wan winter moon did little to drive back the darkness. He heard a stifled moan and peered into the shadows between the stable and his temporary newspaper office. A familiar form took shape in the darkness. Chase shoved the Colt into his waistband and bent down.

"Ira?" Chase whispered.

Ira's eyes fluttered open and he drew in a ragged breath. "Chase, thank God you're still here."

Chase lifted Ira's sheepskin-lined coat and saw a dark stain on the side of Ira's shirt just below his ribs.

"Have you been shot?" The hair on the back of Chase's neck bristled. Chase fancied the burn of watching eyes on his back while he grasped Ira's coat. His half-remembered instincts told him to get Ira inside as quickly as possible, to get out of the open where they made easy targets.

"Not shot." Ira's voice was raspy and full of pain. Chase saw Ira's stallion in the corral. Mist rose from the hot lather on the animal's chest, neck and a half circle on his back, where a saddle had recently lain.

Chase hefted Ira's body and took the man's weight upon himself. Casting wary glances at the darkness across the street, he quickly ducked inside and bolted the door behind him. Chase found a match and lit the lamp. A tendril of black smoke wafted up before he turned the wick down. Ira slumped into the chair beside the desk with a strangled sigh.

"How bad are you hurt?" Chase watched Ira shrug off the coat and peel the blood-soaked shirt away from a long cut.

"Those Southern pigstickers do make a nice clean hole, don't they?" Ira joked but Chase was not fooled.

"I'll go for Doc Lukins," Chase said.

"No. There's no time." Ira looked up at him. He was pale as a ghost and there was fine white line around his taut mouth.

"You're bleeding, Ira. We need to see to that wound, it probably needs sewing up."

"This is just a scratch. We can take care of it later. I left someone at the edge of town. You've got to go to him, show him the way."

Dread tightened icy fingers around Chase's throat. The air in his lungs disappeared. "Show the way where?"

"I know I made you a promise, Chase. I wouldn't ask if it weren't so important. If he's caught, he'll hang. He's got information that must get through. Spies don't get good treatment." Ira coughed and made a hissing sound.

Questions swirled through Chase's head like snow in a blizzard. Cloudy images of Ira's face drifted, without form and substance, among shattered memories from long ago. Chase saw a full round moon and a man. The smell of gunpowder wafted around his head. He remembered raising his Colt, remembered the sound of shots. Chase gulped down the feeling the memory brought and turned away from Goten. He stared at the rough walls of the small room in agony. If only he could remember.

"Chase, you've got to do it. So many more will die if you don't do it," Ira reasoned. "Innocent people, women and children. You have to do it . . . take him to the spot." His voice trailed off.

"Ira, I can't help anyone, not even myself. I don't remember the way or what you're talking about. I don't even know which side you're asking me to help."

Chase turned back and found Ira passed out cold. Ira hadn't heard a word he said about his missing memory.

Chapter Eighteen

Chase slowed his horse beside the deepest shadows on the gristmill road and listened. The night had taken on the same eerie silence he remembered falling over his troops, just before the worst cannon fire rained upon them. He heard phantom noises and shook his head, trying to clear the ringing in his ears. The drone distorted normal sound and make him hear things that were not there. He cast anxious glances into the thicket.

His breath caught in his throat. A new catalog of misplaced memory popped into his head without warning. The forgotten parts of the war returned to him in a rush. Another empty chasm had been miraculously filled, but the time before he rode off and left Linese was a black void without substance.

He kicked the horse and moved him down the shapeless path. He knew not what route he took, or for what purpose, but he urged the horse forward. Perhaps it was by instinct, perhaps it was a buried memory so faint he did not realize it was even in his head. Whatever it was, it pulled Chase deeper into the darkness while he struggled to resurrect the most important parts of his missing past.

A low whistle drew his head around and his hand went to the Colt. For a moment, he wasn't sure he had actually heard it. Perhaps it was just another trick of the relentless drone in his head. The horse's ears pitched forward and orked back and forth. He snorted and the puff of cloudy ist turned translucent in the pale winter moonlight. Now hase knew he had indeed heard the sound.

"Cordell? Is that you?" A whisper came from a dark opse of woods beside the road.

"I'm here," Chase answered, not knowing if he was eaking to friend or foe. His pulse quickened and he waited ith his fingers tight around the butt of the Colt.

A man stepped out from the thick foliage. He held the eins of a leggy bay whose head drooped with fatigue. Chase w the man wore no uniform, but then a spy wouldn't, and a had mentioned that a spy would be hung.

Chase sighed in disgust. He still had no idea which side of e conflict would benefit from his reckless actions this ight, but Ira had said innocent people would die. Chase uld not allow himself to care if they were Southern or nionist—he had seen enough death. He had to help the nocent, if he could.

"It's good to see you again, Major. It's been a long time."

The ringing in Chase's ears became a steady hum. He inced against it and squinted at the man's face while a arp pain narrowed behind his eyes. Fog surrounded the an's face, swirled, thickened and obscured Chase's pained ew. When it started to clear, the ringing and pain less-ed. Then it was gone completely, and Chase remembered e man.

"Stewart," Chase said in amazement. He did indeed ow the man. He had met him on the battlefield many nes, had seen him wear the dark blue uniform of the nion before grapeshot had ruined his hip and brought him ck to Mainfield.

"Goten said he would send someone to help. I never eamed it would be you, sir."

A deep sigh escaped Chase's lips. At least he was offer-g aid to the same side he had fought for. But how had Ira come involved with a Union soldier? Chase had seen the

man beaten for being a Southern sympathizer. More con
fusing questions about Ira Goten formed in his mind.

"We need to hurry, Major. I have information that mus
reach President Lincoln immediately."

"Follow me." Chase wheeled his horse with sudden con
fidence. The knowledge of their path seeped into his limb
from some unknown source. He could not remember how
he knew it or when he had traveled this way before, but h
knew exactly which direction meant safety for Stewart.

The next hour passed quickly while Chase successfull
negotiated the twists and turns in the phantom trail. F
nally he reached a clearing, and even though he still did no
know how he knew it, he knew Stewart's contacts would b
waiting there.

A twig snapped under a horse's hoof. Chase saw fou
mounted, blue-uniformed soldiers materialize out of th
frosty mist at the edge of the clearing.

"Sir?" A bearded soldier addressed Stewart.

"Yes." Stewart looked tired but relieved.

"We are your escort, sir."

Stewart turned and reached across the distance to plac
his gloved hand on Chase's forearm. "It has been good t
see you. God keep you." And with that he turned and fo
lowed the soldiers deep into the foliage before Chase coul
utter a word.

Chase waited with his gun cocked until Stewart was safe
out of sight. The night was quiet, yet all the while Chase ha
the uncanny feeling of being watched. He spurred his hor
and urged him over the frozen ground toward Cordella
with a new sense of urgency.

Something was not right. He could feel it.

The first knifelike pain brought Linese awake. She s
bolt upright in bed and searched the room with her eye
The small clock on the mantel was visible in the golden glo
from the fire the Captain had built, but she was alone.

Two o'clock. The room was quiet, the hard rocker where
hase spent most of his nights was empty. She had been
termined to stay awake until he came home, but had
iled.

"Where could he be?" Her muttered whisper was cut off
the next pain. The third brought a scream of agony from
r lips.

Captain Cordell appeared in his nightshirt beside her bed.
ithin minutes the room was filled with bright candlelight.
e was vaguely aware, through the haze of unbelievable
in, that the Jones girl was mopping her brow with a cool
oth while she writhed and twisted in the mound of bed
vers.

"Chase, I want Chase." Another pain shot through her.
e was in labor, hard labor, and Doc's description had not
me close to preparing her for this. She was going to have
e baby and Chase was not with her. Linese prayed it was
t an omen of what the future was going to hold.

Time became suspended for her while everything in her
e became focused inward on the pain ripping through her.
became a cycle. It came, receded only long enough to drag
a ragged breath and brace herself for the next one. She
d no concept of how much time had passed, until Doc
kins strode bleary-eyed and rumpled into the dining
om.

Linese realized that Captain Cordell was standing beside
e fireplace, fully dressed and warming himself. She knew
had ridden for the doctor in Mainfield and had re-
rned. A long time had passed, and still Chase was not be-
le her.

Doc Lukins tried to mask his concern when he saw the
in of blood on the sheet between Linese's thighs. "Lis-
n to me, Linese. You have to work with the pains. If you
ep fighting them, you'll be worn out before the real work
gins."

"Is Chase here yet?" She gulped in air and forced her-
lf to focus on Doc's face.

"Don't worry about Chase. Concentrate on what yo
need to do for yourself and this baby." Doc's reprimand wa
stern. He dared not show Linese how much he feared for he
and the child. Her pregnancy had been difficult and th
child had grown beyond what he considered a safe siz
given Linese's small stature. Still there was no choice for it-
the child must be born.

"Please, I need Chase." A hard band of pain encase
Linese's belly. Her back felt as if she were being cleaved i
two. She twisted the sheets in her fists and stifled a moan. A
if in answer to her prayer, she heard his steady trea
pounding across the veranda.

"Chase." Relief flooded through her. The candles gu
tered momentarily, then flared bright again when the doc
to the dining room opened and promptly shut behind him

"Linese, I'm here." He was beside her, stroking he
forehead, her cheeks. "I'll keep you safe, I promise."

The smell of crisp winter air clung to his coat. His ha
was damp with night frost. She wondered where he ha
been, but the ensuing pain wiped away her questions. H
kept telling her he would keep her safe. She had to believ
it.

Linese had never known such pain. The sun came up, th
candles were extinguished, and still she had no relief. Sh
watched Doc Lukin's face pinch with fatigue while he pa
ted her arm and encouraged her.

Chase sat at the bedside and held her hands. Each time
pain ripped through her, she clamped her jaw together ur
til her teeth grated, and squeezed his hand until her ow
knuckles ached from the effort.

"Soon, honey, soon it will be over."

His words were calm and confident, only his eyes b
trayed his true feelings. Linese looked into the misty gr
depths and knew Chase was terrified, perhaps more terr
fied than even she was herself.

Day marched into night and the candles were lit once again. Chase dripped cool water into Linese's mouth and gently stroked her brow with a damp cloth. Time had no meaning, no beginning and no end. Life for Linese had condensed into a series of cramps and wrenching contractions. Finally a blessed exhaustion washed over her and pulled her toward unconsciousness.

"Linese, you've got to fight." Doc's harsh voice snapped her back from oblivion.

She blinked and focused on his face. Worry was etched into each deep wrinkle. "You can't give up, Linese, you *cannot*." He grabbed her shoulders with his bony fingers until they bit into her skin. Linese looked into his aging eyes and understood. If she did not muster the strength to bring her child forth, they would both die.

"Linese, I love you," Chase whispered softly.

She summoned the last of her willpower and dredged up the last reserve of strength. While her fingers dug into his hand, she pushed and ignored the hot, tearing pain. An odd gush of warmth between her legs accompanied her own muffled shriek.

"That's it, Linese, bear down—hard," Doc instructed.

A wail tore from her throat. One searing pain folded over her, then blessed numbness. Her limbs were leaden but she inhaled her first pain-free breath in long hours.

A lusty cry brought her eyes open and she wearily pulled herself up in order to see her child.

"It's a girl, Linese." Doc held up a small red, mottled infant.

A sudden pain jerked Linese back into the mound of pillows behind her head. Stark terror blanketed her. Something must be terribly wrong because she felt the anguish of unceasing pain tear through her body once again.

"What is it, Doc?" Chase's voice was rife with fear.

"Oh, my Lord." Doc quickly placed the squirming baby in Effie's waiting hands and looked down at Linese. His face was pale mask. "Oh, my dear Lord,"

Terror gripped Chase. The baby was a girl, a daughte
Memory of his father's ashen face drifted before him.

The Cordell curse.

He heard the words in his head. *The men of the Corde
family are doomed to lose the women they love.* If the Co
dell curse were true, then both Linese and the child were
risk. Both were female, both could be taken from him no'

"Push, Linese," Doc commanded.

Doc's confusing words penetrated Chase's gloom. Push
Why was he asking Linese to push? The birth was over. .

Chase looked at Linese. She was red faced and dete
mined. Love bloomed and expanded within his chest for h
She was his life, his love, and if he had to defy heaven a
hell to be with her he would do so.

"I love you, darling." He wasn't sure she heard him ov
the noise of the soft cries of Chase's second baby. He w
dumbstruck. Blinking like a dazed pup, Chase looked fro
the first baby Effie held, to the squalling infant Doc held u
while he tied the cord off with a piece of twine.

"Twins?" Chase felt the witless smile steal across his fac
A hot lump lodged in his tight throat. The babies wail
loudly in unison.

"It's another girl." The old physician sniffed and chuc
led. "My first set of girl twins in all these years. Linese, y
did a fine job."

Chase looked at his wife in wonder. Exhaustion w
written across her face. Strands of sweat-drenched h;
clung to her cheeks, her blue eyes were ringed by hollows
fatigue. She had never looked more beautiful.

"You've given me two more Cordell girls to love."
kissed her eyelids when they fluttered closed.

Effie bathed the babies while Linese's bed was change
She was padded and propped in the rocker while Chase, D
and Captain Cordell set the room to rights. When she w
once again tucked up in her bed, the girls were laid on
ther side of her, clean and sweet smelling.

Each baby had a tight cap of dark curls around her face. Two pairs of tiny cupid's bow lips were pursed in sated sleep. Linese gingerly peeled back the blanket to check each tiny hand and foot in turn.

"They're beautiful," Chase said. "Just like their mother."

"Prettiest girls I've ever seen," Captain Cordell agreed from his position by the fireplace. Linese saw his eyes were misty. She wondered if he realized they were his great-granddaughters, or if the gentle old soul was simply happy to see new life on Cordellane. Doc rubbed his eyes and nodded in agreement.

"Yes, they are fine-looking baby girls. And now I know why Linese was so big. One baby would've been about right, but two—" The old physician yawned and rubbed his eyes with the heel of his hand. "I better be getting back. The Lawrence boy had the croup, I need to check on him on my way home."

"Thank you, Doc," Linese said.

"Just take good care of them. I'll be wanting to show off my handiwork when you're back on your feet."

"I'll walk you out." Chase stood up but before he and Doc took another step, the sound of anxious knocking drew every eye to the front door. The last time an unexpected visitor had shown up at Cordellane, Sheriff Thompson had been looking for evidence that Chase had been shot.

"I'll see who it is. Stay with Linese," Chase whispered so only Captain Cordell could hear.

"Chase, what is wrong?" Linese asked from her bed.

He turned to drink in the sight of her, holding his daughters in the soft glow of fire and candlelight, and smiled. "Nothing to worry about honey. You rest."

Chase left the room and shut the dining room door securely behind him. He opened the front door and found Hezikiah staring at him.

"Is it the *Gazette?*" Chase braced himself for bad news.

Hezikiah was whiter than a sheet and his hands wer
trembling. Chase poured him a whiskey and the ma:
knocked it back.

"What's happened?" Chase imagined a hundred possi
ble calamities. He envisioned Mayor Kerney and his nefar
ious associates, then he wondered if Ira Goten's recent knif
wound had been discovered, or perhaps Stewart had bee
caught before he delivered his news. Problems swirle
through his head.

Hezikiah swallowed hard and his Adam's apple bobbed
"Southern troops are pouring into Ferrin County. I just g
word from the telegraph office. Mainfield is bound to b
overrun with Southern troops leaving Louisiana."

A few days later, Chase and Hezikiah sat in the make
shift *Gazette* office talking.

"It's ironic, isn't it, Chase?" Hezikiah rubbed his han
over the silent, cold printing press. Mainfield had been o
cupied by Southern troops since the girls were born, but s
far the occupation had been peaceful. "After all you did t
keep the news going . . ."

Chase looked at the silent press and shrugged. "Ther
doesn't seem to be much point now anyway. It's only
matter of time until the South falls. They are short on ev
erything, and are fighting on pride and determinatio
alone." He raked his fingers through his hair and sighe
heavily. "I just want it to end. I'm tired of war, Hezikiah.
want to live quietly and watch my daughters grow. I n
longer have any desire to be a hero and I have little faith le
in causes, no matter how worthy."

Hezikiah smiled and nodded. "Can't say I blame yo
Those girls are cute as buttons. Have you named them yet?

Chase grinned with pride. "Yes. Linese picked the name
Sarah and Marjorie." A rush of affection rolled throug
him at the thought of his wife and babies. He itched to g
home and be with them, and now that the *Gazette* was r

longer being printed, there was nothing to keep him from Cordellane.

The dark shadow of worry about the secrets of his past still hung over him, but day by day he managed to push it further to the back of his mind, while he saw health returning to Linese and his baby girls growing fat. Nothing horrible had happened and Chase had finally begun to believe there was a future for them all now that he had his daughters safe and sound.

A knock on the door brought the men's heads up. The potbellied stove hissed and popped when Hezikiah opened the door. Chase looked up to see two Confederate soldiers standing in the doorway.

"Yes?" Hezikiah asked.

"Is Major Chase Cordell here?" One of the men asked Hezikiah.

"I'm Chase Cordell." Chase stood up and stepped forward. "What do you want?"

"I've come to place you under arrest."

"Arrest? For what?" Chase snorted.

"For the murder of Alfred Homstock."

Chase's belly clinched tight. The man's name seemed vaguely familiar, but he could not put a face to it. He looked beyond the guards to see if Rancy Thompson was with him, and saw nobody but the two soldiers. "By whose authority am I being arrested?"

"I am not at liberty to say anything more about it, sir. You'll have to speak to my commanding officer." The hand around Enfield rifle twitched nervously. "If you will come with us—now."

Chase understood the implied threat. If he was so foolish to attempt to resist the soldiers it could be fatal. "Hezikiah, get word to Cordellane. Talk to my grandfather before you let Linese know what has happened." Chase felt the bite of iron against his wrists when they clamped the manacles shut.

One soldier jerked the chain and nudged Chase in the back with the barrel of his rifle.

"Remember, Hezikiah, speak to my grandfather."

Mainfield was blanketed in an eerie unnatural silence. The daily cacophony of horses' hooves and jingling harnesses was mysteriously gone. Even the spring air of 1865 felt charged with some portent of pending doom. Chase told himself he was being silly, that this March day was no different than any other, except for the fact he was locked in jail.

He rose from the narrow cot and tried to shake off his gloomy thoughts. It was probably all some silly mistake. In fact, Kerney was probably behind the whole stupid plan— one last act of malicious revenge. Whether he liked it or not, whether it was good for business or not, Chase knew the war was going to have to end soon. There simply wasn't enough blood left to keep it going, regardless of what that would do to the profit margin of Mainfield.

Chase relaxed a bit. He didn't even know anyone named Homstock, at least not that he recalled. He tilted his head in a vain attempt to make the ringing go away while he listened to footsteps in the outer office then the heavy thud of a door being shut. Rancy Thompson's voice floated to him on the weird hush that had claimed Mainfield. Chase strained to hear what was being said. The words were spoken in a heavily spiced Southern drawl and the voice was not known to him. Rancy was discussing, no, he was arguing with somebody.

"I am still sheriff." Rancy's voice grew louder. "Is this a military matter, or a civil one, Colonel?"

Chase found himself holding his breath to hear every word.

"I suppose it's a bit of both. The man killed was not a soldier, but he was on business for the Confederacy when he was murdered," the Southern voice explained.

"The least you can do is let Major Cordell have visitors," Rancy said, "no matter how damning the evidence against him is."

"At this time, I can find no incentive to do so, sir. As far as I am concerned, Major Chase Cordell will stay right where he is, without visitors, until a jury is selected and we hold his trial. It is my hope we can proceed with a speedy execution shortly afterward."

Trial. Execution. The words echoed through Chase's head. He sagged down on the hard, narrow cot. Was he in jail because of something Kerney had finally hatched, or had he committed a crime that he still did not remember? He didn't know, and not knowing made his frustration all the greater.

He rubbed his throbbing temples with his fingertips. What was going to become of Linese and his daughters? How would she get along with two newborn babies? He longed to see her, just to look into her clear blue eyes and tell her how much he loved her.

"Selfish bastard," he hissed aloud. How could he put Linese through the experience of coming to the harsh jail to see him?

Later that afternoon Chase heard his grandfather's distinctive baritone drift through the outer office. He held his breath, straining to listen, but all he heard was the sound of retreating footsteps and he knew his grandfather had been turned away. He flopped down on his cot and tried to sleep, anything to numb the terrible ache in his head, anything to shut out the horrible quiet that blanketed Mainfield. When he closed his eyes, Linese's face floated before him and he managed to find peace in slumber.

Chase woke with his heart beating like a piston inside his chest. He must have slept for hours, he realized, when he saw the slender shadows of dusk slanting through the narrow slit that served as a ventilation shaft outside of his cell.

He remained still and listened to the baritone rumble of voices from outside, knowing those voices had woken him.

"I don't care if the Confederacy has declared martial law in Mainfield. This is unconscionable." Hezikiah Hershner's words rang with journalistic indignation. "There's a constitution in this country, or have you secessionists written your own?"

"Be careful, Hezikiah," Rancy's deep voice warned.

"Good advice, sir," a voice agreed. "Be careful what treasonist remarks you make or you might find yourself joining Major Cordell. We could've done something a trifle more harsh with you for having been involved with Major Cordell." It was the same drawling voice Chase had heard earlier.

Chase sat up and dragged his hand over his face. He did not want Hezikiah to come to any harm because of him. Linese would need him to help her—just in case. He swallowed hard and cursed himself.

Was he going to accept this so easily? Was he simply going to resign himself to someone slipping a rope over his neck without fighting for his life? There had to be something he could do.

Several hours later, a voice snapped Chase from his trance of concentration.

"And just who are you, ma'am?" Chase recognized the voice of the burly Confederate officer who had chained him to the floor upon his arrival.

"I am Mrs. Chase Cordell. I've come to see my husband." Linese's voice was steady and calm.

A million emotions ripped through his mind. Had something happened to his daughters? His grandfather? Fear nipped at his heart while his pulse quickened with the desire to see his lovely wife's face. Chase was brought up short by a rude bark of laughter.

"Sorry, ma'am, I don't think we'll be letting anybody in to see the prisoner. Now get yourself on home before you get hurt."

Chase could not discern whether the words were a warning made from true concern, or a threat, but he felt fury sweep through him with the intensity of a wildfire.

"But I must speak to him, see him. It is a family matter of great importance."

Chase heard the desperation in her sweet voice and died a little inside. Dear God, something *had* happened. He sagged onto his cot in abject misery.

It was useless for Linese to try to bargain with the man. They would not let her in, any more than they let in his grandfather or Hezikiah. Worry about Linese and how she would endure such grief snaked through his heart.

The vow he had made to keep her and the twins safe came back to haunt him. He hadn't protected them any more than he could protect Linese from the stark hazard of the future as a widow.

"Perhaps this will change your mind about letting me see him," Linese said softly.

"Well, now, why didn't you get right to the point before, ma'am? I think I can look the other way for a few minutes."

Chase moved to the door and clenched the cold iron bars with his fists. What on earth had she given him to change his mind?

He didn't care. Whatever it was, it was worth it to be able to look at her, to give her comfort, to say he loved her.

The soft, even tread of her feet made him tingle with anticipation. His heart leapt into his throat. The heavy oak door swung open and there she was in the dim hallway.

"Linese."

She was thin and pale. There were circles under her eyes. His heart broke for her. "You shouldn't have come, you're still too weak," he said, but his heart knew he had never been happier to see anyone in his life.

"I had to see you, Chase." She waited until the Confederate officer shut the door behind her. When she heard the creak of the chair in the outer office, when she was sure he had resettled his weight and would not be returning, she turned back to Chase.

"Has something happened?"

She smiled and her face brightened a bit. "No, oh, I never meant for you to think so. We're all fine, just fine, and safe at Cordellane. The Captain and a friend are with the twins." She did not tell Chase the friend was Melissa.

"It isn't safe for you to be out with infantrymen and cavalry roaming the streets." His instinct to protect her suddenly shut out his need to be with her.

"I had to come. I have some information, and it may help."

"What?" A stubborn flame of hope flared inside his chest. He reached out and stroke the side of Linese's face with his fingertips. He longed to hold her.

"The man, Alfred Homstock, was a spy for the South. He was about to expose the route of the Underground Railroad. He had been sent to kill people helping along this part of the route, when he was murdered. I guess it doesn't matter now, with Mainfield occupied, but there is a rumor circulating that the Railroad route cuts across Cordellane property." She frowned and shook her head as if she could banish the story. "I don't see how that can be true. Surely we would've known about it."

"How did you learn this?" Chase caressed her delicate fingers through the narrow bars.

"Hezikiah. I didn't ask how he found out. I didn't care. As soon as he told me, I came here to you. He was leaving Mainfield, going to find the Northern troops that he said are getting closer every day."

She looked at him with blue eyes that held a thousand lifetimes of fear and worry. It cut straight through his soul.

"Does it help? Do you remember anything?" she prodded.

Chase swallowed hard. "Not really." He had struggled, tried harder than ever before, but the only memory he had salvaged was a strange recollection that had no real substance. It wasn't enough to allow Linese to pin her hopes on.

"Chase, you must try." She felt a pang of regret and guilt. Linese cursed herself for ever hoping that Chase would not regain his memory. She hated herself for every selfish minute she had spent worrying about losing him to his past. If he remembered, at least he would be alive. That would be enough, no matter what else happened.

Chase yearned to wipe some of the despair from her eyes. He had to give her hope, no matter how flimsy. "I'm not sure, but I think whatever happened had something to do with Ira Goten." Chase could not risk telling her the dead man might also have been involved with his grandfather's mysterious activities, or the truth about the Captain's madness. His grandfather was in more danger than ever, with the South occupying Mainfield. Chase could not utter a sound that could place the old man in peril.

"I'll go for Ira at once." Linese tried to remove her fingers from Chase's loving grasp. "I'm sure he would help us."

"No, honey, you can't." Chase lowered his voice to a whisper, to be sure the guard in the outer office could not overhear.

"But, Chase, why?" She blinked back tears.

He wanted to hold her in his arms and tell her it would be all right. "I believe he is involved with things that could put him in danger. With the war still going on, I can't jeopardize Ira or anyone else on vague half-recollections."

Linese went pale. "Oh, Chase. Tell me you're not saying what I think you are."

"Linese, I can't put another man's neck in a noose to save myself. I couldn't live with that. And I'm not even sure—"

She stared at him in mute horror. He could see the struggle going on inside her. One tear threatened to slide over her bottom lid, but she blinked furiously and forced herself to breathe slowly in an obvious attempt to master her emotions.

"I will not cry," she said fiercely from between clenched teeth.

"That's my girl. Now, go on home and kiss my babies for me." Chase brushed his lips against her knuckles. "Keep them and yourself safe, and don't give up hope."

"Dear God, Chase, there has to be something. You can't just—" Her gaze ripped into him. "I don't think I could bear it."

"Unless I remember, there is no way I can defend myself against the charge. And there is one other possibility, Linese, as much as it pains me to consider it." He stared hard at her. "Maybe I did what they say. Maybe I murdered that man."

"I don't believe it, Chase." Linese stared into his flinty gray eyes without batting an eyelash. Neither the old Chase Cordell nor the new one could commit cold-blooded murder. "No matter what anybody says, I *know* you are innocent. Whether you believe it or not."

He shook his head in wonder at her unshakable faith in him. "You are a treasure, my darling. Never forget how very much I love you." He leaned close to kiss her when a shot rang out and echoed through the silence outside. He flinched involuntarily when, a heartbeat later, the sound of far-off cannon fire blasted his ears.

Chase had been in enough battles to know there would be no peace once the Union started shelling the town.

"Chase, what is going on?"

"Linese, you must get back to Cordellane right away before the Union troops get in position. Soon Mainfield will be under siege."

The sound hammered at Chase until he felt his insides roil and twist in pain. He put his hands over his ears, but still the sound of war bludgeoned his senses. It mixed with the ringing in his ears and intensified a thousandfold. He curled up on his cot and covered his head with the thin woolen blanket and lumpy pillow, but still he heard it.

Each shot, each blast, sent ribbons of fire swirling from his skull. His fevered blood throbbed through his veins. It hurt to take a breath. His eyes watered while the ringing in his ears grew louder. Waves of nausea swept over him and wrenched his gut. Bile rose in his throat while he fought for control of his shredding sanity.

Just when he was about to shriek for the Confederates to come and put a bullet into his head, to spare him this unbearable agony, it stopped.

He lifted his hands from his ears and listened. The barrage of cannon and shot outside continued without pause, but the maelstrom inside Chase's head had simply ceased. The ringing in his ears was gone, the pain was gone. The discordant sound in his head had completely vanished.

And when it did, he remembered. He remembered. . . .

Chapter Nineteen

Mainfield, Texas
May 30, 1862

Chase stood near the press and read the latest report on th
war. There never seemed to be a shortage of men to die, o
an end to the conflict. More and more lately, he had bee
observing the battles with a kind of inner discontent.

He knew what it was—he just didn't want to face it.

Chase had spent a big chunk of his life trying to live dow
or overcome his grandfather's mental defect. Now that
had reached youthful manhood, he realized how stupid
had been. He regretted the years he had wasted worryin
about what other people thought. He wanted to do som
thing, something that counted. Something that had not
ing to do with proving himself to the citizens of Mainfiel
but something that really mattered.

He had made up his mind to join the Union army and
what he could to shorten the bloody conflict. Chase laid t
paper aside, wrote a note for Hezikiah and locked the do
to the *Gazette* behind him.

He strode to Ira Goten's livery to get his horse while
made plans in his head. He was sure Hezikiah would loo
out for his grandfather, if he asked. There was really not
ing to stop him from joining the fighting. There was n

ody to mourn him if he died—his grandfather would never
ven realize he was gone. Chase swung into the saddle and
new this was what he should have done months ago.

Chase blinked his eyes and the stark images of his past
aded, but they were still lodged firmly in his memory. He
ouched his forehead and discovered it was covered with a
heen of clammy sweat. He did remember—all of it—every
ninute detail of his past.

The recollection he had just relived was so clear, the
nemory could have happened to him yesterday instead of
wo years ago. It was the world he had known, seen, touched
nd walked through, before war had forever altered his
erceptions of the world and himself. He sat down on his cot
nd allowed his mind to go back to the day in May, 1862, the
lay Alfred Homstock died....

The big bay gelding picked his own path down the road.
Chase looked up from his thoughts of joining the Northern
rmy and found himself beside the old gristmill with the sun
lready setting behind him. He had been making plans to
urn the operation of the *Gazette* over to Hezikiah and lo-
ate the nearest Union troops. The gelding stopped short
nd worked his ears back and forth.

"What is it, boy, a squirrel?" Chase rubbed the side of
he gelding's neck to soothe him. Then he heard the steady
rone of voices. He slid out of the saddle and tied the reins
o a scrub oak. Stealthily, ever aware of the danger of ma-
auders and deserters, he crept forward through the thicket
nd peered through the dense foliage. Chase saw them and
ealized he knew each man by face and name.

It sent a shiver of shock through him when they pulled
vhite flour sacks out of their saddlebags. Ragged holes had
een cut for their eyes. They looked for all the world like a
hild's interpretation of a haunt.

At first Chase intended to make himself known, but seeing them in disguise changed his mind. He kept hidden and listened to their conversation.

Mayor Kerney pulled a long, narrow blade from his boot and used the tip to scratch in the dirt at his feet. Chase realized he was making a map. The other men leaned over and murmured their understanding. When they were finished Kerney scraped his boot over the spot and they moved of single file, and mounted their horses. Then they turned and headed east toward the Louisiana border, intent on a raid Chase had heard carefully described....

The burly Confederate soldier flung open the jail door Chase snapped his head up, suddenly wrenched from his newly remembered past. He felt disoriented, unaccustomed to knowing he had no void left in his mind. He blinked and focused on the man and pulled himself back to the present It was silent outside, but Chase knew from sad experience it was a temporary lull.

The soldier was carrying a small metal bowl in one hand and a cup in the other. The smell of food made his empty belly growl. He wasn't sure how much time had passed while he sat in the cell and summoned his old memories, but he was very hungry.

"Come get it, if you want it," the soldier drawled.

Chase rose to his feet and reached between the bars for the food. For the moment he was content to postpone his search into the past, at least until his hunger was sated. He had just managed to maneuver the cup and bowl through the narrow bars, when the door opened again. An imposing Confederate officer with long side-whiskers appeared. The soldier who had delivered Chase's meal snapped to attention and saluted sharply.

"At ease." The Confederate colonel waved his hand carelessly at the soldier. Braided gold decorated both shoulders and he wore an elaborate saber on his hip. He viewed Chase with cold, narrowed eyes.

"So this is Major Chase Cordell," he sneered. "I expected more."

Chase felt a wave of something more than politics between them. The man was hostile in a way that made it seem almost personal.

"You have the advantage of me, sir." Chase eased back down onto his cot. He balanced the bowl on one knee and took a sip of the weak, hot coffee. The liquid slid a long way down before it hit the bottom of his belly.

"I am Colonel Montgomery Homstock." The man dipped his head, never taking his eyes off Chase's face.

Homstock. The same name as the murdered man. A chill of dread snaked its way up Chase's back.

"I won't keep you from your supper, Major Cordell, but I did want to get a look at you." He stepped near the bars and trained his wintry gaze on Chase's face.

"I hope I'm not a disappointment."

The colonel's lips curled into a smile that never touched his eyes. "I hope you can maintain that bravado when your trial begins."

"Aren't those Union guns I heard outside of Mainfield?" Chase goaded with a lift of his brows. "Are you so sure you have the time to bother with the formality of a trial? Why not just shoot me now and drop the pretense of justice?"

The smile slipped for a moment, but the colonel recovered quickly. "The Northern troops won't be able to help you, Major. I am presently making arrangements with the local officials to hold your trial immediately. No matter how the war ends, I'll see you hang. Sleep well, Major, if you can."

With that said, Colonel Homstock turned on his boot heel and left. Chase listened to the steady barrage of cannon shot and knew he would not be able to rest, but he didn't mind. He was determined to relive his past and he hoped, if he scrutinized each memory he would find the answers he needed to defend himself. With a new feeling of purpose, he allowed his thoughts to return to 1862....

After Mayor Kerney and the other hooded men rode off, Chase let the gelding meander through the tall grass and graze at his leisure. He pondered the things he had heard and wondered how he had lived around the men and never discerned their activities. It was amazing to him. The merchants he saw had no political loyalties. They were raiding with one purpose in mind, and that purpose was to bring back loot—blood money—to line their own pockets.

He stopped and rested against the trunk of an ancient oak while he watched the summer moon rise high above the treetops. It seemed grotesque to think of men profiting from the conflict of ideals between the North and the South.

A branch snapped nearby. Chase pulled the Colt from his waistband and peered into the darkness. He had no intention of having his mount stolen by a wandering horseless deserter, whichever side he had been on.

"Identify yourself," Chase demanded. The crunching footsteps abruptly halted. The man was definitely walking, and Chase tightened his grip on his horse's reins.

"Chase? Is that you?" Ira Goten appeared from within a tangled mass of vines and branches. The moonlight gave his lean face a ghoulish appearance.

After a moment of surprise, Chase stuck his gun back in his pants. "Ira, what are you doing out here on foot?"

Ira's eyes flicked away. His Adam's apple bobbed while he swallowed hard. Whatever Ira was about to tell Chase, it was bound to be a lie.

"I, uh, got throwed."

The hair on Chase's neck stood on end. The night became charged with something—danger, deceit, or both. Chase wasn't sure which. Everyone who lived within a hundred miles of Mainfield knew that Ira had been thrown only once in his life. At the time he had been too young to shave

nd drunk as a skunk on elderberry wine. He had not been
rown tonight, and Chase knew it.

"Do you need a ride into town?" Chase nodded at his big
ay, indicating they could ride double, if need be. "Or do
ou want to go to Cordellane? I'll loan you a horse." He
ecided to play along with the deception.

"Naw, but I'd be obliged if you'd walk a ways with me,
ack toward town." Ira shot a glance down the dark trail
oward Cordellane.

No man walked if he could ride, even double, and Chase
as almost sure Ira had been going in the opposite direc-
on, *toward Cordellane,* not to Mainfield as he now indi-
ated was his destination. Chase kept his suspicions to
imself and allowed Ira to set the pace along the path.

"What are you doing out here, Chase?"

The question was asked mildly enough, but Chase sensed
strange tension in Ira. The electric zing of mistrust and
uspicion arced between them.

"I was just riding," Chase said.

"Oh." Ira was silent for a moment but Chase could al-
ost hear the cogs inside his head spinning, digesting the
formation, weighing the words for truth or falsehood.
Come out here often, do you, Chase?"

With each passing minute, Chase felt what the coon must
eel when being trailed by a pack of hounds. Ira Goten was
eeling Chase out, probing him. But why?

"I've always liked the old gristmill road. You can see all
inds of interesting things along the river, particularly in the
oonlight." Chase decided to toss a little bait out himself
nd see what he could snag with it.

Ira's head snapped around. For a moment Chase thought
e was going to say something, then his teeth flashed in the
ale moonlight and he stopped walking.

"How about a drink, Chase?" Ira reached into his boot
op and pulled out a bottle. Before he had his pants tucked
ack in, Chase saw the gleam of a wicked-looking blade
oncealed inside the boot. Ira stood up and uncorked the

whiskey and took a long pull, then he gave it to Chase. Even while he tipped the bottle to his lips, he watched Ira.

"Go ahead, have another," Ira coaxed.

Chase made a big show of wiping his shirtsleeve across his mouth after he barely touched the liquor to his lips. "If I didn't know better, Ira, I'd swear you were trying to get me drunk."

Ira looked as if he had been walloped on the side of the head.

"What a thing to say, Chase. I was just being neighborly." He took back the bottle and recorked it. Then he slipped it back inside his boot before he resumed walking toward Mainfield.

When they reached a small, sheltered clearing, Ira began to cast wary glances at the surrounding trees. It set Chase's teeth on edge and he found himself squinting at the long shadows. He saw the man first, clinging to the shadows like a weasel, his body a darker shade of gray in the night. Chase froze in his tracks and his hand went instinctively to the butt of the Colt. Ira followed his line of vision. Chase sensed the very moment Ira saw the man concealed in the branches.

"Show yourself." Ira bent and deftly slid the knife from his boot.

A form began to move within the trees. Chase drew the gun from his waistband. When the man emerged, his hands were held up and he had no weapon they could see.

"Take it easy, gentlemen." The stranger's words were tinged with a soft Southern slur. Chase thought he might be a deserter, until he got a better look at his clothes. They were of good cut and quality and the fellow wore them in a way that made Chase doubt he'd ever taken an order in his life.

"Who are you?" Chase pointed the gun at the level of the man's belly.

"Since you are holding the gun, I guess I will have to oblige you by answering." An assessing gaze flicked from Chase to Ira and back again. "I am Alfred Homstock. De

ou intend to shoot me now, or may I know your names
rst?"

"Cordell," Chase said while he pondered the unlikely
tuation. It was too much of a coincidence, finding two
en afoot in the woods at night. "What's your business
ere?"

"I've come to meet someone." The man looked Chase
traight in the face and smiled warmly. He slowly put his
rms down at his sides and relaxed.

"Meet somebody? Who?" Chase continued to hold the
un steady.

"You, Mr. Cordell," the man said with complete convic-
on.

"Careful, Chase." Ira's warning whisper came from be-
ide him.

Obviously the man was lying through his teeth. Chase was
ot meeting anybody, certainly not in the sheltered clear-
ng.

"What do you mean you were supposed to meet me?"
lis grip on the Colt tightened.

"I am the man your contact told you about." Hom-
tock's fingers went to his waist, where he pulled aside his
oat and lifted the bottom edge of his brocade vest. He be-
an to unfasten a money belt. "I have gold, lots of gold. It
an be yours. Is this one of the men who work the route?"
Iomstock glanced at Ira with an eager gleam in his eyes.

Chase didn't know anything about gold, or routes. Chase
lamped his jaws shut while his mind went to his grandfa-
her. Was it possible the craziness had affected his grand-
ather so much that he had become embroiled in some
cheme involving gold?

Homstock held the money belt with his right hand and
pened it up with the other. Pale moonlight glinted on gold
oins.

"See, I have brought more than enough. Now will you
how me the way to the Underground Railroad?"

It happened so fast, it was a blur of sound and sight. Ira's arm shot out and a *zing* sliced the night air. There was a wooden *thunk* that echoed when Ira's knife embedded itself in the trunk of a tree.

"Get down, Chase!" Ira called out.

An instant later a sharp crack and a blue spark sent a ribbon of fire across the top of Chase's gun hand. He grated his teeth against the pain and tried to maintain his weakening grip on the Colt. The shot had come from a double-shot derringer concealed in the money belt Homstock still held in one hand. Ira pounced on the man and gold coins rained out of the belt when Homstock hit the ground. The two men struggled for control of the derringer.

Chase looked at his hand. The bullet had done little damage, thank God, even though he was bleeding. He focused on the men grunting and rolling on the ground, but he couldn't risk a shot in the dark.

Suddenly another shot illuminated the pair on the ground. Both men stilled for a moment, then Homstock staggered to his feet and scooped up the money belt. Several more coins fell from it before he draped it over one arm.

"Damn you, Cordell, how did you find out it was a trap?" His labored breathing was harsh. Chase could see a dark stain spreading on Homstock's shoulder where he had been shot with his own gun. "How did you know I had been sent to kill you?"

"He didn't. An informant told me you would be coming to kill the men you found along the route at each meeting place," Ira said. "I didn't know until now it was Cordell you were meeting," Ira said.

Chase felt his grip on the Colt slipping. None of what Ira and Homstock were saying made any sense to him.

"It doesn't matter," Homstock declared with a sneer. "By now my superiors know the names of everyone involved. It won't be long until they send enough men to destroy you all for good."

"No, they won't. They never got the information. The man you sent back won't be reporting anything. At least not in this life." Ira's voice was deadly. Chase was surprised to see he was pointing the derringer at Homstock. "I found him first."

Homstock roared and swung the money belt. The heavy leather pouch full of gold caught Chase across the side of the head. Sparks of light burst behind his eyes and he lost his shaky grip on the Colt.

"You spying Confederate son of—" Ira pulled the trigger on the derringer he had taken from Homstock, but it clicked harmlessly on empty chambers.

Chase sagged to his knees, stunned by the blow from the money belt, while the sound of his stolen horse's hooves echoed through the night.

Chapter Twenty

The returning memory continued to flow like an untamed river....

"Chase, are you all right?" Ira helped him to his feet.

"I'll be fine." Chase was still stunned, but he angrily jerked his arm out of Ira's hand and tried to blink back the stars dancing in his head. "What the devil is going on?"

Ira looked at him speculatively for a moment. "You really don't know, do you? I thought it was an act, but you weren't meeting Homstock here in the usual place, were you?"

"Of course I wasn't meeting Homstock, and I don't know anything about this place. What the hell was he talking about?" Chase picked up his Colt with his good hand and stuck it inside his waistband.

"You really were just riding through these woods." It was more a statement than a question. Ira bent down and scooped up the fallen gold coins from the loamy earth. He shoved them deep into his trouser pockets before he yanked his knife from the tree trunk where he had embedded it in his attempt to kill Homstock.

"Yes, I was." Chase's voice resonated with suppressed anger. "What were you doing? That story about getting thrown and having to walk was a damned lie and I know it."

"I was sent here to save the life of whoever Homstock met. Then I was supposed to kill Homstock, quietly. He's a

Confederate spy, an assassin. If Homstock was telling us the truth, then I was supposed to save a man named Cordell. I thought it was you, but now I realize it wasn't. Here in this clearing, information—and people—are met by Union troops or private escort."

Chase cursed under his breath. "I don't know anything of what you are talking about."

"I'm talking about the Underground Railroad. And assuming that Homstock had no reason to lie, he was meeting a man named Cordell. Since there is only one other Cordell, besides you, then I guess we both know who he was supposed to meet."

Chase swallowed hard. He followed Ira's line of thinking even though logic forced him to resist the thought. "You don't seriously believe my grandfather is capable of such deceit."

"I don't know *what* to think, but that's not important. Homstock is a Southern spy and he is surely on his way to report to his superiors. Once he reaches them, every Southern sympathizer in Texas will be hunting for anyone named Cordell, starting with you and your grandfather."

The truth of Ira's words settled on Chase. He glared at Ira. Anger and concern over his grandfather dissolved the small measure of patience he had left. "I take it you *are* involved with the Railroad?"

"Yes," Ira admitted reluctantly.

"Do you know who the others are, the ones Homstock was sent to kill, I mean?"

Ira shook his head. "No. We try not to know in case one of us is discovered. It's a whole lot easier to keep a secret if only one or two people know it in the first place. All these years I've been working, I never knew your grandfather was involved. Cagey old fox, he had me fooled."

Chase ignored the comment and focused on the problem at hand. "Do you know where Homstock was headed? Which road he would take?"

"Since he learned the last spy was killed, I'm sure he's heading back to deliver this information firsthand. I've heard talk about Ferrin County. Strong Southern ties—rumors. He might've gone that way. Or maybe just straight east into Louisiana and the closest Southern army he can find."

Chase looked up at the moonlit sky and cursed under his breath. Then he started walking.

"Where are you going?" Ira fell into step beside Chase.

"To Cordellane for another horse. I've got to stop Homstock before he manages to talk."

Ira kept pace beside Chase. "Will you loan me a horse and a gun? I was supposed to have stopped the spy before he got this far." Ira's voice was thick with guilt and regret.

Now Chase understood why Ira had been alone in the woods—he was an executioner waiting for his victim.

Ira stuffed the Colt Chase loaned him into his belt before he leapt into the saddle. The rangy black mare snorted and pawed, anxious to be off. She was Captain Cordell's favorite mount, fast and surefooted as a goat. Chase wondered where the old man was. He uttered a silent prayer that he was someplace safe, while his mind struggled to deny that his grandfather was not crazy.

The moon was high overhead and brightly illuminated the woods around Cordellane when Chase mounted a fresh horse. If Homstock left any sign of a trail at all, they should be able to find it in the glow of moonlight.

"I'll go south first, just in case he doubled back on us," Ira told Chase.

"Fine. I'm heading straight to Ferrin County." Chase gathered the reins of the deep-chested roan stallion in his uninjured left hand.

"Chase, if anybody ever asks you about tonight, we never saw each other. You may not have been involved before, but now you are. Lives depend on your silence. Agreed?"

"Agreed. I won't speak of this night. You can trust me to keep your secret, Ira, to the grave if necessary. But I have to ask something of you, as well."

"Go ahead."

"If you are right about my grandfather—and I'm not saying you are—you must promise to keep the secret. If he has gone to all this trouble..." His words trailed off.

"I understand," Ira said.

The words of the two-year-old vow hung in his mind while Chase paced on the end of his chain inside the tiny cell. He felt like a tethered animal. Instead of his memory setting him free, it had shackled him with bonds stronger than mere iron. His own honor and vow of silence held him prisoner now. He forced himself to remember the rest of what happened....

The big roan settled into a steady, rocking gallop. Chase had not taken the time to bandage his hand, but he had stuck a bottle of whiskey inside his saddlebag. He swiveled around and reached for it without allowing the stud to slacken his pace.

Chase took a long drink and then poured some whiskey over his hand. A goodly portion ended up on his shirt, coat and the reins he held, but some of the liquid reached the wound. It burned like being scorched by live embers, but Chase did not want to risk infection from a dirty wound.

By moonlight, Chase followed the straightest path to Ferrin County. Fortunately for Chase, the short road was also the most traveled and he hoped that Homstock would take the longer but more sheltered trail. It would give him badly needed time. He came upon an itinerant peddler who had built his meager camp beside the road. With the glow of the camp fire lighting his face, the old man told Chase someone sounding like Homstock had asked directions to the Presbyterian church in Ferrin County not more than an hour earlier. Chase plunged cross country, driving the horse harder upon hearing he was definitely on the right trail. He could reach Ferrin County ahead of Homstock. While he rode, he concentrated on everything he had learned this night.

He decided, with no small dose of irony, that he had never really fathomed the character of any of Mainfield's men—most particularly his grandfather. Even though he found it nearly impossible to believe, he acknowledged the bitter truth.

Captain Aloyisius Cordell was shrewd, calculating, and had been playing a deadly game of deception in order to help free oppressed people and runaway slaves, but he was not crazy.

The man Chase had been shamed by, the man whose blood he sought to repudiate by proving himself to be the best at everything he attempted, was a crafty old fox.

A burst of pride ignited in Chase's chest and burned away his initial anger. Aloyisius Cordell had fooled them all. Chase would have liked to stay angry for all the years he lived under the stigma of his grandfather's madness, but instead he envied him. The ex-ranger was long on nerve and sharp as a knife blade, Chase realized with a sigh. Now he had an opportunity to be half the man his grandfather was, and he prayed he would measure up.

The dark-shadowed woods blurred by with each lunge of the long-legged horse. Chase was hopeful he would over-take Homstock before he reached his destination. Trying to ignore the ache in his hand, Chase urged the big stallion to give him more speed. He had never killed in cold blood, but the risk to his grandfather, Ira and countless others gave him no options, so he rode hard with murder in his heart.

Chase heard the music first. He stopped the horse and listened. The sound of hands clapping in unison was inter-rupted by an occasional gleeful whoop. Chase moved more cautiously toward the circle of light and found himself out-side the Presbyterian church. He scanned the rows of horses,

earching for the one Homstock had stolen from him ear-
ier. He dismounted and walked among the tethered ani-
mals, checking each one, but his gelding was not among
hem.

Perhaps Homstock had simply let him go when he ar-
ived. Or maybe luck had been with Chase and he had
beaten Homstock. Perhaps he was inside, meeting with his
Confederate contact right now. Dear Lord, Chase thought,
how many men will die to keep these secrets?

He forced himself not to think about it while he walked
oward the church. He brushed off the worst trail dust on his
rousers and raked his hand through his hair. Then he
straightened his coat and buttoned it over the butt of the
Colt. Without a doubt, he was the sorriest-looking man who
ever entered a church, but he was determined to silence
Homstock.

A large crowd was milling near the door when he stepped
inside. Chase mumbled his apologies and shouldered his
way through the throng while he looked for Homstock.
Chase kept himself positioned near the entrance, in case
Homstock should see him and try to flee again. With his
back snug against a thick beam supporting the roof, Chase
earched each corner of the room. After he had checked
every man twice, he grudgingly accepted the fact Homstock was not here—yet.

Homstock had asked directions of the peddler—he was
coming. Chase couldn't consider the possibility that Homstock might get away, that he could have eluded him on the
rail. He resigned himself to waiting inside the church until
Homstock showed. While he was scowling over the idea,
Chase felt curious eyes upon him.

He looked up and found a beautiful girl scrutinizing him
from across the church. Eyes bluer than the Texas sky
probed him. He felt his own gaze flick from her face to the
fourth finger of her left hand without conscious thought.

There was no wedding ring. When he looked back into the
cool blue depths, he knew. Whether or not he lived through

the night, he had to meet the girl who stared at him fro[m]
across the room.

Chase maneuvered his way across the room, dodgin[g]
dancers and men who had been passing a bottle when th[e]
preacher wasn't looking. He stopped a yard from her an[d]
took a deep breath for courage. A smell that put him i[n]
mind of springtime, flower gardens and warm sunshine o[n]
his face filled his nostrils.

"Miss." He nodded his head and allowed his appreci[a]-
tive gaze to skim over her face, her slender neck and th[e]
creamy top of her shoulders. She was all soft curves insi[de]
the simple yellow gingham frock. Pale blond hair framed [a]
face so pretty it was almost painful for him to gaze upon he[r]

"Sir—I—we have not been properly introduced." Sh[e]
lowered her eyes and deftly snapped open a fan that ha[d]
been dangling from her delicate wrist. "I cannot speak wit[h]
you until that time."

He couldn't help but grin. She had done what a we[ll]
brought up young lady should do, when confronted by a[n]
ill-mannered rascal. Undaunted, he took another step t[o]-
ward her. She met his advance with wide doe eyes. His hea[rt]
flip-flopped in his chest and he felt himself preparing to d[o]
the unthinkable.

"Then allow me to introduce myself. I am Chase Co[r]-
dell, of the Tyron County Cordells." He bent at the wai[st]
and did his best imitation of a gallant bow. Chase knew h[e]
probably looked the fool, with his travel-stained clothes an[d]
the bloody gash across the top of his hand. He wondered [if]
he had lost his reason—stopping to court a woman when s[o]
much hung in the balance. He asked himself how he coul[d]
take time to speak to her at all when Homstock might a[r]-
rive any minute. Yet, he persisted in his suit.

"Contrary to what my appearance may make you thin[k]
miss, I am a respectable man. In fact, I own a newspaper."
He grinned proudly.

She peered warily up at him over the edge of the fa[n]
while she seemed to consider his doubtful claim.

"I am Linese Beaufort." She lowered the fan enough for him to see two spots of color on her cheeks.

It seemed to Chase a crowd was beginning to gather at his elbow. He wondered if she had a brother or father who would call him out for making so bold with Miss Beaufort, but nobody challenged him, so he pressed forward while a voice in his head told him to look for Homstock and abandon this reckless endeavor.

"Miss Beaufort, I am most pleased to make your acquaintance, and I feel I must tell you—I am the man you are going to marry."

The group behind him gasped in unison. Miss Linese Beaufort's blush deepened in a manner that made Chase's loins tighten. Innocence and purity shone in her face. Her shock was more tempting and erotic than anything he could have imagined. Instead of regretting his words, he was sure he had spoken the truth.

"You must not say such things, Mr. Cordell." She fanned her face but it continued to flame hot pink with embarrassment. "It isn't proper for you to speak to me this way."

Chase impulsively pulled her into his arms and out onto the dance floor away from the murmuring crowd.

"Mr. Cordell!" she gasped. "What will people say?"

The butt of the gun pressed firmly between them when he pulled her closer and stared into her eyes. She stiffened in his arms. He held his breath, half expecting her to slap his face, or jerk free of his possessive hold, but she remained silent. Chase knew in that moment there was steel beneath her fragile exterior.

She was perfect. She was the woman for him.

Chase held her much too close to be proper, but he didn't care about propriety. Everything he had learned this night had shown him he had wasted too much time in the past, wasted it on things that did not matter. He wasn't inclined to waste another minute because of silly convention or manners. From now on Chase intended to grasp what he wanted of life and live every minute of it to the fullest.

He wanted Miss Linese Beaufort and would have her.

He spun her in a series of turns, and by slow degrees sh relaxed in his arms. When she looked up and met his gaz he thought the ghost of a smile might be tickling the co ners of her mouth.

"Your behavior has scandalized us both, Mr. Cordell. you are not careful, you *will* have to marry me, then you w sorely regret your foolish, impetuous prank."

"Scandal be damned," Chase retorted. "You will be n wife. This is no prank, Miss Beaufort." He raised an ey brow, silently daring her to dispute his intentions.

Her cheeks flamed to crimson and he felt her heart flu ter against his chest, but she met his eyes bravely. "Yo would have to convince my aunt Hesta of that. I'm afrai Mr. Cordell, even you could not prevail against her. It h always been her desire for me to marry a . . . suitable gentl man."

He laughed at her choice of words. This night he had b come a most unsuitable man, with his disheveled appea ance and a gun tucked in his trousers, and murder his late intention. But by God, he was going to have this girl for h wife.

"Please, Miss Beaufort, call me Chase—no need to be s formal with your future husband."

"Mr. Cordell," she continued as if she hadn't heard hin "My aunt has a well-known Beaufort trait—stubbor ness."

"And are you also stubborn?" The more she talked th more he knew this was the woman he had secretly longed fo all his life. She tilted her head to look at him squarely. Th light caught her eyes and made them into blue jewels again her creamy velvet skin and golden hair.

"Sometimes, sir, I am quite stubborn."

"As I am, Miss Beaufort." Chase held her gaze while sh absorbed his words. "As I am." He felt himself smilin again. "Lead me to your formidable aunt now, because I intend to marry you with all possible haste."

Chase watched her gaze flick over to a matronly woman standing by the Presbyterian minister. Their faces were etched with shock. Chase was fairly sure that was the legendary Aunt Hesta.

"Be prepared, miss. If I fail to charm her, I may indeed have to compromise your honor in order to succeed in my goal of marrying you."

A soft gasp of indignant surprise escaped her lips. The fiddle player chose that particular moment to take a break. Linese wriggled out of Chase's grasp and attempted to evade him, but he reached out and clasped his arm around her waist. While she fought to maintain her veneer of control within his most possessive and inappropriate grasp, Chase escorted her to the punch bowl.

Chase had just handed her a cup when the door opened. His position kept him concealed behind a wide beam, but he had a clear view of the entrance. Alfred Homstock leaned inside far enough to scan the church quickly. He hesitated for a moment, a frown creasing his forehead, before he disappeared and the door closed.

"Excuse me, Linese." Chase allowed himself one lingering glance at her face before he followed Homstock outside.

Tied to a bush just outside the torch-lit church was the stolen bay gelding. Chase heard the crunch of boots on gravel. He followed the sound and crept toward the back of the church. The hollow thud of a door drew his eyes to the outhouse, near a copse of trees, where he assumed Homstock was relieving himself.

Chase pulled the Colt from his waistband and prepared to commit murder, but before he had taken another step he heard a muffled groan and running feet. Chase sprinted toward the outhouse and flung the door open. It was empty.

The music inside the church began again with a rhythmic thump. The sound of people clapping, stomping and whooping in time to a rowdy Virginia reel muffled any other sound around him. Chase searched the shrubs and worked his way toward the trees. He moved to the thicket and looked down.

Homstock's eyes were open and lifeless. The ground beneath him was soaking up his still-warm blood. The Underground Railroad was safe for a while longer and Alfred Homstock would not be telling any secrets or meeting any more Cordells.

Pounding hooves drew Chase's eyes. He caught a glimpse of the tired bay gelding and the black mare he had loaned Ira earlier disappearing into the night.

Chase took a shuddering breath and got up from the hard, narrow cot in his cell. The chain on his leg rattled when he moved toward the narrow ventilation slit. All the memory, all the answers, didn't change anything. He could not defend himself against the charge of murder, unless he identified Ira as Homstock's killer.

That was a thing he would never do. Ira Goten had buried his knife blade deep into the Southern spy's back in order to protect the Cordells, as well as the Railroad. Now it was up to Chase Cordell to protect Ira, his grandfather, the Railroad, and quite possibly the entire Union cause by remaining silent about what happened on that night over two years ago.

A hard, tight lump formed in Chase's throat. He had only one regret. By keeping his vow, he would make Linese a widow with two tiny babies to raise alone.

"Linese," he murmured.

The full recollection of their meeting was bittersweet with its intensity. She was like sunshine in the dark, like rain quenching a drought. Now he knew why the sight of her in the yellow gingham dress had been like taking a bayonet in the chest. She had been wearing that same dress when he met her.

"What a young fool I was," he said remembering his wedding night.

He had been with other women before Linese, but he had never been in love with any of them. That difference had robbed him of any finesse he may have possessed. Love had made him self-conscious and clumsy in his lovemaking. Holding her in his arms had stripped him to the bone, laid him open, exposed his soul in a way he had never before experienced.

"God, how I loved her then, and now." Chase raked his hand through his hair. He had thought it remarkable that she loved him when he *couldn't* remember. Now, with his memory intact, he knew it was nothing short of miraculous that she could care at all for a fool as big as him.

He leaned his forehead against the cold, hard bars and cursed himself. His brain had taken everything that had happened to him in his life, then jumbled it up in no particular order. The few memories that were left intact became a confusing tangle that had forced him to stay away from Linese for too long. "How much precious time I wasted." Because of his bewildered state, he had denied his beloved wife and himself time together, time he could never recapture, time they would never have again.

"Linese, it near breaks my heart to see you looking so sad." Melissa pulled her baby, Eathan, back onto the braided rug. His attempts to crawl consisted of pulling himself across the floor on his chubby forearms.

"I'm sorry, I don't mean to be such poor company." Linese gently removed her breast from Sarah's pouting lips. The sleeping baby continued to suckle while she brought one tiny fist up to her downy cheek.

"It's not that," Melissa explained. "I'm happy and grateful to be living here with you. I just wish I could do something to help."

Linese blinked back the hot tears threatening to spill over. She had moved through each hellish day since they took Chase, barely maintaining control of her shredded emotions, while she cared for her daughters and prayed for a miracle. "Nobody can help. Chase doesn't want me to talk to Ira." Linese stopped in mid-sentence, realizing she had been thinking aloud.

"Ira? Ira Goten? Can he help Mr. Chase?" Melissa's eyes gleamed with interest and hope.

Linese silently chided herself for letting Ira's name slip. "Probably not, it's complicated. I can't explain." She could not tell anyone about Chase's missing memory, not without his permission. Linese laid Sarah next to her twin in the crib and pulled the crocheted coverlet over them. She caressed the dark curls on Marjorie's head.

Melissa pitied Linese. It just wasn't fair. Of course, life rarely was fair, but the idea that those babies were to be left fatherless and Linese a widow made Melissa crazy. Everyone in Mainfield had heard about the trial to be held, and the fact that there would *be* a hanging after.

She watched Eathan squirm off the rug and onto the bare floor once again. He had grown fat and sassy living here at Cordellane. Melissa owed Linese Cordell a great debt for giving her shelter when she needed it. Not many respectable women would have done the same. "Linese, would you watch Eathan for a while?" Melissa was determined to find a way to help.

"Of course, I'll watch him. Is there anything I can help you with?" Linese offered.

"No, I just need to call on Doralee," Melissa lied smoothly.

"Do you think it's safe, with the Northern troops so near to Mainfield?"

"I heard they are regrouping—anyway the shooting has stopped for a few days. I'll be fine." Melissa didn't intend to be gone long, just long enough to speak with Ira Goten.

Ira watched the young woman's face while she talked. She was one of those people whose expression told every thought. Melissa was not lying to him, that he was certain of.

"So, Mr. Goten, I came here to see you, to ask if there was anything you could do to help Linese."

"Mrs. Cordell doesn't know you are here?" Ira never took his eyes off Melissa's face, while he watched for any sign of deception in her story.

"Oh, no. She wouldn't like me interfering, but I can't stand by and do nothing. I mean, if there is any way you can help Mr. Chase, that is." Melissa wrung her hands in the faded calico skirt. "I just had to come and ask you to do it."

"I'll see what I can do. Now you go on home. Don't mention this to Mrs. Cordell or the Captain. And don't worry."

"I'll try not to. Linese is nearly sick with fretting. I doubt the old Captain even knows what has happened, or that he understands who Major Cordell is."

Ira smiled at the way the crafty older Cordell continued to deceive Mainfield. He had kept his word to Chase, and never let on that he knew the ex-ranger was sane. "You're probably right, Miss Melissa, he probably doesn't even realize what is going on." Ira smiled. Even when Chase came home from war, they had kept their silence, as they agreed to do two years ago. But Ira had never forgotten Alfred Homstock.

Ira had done what he could to help Chase that night. He had taken the stolen bay gelding, and ridden the black mare like the devil himself. He had been careful not to be seen when he returned the horses to Cordellane. Nobody had spotted them outside the Presbyterian church. For two years he had kept the gun and the gold—and the secrets.

"I'm sorry, Chase, but now I've got to break my promise," Ira muttered while he slipped his knife into his boot top. "You and I will have to talk about that night."

Chase's jaw muscle jumped convulsively while he listened to the conversation taking place in Rancy Thompson's outer office. His entire existence centered around what information he could hear by eavesdropping. Today it was Kerney who came to discuss him.

He listened to Colonel Homstock and Kerney talking about him, while his blood burned with hatred for the wishy-washy politician. At least the colonel believed in what he was doing. With Kerney it was all a matter of profit, just as it always had been.

"It pains me to think that one of Mainfield's own could be responsible for your brother's death, Colonel."

"Really." Colonel Homstock's voice was emotionless.

"Yes. I hope you will allow me to offer my services as judge for the scheduled trial. As mayor of Mainfield, I have often presided over the local court, if the circuit judge was unavailable."

There was a long pause. "You would do that, Mayor Kerney, sit in judgment on one of your own?"

"Of course, Major." Kerney sounded downright eager to put a noose around Chase's neck. He should have known the man would find a way to get even for his lack of cooperation about the articles.

"And doing so would not *offend* your sense of loyalty?" Colonel Homstock asked.

"My greatest concern, and loyalty to, has always been the continued economic stability of Mainfield. And the welfare of its citizens, of course."

"Of course." There was a wry tone in the Southerner's words.

"If getting this trial over with, and bringing Major Chase Cordell to justice, will smooth relations between the town and your troops, then Colonel Homstock, I consider it my civic duty."

Chase flopped on his cot in disgust. If only he were free. Chase would love to meet Kerney face-to-face for just five minutes. The sound of pebbles hitting the side of the jail wall drew Chase's attention. He frowned at the narrow ventilation hole. A tiny scatter of pea-sized gravel pattered across the floor in front of his cot.

"What the hell?" Chase picked up his chain so it would not rattle while he moved closer to the opening.

"Chase? Are you there?" Ira's harsh whisper floated to Chase's ears.

"Ira? What are you doing here?" Chase could not see him through the small aperture, but he definitely recognized the voice.

"I got word there might be something I could do to help you."

"You better leave, it's not safe for you here." Chase warned.

"Safe for me?"

"Ira, you've done all you can to keep my family from harm. Now it's up to me. But I'm glad you came, it gives me a chance to thank you for what you did that night in Ferrin County."

"What I did was nothing, Chase. You don't have to thank me." Ira sounded perplexed.

Chase grimaced. Ira must have steeled himself against the harsh reality of his deeds, the way Chase had seen many soldiers do when they were forced to fight their own kin and neighbors.

"You killed a man to save my grandfather and me," Chase whispered.

"Killed a man?" Ira's shocked words cut Chase off in mid-thought.

"Your secret is safe with me, Ira. Have no fear on that account. The only thing I would ask, is that you keep an eye on Linese and my daughters after—after I'm gone."

"My secret?" There was the sound of shuffling feet outside the narrow slit. "Don't you mean *your* secret?"

Chase frowned and leaned closer. "No. I mean what you did to Alfred Homstock." Chase was beginning to wonder if Ira had lost his memory.

"Dear God, Chase. Are you telling me that you did not kill him?"

"Of course I didn't kill him. I saw you riding off..."
Chase felt his blood congeal in his veins. "Ira, *didn't* you
kill him with that pigsticker of yours?"

"No. I saw the body lying there...I thought you killed
him. All I did was see that the horses got back to Cordellane."

Chase sagged against the wall. "God in heaven. I was
prepared to go like a lamb to slaughter because I thought I
was protecting you from the Confederates."

Ira groaned. "I thought you had killed him to save the
Railroad and your grandfather."

"This is too fantastic to believe. First my grandfather was
accused—now me. I thought you did it, Ira, but if you
didn't, and I didn't, then who did kill Alfred Homstock?"

"I don't know, Chase, but we don't have long to find
out." Ira's voice was a flinty whisper. "The rumor is all over
town. Your trial begins the day after tomorrow."

Chapter Twenty-One

Melissa walked into the library and found Linese silently weeping. She watched for a moment, embarrassed to intrude but unable to turn away and leave Linese to her sorrow.

While the tears slid down Linese's cheeks, she fingered her wedding ring.

"Oh, honey, don't cry." Melissa stepped forward.

Linese whirled around in surprise, obviously embarrassed to be caught unaware in a weak moment. "I wasn't really," Linese protested.

"Why were you looking at your wedding ring like that?" Melissa asked.

Linese dragged her fingers over her damp cheeks and blinked rapidly. She tried to smile but her lips quivered. "I gave my cameo to the soldier, so he would let me see Chase. I have to see him once more. This is the only thing I have left to give him." A strangled sob escaped her lips.

Melissa smoothed Linese's hair away from her face. "I'll watch the twins. And don't give up hope. Things are always blackest before the dawn. I just know it's going to be all right."

"Do you really think so?" Linese wanted to believe the words of optimism.

"Yes, I do. My gram said I have the gift, that I could tell certain things." Melissa smiled. "I have a real strong feeling this is all going to work out."

"I hope you are right, Melissa. I have to believe you are right or I would go insane."

Captain Cordell stood behind the ash tree outside the library and listened to the women talking. He wanted to comfort Linese, but he could not allow her to learn the truth, especially now, with the Southern troops in Mainfield. Linese and the twins were in jeopardy just being under the same roof with him. He could not put them in greater danger by letting her know he was not crazy.

He silently cursed himself for ever putting his family through the lie, but at the time, it had seemed the only way to help all those who were leaving the South. He had mobilized every resource he possessed to save Chase, but so far there had been little news. He had been able to learn only that Alfred Homstock, the murdered man, had been sent to stop the Railroad. That precious bit of information had finally pointed away from Chase. The problem was, only those who were deeply involved with the Railroad, like himself, knew it.

Captain Cordell could not even consider the possibility Chase might hang. He would step forward and confess before he would allow that to happen. He would see the Railroad exposed, and damn all of the people involved to perdition, to save his grandson. He would stand in front of a Confederate firing squad before he would see Chase convicted. In fact, he would go do it now, if it weren't for all the other men his words would sentence to death. But that was the last resort. He had to try everything else first.

If only the damned Southern troops were not occupying Mainfield, then it would all be so simple to sort out. If the Union were occupying Mainfield, then it would only be a matter of revealing himself as a member of the Underground Railroad and claiming that he had done the killing.

a lie, of course, but one he would gladly tell to save Chase. He sighed with frustration and glanced at Linese.

He had wondered how the brave little thing gained entrance into the jail, when he had failed. Now he knew. She had traded away her cameo. Now she was planning to barter her wedding ring. Knowing her plan brought a hard lump to his tight throat.

"I'll have to get them back for her," he whispered. As long as he was forced to remain crazy in the eyes of Mainfield and the Confederate soldiers, he might as well make the best of it. He turned and strode toward the stable, all the while trying to think of a way to save Chase, and praying the Northern army would enter Mainfield soon.

Colonel Homstock stood at the window of the sheriff's office and watched the mayor walk down Mainfield's nearly deserted street. He flinched at the constant barrage of cannon fire beyond the woods surrounding the town.

He refused to believe the South would not win. It had to win. Too much blood had been spent to consider failure after all this time. Too much Homstock blood had been spilled.

Colonel Homstock hadn't slept a peaceful night since Alfred's body had been found—minus the gold—and the news of his death had reached Virginia. He knew in his heart Alfred's death had been the reason for their mother's stroke.

He was bending all the rules of war and martial law, by pushing this trial forward, but he didn't care anymore. Each dispatch received at the telegraph office told the sad truth about the South's lost cause. Realistically, he realized it was only a matter of time before the Confederacy surrendered, but he refused to let the war end with Alfred's death unavenged.

It was a bitter fact that the South had been kept from this remote corner of Texas for two years. Otherwise he would have long ago seen justice done one way or the other.

Major Chase Cordell was guilty. He was sure of it, well almost sure of it. Everything fit. The gold, Cordell's loy alty to the Union, the anonymous information that a hors bearing the Cordell brand had been at the Presbyteria church that night. The final piece of the puzzle had been th fact that Chase had used his crazy grandfather to give him self an alibi, even though the sheriff had tried to make hir believe it was the other way around.

What kind of a man would use a feeble relative to sav himself? Homstock wondered. Major Cordell didn't seen like the cowardly kind, but then what did he care, as long a Alfred was avenged.

He watched Kerney pause on the street and glance to ward the jail, before he turned and entered the bank. H didn't like the mayor. The colonel narrowed his eyes an wondered what it was about the mayor that bothered him s much.

"Is there something wrong, sir?" The soldier's voic snapped Homstock's head around.

"I'm not sure, Leland." He folded his hands behind hi back and paced the length of the sheriff's office. "I must b tired. Lately I seem less and less confident about…things."

Rancy Thompson had been spending most of his tim trying to find some way of saving Major Cordell. Colone Homstock didn't blame the sheriff. He'd probably be do ing the same thing in his position. He might even wonde about the evidence now, if the victim were anybody but hi youngest brother, Alfred. When his brother had been mur dered, he had promised their dying mother he would see th killer brought to justice.

Homstock understood death during war, but his younge brother had been a civilian, forced to stay behind because o their mother's insistence. It was a sorrowful irony tha someone had managed to recruit Alfred as a spy, after a that had been done to keep him safe. That was what haunte him nightly: his brother had died in spite of his efforts t keep him out of the war.

Still, there was something else nagging at him, as well. He strode to the window and stared outside.

He knew he should ride out to the woods, to help in the struggle that was going on, but Alfred's spirit would not allow him. Besides, it didn't really matter anymore. The Confederacy would not stand another day.

That was why he was pushing through Major Cordell's trial. Time was running out for him and the Confederacy.

Kerney stepped out of the bank and Colonel Homstock found himself unable to stop watching the mayor. Sunlight winked off something shiny on the man's chest, forcing Homstock to squint against the painful brilliance. What was it about the mayor? He dressed well, looked downright prosperous.

"Leland?" Homstock turned toward the soldier who stood up from behind the desk and snapped smartly to attention.

"Yes, sir."

"Take some time tomorrow morning, nose around town a bit. I want you to find out everything you can about Mayor Kerney."

"Yes, sir," Leland said. "Are you looking for anything in particular, sir?"

"I don't know," Homstock admitted. "I can respect a man for being my enemy, but I am mightily suspicious of a man who has no conviction or loyalty of any kind. That popinjay Kerney bends whichever way the wind is blowing hardest." Homstock's words trailed off while he thought about it. "And he doesn't have the look of a man who has suffered much through this war." The politician was anxious to be Chase Cordell's judge, anxious to see the trial begin tomorrow. Why? Why was a man who had no personal interest in Alfred's death be so eager? It didn't add up.

"I'll do my best for you, sir," Leland said.

"I know you will, Leland." The colonel pulled on his gloves and his hat before he stepped outside. While he continued to wear the Confederate uniform, he was deter-

mined to wear it proudly. He unwittingly matched hi
footfalls to the sound of nearing cannon fire. He wondere
if the South would survive long enough for him to com
plete Major Chase Cordell's trial and avenge his brother'
death, and he wondered how long it would be before th
Northern troops spilled into Mainfield, Texas.

Linese waited until she saw the Confederate officer leave
the jail. She doubted the soldier would be so easily bribe
if the colonel was in the office.

She pinched her cheeks to give them some color an
wished her eyes were not red rimmed from crying. She hate
Chase to see her like this, but she had to speak with him to
day. Maybe she could say or do something that would spar
a recollection. The Confederate soldier looked up an
smiled when she stepped inside the sheriff's office.

"I—I've come to see my husband," Linese said.

His smile broadened in anticipation. "You know th
rules, ma'am."

Linese pulled the ring off her finger. "Yes, I know th
rules." She placed it on the desk and pushed it toward th
man.

He stared at the plain gold band as if assessing its valu
in cold cash. She tried to ignore the catch in her heart. I
was, after all, only a ring, and well spent in order to se
Chase.

When he scooped up the ring, he nodded toward the doo
to the cell. "Go ahead."

Linese lifted her chin a notch and forced herself to smile
She was determined to be strong for Chase.

Chase looked up when he heard the door open. H
jumped from the narrow cot and nearly tripped over th
damnable shackle chain on his ankle in his haste to get close
to Linese.

"Dearest." He stretched his fingers through the bars an
caressed the side of her face as soon as she was near enough
Her eyes were swollen and red. There were gaunt hollow
under her cheeks.

"Oh, Chase." She closed her eyes and leaned into his hand. Just to be near him made her feel less helpless.

He touched her lips with the pad of his thumb and wished he could hold her. She hadn't been sleeping much, he could tell. She looked too thin, her fragile bone structure was made even more prominent by the paleness of her skin. Being locked away and unable to protect her ate at him.

"Honey, you've been crying," he accused gently.

"I have not."

"You have become a strong woman while I've been away, not at all like the timid, blushing girl I first met, but you are still a terrible liar, Linese Cordell."

She smiled at his left-handed compliment and savored the feeling of his hand against her face. His fingers were warm and rough. His touch sent an arrow of longing through her. If only the cold bars didn't separate them. She yearned to feel the strength of his arms around her, to taste his lips and give herself to him.

"Chase, I've been so worried about you."

"I'm fine, honey. Tell me about you and the girls. I hear the cannons day and night. Has there been fighting near Cordellane?"

"Not yet. The twins are fine, growing like weeds." She looked up at him. Tears pooled in her eyes. "Oh, how I wish you could see them." She blinked furiously in an attempt to keep the tears at bay.

It ripped a part of his soul away to see her in such pain, to be unable to protect her from it and to know it was going to get worse. "I'll see them, honey." He tried to bolster her spirits with a lie.

"If only you could remember something, Chase. Any small detail about your past might help."

Chase looked at her sweet face and felt the floor fall from beneath his feet. He had to tell her. There had been too many secrets between them for too long. He could not keep this from her. "Linese, there's something I have to tell you."

"What, Chase? Have you remembered something?"

"I remember. I remember it all."

Hope filled her eyes, then it traveled down to her lips. The smile and relief on her face was like summer rain on parched earth. It sent a ripple of love and desire flowing through Chase to see how it transformed her.

"Thank, God," she said, and sighed. "Have you talked to Rancy yet? Or the Confederate officer?" Her question spilled out eagerly. "When will they let you come home?"

"It isn't as easy as that, darling." It cleaved him in half to know he was going to crush the life out of her with his next words. "I can't say anything to Rancy or anyone else I remember, but it doesn't make any difference."

"What? You can't mean what you are saying. Of course it makes a difference."

"I do mean it. There are people that would be imprisoned or killed by the Confederates as spies, if I tell what I know. There is one good thing about it." He smiled and stroked her temple. "I remember the day I met you—clearly."

Linese felt a chill climb her back. He had made that remark a moment ago, about her no longer being timid and blushing, and she hadn't even noticed its significance. She hadn't even realized what it all meant.

"Chase, if you remember, then you must defend yourself. Unless…" She narrowed her gaze on him. "Surely you are not telling me that you are guilty."

"No. You were right. I've done a lot of horrible things in war, but I didn't kill Alfred Homstock in cold blood."

"Then you must talk, you must tell the Confederate officer. You have to tell them who did it."

"Honey, I can't. Besides, I don't know who killed Alfred Homstock, I only know who didn't kill him." He could not tell her about Ira and certainly not about his grandfather. She and the twins would need the old fox to keep them safe.

"I can't bear it, Chase." Unchecked tears spilled over her eyelids and down onto his fingers. "I can't live without you."

"Yes, you can, and you will. You will raise my daughters to be just like you. And when they are old enough, you will let them know that I died with my dignity and my honor."

"Dignity and honor be damned!" Linese ranted. Chase watched her eyes come alive with hurt and anger. "You men talk of glory, and honor, while you leave your wives and your sons and daughters to go on without you. I won't listen to this, Chase Cordell, I won't."

She tried to cover her ears with her hands, but he grasped them and peeled her fingers gently away. He wanted her to listen to him, while there was time. "Linese, don't."

A part of him knew what she said was the truth. But what was a man without honor? What kind of man would he be if he sacrificed his grandfather and Ira in order to save his own life? He loved Linese, but he had to be true to himself. Chase had to be the kind of man his daughters would be proud to have as their father—dead or alive. Now that he had his past, he realized he had not been the best man he could have been, but he was determined to be the best he could be, now.

"Linese, darling—"

"No. I won't listen to this, Chase Cordell." She stamped her feet in a frustrated fit of temper. "You had better not let yourself be killed. I—I just won't have it! Do you hear? I won't stand for it." Her lips quivered while she stared at him in defiance. Then a strange calm settled over her. Eyes bluer and harder than turquoise stone pierced him. Silently she whirled and stomped away from him.

Chase wondered if this was to be the last image he would have of Linese, his love.

Chapter Twenty-Two

Linese drove the buggy out of Mainfield like a mad woman. Her heart was pounding from both fear and anger.

"Damn men!" she declared aloud. Chase was ready to give himself up without a fight, like a martyr.

"It's a good thing women bear the children or mankind would cease to exist because of duty and honor."

After a moment, she slowed the horse to a walk. Her anger had burned itself out, leaving her tired beyond imagining. She thought of the twins and was grateful Melissa was with them at Cordellane.

Linese thought back to the days when she had feared Chase slipping away from her. It was Melissa who had helped her then, just as it was Doralee who had helped free Captain Cordell when he needed help.

Women, those were the people she could depend on in a crisis. If anything was going to get done, it would have to be done by women. Linese stared at the budding trees beside the road and thought of the date, April 8, 1865. It should be the time of new beginnings and new life, not a time to be contemplating death.

The crack of rifle fire deep in the woods made her skin prickle with fear and she found herself looking at the thicket. Men were occupied with killing and dying only miles

rom where she sat. It wasn't safe for her to linger on the
oad between Cordellane and Mainfield.

Linese slapped the reins on the horse's rump and re-
umed her journey home. A plan and a ray of hope had
aken shape in her mind. She only had to convince Melissa
nd Doralee to help her one more time.

Doralee and the girls openly admired the dark-haired
wins. Each woman's face reflected deep, private emotion.
inese found herself wondering what sorrows they had en-
ured, what fork in their paths had brought them to their
resent destination in life.

"They are beautiful babies, Mrs. Cordell," Doralee said
vith a wistful sigh.

"I thought we agreed not to stand on formalities. I am
inese, and thank you. They look just like their father."
inese gestured to the settee and chairs in the parlor.

Melissa had done the impossible and found enough sugar
o make cookies. A plate was piled high with them and the
mell of chicory filled the house.

"Please, sit down." Linese swallowed hard. "I have a
ery great favor to ask of you all."

Doralee spread out her skirt and sat down while the other
hree women with her took a seat. She waited quietly while
inese offered cookies and chicory to them all. Finally when
inese knew she could no longer delay, she forced herself to
ay the words she had been struggling all afternoon to find.

"I need your help. I'm asking all of you to tell me if any
f the men who have...been with you...might have said
nything to prove my husband is innocent of murdering
lfred Homstock."

Linese fidgeted with her cup of chicory, half expecting
Doralee to laugh in her face, or get up and leave, if the hor-
ified expression on her face was any indication. The si-
ence seemed to stretch on forever.

"It isn't much to ask," Melissa said softly.

Doralee shook her head. "No, it isn't." She reached over and patted Linese's hand. "You just took me by surprise, that's all." She leveled a gaze on Linese. "Your husband doesn't know what you're doing, does he, Linese? If he did he most likely would not approve, would he?"

"No, he would not approve of my interfering. Chase will let them slip a rope around his neck before he will violate his damned code of honor." Linese tried to control the anger and frustration she felt. "He is innocent, but he refuses to say anything to save himself."

She loved Chase, probably because of the very reason she fumed with anger. But right now, with her daughters asleep in the corner, and the probability of raising them alone so near, it was a bitter thing to admit to anyone, even herself. If he wouldn't save himself, then perhaps one of these women would give her the information so she could.

"Don't be too hard on him, honey. He's not any different than most men. They are mysterious creatures when you get to know them. Let's see if we can find a way to save him in spite of himself."

Two hours later, after Doralee had cussed and discussed every man in two counties, Linese looked at the names she had written down.

"So as far as anyone remembers, these were the only men from Mainfield who were not at your birthday party?" Linese asked while she gazed at the pitifully short list.

Doralee nodded. "It's hard to remember back nearly three years, but as I recall, Tatum Sprague showed up late as well."

"Yes, he did. He drank a lot and was bragging about some raid over in Louisiana." Colleen, a redhead with a slender nose, said, "I thought he was lying to impress me but now that I think of it, he did leave me an extra dollar."

"Lord, that must mean he was telling the truth," Melissa quipped. "He's tight as fiddle string."

Linese wrote down the man's name and put a star beside it. It was not much to pin her hope on, but she had to take

n active part in trying to prove Chase was innocent, since
e would not.

Doralee frowned and gnawed her bottom lip. "Since that
nan was killed over in Ferrin County, I'm not sure any of
his makes any difference."

Linese dipped the quill pen back in the ink bottle before
he drew a heavy black line across the paper, dividing it in
alf. "You're right. But now I realize I was at the Presby-
erian church when he was killed. I never made the connec-
ion at the time. There was so many strangers there that
ight and I was so taken with Chase and his outrageous be-
avior, but maybe there is something I've forgotten, some-
hing that I didn't realize had anything to do with the
nurder. But as you say it was nearly three years ago."

She forced herself to think back, to concentrate, to focus
n the smallest detail that evening. "Oh, Doralee, there is
omething. Something I never even thought about. There
vas someone else from Mainfield, someone who was there
vhen Chase was—but at the time I didn't know who he
vas."

Captain Cordell fixed a blank stare on his face and al-
owed the Confederate soldier to win another hand of cards.
t never ceased to amaze him how confident people became
vhen they thought they were in the company of an inferior.
"How about one more hand?" Leland asked.

"Sure." Captain Cordell leaned back in his chair. He
eard the rhythmic rattle of chains and knew Chase was
acing the floor of his cell. It took all the patience and con-
rol Aloyisius had cultivated during his years fighting Co-
nanche to keep from hitting Leland in the jaw, grabbing the
eys and setting Chase free. It was a tempting thought, but
o have his grandson hunted down like a runaway slave was
ot an improvement over his present dilemma. Only prov-
ng his innocence would be enough.

* * *

Linese looked out the window of her bedroom while she buttoned up the front of her dress. Melissa was going to stay with the twins while she attended Chase's trial. The sun was shining through the budding leaves and dappling the ground around Cordellane. She was struck by the incongruity of it.

April 9, 1865, looked like any other spring day, but it was not. It would never be like any other day again, not when her husband's life was in jeopardy.

"You look nice." Melissa's voice snapped her thoughts back to the present.

"I'm nothing but a jumble of nerves inside," Linese admitted with a halfhearted smile.

"Well, it doesn't show. You look every inch the lady." Melissa stepped behind Linese and helped her push the last of the hairpins in place.

"I've fed the girls—" Linese began.

"I have more than enough milk left since Eathan is nearly weaned. They'll be fine. Don't you fret about them. Just go do what you have to do and I'll be praying for you."

"Thank you." Linese nodded. "Have you seen the Captain this morning?" With all that had been going on, she had neglected him. Guilt and concern flowed through her.

"He saddled a horse and left early," Melissa said.

Linese sighed heavily. "I almost envy him. He has no idea what is happening—the poor dear."

"Probably a good thing. I've heard stories over at Doralee's. He was quite a man in his younger days. If he knew what was going on, he most likely would've already pulled the jail down around that Confederate officer's head, to set Mr. Chase free."

Linese smiled at the thought. "I wish someone would." A hot sting of tears behind her eyes made her blink.

"Now don't you go getting melancholy. It's going to be all right."

"You're right. I'll tell Chase what I remember about that night and he'll defend himself. He has to now."

* * *

Colonel Homstock read the telegram regarding the war once again. He closed his fist and crumpled it into a ball.

"Is there news, sir?" Leland asked with a lift of his brows.

Homstock looked up at the young soldier and shook his head. "Nothing significant." He couldn't tell the young soldier the truth, not now, not today when Alfred's murderer would be brought to justice.

"Oh, Major, I almost forgot." Leland pulled a scrap of paper from his pocket. "You sent me to nose around and I did find one thing that seemed a bit odd. There was one man in Mainfield who had quite a lot of money right after your brother's murder." He handed the paper to Colonel Homstock. "But it wasn't Chase Cordell."

Homstock scanned the page quickly, then he looked back up at Leland. "Does anybody else know about this?" Vague suspicions that he had tried to ignore buffeted his sense of right and wrong.

"No, sir."

"Good, keep it that way. I don't want anything getting in the way of the trial."

The door opened and Rancy Thompson walked in. His clothes were rumpled and it looked like he'd been riding all night.

"Sheriff." Homstock eyed him suspiciously but said no more.

Rancy poured himself a cup of coffee from the pot on the small stove in the corner of the office. "Colonel Homstock."

"Sir, shall I get the prisoner and take him to the court?"

Rancy's head came around with a snap. His eyes narrowed to slits. "I'll be going with you every step of the way."

Homstock nodded. "Fine. Get him, Leland, it's time Major Chase Cordell answered the charges against him."

The report of a rifle outside of town punctuated his sentence. Colonel Homstock wondered if he or the South had even that much time left.

Chapter Twenty-Three

Linese stood beside the steps of the redbrick courthouse and waited. She had to find a way to speak to Chase when they brought him inside. She had to give him the name of the man she remembered seeing that night, so he would defend himself against the charge.

People jostled her around while they gathered in a milling throng outside the door. She heard dissenting remarks grumbled by both Union and Confederate sympathizers. If Chase had a jury of twelve men, she doubted they would be able to reach a decision about his guilt or innocence, but he wasn't going to have a jury.

Upon reaching Mainfield, she had heard that a single man was to hear the evidence and make the decision about Chase's fate. One man was going to sit as judge. She wondered who it would be. One of the Confederate soldiers, or someone from Mainfield? A dark cloud covered the sun for a moment and she glanced up. Thunderheads were building in the west. Linese could smell rain far away. She wrung her hands and glanced inside the courtroom.

It was nearly full. Even the stairway leading to the second-story balcony was congested with men and women trying to find a seat. She supposed it was only natural that so many people would attend. The Cordells had been one of the first families to settle here and were well-known in this corner of Texas. And the fact the *Gazette* had not been allowed to print a word since the Confederate troops arrived made everyone curious. Since the telegraph had been commandeered by the Southern troops, Mainfield had been trapped in a cocoon of silence. People were hungry for news, stimulation.

Linese's chest constricted tightly. To some this trial was little more than a diversion, macabre entertainment, to pass the long hours between sunrise and sunset while the life-and-death struggle went on in the woods outside Mainfield.

She heard the crowd's murmur intensify and turned to see Chase, flanked on one side by Rancy Thompson, and on the other by the Confederate soldier who had taken her cameo and wedding ring.

Her eyes dropped to Chase's hands and she gasped. They had him shackled from wrist to wrist, and another chain trailed down to his ankles where heavy manacles forced him to take mincing steps. She wanted to cry at the sight of him, but she stuffed her knuckles in her mouth and forced herself to remain silent.

Chase located Linese and watched while she went pale. It sent a ribbon of pain shooting through him. Dear God, she appeared so fragile among the assembly, a tiny blond woman with large blue eyes that held too much pain. He wanted to speak with her, but he knew it was impossible.

While he watched, she recovered enough to valiantly begin elbowing and shoving her way to the front of the group. When she was no more than arm's length away, Rancy reached out and grabbed hold of his wrist chains.

"Stop right here," the sheriff commanded loudly.

Chase looked up to see Rancy staring into the Confederate soldier's face. "Hold up, Leland," Rancy said.

"Why?" The soldier looked around uneasily.

"I have something in my boot. Stop here a minute." Rancy released Chase's chains and squatted down. Chase looked down and saw Rancy nod in Linese's direction and then wink. The sheriff had given him one tiny fraction of time to speak with her.

"Chase." She broke through the crowd and wrapped her arms around his neck.

The shackles and chains made it impossible to hold her properly, but he bent his head and nuzzled her damp cheek with his rough, unshaven face.

"Honey, you shouldn't be here," he said, but he was glad she was. He wanted to treasure the sight of her, the smell of honeysuckle, and the texture of her golden hair.

"I had to come. Chase, there is something I must tell you." He heard a tremor of excitement and hope in her voice. He bent lower and felt her warm breath on his ear while she whispered what she remembered. When she was finished speaking, she leaned away and looked expectantly into his eyes.

"You'll tell them now, you'll defend yourself?"

He touched the side of her face with his fingertips. How he loved her, how he hated to destroy her hope. But nothing changed with this bit of new information.

"I can't, Linese. As long as the Southern army holds this town, I can't say a word to save myself."

"That's enough," Leland barked. Rancy stood up and gave Chase a look that was full of apology and compassion.

"Move along, Mrs. Cordell." Leland put a hand out to force Linese away. Rage built up inside Chase. He turned, ready to attack the man for daring to touch his precious wife.

"No, Chase," Rancy said softly. "This isn't the way. Have faith."

Chase swallowed hard and tried to stifle his anger. He looked at Linese one last time, then turned toward the courthouse steps. He put one foot in front of the other and walked toward the door, toward his destiny.

When Chase had disappeared inside, Linese rushed into the courthouse and looked around for a seat. There were none on the lower level and she was forced to climb the stairs to the balcony. Every inch of space seemed to be occupied.

She was nearly in tears when she felt a strong hand on her arm.

She turned to see Captain Cordell. His old eyes looked bright and full of pain. "This way, Linese. Come stand beside me."

She had the ridiculous notion that he was lucid, that he knew what was taking place. She took two deep breaths to calm herself and tried to grasp reality. This was not the time to become hysterical. The Captain was here because every citizen in the county was. No other reason. It was as simple as that.

They took positions side by side at the balcony railing. Linese looked down on the scene below. She watched Chase's dark head while he settled behind a table. Rancy Thompson and the Confederate soldier maintained their positions on either side of him.

She saw the Confederate officer enter the courtroom from the side door. The sound that filled the room upon his arrival reminded her of a swarm of bumblebees when angered. He swept off his hat and placed it on the table, then he slowly removed his gloves. His sword hung at his thigh and he looked every inch the proud warrior.

A strange silence settled over the courtroom. Linese frowned, trying to figure out why it had suddenly turned so quiet, then she realized that the shooting and cannon fire outside of town had ceased.

For the first time, in more days than she could count, there was no sound of war outside Mainfield. It was eerie. Her stomach clenched into a fist-sized knot. The sound of the gavel hitting wood made her jump. She looked at the solitary man who had entered and sat down behind the table in the center of the courtroom.

"Court is now in session. Silence, please," Mayor Kerney ordered.

Linese's knees turned to water. Her hand shot out and she gripped the railing in front of her until her knuckles went white while she fought to keep from fainting dead away.

Now she knew who Chase's judge was, and her last hope for Chase's freedom evaporated like rain on a hot day.

"Colonel Homstock," Kerney said. "Would you like to address the court?"

"Yes, Your Honor." Homstock strode to the middle of the room and looked at Chase. The angle and distance made it impossible for Linese to read the expression in his eyes while he spoke. "Before we begin, I want this assembly to know this trial is not a military action. The murder of Alfred Homstock, a civilian, occurred in 1862, in Ferrin County and has remained unsolved." He turned in Rancy's direction. "Is that correct, Sheriff?"

"Yes, it is correct," Rancy grumbled.

"Is it also true, the accused, Major Chase Cordell, has refused to give any testimony whatsoever on his own behalf?"

"That's true." Rancy's voice was full of frustration. "Chase has refused to talk about it at all."

"You have been investigating this case for some time, I understand, Sheriff Thompson."

"Yes," Rancy said. "Yes, Ferrin County has no sheriff, so I was in charge of the original investigation," Rancy answered.

"Since the victim was my brother, and since I studied law before entering the Confederate army, I'd like to act as prosecutor in this case." There was a collective murmur in the stuffy courtroom. "Is that acceptable to you, Judge?"

Linese's heart was pounding rapidly in her chest. The air in the room was still, thick with tension and doom. It was like watching a staged play in some bizarre disjointed way. She found herself going numb from the neck down while she watched and listened.

"Your request is perfectly acceptable to the court," Kerney told the Confederate colonel cheerfully.

"Then I will begin to lay out the evidence in the cold-blooded murder of Alfred Homstock."

Linese shuddered involuntarily. Hatred and a bitter de sire for vengeance rang in Colonel Homstock's voice. Sh clasped her hands together and prayed silently. Only a mi acle could save Chase now.

Chase wanted to turn around and look for Linese, but h forced himself to concentrate on what Homstock was sa ing. He wanted to search the room, to see if Ira and h grandfather were there, but he held himself rigid and star only at the Confederate officer. He told himself there was r other way, but a part of him grieved for himself and Li ese. He loved her and his daughters, and he found himse praying for a way to escape his fate.

Rain started to fall. At first it was little more than a so pattering, but soon the droplets were beating on the roc and against the windows of the courtroom like angry fist Linese had to strain to hear what was being said below.

"First I offer into evidence this handwritten note."

Mayor Kerney took the paper from Major Homstock. H scanned the page. "For the benefit of the spectators, th note says that a horse bearing the Cordell brand was see tied where the body of Alfred Homstock was found." Ke ney looked up. "There is no signature."

Again a ripple of hushed voices rushed through th crowded courtroom. Linese's stomach roiled violently.

"I would like to call Dr. Lukins to testify," Colon Homstock said.

Linese watched while the crowd below shifted slight! Suddenly Doc appeared, making his way to the single cha positioned by Kerney's desk. She watched while the phy cian raised one hand and placed the other on a worn Bibl The rain prevented her from hearing his oath, but when h lips stopped moving he sat down.

"Dr. Lukins, did you examine the body of Alfred Hor stock?"

Linese had no trouble hearing the colonel's voice, boomed across the courtroom louder than the intermitte thunder.

"Yes."

"How did he die?"

"He had been shot in the shoulder, but the cause of death as a stab wound in the back."

Linese gripped the baluster tighter while the murmur in e room changed pitch. To be killed from behind was the ost cowardly and unforgivable thing a Texan could imag- e.

"Can you determine what kind of weapon was used?" omstock's voice was oddly dispassionate while he asked e questions.

"A slender, long blade that pierced his heart. Death was most instantaneous...."

A clap of thunder obliterated the rest of Doc's state- ent. She watched while he left the stand.

Chase turned in his seat and scanned the crowd. She anted to call out to him, but forced herself to remain si- nt.

"Samuel Green." Colonel Homstock's voice wrenched inese's thoughts back to the witness stand. She watched a nall, balding man step up to the center of the room and ke his oath.

"Mr. Green, what is your profession?" Homstock's voice rowned out the sound of the storm.

"I am a goldsmith. I make and sell fine jewelry."

"Did Chase Cordell purchase a piece of jewelry from you ter his return from war?" Homstock clasped his hands ehind his back and paused in front of Mr. Green.

"Yes, he bought a very fine cameo."

"How did he pay for this cameo?"

The little man shifted in his seat. Even from her vantage oint Linese could tell he was uncomfortable. "He paid with old coins."

Homstock continued to stand in front of him, with his ands clenched tightly behind his back. "Was there any- ing unusual about the coins?"

"What do you mean?"

"Were they common? Have you seen many of the kind?" Homstock's tone made the small hairs on the back of her neck rise. Something about the way he spoke was sl conniving and terribly frightening.

"They were just British coins." Mr. Green fidgeted.

"British coins, you say?" Homstock turned and looke at Chase. His voice was sharp with interest. "They we British coins?"

"Yes, Chase Cordell paid with British gold."

Linese's head was swimming. It was common knowledg the British had been helping the Confederacy. Homstoc turned to face Kerney. Linese saw Colonel Homstock's fi gers whitening with the pressure he was using to keep h hands clasped behind his back. It struck her as odd, but th everything about this day was out of joint and barely seeme real.

"Your Honor, I would like to dismiss this witness a offer some testimony of my own."

Mayor Kerney leaned back in his chair. It was an expa sive gesture that set Linese's teeth on edge. "Of cours Colonel, by all means."

Samuel Green hurried from the witness chair and Col nel Homstock took his place. His posture was stiff and u yielding while he stared in Chase's direction.

"My brother, Alfred Homstock, had been sent to Mai field on a secret mission involving the Underground Ra road. He was wearing a money belt, and carrying a quanti of British gold. That gold has never been found."

The murmur rippled across the courtroom like rollii thunder. Linese shivered inwardly while the impact Homstock's words settled on her.

Chase had bought the cameo for her with gold that ha come from Alfred Homstock.

The evidence was damning.

Mayor Kerney turned toward Chase. The rain lessened f a moment and the courtroom took on an unnatural silenc

"Chase Cordell, do you have an explanation for this?" rney's voice was not as commanding as Colonel Homck's but Linese heard him clearly.

"I have nothing to say." Chase's deep baritone filled the urtroom and wrenched a sob from Linese. He turned in s chair and met her eyes. Longing, fear and regret arced tween them across the crowded courtroom.

Homstock was still for a moment while he stared uninkingly at Chase. Linese couldn't be sure, but she thought s expression was unsatisfied. He took a watch from his cket and snapped open the face. "Then I rest my case."

Linese wanted to scream. She wanted to rush down the airs and flail Chase with her fists. What was wrong with m? Why wasn't he defending himself? Hot tears stung the cks of her eyes and she stumbled away from the railing in ind agony. She was going to be sick. She had to get out-le for some air. Linese managed to get to the ground floor len both the front and side doors burst open with a wet ist.

"Ma'am?" A Union officer grasped her forearms. "Are u all right?"

She stared past the young soldier and found Hezikiah uiling at her.

"Hezikiah? What are you doing?"

"The war is over, Linese." He waved a paper over his ad. "The telegram reached Ferrin County a few hours o." A quantity of blue uniforms began to gather in the eady overcrowded courtroom. "Lee has surrendered—the ir is over. The Union has survived."

The next few minutes were a blur of activity. Linese found rself swept along while the Union officer strode to the ont of the courtroom. He stopped in front of Colonel omstock and saluted smartly. "Sir, will you surrender ur sword to me?" He asked in emotionless tones.

Homstock's jaw muscle flinched once, but he pulled nself to stiff attention. "I will."

Linese watched in silence while the men observed the proprieties of war. In a few moments it was over. The war was over. It seemed ridiculous that it could end just like that.

The impact of what it meant settled on her.

Chase would be free.

She turned to see him looking at her with love shining in his eyes. "May I address the court?" His deep voice boomed over the room. His chains clanked and rattled when he stood up.

Kerney shifted in his chair and his small eyes darted from Homstock to the Union officer who stepped forward.

"What is this proceeding?" The Union colonel drilled Kerney with a glance.

"This is a civil trial, Colonel, it is none of your concern," Kerney snapped.

Linese watched while one tawny eyebrow shot up toward the blue flop-brimmed hat. "Until I have orders to the contrary, everything in this town is my concern, sir."

"Who are you?" Kerney asked with a bit more respect in his voice.

"I am Colonel Thomas Baskins of the Massachusetts 57th."

That information seemed to settle on Kerney like a blanket of ice. Linese slumped into a chair that one of the Union soldiers suddenly produced for her, while she waited to see if Chase's request to speak would be honored.

"May I address the court?" Chase asked again.

"Go ahead," Kerney grudgingly offered.

"Now that the war is over, and the Union forces have entered Mainfield, I am prepared to defend myself against the charge of murder."

The still-crowded courtroom hissed with the collective intake of breath. Linese was grateful she was sitting down. If she hadn't been, she was quite sure she would have fainted on the spot.

Chapter Twenty-Four

Only an hour had passed, but the change in the courtroom made it appear more like days to Linese. She was now seated behind Chase, who had been relieved of his chains and shackles. Captain Cordell was seated on one side of her, Ira Goten had taken a chair on her opposite side.

"Have faith, Mrs. Cordell," he said.

Colonel Homstock and Colonel Baskins sat on the opposite side of the courtroom. The contrast in their uniforms seemed odd, positioned as they were, side by side.

"I call Rancy Thompson as my first witness." Chase's voice drew her attention back to him. She could see hope in his eyes where none had been before.

"Rancy, tell us why you arrested my grandfather."

The sheriff shook his head in obvious disgust. "I had received a note, the note the mayor read."

Chase picked up the paper that was lying on Kerney's desk. "This note? But why my grandfather? Why not arrest me if all the witness saw was a horse bearing the Cordell brand?"

"I had been visited by members of the local businessman's committee. They suggested I do it."

"So you were pressured by Mayor Kerney, and others, to arrest my grandfather for the murder of Alfred Homstock?"

"Yes, I thought it was a stupid thing...." His word trailed off. Linese found herself casting uneasy glances toward Captain Cordell.

"At what point did you decide I was the Cordell you were looking for?"

"I never did decide. It was decided for me. When the Confederates came to town, Mayor Kerney just started telling Colonel Homstock what he been shoving down my throat for weeks."

"Which was?"

"The fact that your alibi had been the old Captain, an if he was with Doralee, then that left you without an alibi."

Chase nodded and Rancy left the witness chair.

"Do you have more witnesses?" Colonel Baskins asked

"Yes, I do."

"Then proceed."

Linese glanced at Mayor Kerney. He appeared unusuall pale, something odd give his florid complexion.

"I call Ira Goten."

Ira smiled warmly at Linese before he strode to the wit ness box and placed his long slender hand on the Bible.

"Mr. Goten, would you tell the court what happened o May 30, 1862?" Chase's voice was smooth and strong.

Ira glanced at the Union and Confederate officers. "I ha been ordered to go to the woods and kill a Confederate sp who was going to assassinate men responsible for runnin the Underground Railroad in this area."

The whisper of shocked voices rippled over the court room. Several loud remarks about Ira's supposed Souther sympathies were heard. Linese realized that he had bee playing a part, allowing himself to be beaten and maligne for a greater cause. Linese heard the steady raindrops pat tering the roof overhead.

"Did you do that, Ira?" Chase stood straight and tall.

"I was waiting in the woods when I ran into you." Ir grimaced. "I had just about made up my mind you were th spy, the man I was supposed to kill, when we ran into Alfred Homstock.''

"Then what took place?''

"He showed us a money belt, asked if it would be enough to buy passage on the Underground Railroad, then he tried to kill you. And you didn't have any idea why.''

Linese saw Colonel Homstock stiffen with interest. She concentrated on his face while Ira kept talking.

"Homstock was shot in the shoulder with his own gun, but he managed to steal your horse and get away. I realized if you were not the man Alfred Homstock thought you were, then there was only one other person he could've been after. He had come to kill your grandfather.''

Linese snapped her head around and stared at Captain Cordell. He smiled uncomfortably under her gaze and a faint blush crept up his weathered cheeks.

"I'm sorry, honey, I did what I thought was best.'' He patted her arm with his big, rough hand and the reality of what he was saying hit her like a cold wind.

"You are not crazy,'' she whispered incredulously.

"No crazier than any other Texan,'' he snorted proudly.

Linese leaned back in her chair. She was numb. How could she have lived with him and never had an inkling that he was sane?

Then she thought back to the day at Doralee's house and the other times, when for a split second she had questioned the story. She shook her head in astonishment. She should have followed her own instincts.

"We got horses from Cordellane and went after him.'' Ira's words snapped her out of her reverie.

The entire courtroom was so quiet you could have heard a mouse tread across the floor. She glanced over the assembly and found them all perched on the edges of their chairs, held in silence by the unfolding story.

"You made it to the Ferrin County church ahead of me,'' Ira continued in a charged voice.

"And when you got there, Ira, what did you do?" Chase probed.

"I saw two Cordell horses tied out front, the one he stole and the one you were riding. Then I found Homstock's body. So I took the horses and headed back to Cordell-lane," Ira explained.

"Who did you think killed Alfred Homstock?"

Ira averted his eyes. "I thought you had. But now I know you didn't."

There was a loud murmuring in the courtroom. It mingled with the sound of pelting rain.

"When I returned from war, what did you give me?" Chase asked.

"A Colt and a handful of gold coins."

Colonel Homstock's hands were clenched into fists on the table before him. Linese saw his eyes narrow more with each new fact Ira revealed about the night Alfred Homstock died.

"Where did you get those items?"

"You loaned me the Colt when we went after Homstock and the gold is what he dropped from his money belt. I picked it up."

"What happened to the rest of it?"

"I don't know. The money belt was not on his body," Ira said with a frown.

"Why didn't you speak of this before now?"

"For the same reason you were prepared to die—too many others were at risk. We made a pact that night to keep silent."

"Thanks, Ira." Chase shook Ira's hand before he got up. "I'd like to call Linese Beaufort Cordell to the witness chair."

Linese tried to blink back her surprise. She made her way to the witness chair on shaky legs. While she took her oath to tell the truth, her mind was racing ahead. What on earth was Chase going to ask her?

"I believe most everyone here knows you are my wife, but for the benefit of our new arrivals, would you state your name."

"Linese Beaufort Cordell." She tried to still the quiver in her voice.

"When did you meet me?" Chase leveled a glance at her and she felt strength emanate from his hard gray eyes. It brought a measure of calm to her when she looked at him.

"May 30, 1862."

He smiled at her. "Where did we meet?"

"At the Presbyterian church social."

"What county?"

"Ferrin County."

"Is that where the body of Alfred Homstock was found?"

"Yes, I believe it was."

"Thank you. I have no more questions at this time."

"Chase?" Linese half rose from her seat in shock. Surely he meant to ask her about the man she had seen. Surely he intended to bring it up now that the war was finished.

"I have no more questions of you." Chase looked into her eyes and she knew it was pointless to argue. Whatever he was doing, it was obviously going to be done his way and in his own sweet time.

"I call Samuel Green to the stand." Chase's voice rang out over the musical sound of rain.

The little jeweler looked more unhappy than ever to be taking the stand, but he slowly made his way back to the witness chair.

"Mr. Green, you testified that I bought a cameo from you with British gold."

"Yes, that's right." He swallowed hard and Linese felt sorry for the little man who squirmed under Chase's unrelenting gaze.

"Have you ever sold anything, to anyone else in Mainfield that was bought with British gold?"

Her breath lodged in her throat. There was something about the way Chase asked the question that made her believe he already knew the answer. Mr. Green frowned and rubbed his fingers across his thick chin whiskers.

"Yes. It was a while back as I recall. I sold a ruby stickpin. It was paid for with British gold."

Linese heard the collective gasp in the courtroom. Chase turned to her and she knew he had solved the puzzle. Now he was going to tell everyone else.

"That is ridiculous," Mayor Kerney blustered, and he leaned forward in his chair. With lightning quick action, Chase leapt around the desk and grabbed the man by the throat. With his free hand he reached beneath the desk, and when he brought his hand up it was clamped around Kerney's fat wrist.

"Now, Mayor, what have you got there?" Chase smiled, but it was not a smile of mirth. "What did you have hidden in your boot?" Linese saw Chase's eyes harden like the cold gray of gunmetal.

"Nobody in this room is to move a muscle," Colonel Baskins's voice rang out. He nodded and she watched Union soldiers position themselves in front of every door and window in the courtroom.

Linese was hard-pressed to tear her eyes away from Chase's grim face, but she looked at the mayor's hand a saw what he was clasping in white-knuckled desperation.

"That's a mighty mean looking blade," Chase said softly, as he let go of his grip on the mayor's neck.

The mayor looked around the room. Beads of sweat had formed on his brow and upper lip. Linese saw panic in his face. "A man needs to protect himself."

Chase smiled again. "Linese, would you take the witness stand?"

She swallowed hard and nodded. Mr. Green practically ran, eager to get away from the bizarre situation taking place next to him.

Linese sat down and Chase turned his attention back to Kerney. "Mayor Kerney, what did you do when I returned to Mainfield with my new bride in 1862?" Chase tightened his grip on the man's wrist and the knife clattered to the desk.

"I—I don't know what you mean."

"Come now, Mayor. Don't you remember paying me a little visit? Don't you remember telling me that you had information that a horse bearing the Cordell brand had been seen in Ferrin County, that a murder had been committed, that you thought my grandfather's continued safety depended on my cooperation?"

The mayor's face flushed to a bright crimson. "I might've said something like that, but—"

"Mayor, how is it that you knew a horse with the Cordell brand was there in Ferrin County that night? Were you here?"

The mayor's eyes flicked from Chase to Colonel Homstock and back. Linese saw his jowls quiver when he swallowed. "Of course not. What a ridiculous notion."

"Then how did you know?" Chase's voice was deadly soft.

"Well, I—that is—I had been in Louisiana, on business. I was riding by and saw the horse. It was the horse Captain Cordell always rides—that big black mare."

"You saw the horse tethered at the church. But you never stopped?" Chase was toying with him like a barn cat with a mouse.

"No. I never stopped." Mayor Kerney seemed very pleased with that answer. "I rode straight on back to Mainfield."

"What kind of business were you on that night?" Chase smiled and turned toward Linese. She felt her heart increase its tempo inside her breast. For the first time she knew what he was doing. He was building to the moment when everyone would know who had killed Alfred Homstock.

"Business," Kerney snapped.

"And would your business have been raiding, looting, gathering what profit you could from the misery of a country torn by war?"

Kerney paled. "Yes! The Businessman's Association had been raiding in Louisiana that night."

A strange ripple moved through the courtroom and Linese saw every eye turn and focus on those men who had been associated with Kerney. It gave her pleasure to know they would profit no longer in Mainfield.

"So, after you raided, looted and burned farms, you quietly rode back home?"

"That's right. It was wartime. You can't fault me for what I did," Kerney snarled.

Linese felt the confidence and love pulsing from Chase each time he looked at her. When he turned to her, she was ready.

"Linese, tell me some more about May 30, 1862. Tell me what happened after the social ended."

"I left late with my aunt Hesta after we cleaned up. When I went to the hand pump outside to wash up, I ran into a man."

"What was he doing?"

"He was washing up at the hand pump."

"Did you know him?" Chase stepped away from Linese.

"Not at the time. He was not from Ferrin County. I only met him after we married and I came here to live in Tyron County."

"What was he washing, Linese?"

"The man was cleaning off a long knife." She pointed. "That knife. I saw Mayor Kerney, behind the church washing his hands and that knife."

Colonel Homstock barely kept his seat. His body vibrated with rage. She saw his hands, still tightly closed into fists in front of him on the table and realized he was trying to control the desire to kill Mayor Kerney.

"Tell us, Mayor, why did you do it? You didn't care who
won the war, so why did you stab that man in the back?"
Chase asked.

"For the gold. I did it for the belt full of gold. The idiot
had stopped to see to the bullet hole in his shoulder. He had
the belt slung over his arm. It was easy, he never heard a
thing." Kerney's eyes had glazed over and a bit of spittle was
forming at the corner of his flaccid lips.

He was mad. Linese could see that now.

"I'm going to take a great pleasure in seeing this man
hang," Colonel Homstock's voice rang out. He stepped in
front of Chase and held out his hand while two Union soldiers took hold of the mayor. "Major, I hope you will accept my apologies."

Chase grasped the colonel's palm. "I do."

"What will you do now, Major Cordell?" he asked.

"I'm going home. I have two daughters that I'm mighty
anxious to get acquainted with."

Linese smiled and felt tears on her cheeks.

"Linese?" When she looked up she found Captain Cordell smiling sheepishly at her. He held out his closed fist. "I
have something for you."

"What?" She still found it hard to believe that her sweet
old companion was as sane and lucid as she was. She held
out her hand. He dropped he wedding ring and her cameo
into her open palm. "Oh, Captain. How did you ever?"

"Nobody ever told that Confederate soldier it isn't smart
to play poker with a crazy man."

Linese's throaty laughter sluiced over Chase and he knew
that he was finally home—finally free.

Chase took her into his arms and kissed her thoroughly.
He had come full circle and met himself in the bargain.

He realized now that the man he had been was not as imperfect as he had once feared, and yet he knew he was a
better man now. Linese's tears of happiness soaked into his
shirt and he made himself a promise. No matter how many

causes, or how great the question of his honor, he woul
never, ever leave her side again.

As if God heard his vow and agreed with it, the rai
stopped and a bright shaft of sunlight blazed through th
windows of the courthouse.

Chase and Linese were free—free of the past—free of ar
curse, real or imagined—free to love each other for the re:
of their lives.

*   *   *   *   *

Author Note

Three separate ideas are responsible for *The Return of Chase Cordell*. Two movies, *Regarding Henry* and *Somersby*. I hated one and loved the other. The third ingredient in the mix was a piece of family history. My great-great-grandfather, Benjamin Everett Caudill, returned to his home in Kentucky from the Civil War, so badly scarred from smallpox, his wife did not know him. From these seemingly unrelated things sprang Linese and Chase.

Mainfield and its citizens are totally fictional, but I have endeavored to keep all dates relating to the Civil War intact. If I have failed along the way, I pray you will forgive me.

This January, bring in the New Year
with something special from

WYOMING
RENEGADE
by
Susan Amarillas

"Susan Amarillas is well on her way to becoming queen
of the frontier romance." —*Affaire de Coeur*

Available wherever Harlequin Historicals are sold.

FREE VALENTINE'S BROOCH! $9.95 U.S. retail value

This Valentine's Day Harlequin brings you
all the essentials—romance, chocolate
and jewelry—in:

VALENTINE Delights

Matchmaking chocolate-shop owner Papa Valentine
dispenses sinful desserts, mouth-watering
chocolates…and advice to the lovelorn, in this
collection of three delightfully romantic stories
by Meryl Sawyer, Kate Hoffmann and Gina Wilkins.

As our special Valentine's Day gift to you, each copy
of *Valentine Delights* will have a beautiful, filigreed,
heart-shaped brooch attached to the cover.

Make this your most delicious Valentine's Day
ever with *Valentine Delights!*

Available in February wherever
Harlequin books are sold.

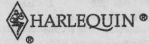

◆ HARLEQUIN ®
®

Bestselling

Harlequin® Historical

author

Ruth Langan

presents

Book III of her exciting Jewels of Texas series

JADE

When the town preacher meets the town madam,
the little town of Hanging Tree, Texas, will
never be the same

The Jewels of Texas—four sisters as wild and vibrant as
the untamed land they're fighting to protect.

DIAMOND	February 1996	PEARL	August 1996
JADE	February 1997	RUBY	October 1997

Heartbreak RANCH

Four generations of independent women...
Four heartwarming, romantic stories of the West...
Four incredible authors...

Fern Michaels
Jill Marie Landis
Dorsey Kelley
Chelley Kitzmiller

Saddle up with Heartbreak Ranch, an outstanding
Western collection that will take you on a whirlwind
trip through four generations and the exciting,
romantic adventures of four strong women who
have inherited the ranch from Bella Duprey,
famed Barbary Coast madam.

Available in March,
wherever Harlequin books are sold.

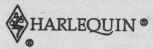

HARLEQUIN ®

HTBK

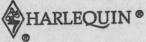

Harlequin and Silhouette celebrate
Black History Month with seven terrific titles,
featuring the all-new *Fever Rising*
by Maggie Ferguson
(Harlequin Intrigue #408) and
A Family Wedding by Angela Benson
(Silhouette Special Edition #1085)!

Also available are:
Looks Are Deceiving by Maggie Ferguson
Crime of Passion by Maggie Ferguson
Adam and Eva by Sandra Kitt
Unforgivable by Joyce McGill
Blood Sympathy by Reginald Hill

On sale in January at your favorite
Harlequin and Silhouette retail outlet.

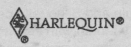
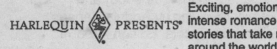
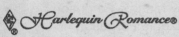

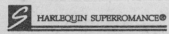